If you picked up this book because you truly want to get away with murder, you will not be disappointed. Simply turn the page and we'll get started.

#HowToGetAwayWithMurder

**UNCORRECTED PROOF COPY – NOT FOR SALE**

This is an uncorrected book proof made available in confidence to selected persons for specific review purpose and is not for sale or other distribution. Anyone selling or distributing this proof copy will be responsible for any resultant claims relating to any alleged omissions, errors, libel, breach of copyright, privacy rights or otherwise. Any copying, reprinting, sale or other unauthorized distribution or use of this proof copy without the consent of the publisher will be a direct infringement of the publisher's exclusive rights, and those involved liable in law accordingly.

# How To Get Away With Murder

REBECCA PHILIPSON

bantam

TRANSWORLD PUBLISHERS

UK | USA | Canada | Ireland | Australia
India | New Zealand | South Africa

Transworld is part of the Penguin Random House group of companies whose addresses can be found at global.penguinrandomhouse.com.

Penguin Random House UK, One Embassy Gardens,
8 Viaduct Gardens, London SW11 7BW

penguin.co.uk

First published in Great Britain in 2026 by Bantam
an imprint of Transworld Publishers

001

Copyright © Rebecca Philipson 2026

The moral right of the author has been asserted.

This book is a work of fiction and, except in the case of historical fact, any resemblance to actual persons, living or dead, is purely coincidental.

Every effort has been made to obtain the necessary permissions with reference to copyright material, both illustrative and quoted. We apologize for any omissions in this respect and will be pleased to make the appropriate acknowledgements in any future edition.

No part of this book may be used or reproduced in any manner for the purpose of training artificial intelligence technologies or systems. In accordance with Article 4(3) of the DSM Directive 2019/790, Penguin Random House expressly reserves this work from the text and data mining exception.

Typeset in 12/15.5pt Minion Pro by Six Red Marbles UK, Thetford, Norfolk
Printed and bound in Great Britain by Clays Ltd, Elcograf S.p.A.

The authorized representative in the EEA is Penguin Random House Ireland, Morrison Chambers, 32 Nassau Street, Dublin D02 YH68.

A CIP catalogue record for this book is available from the British Library.

ISBNs:
9780857507679 (hb)
9780857507688 (tpb)

Penguin Random House is committed to a sustainable future for our business, our readers and our planet. This book is made from Forest Stewardship Council® certified paper.

This book is dedicated to my girls, Rose and Grace.

## *My name is Denver Brady, and I am a serial killer*

I am currently the most successful active serial killer in the Western world. I don't say this to impress you – it's a simple fact.

There are approximately one hundred and fifty serial killers in operation at any given moment. The accepted definition of a serial killer is a person who makes three or more kills with more than five days in between them. I became a serial killer before my twentieth birthday, and I have operated unimpeded since then.

For most killers, murder chooses them.

In my case, I chose murder.

I am not driven by base urges, nor motivated by childhood trauma; this is a cliché, a caricature created by governments, medical professionals and entertainment giants. Their aim is to comfort the wider public. To perpetuate the myth that killers aren't killers simply because we want to be.

I am here to dispel that myth, along with many others.

I am not a psychopath, a sociopath nor a sadist. There is no chemical imbalance in my brain. I was not abused, nor dropped on the head by my mother. I have never hurt an animal and I was neither a bully, nor the bullied, in the school playground.

I chose my vocation in much the same way that you chose yours – or you should have, at least; I simply followed my interests. While my classmates were reading books about children climbing through cupboards into imaginary worlds or dropping down rabbit holes, I was engrossed by the tales of Mary Ann Cotton, Teddy Bundy and Jeff Dahmer.

What started off as recreation blossomed into ambition, rooted in frustration at the mistakes of these high-profile killers. Right when they reached their peak, they made error upon error until they were caught. They were judged. And they were strapped to a chair. These were errors created by their growing base urges. Their inability to master their own desires.

Pathetic ends to supreme reigns.

It was sometime in my early teens that I realized I could outdo them all if I put my mind to it.

So I did. I still do.

And it's precisely because I have outdone my predecessors and contemporaries that I am entirely unheard of.

Across the coming pages, I will teach you everything you need to know about getting away with murder. You will discover my methods and practices. Not only will you learn, in great detail, about the crimes that I've got away with, but also how I've avoided being on the radar of law enforcement. I'll blend anecdote with advice and information for budding killers, such as yourself. I might throw in a joke or two; even serial killers have a sense of humour. Everything I write here will be true, although I do reserve the right to modify details for my own protection – and to have a little fun with you from time to time.

I write this book for two reasons. Firstly, notoriety – I am self-aware enough to know that I crave it. Like any master, I create for myself, but my work deserves to be appreciated. But while I live for my art, I am unwilling to trade my last breath or my freedom for it, as many have been obliged to do – hence the pseudonym. Secondly, I hope to inspire a new generation of serial killers to outperform our frustrating forebears.

As I write this introduction, my mind drifts to a question: how many will pluck this book from the shelf, and for what reasons? Idle curiosity, maybe. A shallow mind drawn in by the cover? Are my words merely a tonic for a boring commute? A diversion from an unhappy marriage, perhaps? A distraction from life in middle-class suburbia? Maybe you fear becoming a victim and want to learn how serial killers operate, so that you can attempt to thwart us and live another day. Your motivations interest me, as much as mine interest you.

If you picked up this book because you truly want to get away with murder, though, you will not be disappointed. Simply turn the page, and we'll get started.

# 1

The problem with breakdowns is that you rarely see them coming. Cars. Washing machines. Laptops. People. It's always so unexpected, and so very inconvenient. If Sam could concentrate on anything for more than a few minutes at a time, that's what she'd think about: how she never saw it coming. One minute she was living the dream, and the next minute her whole world was collapsing around her. Everything she'd ever known crumbled. Everything that had ever mattered stopped mattering. Now, she looks back at herself as if she's been two entirely separate people. Past Sam and Present Sam. Simultaneously the same and completely different.

Past Sam was a successful police officer who trusted in justice, the morality of the law and her place in upholding it. She conquered Kilimanjaro just for fun, and hunted down rapists and killers with unfaltering enthusiasm. She was sexy and strong, and knew what laughter felt like.

Present Sam sits in Dr Pete Thomson's IKEA-chic office, thinking about nothing but the Lindt chocolate balls in the bowl on the coffee table in front of her and trying to ignore the sounds of London's rush hour outside. This Sam watches UK Gold endlessly and knows she should shower more often than she does. She takes her medication and sleeps with no one but Ben and Jerry. This Sam – the only Sam that's left – feels like a shell of herself, the kernel rotted away for ever.

She knows the doctor is talking to her, but she can't for the life of her hear him, especially with those gleaming red balls screaming for attention.

*Fuck you, Prozac,* Sam thinks and she reaches out to take a chocolate.

This week's session has been about managing her physical symptoms. Nothing that happened was her fault, the doctor has reminded her. A breakdown can happen to anyone, anytime, anywhere. But each person who's experienced what the doctor calls a 'negative event' will be left with different emotional and physical symptoms. Sam is still learning to identify and cope with hers. It's been a good session, in fairness to Dr Thomson and those balls—

'Samantha?' he says, penetrating her thoughts with jarring abruptness. She hates it when he uses her full name. It makes her feel so . . . millennial. She could have told him that she preferred 'Sam' in any of their twenty sessions to date, but she could never summon the energy.

'Yes, Doctor,' she mumbles, her cheek distended with the chocolate.

'We were talking about concentration being a major problem still,' he says with a light smile. Sam nods. 'And energy levels? How are they?'

She shrugs.

'What about panic attacks?'

Sam shakes her head. She hasn't had one of those since that day six months earlier, when her colleagues dialled 999 thinking she was experiencing a cardiac arrest.

'Good,' he says. 'Headaches? Yes. We know those are an issue. Taking your medication at the same time each day might help there. Occasional tinnitus when you feel stressed. The usual suspects as far as physical symptoms go, really, but remember that you might experience new symptoms you aren't expecting, and you might feel or do things that are out of character. When that happens, just remember it's OK and be kind to yourself . . .'

Sam glances at the clock. Their session is nearing its close. The chocolate ball pops and the creamy interior floods her mouth. Maybe she should mention the salt she tastes sometimes. Perhaps that's something the doctor could help with.

'Samantha?'

'Mmm?'

'I asked how you feel about going back to work?' She shifts restlessly as he brings up their most debated topic of late. 'Your BDI scores are better than ever, you've established a good routine, your symptoms are under control. I really think it could be in your best interest to consider a phased return. Even one or two days per week could be—'

'Is this you asking?' The melted chocolate muffles her words. 'Or Harry?'

'Samantha . . .' Dr Thomson rubs his forehead in a rare gesture of frustration. 'Yes, Harry is my golf buddy,' the doctor concedes, 'but he is also your godfather. He is your oldest friend, not to mention your Chief Inspector. He only wants what's best for—'

'And *you're* my doctor,' Sam says, hating that she sounds so petulant. 'You shouldn't try to persuade me to go back to work just because Harry thinks I should be there.' It's the same thing she says each time the conversation comes up, which is weekly.

'Samantha,' the doctor says again, and she fights the sudden urge to throw a chocolate ball at his face, hard. 'It would be unethical of me to do that. I am your doctor first and foremost, and in that capacity, I care about you. In that capacity, I also want to challenge you to continue to progress. I fear we've reached a plateau, and you're ready to take the next step in your recovery, which is to return to work. At some point, you have to face what you're so determined to avoid. A phased return really can be beneficial to—'

'No.' Sam pulls both ends of another plastic wrapper and watches the sweet spin open. She palms the ball into her mouth and chews.

'How are you coping financially, Samantha?' Dr Thomson asks. 'Last session you mentioned that you were about to have your sick pay reduced to half-salary? You seemed concerned that—'

'I manage,' she says, and it's the truth – her savings are holding out, but she knows that won't be the case for much longer.

'How about two, maybe three, days a week?' Dr Thomson says, raising his voice slightly. 'That would be a good starting point?'

Sam does some quick mental maths. If she worked two days per week, she'd qualify for full pay again, instead of the half-salary she is now receiving. She could afford to fix the washing machine or replace the torn lino in the kitchen. She could hire someone to deep-clean the house; it'd be nice to see the surfaces again, and perhaps they'd discover the source of the smell in the fridge. She swallows and tries to picture herself walking back into the grand New Scotland Yard building.

'I'm just not ready yet,' Sam says to herself, and the doctor nods. He leans back, scratching his head as if digging for a new angle of attack.

Sam reaches out to take another chocolate, but seeing that there's only one left in the bowl she hesitates, her hand hovering. She pulls back reluctantly, leaving the gleaming treat for the next patient.

'We've talked a lot about your colleague DS Lowry in these sessions,' the doctor starts again. 'Obviously, Harry called in every favour he could to get Lowry out of the Metropolitan Police and far away from you, so you'll never have to see him again. It's a shame he's still in the police at all, but—'

A loud ringing sound starts up in Sam's ears. She closes her eyes but she can still see Lowry's pudgy fingers sliding along her inner thigh; his dull wedding ring, his bitten fingernails spidering up between her legs. Despite the fact that the man was trying to touch her without her consent, Sam can still remember the sudden rush of self-consciousness that her tights and underwear might be sweaty from a day's work. She tastes a familiar salty flavour in her mouth.

'We had no evidence,' Sam says, her tongue thick. 'It was my word against his. The only option was for Harry to persuade Lowry to leave our team of his own volition. I'm grateful, but that doesn't change the fact that I'm not ready to go back there.' Sam looks at the clock again. Still another hour before she can take a tablet to subdue the headache that stalks her through her days.

'I know you and Harry did the best you could under the circumstances,' Dr Thomson says. 'My point is that—'

'Doc, this is all too much. Let's go back to the days when you used to witter on about journaling, or meditation. We once did a whole session on the benefits of walking barefoot on grass. Now, every week you just push me. And so does Harry.'

'We both want what's best for you, Samantha. Especially Harry. He just wants to help you put this episode in the past and get back to solving crimes. You make this city a safer—'

'Give me a sick note for another month, Doc,' Sam says, standing. The doctor sighs and scribbles illegibly on a scrap of paper, then holds out the note.

'Same time next week, Samantha.' Dr Thomson sighs. 'I'll have to let Harry know, since he's footing the bill.'

'Fine,' Sam snaps, snatching the note from him and letting the door slam behind her.

The waiting room beyond the doctor's office is eerily silent despite being full of people. A couple clings nervously to each other in the corner, a pensioner stares out of the window while twisting clumps of her hair, and a young man in a smart suit reads a book – *How To Get* ... Sam can't make out the rest of the title. *How to Get Rich* or something equally desperate, she supposes. Once upon a time, she'd have lingered to catch a glimpse of the cover before googling it and seeing how many stars it had. Now, Sam simply doesn't have the energy to be curious. She descends the stairs and drags open the enormous front door, squinting into the day.

Outside, the May sunshine washes the grey sky with a hint of yellow. There's a cool, light breeze, but Sam is hot from her session and from the oversized Nordic sweater she now wears every day, taking comfort in its bulk. With a ten-minute walk to the nearest bus stop – a real hike by London standards – Sam plugs in her headphones and navigates to her favourite playlist, full of Slipknot and Metallica, guaranteed to shut out the world entirely and not leave her crying like the Bob Dylan albums that used to be her go-to.

As she walks south towards Holland Park, she decides that she'll treat herself to a cuppa and a pastry beside the ornate pond that is located at the centre of what is, in her opinion, London's best attempt at bringing the countryside into the city. Sam loves the huge oaks, overgrown walkways and the way the tiny park manages to feel like a small slice of the Lake District or the Durham Dales, right here in the UK's capital.

A visit to Holland Park will clear her head of the so-called therapy session and help the tightness in her chest dissipate. No doubt Dr Thomson has phoned Harry – DCI Harry Blakelaw, her boss – immediately, to update him. Harry calls Sam, too. Every Monday lunchtime without fail, he rings to see how she is doing. Sam always answers Harry's calls when they come; she knows that if she doesn't, her godfather will turn up at her door with a packet of chocolate Hobnobs and a concerned look on his face. The mess her house is in right now, she certainly wants to avoid any home visits from him.

Sam breathes deeply, pushing Harry from her mind, and turns on to Holland Walk, a narrow alleyway with the park fence on one side and a high wall on the other. At this time of year it's brimming with vegetation and feels like a secret passage. But although Sam loves it, she would be surprised if many women ventured down it alone, especially after dark.

A father and young child on a balance bike come towards her and she moves aside, but the man stops. Sam pulls her headphones out.

'Sorry,' he says. 'I just wanted to let you know that the path up ahead is closed.'

'Oh, really?' she replies. 'Thanks for—'

'Something bad's gone on, that's for sure,' he confides, and Sam notices his neck is flushed and there's a glint in his tired eyes. 'The police took my details and everything. Must be something serious. Apparently the entire park is closed, and there are those people in white suits. You know, like that woman on *Silent Witness*?'

'SOCO,' Sam says, her eyes trailing up the shady path. 'Scene of crime officers.'

'Yeah. Anyway, I wouldn't bother going up. You can't get through.'

An unfamiliar curl of curiosity unfurls within her, and she lingers a moment. A few more people wander back from the direction of the crime scene, all chatting excitedly. Sam stands, uncertain which direction to take. A couple passes her and she catches their conversation.

'. . . must be dead for that amount of fuss,' the woman says.

'Probably just an overdose, love, nothing to worry about,' the man replies.

But they wouldn't close Holland Park entirely for a suspected OD. Something bad has happened. Something very bad. Sam walks slowly, and then with more purpose, along the lane. At the end is the promised police barrier, deep in the shadow of the dense foliage. A young officer turns pedestrians away. Sam approaches, rifling in her handbag and finding her ID. She flashes her warrant card at the tall, blonde-haired officer holding a clipboard, who smiles and nods deferentially.

'Suspected homicide, ma'am,' she says, without Sam having to ask. 'Young, female victim. I'm afraid it's a child. Discovered in the early hours.'

'A known misper?' Sam asks.

'Yes, ma'am,' the officer says. 'A Missing Person Report came in from the father late last night and the description matches. Formal ID of the body still pending but . . .' the officer sniffs. 'She was strangled and positioned underneath a big oak tree over there. The man who found her thought the girl was sleeping. It was sort of . . . arranged, ma'am – the crime scene; organized, I mean.'

'Meaning this might not be the first kill,' Sam muses aloud.

'I couldn't possibly say, ma'am,' the officer says. 'That's just how it looked to me. I was first on the scene.'

'Who's running it?' Sam asks.

'Detective Chief Inspector Blakelaw. He's just left. We haven't been told who the lead detective will be, yet,' the young woman says.

'Thank you, Officer,' Sam says, but the woman is looking away from her now, wiping her eyes.

'It'll never get easier, will it?' she sniffs. 'When it's a child.'

'I'm not sure it should,' Sam says with a sad smile.

The officer shakes her head. 'She was just walking home.'

*Aren't they always*, Sam thinks, and she thanks the officer and walks away, pulling her phone out of her pocket and hitting Dr Thomson's name. When he answers, she doesn't hesitate, worried she'll change her mind.

'OK, Doc,' Sam says. 'I'll go back to work.'

## *How Serial Killers Really Get Caught*

Getting away with murder can be tricky, but it is far from impossible and has been accomplished by men and women with far lower IQs than yours. The fact that you've purchased this book suggests an openness to self-improvement; a desire to learn. These qualities will serve you well.

In this chapter, we'll consider how to avoid becoming a suspect and, ultimately, being caught by police. Let me start by sharing a list of the most common mistakes killers make. This is not a list derived from my own experience – many academic studies exist on this topic. Most of these research papers focus on our greatest role models and their often spectacular blunders – Teddy Bundy driving around with his headlights off, for example.

For your convenience I have collated a few of these studies, and throughout this book you'll find my top tips and personal practices to keep the little piggies from the door. I have focused on Europe and the US only, as these are my territories of expertise – and we all know the rest of the world is a beautiful cesspit of lawlessness, anyway.

**Reasons You'll Become a Suspect – in order of probability**
1. Betrayed by someone you know (20 per cent)
2. Killing people connected to you (17 per cent)
3. Arrested for a different offence (17 per cent)
4. You frequent or are connected to the kill site (16 per cent)
5. Victim escapes or survives (15 per cent)
6. You confess (5 per cent)
7. Caught in the act (4 per cent)
8. DNA/forensic identification (4 per cent)
9. Spotted with the victim by a witness (2 per cent)
10. Killed by your victim (1 per cent)

I accept that the above will be surprising to many of you who have watched *CSI*, *Dexter* or *Silent Witness*. The truth is this: *forensic evidence is far more likely to convict you than it is to identify you as a suspect*. Obvious exceptions exist, and if you don't know who I'm talking about then are you even a true-crime fan? You should put in some proper study time. What's clear from the above is that you need to give the greatest attention to the people around you, your criminal history and your choices of victim and kill site. These account for the majority of problems you might face down the line.

I can imagine many of you are shocked that far more serial killers aren't tracked down by those mythical beings known as 'profilers'. These soothers of public conscience are neither use nor ornament, as my granny would say, and I'll tell you more about them as we go.

I've always demonstrated a natural talent for avoiding suspicion. I made my first kill when I was just twelve years old and no one suspected a thing, despite the fact that it was in broad daylight with multiple witnesses. I was certainly a natural talent from the outset, but this accomplishment so early in my life was a revelation, for I was a quiet child, mediocre in school; I was a short pre-teen, too, and rather weedy. In spite of my puny frame, I killed a much bigger boy in the summer holidays, not far from my home.

I remember it so clearly, and the reimagining of my first time brings to mind a quote from *Great Expectations*. I doubt many of you will have the intellect for it, but I'll try you. The great Charles Dickens said:

> *Pause, you who read this, and think for a moment of the long chain of iron or gold, of thorns or flowers, that would never have bound you, but for the formation of the first link on one memorable day.*

I can see my skinny little self stood there, in that quarry, on my most memorable day. My first victim, still alive and fresh, lugging his raft towards the water. Little did either of us know that he would be the first link in the long chain of the most successful serial killer in your lifetime.

This was the moment when it all began.

The moment Denver Brady was born.

# 2

Sam barely sleeps that night, or the next. She dreams she's being chased through Holland Park and she can feel his fingers sliding up her legs, no matter how quickly she runs. She wakes sweating and pads downstairs, turns on the news. On her old TV, she sees her godfather. *Detective Chief Inspector Harry Blakelaw*, the banner at the bottom of the screen reads, and Sam grabs the remote and turns up the volume. His voice sounds different on television: less of the Essex boy and more like the Broadstairs gentleman.

'. . . Charlotte was just fourteen years old,' Harry is saying to the reporters, 'a straight-A student, popular, with a loving family and her whole life before her.' Harry pauses, swallows, clears his throat and continues. 'We're appealing to anyone who was in or around Holland Park on Thursday evening into the early hours of Friday to come forward. Often, witnesses have seen much more than they realize, so please, even if you think you saw nothing out of the ordinary, contact the Metropolitan Police if you were in the area.' Harry reads out a telephone number and then takes a few questions, but it's an active investigation so there's very little he can say.

The feed switches to another man standing outside what appears to be a red-brick school building, and the banner now reads: *Hugo Wentworth-Brand – Headteacher*. 'Charlotte is . . . was . . . a wonderful girl,' he says, running a hand through his dense white hair. 'She was especially talented at netball, playing centre for our school team. Her father never missed a match. Charlotte was highly capable academically and had Oxbridge aspirations, hoping to follow in her father's footsteps. Teachers and pupils alike adored Charlotte. Wicked sense of humour, too . . .' The headteacher smiles, tears in his eyes.

'What's your fondest memory of Charlotte?' asks the reporter.

The headteacher smiles again and wipes his cheek. His chin wobbles slightly as he says, 'Thank you, gentlemen, that's all I can manage for now.'

A sudden knock on the door brings Sam back to her untidy lounge. Wondering who could be calling on a Sunday morning, she makes her way into the small hallway, between her lounge and kitchen, and picks up the last couple of days' post from where it's landed on the mat, then peers through the glass in her front door. A man in a bright-green Asda uniform stands holding a crate of groceries. She slides off her deadbolt and security chains, then awkwardly drags the door open. The man doesn't even look at Sam as he reels off this week's substitutes and she's grateful he doesn't notice that she looks like exactly what she is: a woman who's spent the weekend in the same pyjamas, without showering or even brushing her hair.

Sam dumps the crate out on to the hall floor, thanks the driver and locks the door again. She grabs a packet of chocolate Hobnobs and munches through them as she moves the groceries, one item at a time, into the kitchen cupboards. The kitchen lino is sticky underfoot and her slippers make a sucking sound as she moves about the room. She promises herself that, once she's back at work, she'll get on top of the housework, too. She rinses her dusty fruit bowl under the tap before putting the fresh green apples in it. It's been a while since she's bought any healthy food, but Mondays are always a good day to begin a new chapter.

She heads upstairs to the small landing that separates the two bedrooms and only bathroom. She tips her already-overflowing laundry basket upside down and begins to sort her clothes, placing the darks into her old hiking backpack, ready to head to the laundrette tomorrow after work. She can take the whites on Tuesday.

Drained by the small exertion, Sam makes her way back downstairs and rewatches her favourite episode of *Only Fools and Horses*, the one where Del Boy disguises Rodney as a schoolboy to win a free holiday. Sam usually laughs aloud at the sight of the young Nicholas Lyndhurst in his roller-skating gear, but today she can't shake off her thoughts of a dark corner in Holland Park and a fourteen-year-old girl called Charlotte.

The morning of her return to New Scotland Yard, Sam rises early and jumps straight into the shower, lathering her dirty-blonde hair twice before combing it straight into a ponytail. She eats two slices of peanut butter on toast, and one of the apples from the fruit bowl.

It's not until Sam goes to pull on her work clothes and the buttons of her suit trousers won't meet in the middle that she realizes there's going to be a problem. No amount of pulling or wiggling can get her body inside any of the clothes that Past Sam had slid into with ease. She rummages deep inside her wardrobe, frustration mounting. She literally has nothing to wear. She pulls back the wardrobe door, ready to slam it with a force that the old hinges would be unlikely to survive, but stops herself. She takes a deep breath in through her nose, holds it, exhales, and makes her way calmly out of the bedroom.

Tipping out the old backpack that she'd placed in the hallway, Sam retrieves the black leggings she's lived in for longer than she cares to remember. She sniffs them tentatively, then winces. She has no choice, though. She'll just have to stand a metre away from anyone at all times.

'Fuck you, Prozac,' she mutters as she pulls the leggings on and repacks the bag. She finds an old, semi-smart polo neck at the back of the cupboard and stretches it over her head. It smells musty and she finds herself coughing as she emerges from the tube-like collar. She pulls out her old beige trench coat from the cupboard under the stairs. As she slides her arms into it, Sam catches notes of the luxury fragrance she used to spritz on each morning before she left for work. She can't believe how well the scent has lasted. Six months and still going strong. *Rouge Malachite has more fortitude than I do*, she thinks, remembering the day she bought the bottle for herself as a birthday present. She can't imagine ever finding the energy to spray perfume again, let alone going to a shop and buying it. Nonetheless, she enjoys the scent as she fastens her coat all the way up, to under her chin. The buttons strain in their holes but Sam doesn't care. The tightness of it will help to keep her upright.

Picking up her handbag, she steps out into the brightness of the day, locks her front door behind her and walks down the path. She ducks to avoid an overgrown bramble and lifts the little garden gate open. Hers is by far the messiest garden on Acklam Terrace. Most of the neighbours have replaced their grass with decorative pebbles or marble-coloured paving, but Sam has always loved snatches of metropolitan countryside.

Sam takes the narrow alley past St. Paul's – not the Cathedral, but Clapham's own church of the same name and lesser fame. It's a pretty building in Sam's opinion; just as worthy of a visit.

Sam emerges on to the high street and looks longingly at her go-to café, Bubbles and Beans, which she'll be forced to bypass today thanks to her wardrobe issues. She jogs across the road and joins the orderly queue at the bus stop just seconds before a red double-decker squeals to a halt.

The bus is packed and Sam wedges herself into the corner near the emergency exit. She spends the journey concentrating on her breathing. In spite of her headphones and the heavy-metal playlist, she can still hear the woman next to her reciting English verbs into an app. Bodies sway as the bus stops and starts again. Teens in various school uniforms hop on and off. People sneeze noisily into tissues. A toddler writhes and a businessman yells into his phone – when Sam sees his eyes travel over one of the schoolgirls' knees, she feels salt rise in her throat.

More passengers pile into the bus as it heads into central London and bodies begin to brush up against her. Sam's arms tingle. By now, her mouth tastes like the ocean. Unable to bear it any longer, she hits the bell and jumps from the bus two stops early. Ten minutes later, she's walking along the Thames embankment towards New Scotland Yard.

As she walks, Sam keeps her eyes away from the mangling murk of the river. Every time they ventured down to the sandy banks of the river in Somerset where Sam had spent summers splodging with friends from her primary school, her mum used to warn her that water killed more people than lions and tigers and bears ever had.

'Fresh water is the most dangerous of all,' Mum had said, squeezing on bright-orange armbands as Sam darted embarrassed looks at her friends who were already waist-deep. 'Salt and chlorine add buoyancy, but in fresh water like this you'll sink in seconds.'

'No one else has to wear these,' Sam had hissed at her mother. 'I'm not a baby.'

Mum kissed her nose. 'You'll always be my baby.'

Sam reburies the memory with a few deep breaths. A moment later, the 1930s classical facade of what was once called the Curtis Green building is in front of her. The word *New* is simply to highlight that the building has been updated, not, as many people think, because there is any *new* ideology behind the policing that goes on there. Her father, a Detective Inspector himself, hadn't lived long enough to see the work on the building completed. It was probably for the best. Detective Hansen had loved tradition. He'd have hated New Scotland Yard and all its modernity.

In front of the rectangular stone face of the main building, next to the world-famous spinning sign, is a glass anteroom through which all must pass. Sam signs in, and the receptionist tells her that DCI Blakelaw will be down to escort her inside and that a new security pass will be ready for her tomorrow.

Sam sinks into the black leather sofa in the waiting area and lets herself be swallowed by dread. She wipes sweat from her upper lip then buries her nose in the collar of her trench coat and breathes in air that smells like a stronger version of herself. *Just keep breathing.* She lets her mind wander out of the building and back to Holland Park, imagining Charlotte walking home. The terror the girl must have felt when she first noticed footsteps behind her. *What have I got to fear?* Sam reminds herself that Harry is here to watch out for her, and Lowry has been transferred over a hundred miles away from London.

By the time the towering figure of DCI Harry Blakelaw is striding towards her, Sam has calmed her heart rate. She stands and greets Harry as her old self would have done, although the once-familiar hug is a little stiff and awkward. Harry asks how she is and tells her that she looks well. She looks well to everyone, she supposes. On the outside.

Together, they take the lift to the fourth floor. As they wait for the doors to close, she prays that no one else boards and forces themselves into her personal space. Mercifully, no one does, and Harry brings her up to speed with the team as they ascend. Anna has transferred, he explains, saying how sorry he is because he knows she and Sam were good friends. *Until I ignored her for six months and didn't turn up to her wedding, even though I was supposed to be her bridesmaid.* He doesn't mention Lowry at all, but talks about another couple of officers that Sam used to be friendly with who have changed teams or left the force entirely, meaning there won't be many people here that she knows well.

'Except yours truly.' Harry smiles. 'We'll get through this

together.' He gives her a friendly pat on the shoulder, a gesture that Sam recognizes from childhood. She leans into his warm hand and smiles back at him.

The lift doors open out on to the same open-plan space that Sam was carried out of all those months ago, paramedics holding her by the armpits. The office is entirely the same and entirely different, all at once. Police officers of varying ranks from the Homicide and Violent Crime divisions sit around desks, chatting, drinking coffee, and typing at keyboards.

The space is a huge rectangle filled with islands of cheap wooden desks, each piled with lever-arch files and overflowing in-trays. There's a small kitchenette against the far wall that serves the fifty officers and a dozen or so civilians who work on this floor. (Ironically, Sam remembers, fridge theft is commonplace.) Alongside the kitchenette is the breakout space: three small sofas, a dusty glass coffee table and a TV that's always on but usually muted. Each corner of the fourth floor contains a soundproofed glass box. One is Harry's private office; a second, much larger one is used for team briefings; and the other two are smaller meeting rooms. The carpet is brown and sticky, and the strip-lighting is overly bright.

Sam trails Harry to his office, noticing a few heads turn to follow their progress. A couple of officers call morning greetings to the boss, and Harry returns them without breaking stride.

Sam catches a glimpse of Lee Chen sitting at DS Lowry's old desk. She can still picture him sitting there, just a few feet away from her, chatting with colleagues and showing them photographs of his daughter. Suddenly, Sam feels like she just swallowed a mouthful of seawater. She offers Chen a weak smile. He must barely recognize her – they met only a handful of times – but he nods and waves in return. A pair of officers – a tall, dark-haired man and a blonde woman with her back to Sam – laugh together at a desk. They look so young and carefree, and she knows that once upon a time, not so long ago, she must have seemed just like that, too.

'Sam?' Harry calls, waving for her to follow him into his office.

He holds the door for her and then gestures for her to take the seat opposite him and his giant desk. Something's different in the office, but she can't pinpoint what. Fewer plants? Perhaps no one has watered them during her absence. She's sure there used to be a photo of her and Harry on his desk. The one of his wife, Beryl, is missing too. In fact, the only photograph that remains is a faded print of him and Sam Hansen, her father and namesake, taken in the eighties. She decides not to allow herself to read too much into such a trivial change.

Harry is talking but she's missed the beginning, so can only offer a 'Mmm?' when he breaks to allow her to respond.

'I was just saying again how good it is to have you back. The Met has missed you. I've missed you.'

Sam nods and jerks the corners of her lips upward as best she can as Harry begins talking again. She can tell by his tone that he is taking her phased return seriously, and with a dart of alarm, senses that he might be leaning towards keeping her out of the murder investigation altogether.

'Actually, sir,' she says, 'I want to be considered for SIO in Charlotte's . . . I mean, the Holland Park murder.' Harry makes to interrupt her, so she carries on quickly. 'I know I've just come back to work, but no one has a better solve rate than me. Especially when it comes to women and girls. The crime scene was organized, and we could be dealing with someone who's killed before. You need experience on this one, and that's me. I'm your best detective—'

'Sam,' Harry says, not meeting her eye, 'that was *before*. You *were* my best detective. But you've been away for so long that I can't throw you back in the deep end with a child homicide.'

'But—'

'No buts, Sam,' Harry insists. 'I talked to Pete—Dr Thomson, and we've got to take this phased return slowly and seriously. You'll work Monday to Wednesday only, for the first month. HR will email you with check-ins, so please engage with them.'

'Sir,' Sam lowers her voice, 'the reason I am so motivated to return to work . . . the reason I have overcome my—'

'Sam,' Harry says, holding up his hands in surrender. 'I get it. You came back for Charlotte. I thought you might, erm, feel a connection to her case.'

'Yes,' she admits. 'And honestly, Harry, if you put me on a different case, I doubt I'll have the motivation for it.'

Harry nods slowly at her lightly veiled threat.

'Fine. You can be involved in the Charlotte Mathers case, but not as SIO,' Harry says, after a moment. 'What I need you to focus on is . . .' Harry continues but Sam's distracted by the way her godfather tugs at his own eyebrows as he speaks. It's a habit he's always had, but it's never bothered her before. Now, though, it's incredibly annoying and she can't concentrate on anything else. Even her disappointment at not being considered for SIO doesn't sting its way through as she watches his fingertips grasp his right eyebrow and pull it. She bites her cheek and fights the urge to tell him to stop.

'Sam?' Harry cuts into her thoughts. He's stopped talking again and is clearly awaiting her reply.

'Yes, sir,' Sam says, hoping that this response covers everything.

'Good,' Harry exhales, with what sounds like relief. 'I think you'll like her, the new DI. *Tina* Edris, that is. She's a . . .' Harry waves his hand in Sam's general direction, 'you know . . . a woman.'

'Yes, sir.' Sam smiles, supposing that Harry is being thoughtful by assuming that she'll feel safer reporting to a female senior officer. She resists entertaining other possible interpretations of his comment, choosing always to see the best in him as he does in her. She watches as he tugs his eyebrow again. *It's a 'he said, she said*'. The words pop unbidden into her mind. *You know how these cases go*. Sam shakes her head lightly to rid herself of the unwanted memories, but her eyes flick involuntarily towards Lowry's desk. *Harry did his best for me,* she reminds herself. She takes a deep breath, holds, exhales.

'Sam?' Harry pulls her focus back to what he's saying. 'I was just saying . . . Charlotte's body was found in the early hours of Friday morning over in Holland Park. She was strangled and left beneath an oak tree, with her initials carved into the tree itself. Well, not just *her* initials. The exact inscription was CM + DB, inside a heart. CM is obviously Charlotte Mathers. DB, we are assuming, is Denver Brady.'

'A boyfriend?' Sam asks.

'No, Sam. I just . . .' Harry sighs. 'Let's go over it again. Denver Brady is the author of a book called *How to Get Away With Murder*. A copy of that book was found among Charlotte's belongings at the crime scene. I want you to run a line of enquiry within the homicide investigation to find the author, Denver Brady. DB.'

'*How to Get Away With Murder*? As in, a dummy's how-to guide to committing murder?' Sam rubs her forehead.

'Exactly. Some Charles Dickens, Ted Bundy wannabe claiming to be able to teach people how to kill and get away with it. Just what we need. As if the Met isn't stretched enough as it is,' Harry says. 'The victim's father is certain that the author is to blame for Charlotte's murder. Not only was *How to Get Away With Murder* found at the scene, but there are similarities between Charlotte's death and what Brady claims, in his book, to have done to another girl. Plus the initials in the tree trunk, of course. "DB" for Denver Brady.'

'You told the family about the book and the initials in the tree trunk?' Sam asks. 'Wouldn't we normally withhold that?'

'It's simple,' Harry responds a little defensively. 'We had to know if the book belonged to Charlotte. If her family had seen her reading it or—'

'If the killer left it at the scene himself.'

'Exactly.' Harry nods.

'Tell me about Charlotte.'

'Fourteen. High achiever. Sporty. Popular. Lived with her father, Nigel, and her uncle, Jack. Neither could say for certain if Charlotte owned *How to Get Away With Murder*. Apparently, the girl always had her nose in a book. A bit like you used to, I suppose. I remember that one time the school librarian called your dad because she was worried about the—'

'. . . nature of the material I was reading.' Sam smiles, remembering. 'Truman Capote's *In Cold Blood* and—'

'That one about Ted Bundy,' Harry chuckles.

'*The Stranger Beside Me*,' Sam confirms. 'You had to convince my dad to—'

'Give you a book allowance.'

'Give me a book allowance.' They speak in unison, smiling. Harry's eyes move to the picture of Sam's father on his desk, and Sam looks fixedly out of the window at the saxe-blue city sky.

After a moment, Harry clears his throat. 'In my opinion,' he says, reaching for his eyebrow but halting midway to turn on his computer instead, 'it's far more probable that the victim knew her killer – we are all familiar with the statistics. When a child is murdered, it's almost always by someone they know. But there's a slim chance that this Denver idiot really exists and is in some way connected to Charlotte or her family. We need to find him, even if just to rule him out of our inquiries, and we absolutely cannot let any serial-killer notions leak to the press. It would send the country's imagination into overdrive and completely derail Charlotte's investigation.'

'Catchy title,' Sam observes. '*How to Get Away With Murder* has a real ring to it. I'd definitely pick it up if I saw it in Waterstones.'

Sam smiles but Harry simply nods and continues. 'Obviously, you're on light duties, with this being your first investigation back after, what – almost a year? Eight months?' *It's six months and nineteen days, but who's counting?* 'So DI Edris will be Senior Investigating Officer and you'll run the book enquiry team. You'll report to Edris primarily. And me, of course. You'll work three days per week, strictly no more, and—'

'I'll run an enquiry team?' Sam asks, perking up. 'How many?'

'You'll have a TDC under you, and access to the civilian team.'

'A book enquiry team of just two?' she challenges. 'Me and a probationer to catch a potential serial killer?'

In response, Harry just holds out a flimsy brown case file along with what appears to be a skinny novel. Sam takes them from him. There's very little in the file itself, and she guesses it's been hastily thrown together over the weekend, probably a task delegated by Harry to a junior. She sees a simple case summary and a system-generated progress report, along with a smaller envelope that presumably contains crime scene photographs. It's clear that Sam will be bringing herself up to speed as best she can.

Harry begins clicking his mouse and cursing modern technology. She waits, her eyes drifting around the room, trying to find a comfortable spot to rest. She wonders if her new apprentice will have been briefed to keep an eye on her. If they'll have been warned about the unstable female, possibly suffering from perimenopausal hysteria, back on the job after spending six months at home after she lost her grip.

'What's-his-name, your trainee, has been briefed,' Harry says, as if reading her mind. 'On that subject . . . make him work for it. He came in on one of these fast-forward schemes. Shortcuts to get bums on seats, when what we need is more like you and me. Grafters. Doers. Not box-tickers. So, make him pull his weight. Do the heavy lifting. Save you getting stressed out. Six-figure degrees and a rich daddy MP can only get him through the door, but he earns the rest. OK?'

'Yes, sir,' she says. *Great,* she thinks, *a newbie to manage.*

'Good. You'll meet DI Edris before the next briefing. I think she's attending the post-mortem today.' He clicks again, oblivious to Sam's stomach lurching at the word *post-mortem* and the accompanying mental images of cold, sharp steel and chilled young flesh. 'It's great to have you back, Sam. Don't stretch yourself and don't miss any sessions with Pete, OK? They're mandatory.'

'Yes, sir.'

'And Sam, anything you need or if you . . . you know . . . feel overwhelmed again, please say. You're not the first Sam Hansen I've said this to: my door is always open.' The DCI clears his throat, and Sam can see the moisture in his eyes as they linger again on the picture of himself and her father.

'Sure,' Sam says, then adds, 'Any tips, Harry? On where to start with *How to Get Away With Murder*?'

Harry looks flattered. 'You don't need my help to investigate a book, Sam. Just find Brady quickly and rule him in or out. Personally, I'd start by comparing the description he gives in the book to Charlotte's crime scene photos. There are some disturbing similarities.'

'Any chapter in particular?' Sam asks, flicking through the pages of the book and resisting the urge to sniff them.

'Yes,' Harry says. 'Don't stop reading until after the chapter about Sarah. That's the one with the most links to Charlotte's murder.'

## *Popping My Cherry*

It was an extremely hot and still day, the kind rarely enjoyed in England. Owing to that particular area's past, the landscape was littered with abandoned quarries. Over time, these places filled with groundwater and became havens for wildlife, including the local youth. On warm days, villagers would head to the quarry to sunbathe, socialize and swim. The shale floor felt not dissimilar from sand and the rock bounced the heat around inside the quarry, making the place a suntrap. If it was a good day, the ice cream van might stop nearby.

That day, it didn't. I'd gone to the quarry with my cousin, Bobby, who was a couple of years older than me. At twelve, that small age difference can feel like a lot, and, given my small stature, I noticed the distance between us keenly.

The quarry was only five minutes from the village market square, and Bobby knocked on his friends Gordie and Jono along the way. Gordie had a nasty habit of calling me 'Tiddler', and sometimes my cousin would join in. I preferred Jono, who was a milky, doughy creature with a stutter. I tended to keep myself to myself whenever the three boys were together. That day, I sat on the toasty shale, reading, while Bobby and his pals worked on the raft they had spent the summer building. From my shady spot, I could see their already-tanned skin turning increasingly pink at the shoulders. The grown-ups were all at work and, for the most part, we had the place to ourselves.

The boys had, over the preceding weeks, acquired four barrels and lashed four planks to them to form a square floatation craft that was quite impressive. That day, they were building oars from pilfered baking trays that they nailed to the ends of old broom handles.

I recall quite vividly the minutiae of the day. I was reading a book about Mary Ann Cotton that I'd waited months for the library to acquire. I'd only picked up Mary Ann that morning, when Bob and I had gone into town to buy ourselves some pop for our day at the quarry. The librarian, a nosey old hag, asked if my mother knew what I was reading and I poked my tongue out at her.

It was sometime around 2 p.m. Definitely after lunch, which we hadn't brought. My hunger added to my anger at discovering that Mary Ann Cotton was likely entirely innocent. I was about to throw the book into the quarry depths when it all began.

The raft was being launched. Younger children gathered around as Bobby, Jono and Gordie pushed the craft out on to the water, each jumping aboard, perched above a barrel. The little children cheered, but it was immediately obvious to me, watching from the shade, that the boys would have a problem. The raft was a square construction and the fourth barrel, without a sailor aboard, was lifting out of the water. They'd all tip off. Jono's milky flab, coupled with Gordie's height and muscle, made the endeavour impossible. They'd ignored the simple laws of physics.

*Idiots*, I thought, as I tilted my face skywards and breathed deeply, turning my mind back to the final chapter of my book on Mary Ann Cotton and the day the prison officer in Durham Gaol had escorted her to the scaffold. I pictured her trembling lips and pinioned hands. I wondered if she had protested her innocence, or better still, begged for—

'Oi, Tiddler!' Gordie was standing over me, dripping. I'd been so deep in thought, I hadn't heard him approach. 'It's your lucky day,' he said. 'We need a fourth man for the raft.'

I glanced from Gordie to the shoreline where my cousin Bobby and the fat boy, Jono, were waiting. They were all at least a foot taller than me and significantly heavier.

'No,' I said firmly. Gordie stared at me, so I elaborated with, 'I can't swim.'

'Just come and have a look,' Gordie said, 'you don't have to get on it.' He placed his hands on his hips and, reluctantly, I took a step. He put a sweaty arm around my shoulders and I could smell his musk. Not entirely unpleasant, but nothing like my own body produced yet. 'Tiddler will be the fourth man,' Gordie called to the others.

'No,' I said again, trying to back away. 'I can't swim!' Gordie held me firmly around the shoulders and I didn't meet Bobby's eye because he knew only too well that I was, in fact, a fine swimmer.

'Don't worry, Tiddler,' Gordie said. 'You can sit in front of me. I'll look after you.'

'I c-can't swim too great, neither—' Jono began, but Gordie cut him off, calling him a chicken and dragging me forward. Gordie manoeuvred me over one of the front barrels. I was still fully clothed, in torn denim shorts and an overly small black cats shirt that had been Bobby's. The boys launched me on to the water. The barrel was between my legs like a battered, round horse and my feet dangled in the water. It was startlingly chilly and my skin pimpled as the others mounted their barrels and began to row. I watched as the water changed colour beneath me and I saw the skeleton of an old car in the murk below. There were no fish and few plants, just dark depths.

We'd reached the middle of the quarry, the deepest point, when the raft failed. Looking back now, it was inevitable, wasn't it? Before we had chance to realize our peril, the planks had detached and we were clinging to debris. Gordie immediately swam to shore with an impressive front crawl. My cousin bobbed on a barrel a fair distance away from me. Jono was holding on to a plank close by. I was treading water, trying desperately to hold on to my barrel, it kept spinning round and I was too small to reach over the top of it, as Bobby had done.

'Swim to Jono, he's really close to you!' Bobby called as the barrel spun again, plunging me into the cold blackness. The icy water filled my ears and tingled against my scalp as I gulped. My legs burned and my feet cramped inside my sandshoes.

I remember very clearly thinking that I was going to die. I had once read somewhere that fresh water was far less buoyant than salt water or that used in swimming pools. I was facing my final end. I thought of Mary Ann Cotton, swinging. I thought of Ted Bundy strapped to Old Sparky. I pictured the lethal injection closing the eyes of John Wayne Gacy. I thought about how no one would write a book about me. I would just be dead. Forgotten. No one would even remember that I had existed.

As if in response to my thoughts, I abandoned my barrel and swam to Jono. I gripped his outstretched hand, my fingers twisting in his. It's incredible the impressions we have in extreme moments, for despite the peril of our present situation, I noticed that Jono had been eating hot cross buns. Even though they were now dripping wet, his hands were sticky with molten syrup and the ripe sultana smell lingered on his breath.

My cousin had drifted further away. Everyone on shore was shouting. I didn't make a sound. I only focused on my fingers. On Mary Ann Cotton. On Ted Bundy. I manoeuvred my grip so that Jono and I were no longer holding hands but, rather, our fingers interlinked as if we were about to play a game of Mercy. I watched Jono's face. I could see he was tiring. Panting. Snot hung from one of his nostrils. His big lips flapped. He'd sink like a fat stone. The thought gave me a tingle that, being only twelve, I'd never felt before. I gripped his hand as tightly as I could and I pushed.

Down.

As hard as I could.

Jono gasped and vanished. I pushed more. Stretching every muscle. Below, I could feel Jono fighting to be free. I would not let go. A hard pleasure electrified me, pulsing from my fingers to my toes. I grunted. The guttural sound from the back of my own throat only made me push harder.

The other boys were shouting, their voices echoing off the stone of the quarry. They'd realized Jono had gone under. Voices were everywhere. The plank, freed from

Jono's weight, easily supported me. Jono was now below me, his fat fingers desperately clawing at my hand and inner thighs, gouging my flesh. The water was so deep. So cold. If Jono had only had the sense to pull me down, instead of trying to push up, I'd have had to let go. Stupid boy. Evolution at work. After another moment, I felt a juddering and then Jono's hand relaxed, flopping against me. I stayed there for a moment, enjoying the way his fingers felt between my legs. When I could truly stay afloat no longer, I let Jono go and swam slowly to shore. I was barely able to mask the satiation radiating from my face, from my body, for the whole world to see.

I lay on the hot shale, panting, watching a wisp of cloud floating overhead. As I basked in the bosom of the warm quarry, I felt, for the first time in my short life, true joy. I thought of what I'd just become and what lay before me still. Look at me, Mary Ann. Look at me, Ted. Look at me, Jeffrey. Look at me, Mr Gacy. I am on my way to becoming you, and more. I'll be everything you couldn't be – alive and free.

Some men who'd been working nearby had arrived on the scene and now swam out to the wreckage in hope of finding Jono. Gordie sat weeping. My cousin yelled to the men to keep looking. More adults arrived. I saw Jono's mother on the shore and I stood to go and give her the bad news but a large man intercepted me and piggy-backed me home.

The headlines were wonderful. I remember cutting them out and taking them to show Bobby, who was confined to his bed and puked water for a week. He mourned his friend terribly and felt, I think, guilty for what had happened. Jono's equally milky mother visited

Bobby daily, sang hymns and placed a framed picture of Jono by my cousin's bed.

'There's nowt as queer as folk,' my uncle sighed when the woman had departed. He was a man of few words.

Following the trip to the quarry that summer, a lightness came over me that lasted for months. Each night in bed, I felt Jono's fingers clinging to me. Some nights, I clawed at my own legs in my sleep. In the daytime, I began to hum. Sweet little tunes as I went about my business.

No one noticed my newfound joy except Bobby's mother, who began to reach for his hand whenever I was close by. I realized that if I wanted to pursue my newly discovered passion, I would have to take care to educate myself and become the best version of myself that I could be. Fortunately for you, my natural talent, coupled with tenacity and grit, meant that I went beyond my own wildest dreams.

I became the best, and that entitles me to bestow my sagacity on whomever I choose. And I choose to help you become the best serial killer that *you* can be. Assuming that you're not entirely stupid, you will experience some success if you follow my guidance. I'll also let you get to know me more personally. I'll tell you all about Sarah, Sean, Amy, Betty and Melanie, and a few more besides. I hope you're as excited as I am to get going. Remember to take notes and to take breaks. Have a KitKat. Drink lots of water. This is going to be a real page-turner. The juiciest bits are coming right up.

# 3

Sam's desk is clean and clear, which means someone has been told to ready it for her return. New log-ins have been written neatly on a Post-it adhered to the bottom of her monitor and when she opens the top drawer she finds a packet of chocolate Hobnobs and another note, saying *Welcome back, Samantha.* The use of her full name suggests that whoever Harry asked to write it is new to the floor. Her trainee, perhaps. There's a brand-new work phone for her, which she turns on and finds fully charged and ready to use.

Sam sits back in her chair and peers around at her surroundings. This room was the centre of Past Sam's world – her raison d'être, the place she felt most alive. Now, Present Sam notices the cheap carpet, the battered binders that have overflowed from shelves, on to the floor. A room so loud that she can barely hear herself think. Not all are police, many of them are civilian indexers who type away all day long, their fingers flying at an unholy speed for barely a living wage.

Sam takes in the whiteboards that are scattered all around the room. Writing is scrawled in various colours. In the centre of one board, Sam sees a photograph of a beautiful red-headed child. Her heart skips and she swallows hard. Charlotte Mathers. It must be. Her face printed on a piece of A4 that's already curling at the corner. The girl doesn't even look fourteen years old; maybe closer to twelve. All chubby cheeks and freckles. Just a baby, really. Sam pulls her eyes away. Sniffs. But she can't help but look back at Charlotte, and her mouth floods with the taste of salt. She closes her eyes and takes deep breaths. She can feel glances from her colleagues, but no one comes near and she suddenly misses Anna deeply. She misses Past Sam more. Her chest begins to tighten and she holds her head in her hands.

'So young,' Sam whispers quietly to herself. 'So lovely.'

'Why, thank you.'

A voice from behind makes Sam turn in her chair. She finds herself confronted by a flawless, smiling face. He puts her in mind of those cookie-cutter-perfect young men that used to be splashed across the cover of *Smash Hits* magazine and swooned over. From his stylish boat shoes to his boyband curtains and everything in between, he is polished and groomed to model standards. He grins at his own joke as Sam rises gracelessly to her feet.

'My new TDC, I presume?' She's pleased to register the surprise in his blue eyes when her long bones bring her up to his level. She straightens to her full 6ft height.

'Yes, indeed,' he beams and offers a hand, which Sam ignores. 'Adam Taylor, your Trainee Detective Constable, reporting for duty. I'm new on this floor,' he says, eyeing their surroundings like a child at a a fairground. 'I've never been in the Holmes Room before. Wow, this place is incredible. I've just come over from the Community Safety Unit. This is my second placement as part of the new entry programme. I've heard a lot about—'

'Ma'am,' she interrupts.

'Pardon?' Taylor asks, in his perfect RP, his smile beginning to falter.

'You need to say *ma'am*.' Sam says. 'Reporting for duty, *ma'am*. Or better yet, a simple *Yes, ma'am*. I've no need for your verbosity, Taylor. Nor your personal history. Nor your bad jokes.'

A crimson flush creeps up the young man's smooth throat. Sam's never enjoyed pulling rank or chastising people before, but something about his ill-timed quip and too-easy smile has sent heat through her.

'In fact,' she continues, stepping deliberately into his personal space, 'I've no need of anything from you right now, Taylor, save your tea-making skills – which I hope are up to standard? No sugar. A little milk. Most importantly, a clean cup, washed by your own, beautifully manicured hands.'

Taylor's jaw slackens and he stares unbelievingly at Sam, who stares right back. After a moment, he straightens, closes his mouth and sucks in a breath.

'Yes. Of course. Tea. Yes,' he stammers.

'Yes, *ma'am*,' Sam corrects again.

'Yes, ma'am,' Taylor mumbles.

The young man starts towards the kitchenette, and Sam notices some of the other staff turning away to conceal their smiles. *In for a penny, in for a pound*, Sam thinks, before raising her voice and adding, 'TDC Taylor?' The young man turns. 'While the tea's brewing, you can take yourself down to the lower basement and borrow some footwear that conforms to police uniform code SL354. Unless Christian Louboutin has started reinforcing the toes in his loafers?'

Taylor's face now perfectly matches the soles of his £750 shoes. A few officers nearby chuckle, without looking away from their monitors, knowing full well that there is no code SL354, and no lower basement in the building, either. Taylor nods and hurries away. When the young man is out of range, Sam slumps exhausted into her chair. *Where did that even come from?* she wonders. A wave of guilt washes over her. *I've got to be better than that.* She promises herself she'll start as soon as he gets back.

Straightening in her chair, she opens the brown case file that Harry gave her and scans the documents. Charlotte Mathers' picture is clipped to the inside of the cover – a different one from the one on the whiteboard; a professional school photograph. She forces herself to breathe as she takes in every detail. Her finger traces the girl's pale cheeks. Charlotte's smile reaches up to her green eyes in a way that Sam knows is missing from her own school photographs when she was this age. Charlotte must have been truly happy at the moment the camera snapped this shot.

Charlotte wears a green uniform, beaded with gold, an understated 18-carat Rolex on her wrist. Her curly red hair reminds Sam of Merida from the Disney movie *Brave*. Sam's vision blurs as tears rim her eyes. She wipes at them before they have a chance to spill on to her cheeks, or on to Charlotte's.

She flips to the file's summary page. Murdered by strangulation. No evidence of sexual assault. Time of death between 10 p.m. and midnight on Thursday. Just hours before Sam's meeting with Dr Thomson, less than ten minutes away from Holland Park. The child's body was posed, as if sleeping, against the trunk of an oak tree, beneath a carved love heart containing her initials and those of an unknown person: CM+DB.

Sam does not open the envelope marked 'Crime Scene Photos'. There's no way she can handle that today. Instead, she opens a fresh notebook and writes *'Who is Denver Brady?'* at the top of the page. Then she reaches for *How to Get Away With Murder*. There's no blurb or quotes from the *Guardian* about what a masterpiece it is, so she opens to page one and begins to read . . . *My name is Denver Brady, and I am a serial killer.*

By late afternoon, Sam is only three chapters in. She remembers a time when she could fly through a book the size of this one in a single sitting. Now, though, she's moving at a snail's pace, unable to concentrate and having to read most sentences twice. It's gruelling.

Denver's grimly detailed description of his murder of a boy has left Sam with a tight feeling in her chest that she knows will build into something debilitating if she doesn't manage it. She marvels at the effect the words of others can have; even through pages, Denver has made her feel sick. It's the way he sexualizes Jono's murder, coupled with his compelling voice and vivid description. One line in particular circles in Sam's mind: Denver's eerie comment about the buoyancy of fresh water, which echoes what her mother used to say to her as a little girl. There's something about hearing her lovely mum's words from the mouth of a murderer that leaves Sam reeling. She glances down at the list in her notebook.

*Who is Denver Brady?*
- *Grew up in a 'village' with a market square and a library.*
- *Lived (lives?) near a quarry with a shale floor. Could mean a limestone, sandstone, clay or shale quarry.*
- *Had a cousin called Bobby. Could be Robert or Robin.*
- *Friends: Jono/Gordie – could be John or Jonathan/Gordon or George.*
- *Thinks Mary Ann Cotton is innocent and is angry about that – why?*

Sam needs to take a break from Denver for a while, but the last thing she wants is to stop pushing forward with her investigation. She decides she'll bring herself up to speed with the provisional interviews the homicide team will have conducted. That way, she's making progress for Charlotte, while still looking out for herself. Besides, being au fait with the details of Charlotte's life and murder will help her spot connections if and when she comes across them in Denver's book.

Sam powers up her computer terminal, navigates to Charlotte's digital case folder and finds the interview videos. She clicks on the first file and puts on a headset so she can listen. The girl being interviewed identifies herself as Jessica Patel. Even though Sam can only see the backs of their heads, she doesn't think she knows the officers conducting the interview: a blonde-haired Detective

Constable – perhaps the officer Sam encountered in Holland Park? – and a male officer.

'For the purposes of today, Jessica,' the blonde officer says, 'you can call me Chloe. You don't need to say DC Spears, okay?' Jessica nods, her hands twisting inside one another on the steel table.

'How old are you, Jessica?' DC Spears asks.

'Thirteen years, ten months, two weeks and six days,' she says. 'I'm in Year 9 at school. So is Charlotte, but she's older than me.' Jessica looks back at the woman sitting close behind her, presumably her mother. To Jessica's left is an older man wearing a turban, who must be the family's solicitor.

'Tell me about Charlotte,' DC Spears says. 'What was she like as a person?' They wait for a moment as Jessica takes a few deep breaths. Her hands continue to twist, white knuckles and red fingertips.

'Charlotte is . . . was . . . one hundred and sixty-two centimetres tall and a UK-size seven shoe. She was in the top set for all classes and achieved on average a grade eight in her subjects. She just had her braces removed after sixteen months of treatment. She plays Centre in the school netball team and has a ninety-three per cent success rate delivering the centre pass and receives forty-three per cent of our POMs. Charlotte—'

'Tell them about Charlotte's pranks,' the woman behind Jessica says softly, giving the girl's shoulder a gentle squeeze. Then, turning to the officers, she adds, 'Jessica finds comfort in numbers, Detectives. Go on, sweetie. You're doing really well.'

'Charlotte was a real prankster.' Jessica smiles. 'Never cruel pranks, only ever funny ones to make people laugh. There are over seventeen pranks that I can recall in detail, but I estimate more than twenty-five total pranks.'

'That's great, Jessica,' Chloe Spears says, nodding. 'What was your favourite one of Charlotte's pranks?'

'Mmm,' Jessica casts her eyes to the ceiling in concentration.

'Probably the time she renamed all the contacts in my mum's phone.'

'She changed them all to celebrities,' her mother says. 'My auntie rang me and it showed up as Jason Statham. Charlotte had even added a topless photo of the actor, which flashed up on my screen.' The woman smiles, then shakes her head sadly.

'My absolute favourite was Charlotte's Steve Buscemi phase,' Jessica continues, and her mother laughs. 'Charlotte loved old movies, mainly ones from the nineties. She was obsessed with action films like *Con Air* and *The Rock*, and romance movies like *10 Things I Hate About You* and *Never Been Kissed*. Anyway, there's this one movie, I think it's *Con Air*, with a guy called Steve Buscemi in it. He has kind-of a funny face. Charlotte printed out more than twenty photos of Steve Buscemi and snuck into the headmaster's office. She took all his framed certificates down, and all his family pictures too, and replaced every picture with a different photo of Steve Buscemi.'

'That's funny,' Chloe says.

'Yeah, Charlotte is . . . was . . . very funny.' Jessica looks down at her hands and then rubs her eyes. 'It was days before old Wentworth-Brand noticed what she'd done. That was the funniest assembly ever. He came in holding a framed photo of Steve Buscemi. One hundred per cent of pupils were in hysterics. Even Old Wen-B saw the funny side, in the end.'

'Did Charlotte have a boyfriend, Jessica?' the male officer asks, and the atmosphere in the room shifts.

Jessica shakes her head, clenches and unclenches her fingers. 'Charlotte had a huge crush on this guy from—'

'What's his name please?' the male officer asks, pen poised.

'No, you don't understand,' Jessica says. 'He's called Charlie Heaton—'

'And does Charlie go to your school?'

'No, Charlie's from *Stranger Things*.'

'What's that?' the officer pushes.

'It's a TV show,' DC Chloe Spears clarifies for her colleague.

'Charlotte didn't have any real-life crushes,' Jessica says. 'We're only thirteen – well, Charlotte just had her fourteenth birthday ... All we do is go to school, do homework, play netball, hang out and watch shows. Sometimes we go to the cafe for bubble tea. Charlotte loved mango balls in hers, which costs an additional two pounds fifty, but she thought it was worth it.'

'They're just children,' the woman behind Jessica says, her voice soft.

'Was Charlotte raped?' Jessica asks suddenly and her mother gasps. 'That's why you're asking about boys, isn't it? I read that the Metropolitan Police drops more than ninety-five per cent of rape cases without charging the men who—'

'I'm afraid we can't disclose—' the male officer begins, but DC Spears holds up her hand to silence him.

'We have no evidence of sexual assault, Jessica,' she says in almost a whisper.

Sam smiles. There's no way that Spears should have disclosed that information, but Sam is pleased she did. In the video, Jessica begins to cry and say 'good' and 'thank God' again and again. Sam feels a wet drop land on her wrist and looks down, only then realizing that she is crying too. The tightness in Sam's chest has now established a vice-like grip and she rises from her desk, quickly closing down the video clip without reaching the end of Jessica's interview. She promises herself she'll watch the rest later, forcing herself not to think about Past Sam, who would have moved through such a recording with quiet determination and her emotions in check.

At the next desk over, her trainee DC has found his way back from the non-existent lower basement and now has his nose in

*How to Get Away With Murder.* He's scribbling notes and highlighting his copy as he goes. Everyone else on the fourth floor is still working, and likely to do so well after their shift ends. Sam hesitates for a moment, then stands. She pulls on her coat and slides Charlotte's file into her handbag, along with Denver's book. Her first day back at work is over; she can't take a moment more. She's not only exhausted, she's famished, too.

London is already full of evening traffic – theatre-goers and commuters on their way home mingle with tourists and university students. Across the river, directly opposite HQ, the London Eye turns steadily and the tiny people in the glass bubbles look out at Big Ben, the Houses of Parliament and Tower Bridge. Sam doesn't want to be among the throng longer than she has to, but she can't face her messy terrace house right now.

She makes her way along Embankment, then towards Charing Cross Tube station. The Kit Kat Club is advertising a show starring Eddie Redmayne and Elton John, which strikes her as an unusual combination. For a moment, she pictures Eddie swaying along to 'Candle in the Wind' and she realizes she's smiling to herself. Her chest is easing. A little further along the street is a secret alley called Craven Passage. Sam turns down it towards the Ship and Shovell, a brightly painted pub with a blood-red facade, barrels for outdoor tables and seats hidden in ancient alcoves.

Inside the Ship and Shovell is Victorian England, and Sam relishes the trip back in time, as well as an anachronistic but delicious chargrilled double cheeseburger, which she ordered at the bar. As Sam sinks into a desperately creaky hundred-year-old chair, she exhales deeply, looking up at portraits of British ships and explorers from days of yore. Perhaps some of her ancestors came to this pub. Maybe they ice-skated on the Thames and wore face masks indoors so as to not suffocate from the fog that seeped into their homes. Did Denver Brady's ancestors skate on the Thames, she wonders?

If Denver even exists at all. He feels very much alive in Sam's mind, but she knows better than to trust her tattered instincts. What niggles at Sam as she devours her dinner is Denver's specificity. The shale quarry. The book on Mary Ann Cotton. His cousin, Bobby. Jono's stutter and pale skin. The devil's always in the detail, as the saying goes.

As any true-crime fan knows, though, communication can lead the police straight to the door – so why do it? Perhaps that old adage that every serial killer wants to be caught holds some truth. And who can blame them? A world of celebrity awaits. Maybe Denver wants to be found, or maybe he'll divulge more about his true reasons for taking up the pen in the coming chapters.

There are other cases of serial killers who've written books, Sam remembers. Denver isn't alone in that. Sure, most tend to write treatises aimed at justifying their crimes, like the *Unabomber Manifesto* by Ted Kaczynski. *Didn't police catch Kaczynski by using that book?*, she wonders. Then there are the numerous serial killers who have written books after they were caught.

How many killers have flaunted themselves as publicly as Denver while still at large? One comes to mind immediately: Happy Face, an American serial killer whom the police misidentified and left to operated unimpeded across the country for years, just as Denver claims he has. Rather than a book, he contacted the police with notes and long letters.

Then there's the Zodiac Killer. He sent letters and ciphers to law enforcement via newspapers, and even called up a talk show for an on-air interview. Years later, a man named Eddie Seda became a fame-seeking copycat of Zodiac, choosing victims according to their star sign. Could Denver be a real killer, and Charlotte's murderer an admiring copycat? That would mean the Met has two killers on their hands. Sam swallows the thought. She takes a sip of her lime and soda and refocuses.

Wearside Jack taunted the police with voice notes sent on

cassette tapes. He claimed to be the Yorkshire Ripper but was in fact innocent of murder – a fantasist who diverted valuable attention and resource away from the investigation. Is it possible, she wonders, that Denver's book is completely fictional, the product of overexposure to crime entertainment and a deep-rooted fear of vaginas? Charlotte's real murderer could have simply taken Denver's work of fiction and used it to deflect police attention towards finding the author of *How to Get Away With Murder* instead of the child's actual killer.

Sam places her knife and fork together and dabs her mouth with her napkin. So, Denver could be a serial killer who murdered Charlotte; he could be a real killer who did not kill Charlotte but inspired a copycat; or he could have made the whole thing up and simply be a distraction. Any of the three options are equally possible at this stage.

The pub is getting busy and loud, but Sam still has no desire to return to her lonely home in Clapham, so she orders herself a mocktail. Sam's never been a drinker – she's always considered the drunk detective too much of a cliché. The one time she allowed herself to let her hair down was when she and her ex-colleague commiserated over a grisly cold case they couldn't get reopened. The night that Phil Lowry accidentally bought a whole bottle for her, instead of a single glass. She should have seen it coming.

Sam takes a slow sip of her virgin drink, savouring the fruitiness, and pulls Charlotte's file from her bag. The file should never leave the office, strictly speaking, and she takes care that no one else is close enough to see as she pushes the envelope marked 'Crime Scene Photos' aside and begins to read the front-page summary.

Charlotte Mathers was walking home when she was killed. Charlotte went to her friend Jessica Patel's house every Thursday after netball practice and Nigel Mathers usually collected his daughter at 8 p.m. sharp. On the night in question, Nigel had fallen asleep and failed to arrive, even after numerous missed calls from his daughter.

When her dad didn't show, Charlotte had told her friend she would simply walk the thirty-minute route home. Jessica said Charlotte was completely herself that evening, and confirmed that Nigel had failed to collect Charlotte a few times before and this always worried her, so she'd been eager to get home. Jessica's older brother, Jamil, backed up his sister's statement, saying that Charlotte left their house on foot at around 9 p.m.

'So no one knew Charlotte would be in Holland Park that night,' Sam says quietly to herself.

She loads up Google Maps and traces the route from Jessica Patel's house to Palace Gardens, where the Mathers lived. Charlotte would have saved maybe fifteen minutes by cutting through the park. She remembers walking down the shady passageway alongside Holland Park after her session with Dr Thomson; Charlotte must have been so scared, venturing into the park alone. The girl no doubt consoled herself that it was just after sunset and there were still people around. Sam swallows hard and takes another sip to wash away the lump in her throat.

Nigel reported Charlotte missing at 4:35 a.m. on Friday morning when he woke up and discovered his daughter was not in her bed. He called the Patels' home at 4:28 a.m. and immediately dialled 999 once they told him his daughter had walked home the night before. Charlotte's body was found in the early hours of Friday morning by a dog walker.

*It's always a dog walker*, Sam thinks. She inhales deeply and rubs her eyes. Charlotte was just fourteen. A hot anger rises in her stomach and she gulps a large mouthful of her drink to cool it.

Sam's fourteenth year had been the worst of her life, but Charlotte looked happy in her photo. She deserved so much more. She was just walking home.

'I'll get you, you bastard,' Sam murmurs, running the back of her hand across her top lip.

Next, she reads the initial forensics report. It's not very long because there's little to go on. Two sets of footprints were found at the scene. One was Charlotte's size-seven school shoes and the other was a man's boot, size twelve.

'Poor kid.' Sam finishes the last of her drink.

She rolls over the details of the case again as she walks back along Craven Passage. Every few steps, she casts a glance over her shoulder. A murderer is roaming the streets of this city and she analyses the face of every man she passes, looking for traces of evil, any indication that he could kill. The tightness in her chest lingers, but she feels a renewed determination to bring another predator down – to stop this man before he can strike again. *I can do this*, she tells herself. *I will find him.*

A scruffy little dog is tied to a drainpipe on the corner and Sam watches its skinny frame shivering pitifully as she waits to cross the road. It looks up at her imploringly from under wiry eyebrows. *You don't want to come with me, pal*, she thinks, *I can barely look after myself.* The dog whines and strains towards her, stretching its raggedy rope.

'Sorry, little one,' Sam says as she turns her back on the mutt and walks away, assuaging her guilt by resolving to call the RSPCA the second she gets home and charges her phone. She yearns for a cup of tea and an hour of vintage *Only Fools and Horses* – her version of self-care. But tonight she has a date with a wall of washing machines at the laundrette on Clapham High Street.

She decides she'll take *How to Get Away With Murder* along and try to make progress with it as she watches her undies splash around in lather. She'll add to her notes and use page markers, as she'd seen her trainee doing earlier. The thought of him brings guilt with it, so she pushes his image out of her mind and picks up her pace.

Sam's almost to the Tube when she hears the sound of footsteps behind her.

## This Little Piggie Went to Prison

Before we get into more specifics of getting away with murder, a basic grasp of how the police catch and convict killers will serve you well. If you are yourself a police officer, a lawyer or have read every Val McDermid novel that's ever been published, you can probably skip this chapter. For the rest of you, here we go.

*For every twenty serious crimes committed, there is only one conviction.*

The intelligent enough among you will have derived two important lessons from the above information:

1. The villains don't always get caught.
2. If we get caught, there is often insufficient evidence to convict us.

Not getting caught should always be your number-one priority. However, it might happen, so you need to take action now to avoid the chances of you being convicted if it does.

By understanding the basics of police structure and procedures in your country, you should be able to improve the likelihood of getting away with murder. I will cover UK policing below, but the valuable points I make can be applied in the United States, across Europe and beyond. I recommend that you conduct further research depending on where you are, because knowing your enemy is a powerful thing, wherever you may be.

## Policing by consent

In the UK, our police operate in accordance with the nine principles put forth by Robert Peel in the early 1800s. This is known as 'policing by consent' and is the treasured, traditional foundation of our law enforcement to this day.

Like our American spawn, the British police force is divided into territories and jurisdictions. However, British officers can operate outside of their jurisdiction, and physical county boundaries don't really come into play here as they do in the US. Of the forty-three police territories in the UK, almost a dozen are in 'special measures' meaning that they are below the required standard – failing, in other words. This includes the notorious Metropolitan (London) Police.

Outside of the police, there are other law enforcement agencies, such as MI6 (Intelligence) and the National Crime Agency, and they will find you quicker than Liam Neeson with a kidnapped daughter.

## Stretching the police

Now that you understand a little about how the police force is set up, it may have occurred to you that you should spread your activities across the widest possible geographical area – crucially, across police borders. Stretch the already flimsy police communications and avoid a single detective looking for you for more than one crime within their jurisdiction. As you'll never be committing crimes near where you live (or places you frequent), this alone will offer you enormous protection from geographic profilers and any triangulation theories.

Police officers themselves are regular people who often do a mediocre job to earn a crust and just want to get home to Netflix in the company of Ben and Jerry. There are no Kay Scarpettas or Nikki Alexanders in real-life pathology labs. Nor are there any Sherlock Holmeses or Columbos heading up investigations. Police officers are flawed, and often not particularly intelligent. They also work shift patterns, which can leave them exhausted and not at their best. The police are understaffed and officers are often kept back hours over their shift finish-time. Police officers experience more trauma in a week than most people will in a year, and there is little to no mental health provision within the force. Leadership can also be poor, as a lot of higher-ranking officers are corrupt old men.

### *Avoid commonality*

Following the discovery of a piece of your artwork, a variety of people will file reports and take photographs, and then a few will investigate. An SIO (Senior Investigating Officer) will be appointed, and he (or sometimes even 'she') will allocate small enquiry teams of DCs (Detective Constables) to investigate. These 'beat bobbies' will bring information back into the investigation in the form of notes or sometimes recorded interviews with witnesses. This documentation will be transcribed and filed on the central police database called HOLMES: the Home Office Large Major Enquiry System (named after Sherlock, but nowhere near as smart). HOLMES is operated by minimum-wage civilian indexers whose job it is to catalogue and tag everything the enquiry teams discover, and is searchable, like Google. Searches made are processed using keywords such as 'stabbing', 'decapitation' or 'strangled the cat'. So, *avoid commonality between your crimes.* Herein lies an important lesson around modus operandi, or MO.

Remember the Wet Bandits from the classic nineties Christmas movie *Home Alone*? Harry Lime and Marv Murchins were successful burglars (played by Joe Pesci and the other guy, whose name no one ever knew – got hit in the face by an iron: that one). Despite their lack of smarts, Harry and Marv understood the importance of research and preparation. Posing as a police officer, Harry approached the enormous mansion of Peter and Kate McCallister (heaven knows what Pete did for a living, or maybe Kate – no, this was the nineties; women still knew their place, for the most part). I digress. Harry finds out that the McCallisters are going to Paris over Christmas, so he and Marv make plans to rob the house. Young Kevin, their son, left home alone, discovers the plan and enjoys torturing the burglars instead of dialling 911. (Kev would definitely own a copy of *this* book.) Anyway, Harry and Marv are eventually arrested by Chicago Police Department. As Harry and Marv are led away, the police officer tells them that the cops know which houses the pair have previously burgled because of Marv's penchant for blocking all of the sinks and setting the water running. Marv wanted to be a notorious Wet Bandit. Thanks to Marv's signature move, however, they were connected to far more crimes than the one they were caught for. Harry and Marv have a valuable lesson for us all when it comes to law enforcement: you need to vary everything about your crimes if you can, or copy someone else's MO. Clever police work involves reviewing your past moves and using them to predict your future ones. Like chess, but more fun. So, don't be a Wet Bandit.

Fortunately, most police officers aren't too bright. I had my only run-in with the police after my second murder. I didn't rate police intelligence levels even back then, and they've only deteriorated since.

I was studying for my A-levels at the local college at the time. The college was a fairly large, stand-alone sixth form, with a wide catchment area. My cousin, Bobby, had done well there and had gone off to university, so I was alone most of the time.

I opted to study psychology, a relatively new subject for the college, along with some other more mundane topics. Since Jono, my interest in murder and the minds of those who kill had only deepened. I was no longer seeking to understand Teddy and the others, but myself as well. At college I made some friends, but, not enjoying football, I mainly hung out with an academic crowd, who I found fairly dull. I could have taken up sport; my body was no longer so scrawny and I'd grown to a full six feet, but I had no interest in games.

As far as my small group of chums went, I was the best-looking by some way. At lunchtime, it was something of a tradition for the boys from our college to cross the fields and hang around the walls of the all-girls convent school. There were plenty of girls in our own college, but there was something that drew us to those convent walls each day, seeking a glimpse of the heavenly creatures inside.

That was how I met Sarah.

# 4

Sam's jeans and cobalt-blue shirt are still a touch damp as she wiggles into them the next morning. She's a little later getting up than planned. In her dreams, DS Lowry was a snarling dog running his claws along her skin, up her leg and over her backside. She pushes her nightmares out of her head as she eats breakfast. At least she has freshly washed clothes to wear to work today.

A whimpering sounds from Sam's lounge, and she opens the door to see a scruffy little creature curled up on her sofa.

'And what on earth am I going to do about you?' Sam asks it, offering up the rest of her toast, but the little creature tenses, trembling and burying its head deeper into the old blanket she'd put out for it last night. An unpleasant smell hits her and she looks accusingly at the little dog that had tugged free of its rope, followed her home and guilted her into letting it in. It's skinny and dirty, with a wiry coat that might be brown or white, for all she can see through the muck. The fur is a little longer around the back legs where clods of dirt have matted up, dangling unpleasantly – and, apparently, aromatically. Its eyes are too big for its head, and carry a look of perpetual sadness.

Sam decides the little creature needs some space so she sips her cup of tea and pops her Prozac out of the blister pack. The tiny green pill leaps from her hand on to the carpet. She bends to retrieve it but soon thinks twice when she sees that it's lodged itself in a fluffball up against the skirting board. *I must clean this place up*, she thinks, and her mind is instantly flooded with nasty thoughts about herself, her lack of motivation and general worthlessness as a human being. The dog gives a little whine, interrupting her inner scolding, and she takes a deep breath.

'Are you sure you don't want to find a better stranger to follow home?' she asks the dog, whose head turns on an angle, as if unsure of her meaning. 'My house looks like the kind of place Liam Neeson would rescue his daughter from,' she says. The dog remains silent.

Sam pops a fresh pill from the pack, washing it down with the last of her tea. Before she leaves, she warms a bowl of Weetabix for her uninvited guest and leaves the food and a bowl of water in the kitchen, next to her old 'sick blanket' that her mother would pull out any time she was poorly.

As she waits for her frothy coffee at Bubbles and Beans, she calls a couple of animal shelters, but is amazed to discover that none of them have room. Eventually, a shelter in Battersea relents but asks if Sam can hold on to the dog for a week or two first.

'I know what they're hoping for,' Sam says to no one once she's ended the call. 'And they can forget it.'

Sam's never owned a dog before and, as the bus rocks its way towards New Scotland Yard, she mulls over what it might need for a week. Only a week. Two at most. Food. A lead and collar. Definitely some strong shampoo.

The bus is quieter today, but Sam still turns up Slipknot and Paramore as loud as possible to keep the sound of the rest of the world from reaching her. She only managed one chapter of *How to Get Away With Murder* last night. It was excruciating, reading over and over again as her eyelids sagged from the exhaustion of her first day back at work. Plus she lost a lot of time to caring for her unexpected guest. She reaches into her bag and, in a shaky scrawl, updates her list as the bus makes halting progress through the London rush hour.

- *Studied psychology A-level.*
- *Went to sixth-form college near a walled, all-girls convent school.*
- *Likes Val McDermid and Home Alone (but who doesn't?).*
- *Does not respect the police.*

She disembarks at the correct stop today and heads to the front desk to collect her new security pass. In front of her, a young woman is arguing with the receptionist, who is insisting that no one is available to see her. Something about her voice is familiar to Sam and when the girl turns around she sees that it isn't a young woman at all, but thirteen-year-old Jessica Patel.

'Jessica,' Sam says, automatically. The teenager looks her up and down, making Sam feel very wanting in the appearance department.

'Who are you?' she asks.

'DI Samantha Hansen. Sam.'

'Are you working on Charlotte's case?' Jessica asks.

'Yes – well, kind of.'

'No one will give me an update,' Jessica complains. 'I've been waiting for twenty-eight minutes.'

'Shouldn't you be in school?' Sam asks. 'Do your parents know you're—'

'I just want an update, please.' Desperation suffuses her voice.

'OK,' Sam says, stepping away from the reception desk and into the empty waiting area. 'Sit down, Jessica.' Sam explains that police investigations need to be confidential. She describes how police withhold a lot of information from everyone, including friends and family of the victim, in order to ensure their prosecution is as strong as it can be when they make an arrest.

'So you're confident you'll catch him?' Jessica asks. 'How certain are you? Can you give me your answer as a percentage, please?'

Sam takes a slow breath. She recognizes this moment. In books and films, when Sam hears detectives promising to find the killer or the rapist or the missing child, she knows she'll stay transfixed as the police character torments themselves with their failures and the victim holds the promise over them for ever.

'We can never guarantee outcomes, Jessica,' Sam says, her voice gentle.

'Well, what's your personal success rate?'

'I shouldn't—'

'Do you know the percentage?'

'Ninety-four per cent across all cases,' Sam says, 'ninety-eight per cent in all homicides. But Jessica, you need to understand that I'm – well, I've been ill. I can't promise—'

'Over how many years?' Jessica asks.

'I've been in homicide for more than ten years.'

'I can't calculate precisely, without the exact number of cases per year and variations year to year, but the probability that you will solve Charlotte's murder is extremely high. The unknown variable is your recent illness. Is this your first case after illness, and how long have you been absent from the job? Do you have ongoing symptoms or weaknesses? These factors will significantly influence—'

'Jessica,' Sam interrupts, panicked by the barrage of personal questions. She takes a second to unwrap another mint from her pocket, not meeting the girl's eye. They sit in tense silence for a moment, then Jessica sighs and stands to leave.

'Look, Jessica,' Sam says, 'I will do my very best for Charlotte. I promise.'

The child hesitates. Nods. Then she takes something from her pocket and places a small, round object into Sam's hand. It's a miniature sports ball with the letter C in the middle, attached to a chain with a keyring at the end.

'Keep this with you, until you find Charlotte's killer,' Jessica says.

'C for Charlotte?'

'No, for Centre,' Jessica says. 'The position Charlotte played in netball. I gave this to her for her fourteenth birthday. Nigel found it in Charlotte's room and . . .' The girl begins to cry then. First slow tears that spill down her cheeks, then bigger sobs, until she's heaving against Sam and mumbling incoherently.

'Jessica!' A woman appears beside them, scowling slightly at Sam before sitting down and pulling Jessica into her arms.

'Mrs Patel,' Sam says, 'I'm Detective Hansen. Jessica came in hoping for an update—'

'As soon as I saw she was here, I left work and came straight away.' She holds Jessica tight against her chest: 'Oh, sweetie . . .' Looking up at Sam, she continues, 'It's been so tough on her. On us all. We love Charlotte. Loved.'

'You saw she was here?' Sam asks.

'We all track our children, Detective,' the woman says. 'As soon as I arrive at my desk, I check on everyone. Mainly because Jamil, my son, stays up all night on video games and then sleeps in, and I have to call the gardener to bang on our front door and wake him up.'

Mrs Patel stands, pulling Jessica up gently and telling her she has a taxi waiting. Jessica takes a few deep breaths and then looks at Sam.

'Keep the keyring with you, please, Detective Hansen,' she says. 'I want it to remind you of Charlotte for each of the one thousand, four hundred and forty minutes in the day.'

Sam sees the Patels out to their taxi before taking the stairs up to the fourth floor and making herself a cup of tea. She places the miniature netball in her pocket, feeling the pressure of it against her flesh as she moves. As she arrives at her desk, Sam looks out of the window and sees a large seagull cruise by. She lets her eyes follow the bird as it spirals down to the street level in search of food. It lands on the front steps of the building and pecks at a crisp packet. Several journalists linger close by, presumably hoping to discover the latest progress on Charlotte's murder for the morning news. Sam watches as the journos suddenly jump up and run over to two men who are approaching New Scotland Yard.

The men are of similar height and build, one with black hair and the other sandy-brown. They're walking awfully close together, and Sam realizes that one appears to be supporting the other, almost holding him up. The journalists ram microphones and camera lenses at them. Two smartly dressed figures descend the steps to meet the men, sending the seagull and reporters leaping backwards. One is DCI Harry Blakelaw and the other, Sam assumes, is the SIO in Charlotte's murder investigation; the woman's name has slipped Sam's mind. The two men, Sam deduces, must be Charlotte's uncle and father. Jack and Nigel Mathers.

Forgetting all about her trainee, Adam Taylor, who is hovering nearby, waiting for Sam's instruction, she moves quickly to the lift. She jumps aboard and jabs at the button for the basement, where the custody suite and interview rooms are.

As she descends, Sam notices a glossy poster featuring a mnemonic to remind officers of new cognitive interview techniques. TED's PIE, it says, with each pie-slice in the picture containing question openers. *T = Tell me. E = Explain to me.* And so on. The sight of oozing apple and sugared pastry makes Sam's stomach rumble and she promises herself a trip to Greggs at lunchtime. She closes her eyes and casts her mind back to the days when she and Harry would interview suspects together, and the old-fashioned techniques they used. Her godfather taught her how to make the hard nuts crack by letting them think they're in control then slamming them with your strongest piece of evidence – something they don't know you know. He taught her how to lull a softer suspect with small talk, drinks, tiny favours that endear and create a feeling of friendship. They'd even used the old good-cop, bad-cop from time to time. Together, they'd teased confessions from the worst kind of human beings. Harry knew all the tricks in the book. He once let a drug dealer bring his pet pug into the interview; the perp sang like a canary after that. *The gear's in me nan's cupboard at the bottom of the kitty-kibble bag. Don't tell her. She'd never forgive me for what happened with Cindy Clawford.* For a week after that, Harry emailed her videos of pugs on skateboards and performing summersaults, making her smile every time.

Sam remembers that Harry prefers interview room number one, so that's where she heads when she steps out of the lift. It's the room that makes the suspect most uncomfortable, with its flickering light, small hard chairs and useless fan. Sam walks quickly to the observation room attached to the main room, swipes her pass and enters, leaving the light off and standing behind the door. Hiding, despite knowing no one can see her from the attached room.

A minute later, the lights in the interview room flicker to life and the lighter-haired Mr Mathers takes a seat. Someone opens the door to the observation room to check that it's empty. Sam holds her breath, flattening herself against the wall, and the door closes again. Sam stays where she is, frozen. After a moment, she steps forward and looks through the one-way mirror. Harry and the female SIO are seated with their back to her. Sam presses a button on her side of the mirror so she can listen in. The woman activates the recording system and reintroduces herself as Detective Inspector Tina Edris. The man being interviewed looks shattered. His green eyes are red-rimmed and his hands rest on the steel table as if he doesn't have the strength to lift them.

'If you would please state your name for the recording,' Tina says gently.

'Jack Mathers.'

'And I am DCI Blakelaw, here to observe,' Harry adds, and Sam notices Tina's shoulders twitch. It's clear that the Met's newest DI does not want babysitting by her boss.

'Mr Mathers—' Tina begins.

'Jack,' he says, but doesn't try to force a smile.

'Jack. Just to remind you, this is a voluntary statement to help us with your niece's homicide investigation. I know we've already taken a preliminary statement, but it's standard practice for us to speak to key witnesses more than once in such cases. There may be some repetition today, but please believe that this is vitally important to the case.'

'OK,' he says. 'Anything we can do to help you catch him, we'll do.'

'Please begin by talking us through your movements on the night of Charlotte's murder.'

Jack takes a deep breath. 'I didn't see Charlie – Charlotte – that day. She'd left for school before I came downstairs. I didn't . . . get to say goodbye to her that morning. Jesus, how is this happening?' He breaks off, looking around the room.

'Where were you that evening, from five p.m. until midnight?' Tina asks.

'I was at home until around six p.m. Then I went to a retirement do. An old mate I worked with years back. 'Til maybe one in the morning. I shared an Uber home—'

'And where was the party held?'

'The Pig and Butcher in Brenham. It was a decent night, everyone was really friendly and . . .' he trails off. 'As if any of it matters now. As if *anything* matters.' Sam watches his face. There are clear similarities between him and Charlotte. The sandy hair with hints of auburn, the green eyes and creamy skin. Jack sniffs loudly and drags his hand down his face. He reaches for a cup of water, lifts it, trembling, to his lips.

'Can you confirm that you stayed at the party the whole night, Mr Mathers?' Tina presses.

'Yes.' Jack nods. 'Charlie, she's just a baby. It feels like only yesterday I was teaching her to ride a bike. Oh, Jesus . . .' Jack's chin wobbles and he looks, for a moment, like a child himself.

'You never left the Pig and Butcher?'

'I went to the corner shop for some vape juice. But that took, like, ten minutes. Twenty at most,' Jack says, tears now rolling freely down his face.

'So you left the Pig and Butcher for no more than twenty minutes? It couldn't have been longer?' she asks. Jack shakes his head.

'You saw your brother that night, before you left,' Harry suggests. Harry had told Sam on Monday – that was only yesterday, she realizes – that he thought someone close to Charlotte was likely responsible.

'Yeah. I saw Nige at around six. Just before I left,' Jack says, lightly tapping his own cheeks as if trying to wake himself up.

'What was he doing?' Tina asks.

'He'd just got home. Nigel gets in at six every day.' Jack sniffs again. 'He runs on his treadmill. Takes a shower and sits in his armchair with a whisky. Then he and Charlotte—' Jack breaks off at the dead girl's name, and takes a deep, calming breath. 'Charlotte and Nigel eat whatever Sonja, the housekeeper, has prepared. They eat late, around seven-thirty. My brother is a man of routine.'

Sam's eyebrow raises. She knows Charlotte grew up in Palace Gardens, an exclusive terrace of white marble homes, but a housekeeper? That's another level of rich. Sam pulls her phone from her pocket and quickly googles Nigel Mathers, clicks on LinkedIn. The man in the image is barely recognizable as the man she just saw enter the building, but it must be him. *Hedge fund manager. Figures*, Sam thinks, sliding her phone away again.

'On Thursdays, Charlotte and Nigel's routine changes?' Tina asks, and Jack shrugs.

'I suppose. I never really paid attention until this happened. But yeah, Charlie goes – sorry, I mean Charlie *used to* go – to a school friend's house on Thursdays after netball and Nige picked her up. I don't know the exact details,' Jack says. Sam rubs her thumb over the small netball in her pocket.

'Do you know where the school friend lives?' she asks.

'No,' Jack says.

'You have a bit of a history, Jack,' Tina says. 'Talk to us about that.'

'My history?' Jack blinks.

'You served some time, back in the day,' Tina says.

Jack's pale face reddens. 'That was stupid kids' stuff, and I paid for it. Six months in juvy and my own dad never spoke to me again. Cut me off entirely. I was seventeen, for God's sake.' The man covers his face and his shoulders heave, but Tina doesn't let up.

'Jack, we need to find who hurt Charlotte and—'

'Well, it wasn't me!' he yells, his face a picture of pain. 'I loved that kid. Why are you doing this? We all know who killed my niece. Why haven't you—'.

'Who do you think murdered Charlotte, Jack?' Tina asks and he just stares at her, his mouth open.

'Brady killed her,' Jack whispers. 'You told us Denver Brady's initials were found at the scene. We googled around and found Howtogetawaywithmurder.com. Nigel bought the sick little how-to guide. What are you doing to catch *him*?'

'At the moment, Mr Mathers, we're keeping all lines of enquiry open. I can assure you we are taking that element of the case very seriously. We—'

'We don't need assurances. We need you to find the man who murdered Charlie.' Jack heaves one giant sob, then stands and moves slowly to the door. 'I'm sorry,' he says as he opens it, 'I can't take any more today. I'll send Nigel in, but please, he's been through enough. Just go easy, OK?' Jack lets the door click shut behind him.

'He's convinced that Denver—' Tina whispers but Harry cuts her off.

'We'll find Charlotte's killer the same way we find the rest. Means. Motive. Opportunity.'

'Sir, whether we like it or not, *How to Get Away With Murder* is an important part of this investigation,' Tina says. 'I'm concerned that this is my first homicide investigation at the Met and this vital element of my case has been put under the command of a DI in her first week back following a significant—'

'Detective Hansen has over ten years' experience and an exemplary arrest record,' Harry cuts in.

'Sir, I just feel that it sends the wrong message. We need to be *seen* to be taking the book seriously, just in case, and giving it to—'

'Your concerns are noted, Tina, but as DCI I feel that a combination of your fresh talent and Sam's experience is best,' Harry concludes.

Tina pauses for a second, chews her lip, watches him shrewdly. 'It certainly protects you from any criticism, sir. Having two female Detective Inspectors involved.'

Sam notices Harry's neck flush red, but before he can respond there's a knock at the door and a man shuffles in. His suit hangs limp and crumpled about him. He has dark hair with hints of grey around the temples, greasy and matted at the back. His skin is pale with a yellow hue and he sits down awkwardly. A wave of sadness washes through Sam. Nigel Mathers' eyes are glazed and he downs a cup of water that Tina hands him. The police officers make a few comments, give the obligatory caution, and then begin with some easy questions. It's immediately obvious to Sam that this is a broken man.

'I just fell asleep,' Nigel slurs. 'It's my fault. My beautiful girl . . .' he dry-sobs, as though the tears have all run out. 'It's my fault. She wanted her own Uber account and . . .' A glob of spit falls from his mouth and he instinctively catches it in his hand, then looks up at the ceiling as if rain might be falling. 'There was a man . . .'

'What man, Nigel?' Tina asks.

'On Netflix,' he sniffs. 'A taxi driver who was picking up girls.

So I said, *No, Charlotte, I don't want you in cars with strange men.* Oh God . . . She said, *Dad* . . . Now I'll never hear her say Dad again. Am I even still a dad? If my only daughter is . . .' Sam can't understand what Nigel says after that and they wait until he falls silent.

'Mr Mathers. Nigel,' Tina says, 'The night Charlotte died, can you confirm your movements? Did you arrive home from work at your usual time?' The man nods and mumbles, and Tina asks him to answer aloud for the benefit of the recording.

'Did you leave the house that night, Nigel?' Tina says, and he opens and closes his mouth, his dark eyes roaming the corners of the floor.

'Please catch . . . catch him. Catch DB. Please, catch Denver.'

Nigel begins to rock. Tina looks at Harry and shakes her head. This interview can't continue. Nigel is clearly sedated and anything he's said in this state won't stand up in court anyway. They thank Nigel and close the interview down, shutting off the lights and leaving both rooms in the dark.

Sam slumps in a chair and fiddles with the little netball to calm herself. The sight of Jack and Nigel Mathers, their raw grief, has shaken her before the day has even begun. Despite Harry's suspicions, Sam doesn't believe that Nigel murdered his daughter. She just sees a shell of a man, heartbroken by loss. The uncle is obviously devastated, too. Neither man seems to be putting on an act, but Sam knows you can never be certain. She pockets the keyring and rubs at her temples.

Her mind turns back to Harry and Tina's conversation just moments ago. Tina clearly implied he's involving both her and Sam to shield himself, just in case the words 'serial killer' hit the headlines. Sam shakes her head instinctively. She won't believe that. Harry simply wants the benefit of her experience, plus Tina's only just a DI, so of course he's treading carefully with a high-profile case. They need to find Charlotte's killer, and 'DB', quickly.

'Denver Brady,' she whispers, feeling his full name on her lips for the first time. She closes her eyes and turns the three possibilities over in her mind again: Denver the serial killer; Denver the killer with a copycat; Denver the fantasist red herring. 'Which are you?' she whispers.

Sam stands, makes her way from the interview rooms and takes the lift back up to the fourth floor. As she ascends, she feels the corner of *How to Get Away With Murder* pressing into her side, through the soft leather of her bag. She has blocked out the next few hours of her morning for reading through it and she intends to take notes as she goes.

The lift doors ping open and she sees Adam Taylor loitering, two cups of steaming tea in his hands. He smiles, wishes her good morning and gabbles something about a man named Basil.

'Let's do this later, Taylor,' Sam says, cutting him off, as she takes a mug of tea from him and sits down at her desk, then reaches into her top drawer for a headache tablet.

'But, ma'am.' He lowers his voice as if embarrassed to ask. 'What should I be doing to help?'

'Isn't it obvious?' she snaps, wishing to God that her trainee was a crime fiction fan. She swallows the pills and pinches the top of her nose, trying desperately to alleviate the pressure building across her brow and over her eyes. 'I need you to pull out any potentially identifying information you can find in the book – names, locations, MOs and so on. Then set up database searches to look for any real-life victims that match those described in the book. Do you know how to do that? Good. We'll monitor the results and sense-check any hits we get. We also need to find out how the book is printed, distributed and sold.' She opens the book to the copyright page. 'This isn't a publisher I've ever heard of – I reckon he paid to have it printed and then uploaded it to his own little website. Check out Howtogetawaywithmurder.com.'

'Yes, ma'am,' he says, jotting furiously in his Moleskine notebook. 'Shall I have the site taken down?'

Sam thought for a moment. 'No. We need to find out more before we do that. Plus, we don't want Denver to know we're on to him.' Sam blows on her tea before taking a scalding sip. 'Copy me in on everything and let me know if you want help. Right now, I need to read the next chapter of *How to Get Away With Murder* before this migraine gets me.'

## *How do You Solve a Problem Like Marry Her?*

I first noticed Sarah over the convent walls, playing rounders. Her curly auburn hair looked to be on fire as she ran from base to base and the other girls scrambled to bowl her out. They all wore A-line skirts below the knee, brown with yellow trim. It was truly disgusting garb. Yet, somehow, Sarah looked wonderful in it.

One day, Sarah hit the ball so hard that it flew out of the school grounds and into the undergrowth on the other side of the convent walls. She dropped her bat and came to lean over the wall to see if she could spot the ball. I was sitting reading with my friends on a grassy bank opposite – our usual vantage point from which to watch the girls, who rolled their skirts up high during games in order to be able to run unhindered, making excellent viewing. The ball had vanished. Being an empath, I immediately perceived the need for help in locating it and got up to volunteer my assistance.

'It's there!' Sarah called. Other girls had joined her now, peering over the convent wall at me as I rummaged for the ball. They giggled and whispered to each other. Brambles tore at my jeans.

'What's your name?' one of them shouted.

'Bobby,' I said, giving my cousin's name, which for some reason set them tittering.

'I'm not out,' Sarah said to her friends. 'I'm still batting once Bobby's found the ball.'

'You got MSN, Bobs?' another girl shouted. For younger readers who can't remember the nineties, MSN was kind of like WhatsApp, but on a computer as we didn't have mobile phones yet.

'I don't use MSN,' I said, kicking my way through a fern to try to find the elusive ball. In truth, I didn't have a computer at all. My family was, I confess, on the breadline. I had always received free school meals and endured the shame of sitting still while classmates handed in packets of money each Monday morning.

'It's over there,' Sarah called, 'just there. Behind that ash tree. You're miles away.'

I moseyed slowly towards the ash, pretending not to see the ball. Soon I was so close to it that Sarah would think I was blind if I didn't pick it up. So I did, and I turned, looking up at her. Even from where I stood, below the convent wall, in the cold shade, I could see the warm freckles on her skin. Green eyes. Her flaming mane, wild and free.

'Pass,' she instructed, cupping her hands for the ball. I nursed it a little longer, giving her what I hoped was a cheeky grin.

'What'll you give me for it?' I said, in a rare moment of flirtation.

'Nowt!' she said. 'Pass it!'

'Sometimes the lads leave us notes under that rock there,' her friend shouted to me, then received an elbow from a fat girl who hadn't spoken at all.

'What? He's all right,' the first girl said, rubbing her arm.

'He's minging,' said the fat girl, and I'd have flayed her on the spot if the high walls hadn't been dividing us.

'Pass the ball,' said Sarah, and I threw it to her. She turned away and went back to the game. Several other girls stayed, leaning over the wall and chatting to my friends, but I lost interest and withdrew. The girls stayed well beyond their lunch-break, until a tiny nun came along and yelled that the bell had gone.

I was desirous of seeing Sarah again, but I did not like the idea of a shared location for leaving notes. I resolved to leave one brief snippet under the rock, instructing Sarah to write to me by way of a nearby statue with a loose foot. I waited two weeks but then, one fine day, I tugged the Mother Mary's ankle and there it was. A riveting correspondence ensued. Very romantic, I know. Risky, too, although I did beseech Sarah to burn my notes after reading, and I believe she complied for fear of her God-bothering father. After many months of wooing in this way, and at significant cost to the Virgin's limb, Sarah finally agreed to meet me after school. She'd tell her parents she had rounders practice and tell the nuns she had a dental appointment. That gave her about an hour and a half to spend with yours truly.

I hid in the bushes by the river and waited for her. Then we wandered a route I knew well, up towards the reservoir, through the farmer's fields with pink hawthorn hedges. We sat beneath an oak tree and I promised her I'd carve her name into it next time. As it turned out, there wasn't to be a next time. It was my first kiss and it was full of orange flames as her hair shone through my closed eyelids. It was as terrible as everyone's first kiss, I suppose. She climbed on to my lap and we practised until she was making sweet little moans. Things turned a little sour when her fingers moved towards my special place and I had to calm her down. She assured me that she would not pressure me and that she didn't believe in carnal sin. Had I ever thought about my wedding?

I desired a subject change, so I gently pulled her beside me and began asking about her interests, and sharing mine. I don't know at what point things took a turn for the worse, but suddenly Sarah was on her feet and, would you believe it, called me a *freak*. Me. It's possible that she simply hadn't understood my disappointment about the innocence of Mary Ann Cotton, but Sarah began to back away from me.

I took hold of her wrist, pulling her on to my lap with my arms tightly around her. I held her close as I tried to make her understand that we were simply chatting and my interests were purely theoretical. She writhed and squirmed. Then she turned hateful – biting down on my arm, drawing blood! I yelled and released her, and she proceeded to try to run away from me as if I'd attacked her, and not the other way around. I ran after her and as I tried to stop her, we both fell, landing heavily.

As soon as I was astride her, my weight forcing the air from her lungs and my knees pinning her wrists, I knew that I wouldn't fight it. I let my fingers find her delicate white neck and I gave a little squeeze. A thrill ran through me, far stronger than anything I'd felt during the kissing. We spent some time together until she could take no more and, as the sun fell low, I closed her beautiful green eyes for ever. Before she stiffened, I lifted her carefully and positioned her snuggly beneath our oak, as if she'd curled up and fallen asleep.

I rinsed my face and hands in the river and walked back to college, sneaking into the study hall, which was open until 8 p.m. each school night. When the janitor kicked me out to lock up, I chatted to him, ensuring I described the essay I was working on and how I'd been there all evening, trying to get it done.

The police visited our college a week later. We were all briefed in assembly and then many of the boys who hung around the convent were interviewed individually, including me. The detective was a fat man with a bald head, who had a young female PC with him to take notes.

'Now then, son,' he said to me. 'Did you know the girl? Sarah . . .' I forget her surname.

'No,' I said.

'But you've seen her? When you and your friends hang around down there by the convent?'

'Do you have a picture?' I asked and he produced one. Not a complimentary photo of Sarah, I must say. She looked more like Geri Halliwell than herself. 'Yes, I've seen her at the convent. But that's all.'

'Ever talk to her?'

'I don't think so.'

'You don't think so?' he pressed.

'Yeah,' I said, feigning what I considered typical teenage nonchalance.

'Where were you last Wednesday night?' he asked. I took my planner out of my bag, laid it flat on the table and flipped through it, finding the relevant week and letting the officers see it. I'd written in big letters in the Thursday slot: *SKINNER ESSAY DUE*.

'I had a psych essay due the next day, so I think I stayed back to type it up.'

'You think?' the detective pushed. I shrugged. Normal teenagers don't know where they were yesterday, let alone last week.

I never heard any more about it. The hoo-ha around the murder continued for some months. Eventually, the case cooled and no one was apprehended. The police presence increased around the town and there were a lot of news conferences and posters in shop windows, but the police seemed to do very little actual investigating. I suppose they didn't have a lot to go on. It did feel like a bit of a close shave, to be honest. The number of panda cars that suddenly cruised around our area was anxiety-inducing, so I decided there and then that I'd stop shitting where I lived and develop some proper victim-selection principles. I'll share those with you shortly.

As for my second victim, I consoled myself with the knowledge that her soul would receive more prayers than anybody else that year, what with the nuns partially to blame. Then Princess Diana was killed and Sarah was trumped. I didn't want my Sarah forgotten, so I went back to our special spot and carved our initials into the oak tree, surrounding them with a love heart. It took a long time and I went to no small amount of effort to ensure that I carved deep and neat.

Speaking of cutting deep, let me tell you another story.

# 5

A stunning young officer has one buttock planted on the edge of Sam's desk when she arrives back from lunch, a bag of kibble, some puppy pads and a few other pet items under her arm. The blonde tosses her glossy hair as she laughs at something Adam Taylor has said. The TDC springs to his feet when he sees Sam approaching and the officer's eyes run up and down Sam's body, taking in every shabby, slightly stodgy inch of her. Sam recognizes the woman as both the one from Holland Park and the one from the Jessica Patel interview recording she'd watched yesterday. Sam tries to remember her name, but fails.

'Ma'am,' Taylor starts, 'I was just—'

'Get a room, Taylor,' Sam orders, and the young man's face turns instantly puce.

'Ma'am, you've got the wrong end of the—'

'Not interested, Taylor,' Sam snaps, cutting him short, and unloads her purchases on to her desk. 'Find a room.'

'The DI means a meeting room, Adam.' The young woman smirks, retrieving a dog collar that has landed on the floor near her feet.

Red-faced, Taylor slopes off and Sam sits, quickly checking her emails and the database search output. She notices several emails from HR: welcome-back messages and well-being check-in appointments. She ignores them, opening a browser and typing in *Howtogetawaywithmurder.com*.

She's surprised to be met with a stylish website. The homepage features a simple image of Denver's book and an 'Add to Basket' button beneath. Customers can choose between the hard copy and the e-book, and both seem averagely priced. She clicks on 'A Message from the Author'.

Dear Reader,

Welcome. I'm the author of *How to Get Away With Murder*. I hope you enjoy my first book, and if you do, please leave a killer review. May I humbly suggest the following hashtags: #howtogetawaywithmurder and #teamdenver
    It means the world to me to read about what you've discovered among my pages. I appreciate every single one of you. If for some watery reason, you feel inclined to leave a negative review, pray that you know how to hide your IP address. Ellie1985, I see you. Hope you enjoy your son Archie's football match tonight. Go Blackheath Cubs FC.
    Just kidding. But seriously, serial killers have feelings, too. Kindness costs nothing.

Warm wishes,
Denver Brady, S.K.

Sam rolls her eyes and goes back to the homepage, where she adds a book to her basket and proceeds to checkout. As she suspects, the payment gateway is provided by a secure third-party plug-in, WorldSecurePay. Sam smiles as she copies the payment URL and sends it to DC Chen, head of the technical enquiry team. A warrant may be needed, but they'll be able to request the details of the bank account receiving the money from the sales made via Howtogetawaywithmurder.com.

Closing her email, Sam quickly navigates to the police database. There are no hits on any real-life Denver victims yet. She broadens a couple of the search criteria, but Taylor's done a good job overall and she sets it running again. The database will identify any unsolved homicides where the victim's name matches any of Denver's victims: Sarah, Jono and so on. Taylor has set up multiple searches for a man named Basil, who appears to have been attacked but not murdered, unlike Denver's other victims. It's more likely that they'll find the homicide victims first. There are only around six hundred murders per year in the UK compared with countries like America, where there are around twenty thousand. They only have forenames and approximate times frames to go on, but if the cases are there and their search terms precise, the database should flag them. Sam doesn't dwell on the obvious caveat: Denver could have easily substituted a victim's real name with a fake. But they have to start somewhere.

Gathering her copy of *How to Get Away With Murder* and Charlotte's case file, Sam stands to follow Taylor to the briefing room, but realizes she's being observed. The pretty young officer is lingering and clearly has something that she wants to say, but rank and etiquette seem to have tied her tongue. Sam stands and waits.

'Ma'am . . .' the young woman begins, 'you have a little something . . .' She gestures with her fingers and Sam looks down her shirt to where a glob of ketchup has landed on her boobs and slalomed further down her chest. Once upon a time, before DS Phil Lowry violated her and sent her spiralling, Sam kept a clean, pressed shirt in her locker, along with make-up, deodorant, a hairbrush and a host of other items that normal women needed to smell, look and function perfectly. Now the only thing in there was dust.

Sam shrugs off her embarrassment and says, 'Thank you, Officer . . . ?'

'DC Spears, ma'am,' she says; and then, tentatively, 'People call me Britney, ma'am, among other things, but my name is actually Chloe. I'm on the witness team. We're working on interviews and statements for the Charlotte Mathers case.'

'Nice to meet you officially, Chloe. I thought you handled Jessica Patel's interview very well.'

'Thank you, ma'am.' Chloe blushes. 'Adam mentioned that you're leading the book enquiry team? I've just started reading it myself. I know that it isn't anything to do with my role in the investigation, but I saw a copy on Adam's desk and, well, I'm struggling to put it down, to be honest. I love a good crime book.'

Sam smiles. 'Well, DC Spears, welcome to the Met's first book club.'

'What are your thoughts on Denver so far, ma'am?'

'I'm keeping an open mind at this stage and I'm still reading, so I don't want to leap to conclusions. There are three possibilities that I'm working with.' She listed them, gratified by Chloe's rapt attention.

'Meaning we either have one serial killer, two killers or a made-up story that inspired murder. Wow. My mind is—'

'Spears . . .' Harry leans out of his office door. 'Aren't you meant to be interviewing the headmaster?' Chloe looks at the huge clock on the far wall.

'Shoot,' she mutters, spinning away from Sam. 'On it, sir.'

Chloe Spears jogs to the lift and Sam spots Taylor, his face now its usual colour, waiting at the door to the small glass meeting room in the corner of the fourth floor. The room is tiny, and when she takes a seat she notices that their bodies are uncomfortably close to one another. She suddenly finds herself wishing she had spritzed some of the old perfume she used to wear.

'Sorry, Taylor,' she starts, shuffling uncomfortably and knocking her knee accidentally against his. 'I was just looking at Denver's website.'

'It looks decent enough,' he says, 'but I ran a SimilarWeb report and there's very little traffic hitting it. What little there is seems to be coming mainly from Reddit. One particular sub is driving most of the visitors—'

'Sorry . . . Reddit?' Sam scrunches her brow.

'Yes, ma'am.' He pulls out his phone and she scrolls on it as he talks. 'It's a website of online communities known as "subreddits" or "subs" – basically, forum-style group conversations organized around the shared interests. Anyone can join and anyone can post. If a user's post is interesting to others, people can upvote it so it gets more attention.'

'OK. So, Denver joined a chat room to self-promote?'

'Basically, ma'am, yes. With Google or other search engines it'd take longer, require more skill and cost money to drive people to his website. Reddit has loads of subs about serial killers and Denver has basically hijacked the conversations and promoted his book there.'

'Send everything you have to DC Chen.' She hands back Taylor's phone. 'I've emailed him to pursue the payment provider Denver uses on the site and, with any luck, we can follow the money right to Denver's door.'

Taylor's head sags. 'I should have thought to check the payment gateway . . .'

'Let's talk about the book. What're your thoughts so far, Taylor?'

'Well,' he begins, flipping some pages of his Moleskine, 'I think we need a profiler, ma'am.'

'A profiler?' Sam swallows her tea. 'I'm sorry to burst your bubble, Taylor, but offender profilers are pointless.' He opens and closes his mouth. 'I know,' she says before he can object. 'You've seen them on television, read about them in books? These heroes with a sixth sense who can tell you what a serial killer had for breakfast or how his awful mother waved a pair of scissors at his . . .' Sam takes a deep breath. Taylor crosses his legs. 'Sorry,

80

you're new and I'm supposed to be mentoring you, not jumping on my soap box.'

'It's OK,' he says, rather awkwardly. 'I just thought a profiler would have a field day with Denver.'

'I'm going to refer you to two cases, Taylor,' Sam says, taking his notebook and writing *Rachel Nickell* and *Beltway Snipers* on a fresh page. 'These will help you understand how offender profilers can derail an investigation entirely. Geographical profiling is much more useful, but *How to Get Away With Murder* is deliberately vague with place names and there's just not enough data to construct a geographical profile. In terms of compiling information about Denver, based on his book, we'll be doing that ourselves over the course of the investigation.' Sam hands him her *'Who is Denver Brady?'* list and explains that she'll type it up and add it to a shared folder so they can both build on it. 'This is as good as any offender profile, Taylor,' she promises. 'I'll share it with DI Edris too.'

'I, er, was also going to suggest we draw up a Denver timeline,' he says hesitantly.

'Great idea, Taylor.' She nods and he exhales, relieved.

'I've already started, actually.' Taylor unfolds a piece of A3 paper from the back of his notebook and Sam is reminded of watching *Blue Peter* or *Art Attack* with her mum. They both used to giggle when the host said, "Here's one I made earlier."'

Taylor holds up the paper. 'Denver tells us he's twelve when he kills his first victim, Jono,' Taylor says, 'the boy in the quarry. And Denver's in sixth-form college when he kills Sarah, the convent girl. From Denver's narrative, we know that was the same year that Princess Diana died, 1997. So, Denver was between sixteen and eighteen years old in '97. This means that Jono was killed in the early nineties. I've gone with 1993. Making Denver—'

'Not much older than me,' Sam says, a little stunned. 'I remember Dad and Harry worked the cordon at Diana's funeral – I was right at the front with them. I was about Charlotte's age at the time. It was like nothing you can imagine: mountains of flowers, everybody in tears. So . . . Yes. Denver is about my age.'

'Well, for the record, ma'am, you don't look—'

'Please don't, Taylor. I can't handle compliments from twenty-year-olds at the minute,' she says a little harshly, making him blush crimson.

'I'm twenty-nine and I'm—' Taylor begins, but Sam has already moved on.

'We know that Denver killed at least one other person *before* his twentieth birthday,' she says, 'because the first thing he tells us is the definition of a serial killer, and that he became one before he turned twenty. It's as if he's slapped a huge clue in our faces on page one. The arrogance.'

'He doesn't tell us who his third victim is,' Taylor confirms. 'I've almost finished the book and the victim after Sarah is killed in about 2006. I haven't added them to the timeline yet, but I will.'

Taylor places the sheet on the floor so Sam can add a further point at the bottom.

*How to Get Away With Murder – Timeline*

- *Denver is born – approx. 1981.*
- *Denver kills Jono (Quarry. DB age 12) – 1993.*
- *Denver kills Sarah (Convent. Physical evidence: letters) – 1997.*
- *Denver becomes a serial killer by age 20 (Missing victim?) – 2001.*

'This is good, Taylor,' she says. 'Keep building this timeline. I've checked our searches for real victims, so let's hope for a stroke of luck there soon. While I work on the money trail from the website, I want you to really push to find out where Denver's book was printed. Telephone every printer in the country if you have to.'

'Yes, ma'am,' he says, writing down her instructions in a way that pleases her far more than his compliment about her youthful appearance.

Sam turns over her copy of the book and examines the ISBN. Surely, they'll be able to trace the printer.

'Taylor?' she says after a moment and he nods, leaning forward, pen poised. 'A personal question, but . . . have you ever owned a dog?'

'A dog? Er, yes, ma'am,' he says, a tad flummoxed. 'My family keeps gun dogs. Spaniels for the most part. Some labs, a few old beagles.' Sam pictures a country lodge and men in tweed jackets with rifles pointed at pheasants. 'Jess, she's called. My border collie,' Taylor says, and Sam returns her focus to him.

'Tell me, Taylor,' Sam asks, 'what does a person do with a dog while they're at work?'

'I think most people use dog walkers, ma'am,' he says, with a slight blush. 'Or family. Friends. Neighbours, perhaps. Our dogs . . . we have a gamekeeper, Barney. He takes care of them.'

Sam remembers that Harry mentioned Taylor's father is a wealthy man. A London MP with gun dogs and a gamekeeper called Barney. They must have more money than some small counties. Why on earth would such a privileged young man join the Metropolitan Police?

'What will you be working on, ma'am?' Taylor asks, as if keen to change the subject back to work.

'The money trail, like I said.' Sam gathers up her things and stands. 'I'm also going to send the e-book of *How to Get Away With Murder* to a linguist I know – Claire – she's a bit of a genius. If she agrees to help, and Harry approves a budget for it, she'll be able to pick up any regional dialect and phrases that Denver uses.'

'That sounds great,' Taylor says, then quickly adds, 'ma'am. I'll put the kettle on.'

'Make mine a coffee this time, please,' she says, holding the door for him. 'After all that, I'll need to get back to reading *How to Get Away With Murder* – and my concentration needs all the help it can get right now.'

Sam's re-reading the chapter about Sarah. Denver has just described strangling the girl beneath an oak tree and she is comparing his description to the written crime-scene summary of Charlotte's murder, because she still cannot face looking at the photographs. The similarities leave Sam's mouth salty and she opens a new box of headache tablets before swallowing two dry. The cup of coffee Taylor left on her desk an hour ago is overly milky and she's let it curdle in front of her. She can feel the pills inching roughly down her throat. Her palm is throbbing, too, and when she looks down, she notices she has Charlotte's netball keyring in a vice grip. She shakes out her hand and picks up her pen.

- *Low-income family: no computer, free school meals.*
- *College is near a stream, a reservoir and a field with a single oak.*
- *Denver and Sarah exchanged letters – physical evidence (1997).*

She opens the email from DC Chen and scans down to the important part – the details from WordSecurePay. The money from Denver's website, his takings from sales of the book, is being sent to a student bank account in Glasgow. Anticipation mounting, Sam calls the bank. She's on hold for an age, speaking to multiple people, verifying her credentials each time.

'Take your time,' she says sarcastically. 'It's not like there's a killer on the loose.'

After all that, they refuse to budge on the need for a court order before they will disclose more details. By the time Sam's hung up, her head is splitting. She holds the cool back of her hand against her forehead.

She fires off an email to the civilian team to get the court order moving asap., then heaves a huge sigh. Every step she takes, there's more paperwork for her to complete and *How to Get Away With Murder* lies closed on her desk, Charlotte's little netball lying beside it.

A loud thud sounds from Taylor's desk as he slams down the receiver then immediately picks it up to dial again. Without anything else to go on, he has resorted to calling every printer he can find online and Sam sees a spreadsheet grow larger on his screen as the young officer simultaneously speaks to another receptionist and adds to his list.

Sam decides she'll make a strong coffee then sit down and read Denver's next chapter with the help of the tablets she can still feel scraping their way towards her stomach.

'Detective Inspector Hansen?'

She looks up, wincing as the sudden movement doubles the throbbing in her head.

'Good afternoon,' Tina Edris says, extending a hand. Sam notices her discreet French manicure – Past Sam's go-to choice. 'I'm Detective Inspector Tina Edris. Senior Investigating Officer on the Charlotte Mathers homicide investigation.'

'Please just call me Sam,' she says, holding out her clammy hand, which Tina grips firmly and shakes once. She curls her hands in her lap, not wanting her own ragged nails on display. Sam breathes Tina in: a jasmine citrus scent, white satin blouse, deep brown eyes that are almost black. No make-up or jewellery, save a beautiful Swiss Swatch and a simple pearl stud in each ear. Tina's black hair is slicked back into a high up-do, and she puts Sam in mind of Nefertiti.

'Nice to meet you,' Tina says. 'Do you have a moment? I'm hoping to discuss your role in my investigation and how we can best work together.' Tina speaks slowly, seeming to choose each word deliberately before saying it quietly, without any accent. Sam supposes this is a technique to ensure she's listened to and not talked over.

'Yes. Sure. Let's talk,' Sam says and Tina nods her head to the small meeting room. Sam stands rather wobbily and is relieved that Tina has already started walking away. She pops a mint in her mouth and follows. Inside the small meeting room, they sit facing each other.

'Firstly, I should say welcome back to work,' Tina begins. 'How are you finding it so far?'

'Fine. Thanks,' she assures, almost truthfully.

'Excellent. So, as SIO, you'll be reporting to me and I'd like to set expectations here and now. Good rules make good friendships, as the wise man said,' Tina smiles, but it doesn't reach her eyes. Sam waits. 'To business, then,' Tina continues. 'As you know, you will be responsible for the book element of the Charlotte Mathers investigation. I would like to ensure that we're on the same page with *How to Get Away With Murder*. Excuse the pun.' Sam tries to smile but her head spins, forcing her to look at the floor and focus on her breath.

'. . . Detective Hansen?' Tina's brow wrinkles. 'I asked how you plan to approach your element of the investigation?'

'Well,' Sam says, swallowing hard. 'I've started reading the book.'

'What do you make of it so far?' Tina raises an eyebrow. 'I read it over the weekend.'

'Oh, great.' Sam pinches the top of her nose, praying that the tablets kick in quickly.

'I'd like you to focus exclusively on finding the author,' Tina says, pulling out her notebook and reading from a neat list. 'I'd like you to identify where the book is selling – how are people buying it? Find out where the profits from the sales go, how the book is printed and—'

'I'm doing all that,' Sam says through her mint.

Tina continues to read from her notebook: '. . . and set up searches for all named victims. Especially Basil, who survived

Denver's attack.' Tina takes a breath, flips a page and continues. 'You should know that I visited the lab today and the copy of the book that was found among Charlotte's belongings had only her fingerprints on it. We can't determine whether those were made pre- or post-mortem but the lab found several on the outer cover and nothing on the inner pages, which indicates that Charlotte read little, if any, of Denver's book. She may still have owned the copy of it found at the scene, though, so it's still important. As I'm sure you know, reading and collecting books are separate hobbies. Obviously, both the presence of Denver's book and his initials on the tree trunk are details that have been withheld from the press.'

'Have you spoken to the housekeeper yet?' Sam asks. 'Charlotte's teachers need looking at, the men especially as males commit over eighty per cent of homicides. We need to focus on anyone who knew Charlotte might be walking home that night. Charlotte's online activity—'

'I'm doing all of that,' Tina says, her mouth a tight line. 'I'd like a weekly report from you and I'd like you to focus *exclusively* on finding the author of *How to Get Away With Murder*. Nothing else.'

'You need to pull all CCTV footage of Charlotte in the park,' Sam says. 'There are restaurants in there, a hotel even, they'll have security—'

'To achieve my objective and solve this case swiftly,' Tina says, raising her voice slightly, 'I need every officer to concentrate on their own task. To follow instructions, even if they're returning to work following extensive sick leave. I cannot tell you how hard it has been for me to get to where I am today and I will not allow a team member's misplaced idea that those instructions don't apply to her to jeopardize my investigation.'

'Absolutely, Tina,' Sam says through gritted teeth.

'Thank you.' Tina stands. 'By the way, what are your thoughts on Basil?'

'Oh.' Sam's cheeks flare with heat. 'Erm . . . I . . .'

Tina scrutinizes Sam's face. 'Please tell me, Detective Hansen, that you have read *all* of *How to Get Away With Murder*?'

'Of course I have.' Sam tries to sound offended, but even to her own ears, her protest is hollow.

Tina simply shakes her head, lip curled in disgust, and lets the door slam closed behind her.

'How'd it go?' Taylor asks as Sam returns to her desk. She presses her hands to her burning cheeks.

'Coffee, Taylor,' she mutters. 'Please. Strong.'

'That good, eh?'

Sam gives him a look that sends him directly to kettle without further comment. She checks her watch and decides that a third paracetamol won't kill her but might take enough off this headache to let her concentrate for an hour. She swallows it, then picks up the damned book and turns to the next chapter.

## How to Win Friends and Influence People

Nothing hurts as much as being betrayed by someone you love. I myself was betrayed by a family member. It cut me deeply and I wish I could say more about it without giving too much away. Perhaps in a later chapter. Remember that a whopping 20 per cent of serial killers become a suspect this way: someone they trust points the finger at them. In fact, this dreadful fate befell many of the greats.

Ted Bundy's girlfriend called the authorities on him twice. The first time after she read a news report detailing the killer's vehicle and saw a sketch that resembled Teddy. She tried again after finding crutches in his car. Luckily, the police dismissed her on both occasions and our hero enjoyed many more months of freedom.

Ted Kaczynski's own brother dobbed him in. After the Unabomber reached the peak of his career and finally achieved publication for his manifesto, his sister-in-law recognized the style of the writing and a few key phrases TK had used. The woman then persuaded her husband, Kaczynski's brother, to call the police.

'You can't eat your cake and have it too,' the brother said to the cops. 'My brother Ted always uses that phrase. He must be the Unabomb killer.'

I paraphrase, but you see the point: many have fallen

foul of law enforcement because those they loved most turned on them. Let's think about how you can avoid such a betrayal by the Judas at your own table.

The most important lesson I can teach you here is how to find your lobster. There's an old saying about being able to choose your friends but not your family – that's codswallop. You can choose both. You must surround yourself with the right people. That can mean cutting off any clingy parents or siblings who are overly intrusive and prone to radical behaviour such as asking where you are all the time or turning up at your home unannounced. Don't let silly sentimental ties be your undoing.

Having a partner or spouse can be troublesome but highly useful if you select the right candidate. Firstly, try to secure a relationship with someone who has a job that screams 'nice'. Women who run shelters for abandoned animals, child-minders and dinner nannies can be priceless pawns in your cover-family line-up. Single mothers are good and easily attainable, but that obviously involves living with children and we can't all stomach that – better to spawn your own if you're willing to go to these extremes. Consider your partner's age with care. Young women can be troublesome. Do you really want to be with someone who photographs their food before they eat it? While a nineteen-year-old might look hot in your shirt, she will not be able to iron it for you. Women in their forties are your best bet. They have been through the mill and generally have far lower expectations of the men in their lives. As long as you don't beat them and put out once or twice a month, they will be largely self-sustaining.

It's a tragic fact that it will be far more dangerous

and difficult for a female serial killer to find a good partner. Women account for only around 15 per cent of all serial killers – *that we know of*, at least. I have always believed that women are superior to men as murderers and this number is likely a massive underestimate. If you're looking for Mr Right, never accept a man who still lives with his mother. There is no greater risk to your mental well-being. You can guarantee that, no matter his age, Mummy's little prince has never cleaned a toilet before. He'll tell you that he's very happy to help you, but he just *can't see what needs doing around the home like you can*. You will end up killing him, and you need to remember our principles. Select a man who has lived alone for a long time. One who is grateful for human female companionship, and won't ask too many questions about where you are and who you're spending your time with. Perhaps try video-game stores or your local Dungeons and Dragons club. Women are far more flexible than men, and I urge my female readers to consider dating other women instead of persevering with mediocre males. Or embrace spinsterhood. Perhaps acquire a cat, join several book clubs, take up crochet or learn to bake cakes that look like household objects. I am certain you will be happier.

Avoid intelligent partners. Normal IQs are between 80 and 120, with 100 considered average. Around 80 is the real sweet spot. You don't want an absolute vegetable, just someone who won't ask too many questions or see through your lies.

Interestingly, while we're on the subject of IQ, we serial killers are thought to be 'below average' in terms of intelligence. According to the Serial Killer Information Center, the average serial killer is believed to come in at 94.5. This is simply further evidence that the police have no clue about how many of us there are, and have failed to catch those of us who are smarter than Joey Tribiani.

I don't want to discourage you if you think you aren't the sharpest knife in the block, though; many stupid serial killers have achieved great things. The Green River Killer barely scraped through high school, yet he murdered over ninety people. It took law enforcement almost twenty years to catch him. He got so bored waiting that he even wrote confession letters to newspapers, including unique knowledge of the crimes he'd committed that had not been released to the press. The famous profiler on the case dismissed the letters, calling them a 'feeble and amateurish attempt to gain some personal importance'. Green River went right on killing until a random DNA breakthrough led to his capture and arrest in 2001. I love profilers, me.

A valuable digression, but now, back to choosing your family.

Once you have secured your significant other, be sure never to ask them to engage in anything other than vanilla bedroom activities. Ted Bundy took a big risk when he asked lovers to pose dead during sex. Big no-no. You need to be the model partner, parent and professional. Never show any psychopathic or narcissistic traits in your relationship. Don't beat your lover, control them or lose your temper. The best way to do this is to create a lifestyle whereby you're apart as much as possible.

Finding ways to have your spouse or family completely dependent on you might also help, as they are far less likely to betray you under those circumstances. For example, if their visa depends on being married to you, or if you're very wealthy and they would otherwise be dirt poor – Thai brides, Nigerian princes awaiting their inheritance, and so on.

I'd recommend having a lot of acquaintances – golf buddies, book club pals – but no one too close who expects you to share emotions. I fear that I can't say too much more than I have about my own familial situation. I already told you about my cousin Bobby, and divulging more detail puts me at risk. I can say, however, that I did have a best friend named Tony who I cherished with all of my heart. We went everywhere together and he knew all my secrets. I told him about Jono and Sarah and he listened unjudgingly to all of my thoughts about Ted Bundy, Jeffrey Dahmer, Mary Ann and the rest of the gang. For my part, I shared my food with Tony and didn't hold his halitosis against him.

I suppose I ought to take this opportunity to dispel the long-standing myth that serial killers hurt animals. This is simply untrue. There may be the odd example of serials who hang kittens from washing lines, but those are few and far between. If the little boy over the road torches ants with a magnifying glass or ties cats' tails together, it's far more likely that he's destined for a life as a dentist than a killer.

Because this myth is deeply entrenched in society, largely thanks to the fecklessness of profilers, let me give a few examples to counter it. Britain's most prolific serial killer, Harold Shipman, aka Doctor Death, killed hundreds of people. Hundreds. Yet he was an animal-rights campaigner and cared diligently for his pet poodle and his little bunnies, which he adored. Dennis Nielsen murdered at least twelve men and boys, but cried when he discovered that the pound had euthanized his collie Bleep, following his arrest.

My Tony was the best boy you could ever meet. I found him one day tied to a tree. Not long after Sarah died, I was walking through a small wood that separated my cousin's house from my own. It was stunning at that time of year; bright-pink hawthorn blossom sprinkled like confetti in my hair as I made my way along.

I was usually alone in the woods, but that day I heard children shrieking and strange yelps, and suddenly a pebble hit me in the chest. I spun to find who'd thrown it, but the kids were long gone. I was about to go on my way when a pitiful whining started up, somewhere off to my right.

I followed an overgrown path and came to a small clearing. He was tied to a tree, lying on his side, licking his front legs. As I approached, he growled but seemed to lack any real fight. Around him were dozens of small rocks, like the one that had hit me, along with sticks and other instruments of torture. 'Sshhh,' I soothed, 'good dog.' He eyed me and whined. I noticed bloody patches. Protruding hips and ribs. 'Poor thing,' I crooned. He flopped his head up fully to look at me and I saw then that there was a vicious, bloody hole where his eye should be. I jumped back – I've never loved gore. Oh, I know, the irony.

I spent a good hour coaxing him to let me near. Eventually, I managed to untie him and carried him home, where there was surprisingly little objection to my having a dog; my family thought it would be good for me. I was relieved at this because I'd already decided that were my mother to try to take the little creature from me and ship him off to some God-awful shelter, I would have broken my own rules and staved her head in with a tin of Spam. While that proved unnecessary, I did, however, have to begin working weekends in a meat-packing warehouse to pay Tony's vet's bills.

We were inseparable, Tony and I. Soon, I discovered that a dog was not only a wonderful companion, but an excellent accessory for an aspiring serial killer. Let me explain why.

A man walking alone at night will set any woman's teeth on edge. She'll lace her car keys between her fingers, as if that does anything, or call someone and ask them to stay on the phone with her as she walks home. A man walking a dog at night? Normal. You're just a dog-walker; you're the person who finds the body, not slices and dices it. People with dogs also interact an awful lot. They chat and pretend not to notice as their canines lick each other's arseholes. If you enjoy chatting with your victim before the big day, a dog might help you make the connection.

Interestingly, our friends in law enforcement don't own many pets. Statistically, police officers are more likely to be non-pet owners than other professions. Even dentists rank higher. I believe that Tony, were he not a dumb creature, would have thanked his lucky stars that it was a serial killer who found him that day and not a copper. With me, he had a home for life. Who knows what dreadful shelter he'd have ended up in, had someone paid to protect and serve discovered him? This should give you pause. If you're just a regular reader and not set on your career path just yet, really think about which side of the fence a true psychopath belongs on. If you really want to get away with murder, a police badge might not be a bad idea.

You may consider other pets, but do be careful, particularly if you're a single man. Have you ever met a normal single dude with a budgerigar? Snakes and lizards are exclusively owned by weirdos, too. Who wants to keep grasshoppers and mice in the fridge? Sadists, all.

To complete your perfect family set-up, I heartily and unreservedly recommend a dog like Tony. It was thanks to Tony that I met victim number twenty-four, a young woman called Melanie. But I'm getting ahead of myself here. First, I need to teach you about Blondie, and the principles of victim selection.

# 6

Sam snaps the book closed and takes out her notebook and pen, to add to her list.

- *A straight man, potentially with a family.*
- *Had a one-eyed dog – Tony.*
- *Worked in a meat-packing warehouse.*

Her phone vibrates with more email notifications and she quickly checks her inbox. She finds a handful of messages from HR, asking her to schedule a meeting to review her return to work. She'll deal with those later, she tells herself, as she spots a response from the civilian team. She opens it immediately, but the email simply confirms that an application for a court order compelling the Glasgow bank to disclose the details of the account holder has been submitted. Sam will be notified when the information comes back, but she might have to hang on for a few days.

Sam rolls back her chair with an angry kick. 'Well, let's just hope our killer hangs on too,' she mumbles.

Glancing at the clock, she swears as she sees she's five minutes late for the team briefing. As she marches towards the briefing room, she feels defeated and a little off-kilter following the latest chapter. Denver's words about rescuing a dog unnerve her. It's a coincidence, she tells herself. Denver wrote his book months, if not years ago; she found a dog this week. Lots of people come to own dogs under unusual circumstances. It's just an author's trick, taking a widely shared human experience and leaving his reader feeling like he can see into her life.

Sam's nose wrinkles when she sidles into the briefing room, breathless and clammy. Too many bodies, not enough ventilation. The Charlotte Mathers homicide investigation is large, with multiple enquiry teams. Coffee steam mixes with sweat and cheap aftershave. Tina Edris is at the front, already talking and gesturing to whiteboards on wheels, as well as a digital presentation on the main screen. Harry nods and smiles as Sam enters, then discretely checks his watch. Sam feels her cheeks burning as she shuffles to the closest empty seat which is, of course, on the opposite side of the room. She spots Taylor sitting next to Chloe Spears and he lifts his hand in a small wave.

'We've nothing to go on beyond the footprints and fibres,' Tina is saying as Sam sits down, 'and there's not a lot we can do with those. The lab has confirmed the assailant was wearing a black waterproof jacket and denim jeans from Marks and Spencer, along with a pair of size-twelve walking boots. We also have a long, yellow synthetic fibre, consistent with a costume hairpiece, so the perpetrator may have worn a disguise. Obviously, we'll thoroughly examine all of it, but he's bought mainstream items without distinguishing features, so it's a needle-in-a-haystack situation.'

'What about the carving on the tree?' Sam asks. 'Any idea what tools were used, if there are glove fibres etc.?'

'Er . . . yes,' Tina wavers, as if surprised at the precision of the question, and Sam feels a grim satisfaction at the opportunity to remind her SIO that she's a damn good detective, too. 'The lab brought in an expert who's confirmed that it would have taken at least thirty minutes, and there's a list in your briefing pack of the tools most likely used. The carving was fresh, no more than a day old, and given that no one knew Charlotte would be in that park that night, we have to assume that our perp was on site for at least an hour and carved it on the night in question. Someone must have seen something in that time. Detective Constable Spears, where are we with witnesses?'

'Yes, ma'am.' Chloe stands and someone hums *Hit Me Baby One More Time* under their breath, attracting a scowl from Edris, who looks to Harry for intervention. Harry stares fixedly out of the window and a second baritone joins in. Tina stares after Harry, her jaw twitching. Chloe attempts to ignore the humming and begin her report on witnesses but—

'Shut the fuck up!' Sam snaps, the words shooting out loud and hot. The humming ceases instantly. Everyone stares at Sam, who is just as shocked by her outburst as they are. Still, she keeps her face calm, straightens in her chair, and thrusts her chin forward in defiance. 'As you were saying, Chloe.' Sam and Taylor give the young DC an encouraging nod. Chloe begins her report – there's perspiration on her brow, but a hint of a smile on her lips.

'We spoke at length to Jessica, her brother Jamil Patel, and their parents, Allan and Ira Patel. Charlotte was in a good mood and ordered a Deliveroo dinner for herself and Jessica. Jessica says that Charlotte seemed worried when her father, Nigel Mathers, didn't arrive at 8 p.m. to collect her as normal. Nigel had only failed to show up twice before and Jessica says that it rattled Charlotte so she set off walking at 9:03 p.m. exactly. Jessica Patel has a thing for numbers, so I'm pretty certain she's accurate on that.'

'Why didn't one of Jessica's parents drive Charlotte home?' Sam asks. Chloe nods as if expecting the question.

'Allan and Ira Patel left their home at 7:34 p.m. to go out to dinner with friends. We've taken statements from all the guests, who confirm they were there all night. Jessica's brother, Jamil, who's eighteen, remained in the home. He corroborated Jessica Patel's statement, saying that he heard the front door close when Charlotte left, at around nine.'

'What about the Deliveroo driver?' Harry asks.

'Far away by the time Charlotte left,' Spears confirms.

'What about the door-to-door?' Edris asks, and again, Chloe nods.

'Nothing meaningful, although plenty of people saw Charlotte,' she says. 'DC Chen has camera footage of her, too. Every witness confirms that Charlotte looked any other schoolgirl walking along the path. We've added full statements into HOLMES.' Spears rubs her eyes and Sam guesses that she isn't getting much sleep.

'Any witnesses from inside the park itself?' Edris asks.

'Lots of statements taken but, again, nothing out of the ordinary. No one saw Charlotte with anyone, and no one saw someone carving a tree.'

'I'm hoping that Nigel Mathers will agree to doing a press appeal,' Tina says. 'The case is all over the newspapers but we're not getting anything useful from the public right now. Someone must have seen something. Also, try to focus on who, other than Jamil and Jessica, would have known that Charlotte would be walking home that night; unless it was a stranger attack, which I believe unlikely, someone must have.'

'Yes, ma'am,' Spears nods, and sits back down.

'Detective Constable Chen . . .' Edris turns to face the team's technical expert. 'I'm assuming that Charlotte's phone and laptop are priorities for your team?'

'Yes, ma'am,' Chen says. 'Not just Charlotte's. My team has Jack and Nigel Mathers' phones, too. I can confirm that Nigel's phone never disconnected from his home wi-fi that night. He called Charlotte's number repeatedly from about four a.m., then the Patels and 999. As for Jack's phone, that was connected to the wi-fi at the Pig and Butcher, a pub in Brenham. Jack got an Uber home, pinging several masts en route, and the phone then connected to the Mathers' home router. The phone evidence fits with both men's statements.'

'And Charlotte's online activity that night?'

'So far, everything the teams are bringing in stands up on the digital front.'

'What about the pregnancy test?' Harry says. 'Surely that's a crucial piece of—'

Sam's mind is instantly reeling. *What pregnancy test?* How had she missed such an important detail? She flips through the case file. Sure enough, a pregnancy test is listed among Charlotte's possessions. *If only I'd looked at the crime-scene photos*, Sam thinks furiously. What else might she have missed? *And I was dumb enough to think I was ready to be SIO and run this investigation.*

'Sir,' Chen says, 'I've scoured Charlotte's online shopping accounts and her bank account. She spent sixty quid on Nando's the night she died and beyond that it's just the odd study item or clothes. Nothing that raises any flags and certainly no pregnancy test. No messages to or from a potential boyfriend either.'

'What about the brother, Jamil Patel?' Harry asks. 'Any messages between him and Charlotte?'

Chen shakes his head. 'Nothing. His number isn't in Charlotte's phone, and they're not connected on any social media.'

Sam takes a swig of water and lets the details sit in her mind alongside her headache. Others talk around her and she knows she's missing what's being said but something about Chen's information is niggling her. Sam pictures Nando's. She sees the sticky wooden tables. The cockerel on a stick that the waiter removes once he's remembered to check that you're happy with your food. Adrenalin fizzes through her.

'Chen,' Sam says, cutting off whoever is now speaking, midflow. Every face turns to her and her head pounds unforgivingly. Adam Taylor's eyes bore into her from across the room. He looks worried, but she can't bring herself to wonder why.

'Look again at the brother,' she says.

'What have you got, Sam?' Harry asks.

'Charlotte spent too much,' Sam says.

'Go on,' Harry says, smiling.

'Sixty pounds. It seems to me that Charlotte ordered enough food for three. Charlotte, Jessica *and* Jamil Patel,' Sam says. 'Let's just take another look.'

'Great call, Sam,' Harry says with an approving nod.

'Where have you got to with identifying Denver Brady?' Tina asks.

'Yes... Er...' Sam rises to her feet and takes a long slow breath. 'The book sells online as both a physical copy and an e-book from Howtogetawaywithmurder.com, which Brady got people to visit via Reddit. We are prioritizing trying to find the printer of the physical book, as well as following the money from the online sales. The profits from the online sales are landing in a bank in Glasgow – we're hitting them with a court order.

'We're leaving the site up for now, to keep the money trail warm and not alert him to the fact we're looking for him. We're also running searches against all the victims Denver mentions in *How to Get Away With Murder* to see if any real-life crimes match his descriptions. Should that happen, we'll dig into each case and see if it's connected to Charlotte in any way. At that point we could also create a geographical profile to determine if Charlotte is linked to any of Denver's victims or the places they lived and died.' Sam ends, then sits down. She feels exhausted and chastises herself for forgetting to mention the linguist who's agreed to scour the book for lexical clues, but can't bring herself to stand back up again.

'Look, folks,' Harry sighs. 'We have very little on the table here. We need a big push this week – and Edris, sort a press appeal please. Thanks everyone. Keep at it.'

The briefing room empties slowly, and Sam makes her way back to her desk then flops into her chair. *How did I miss a pregnancy test?* she thinks to herself, heaving a sigh. She navigates to the central database and pulls up the report from the forensics lab. One, unopened, pregnancy test had been found among Charlotte's scattered belongings, close to her body. The only fingerprints on the packaging were Charlotte's. They could, of course, have been made post-mortem, but the other, more straightforward explanation is that it was actually Charlotte's. Sam pulls up a photograph of the pregnancy test. It's the first real crime-scene photograph that she's managed to look at and she notices her heart rate increase, sending a slight tingle down the insides of her arms. She takes slow breaths as she stares at the image . . . 'Seeing those two blue lines was the best and worst moment of my life, rolled into one,' Sam's mother had told her. 'The best because I knew you were coming' – she'd smiled, kissing Sam's nose – 'and the worst because I knew my parents would never forgive me.' To this day, Sam has never met her maternal grandparents. She doesn't even know their names.

'Why didn't Granny and Granda want me?' Sam had asked, one morning. It was her school sports' day and there was a Grandparents' Relay, which she'd be entering with Old Joe, the school caretaker.

'It wasn't you they didn't want, darling,' Mum had said. 'I was so young. Just sixteen.'

'That's old!' Sam had said.

'To an eight year old it is.' Mum had smiled. 'Your dad was older and your grandparents didn't like that. We had a big fight about it. We still sometimes fight about it, whenever we try to speak.'

'I know that,' Sam had said, swelling with her infant detective skills. 'I know you fight with someone because I saw your ears.' Her Mum had turned pale then, pulling her hair self-consciously forward and the collar of her polo neck up.

'DI Hansen,' Taylor says, and Sam swipes quickly at her cheeks. 'Do you have a minute? I was thinking that we could maybe grab a bite and talk about Sean?'

'I've got to head off, Taylor,' Sam says. 'Who's Sean, anyway?' she stands and tugs on her coat.

'You know, Sean from *How to Get Away With Murder*? The guy on the bridge?' Taylor says, and Sam nods, not wanting to admit that she still needs to finish the book.

As she lifts open her garden gate, Sam hears a high-pitched whining coming from inside her house. The little scruff is waiting for her as she opens the door, its tail wagging so much that its entire back end sways from side to side. Sam is surprised at how much her heart swells at the thought that someone has missed her and is pleased she's home.

Sam uses toilet roll to collect and flush a little parcel the dog has left in the corner of the kitchen floor. She mops up a couple of puddles, bleaches the floor and then puts a scoop of kibble into the chipped breakfast bowl she's using as a dog dish. The dog trots over with an uneven gait, and Sam notices that one of its hind legs operates at an odd angle. She puts a puppy pad down in the corner of the kitchen, a needs-must until a spot opens up for it in the dog shelter. As the little creature eats, she takes out her phone and taps in 'dog care for beginners'.

'I think, little scruff,' she says, sniffing in its general direction, 'that we need to try a bath. I know we've only just met, but you're going to have to trust me.'

The bath is dusty, Sam only ever using the shower, so she rinses it out before filling the tub with warm water and pouring in some Tresemmé. She watches a quick YouTube video and then carefully carries the dog upstairs and bathes the little mutt. In the process, she discovers 'it' is in fact a 'he'. The little body is painfully thin and Sam concentrates on not rubbing too hard over the protruding ribs and his wonky leg.

She lifts him gently out of the tub and he shakes himself, spattering water everywhere. She runs to the airing cupboard and grabs one of her mum's guest towels, wrapping him tightly and carrying him back downstairs.

'I think, boy,' she says, scrolling through Google, 'that you're like something called a Border Terrier. But you're a bit too small and a bit too grey, so maybe some sort of mix.' In response, he wobbles down the hallway and scratches at the front door.

'I suppose that means you'd like a walk.' She locates the carrier bag from her lunch-break shop and tries to fit the collar. He doesn't make it easy; he licks her hand constantly, making Sam's nose wrinkle. The collar hangs bulky and low on his neck. It's clearly far too big.

Cursing, Sam slides off the collar and opens the under-stairs cupboard, grabs Past Sam's Chanel neck scarf and ties it into a makeshift collar. She tries to clip the new extendable lead to the headscarf but the bulk of the silk is too much for the clasp, so she runs upstairs to find something suitable.

'I couldn't find a belt, so these will have to do,' she says, securing the foot of an old pair of tights to the neck scarf. 'Very handsome. You're better dressed than me,' she says, averting her gaze from her old leggings with the faded knees and a hole on the shin, and her comfy Skechers, whose fabric is barely clinging on at the toes.

The walk is slow, as her new companion stops regularly to sniff about. She doesn't think he's in too much pain from the wonky leg; he stills uses it normally, but he looks a little like he's on the catwalk, swishing his hips. Somehow, after the bath, he looks more pathetic than ever. Still, his gentle pace suits Sam because she's barely left the house for months, and her head is swimming with Denver and all the details of Charlotte's case.

The evening is cool but calm and, without fully intending it, Sam lets her feet drift in the general direction of Charlotte Mathers' home address on Palace Gardens, in one of London's most affluent boroughs.

Sam peers around, gaping. The terrace of white houses where

Charlotte lived is beautiful. Bulging hanging baskets strain with the weight of plush petunias and glossy ivy. Sleek cars fill every parking space. Polished marble entryways gleam before each door. Sam leans up against a fence that's clearly been repainted a lot more recently than her own fingernails.

A smartly dressed couple emerges through one of the heavy, black-gloss doors. The woman wears an oatmeal wool coat and her hair bounces as she walks. The man offers her his free hand. In the other, he carries a full-sized umbrella with a hook handle, which he swings, tapping its top on the ground in harmony with his stride.

As they pass a colourful tower of flowering pots, Sam hears them greet a man who's bent over, tending to some primroses. She watches him for a moment and then approaches.

'Excuse me,' she says, 'are you the gardener here?'

'That's right, among other things,' he says, standing slowly and rubbing his hands on the back of his trousers. He bends down to greet the dog, who hides behind Sam's leg and makes an odd rattle that she takes for a growl.

'Always work in this area, do you?'

'I do, chuck. Why'd you ask?' The man, who must be around fifty, begins to look a little uncomfortable.

'My name is DI Hansen,' Sam says, showing her warrant card, 'from the Metropolitan police.'

Understanding dawns on his face. 'This about that girl?'

'Charlotte Mathers, yes. She lived in number forty-five.' Sam points. 'Did you know her?'

'Awful what happened. My wife is following it on the news. She won't leave the house – reckons the killer will strike again.'

'Your wife's not wrong to be concerned, I'm afraid,' she says, honestly. Past Sam would have towed the line and reassured the man that the risk was slim, but she can't stomach that. The killer could strike again tomorrow, for all they knew.

'I saw the girl,' he says. 'Wears a bright-green uniform. Her old man drives a Bentley. Lovely motor. That's it, there.' He points to a gleaming black car that's four times the size of Sam's Ford Fiesta. 'I'm Jim, by the way.' He grins and wipes his hand again before offering it to Sam.

'Nice to meet you, Jim,' she says, then adds, 'Look, I'd really appreciate your observations on number forty-five. You might have some knowledge that could be valuable to us.'

'Well, not much I can say. I just do the baskets, a bit of gardening, litter when there is any.' He smiles with pride at the pristine area.

'Who have you seen coming and going there?'

'Well, the girl – I see her most days.' Jim scrunches his forehead in concentration. 'That green uniform is hard to miss. The dad I don't see much. The Bentley is usually gone early in the morning. Rumour is he's a big banker and he's loaded, but he cleans his own car; and the housekeeper – he's cut her hours down, you know. So maybe things is a bit tighter than they look.'

'Any other changes you know about?' Sam asks, typing notes in her phone.

'Another bloke stays there – a brother.' Jim shrugs. 'Friendly enough chap.'

'Friendly how?' Sam pushes.

'Chats, like. Comes outside to smoke. I reckon he's not allowed to in that posh house. Mind you, if I owned a house like that, I wouldn't let folk smoke in it neither. He never drops his butt, always uses the ciggy bin.' Jim points to a wall-mounted cigarette disposal unit at the end of the street.

'What does the uncle chat about, Jim?'

'Oh, this and that. Weather. Football – he's a Gooner. He's into his sports despite being a smoker – cycling, running, the usual.'

'Thanks, Jim. Do you mind if I take your number in case I need to chat to you again?'

They exchange details and Sam strolls along to stand directly outside number forty-five. Charlotte's home. There's a matching pair of bay trees in glossy ceramic pots flanking the door and Sam sees a woman inside, polishing a window.

As Sam begins her walk home, she emails her notes to Chloe Spears, copying in Tina, and attaches Jim's contact details. She's walked a few streets when she notices that the little dog is shivering. She glances at her watch and is shocked to see that they've been out of the house for two hours. He whines and sits down, his back legs trembling. Sam immediately curses her own stupidity. Of course a malnourished dog can't walk for miles across London. As if sensing her self-loathing, he lies down on the pavement and rests his head on her old trainer.

Sam sees a bus stop across the street. 'Come on, boy,' she says. He wobbles to his feet as a bus pulls up and hisses to a stop. They step aboard and Sam taps her debit card, then moves to sit in a seat near the front. The dog crouches beneath her legs, making a high-pitched sound. She lifts him gently on to her lap, opens her coat and wraps it around him. As the remaining passengers board, Sam fiddles with Charlotte's keyring, tightening the little chain around her finger until it throbs, and then releasing it. She lets the conversation with Jim run through her mind.

The bus pulls off and a few stops later, the dog begins to snore. Sam notices a hippy couple staring at her. After an awkward moment the woman stands and crosses the aisle to sit next to Sam. She smells like incense and self-righteousness.

'Excuse me, miss,' she says in a northern accent – one of the friendly ones that isn't too nasal. 'I wanted to give you this.' She hands Sam a card. It's pale green and proclaims *We're Here for YOU*, followed by a phone number. 'We work with a Christian charity and we can help with pets, too. Food. Vet's bills. I can take you both for something to eat now if—'

Sam stares at the woman, bemused. She is peering at the dog

with her eyes full of pity, taking in its scarred snout, the wonky leg dangling from beneath Sam's coat, the odd clump of dirt still hanging on. The old tights instead of a proper dog lead. Sam's frayed shoes.

When Sam finally gets it, her face turns to fire. 'You've got the wrong idea,' she says.

'It's OK.' The woman drops her voice. 'I'm only trying to help.'

'I don't need help,' Sam snaps, but the woman simply nods as though she's heard it a million times.

'We really are just trying to help people who are—'

'Oh for God's sake,' Sam hisses, as the bus doors swing open. 'He's wearing Chanel!'

She carries him the last half-mile home, her arms burning even though he can't weigh more than a four-pint milk bottle. It's growing dark and Sam notices the woman ahead glancing back to see who's fallen into step behind her. She wonders if Denver ever followed a woman down the street at night, making the hairs on the back of her neck prickle as she laced her car keys through her fingers or made a fake phone call. Sam forces open her garden gate and, once inside, wraps the little dog in a blanket and lets him rest on the sofa. She takes a seat next to him, looking around the room.

'This mess just won't do, will it, little one?' she says. 'This is no way to treat a guest.'

She pulls out her phone and, after a few failed attempts, manages to find a cleaning firm that takes bookings online. They have a discounted cancellation slot tomorrow. *Perfect*, Sam thinks, selecting the 'Deep Clean' option and typing in her address. It's only when the confirmation email arrives that she realizes the problem: no pets to be present during the clean.

'Not to worry,' Sam says, rubbing the soft silk of his ear. 'I don't work Thursday and Friday, so we could visit the vet tomorrow and have them look at that leg.'

The dog doesn't answer and Sam is distracted by a text message from Harry.

hello sam how was your first week back nigel m has agreed to do press conference tomorrow morning harry

Sam is about to send a thumbs up emoji, but decides to make the effort.

Hi Harry, my first week back was fine, thanks. As I'm not working tomorrow, I'm taking the dog to the vet in the morning – I'll be sure to catch the press conference when I get home. Sx

Harry responds immediately:

good to hear I knew you were ready to be back at work your old man used to say the devil makes work for idle hands it will be good when dog is gone nothing but hassle i am up to page XX of denver book is he lying? how does what he is saying fit with charlotte m what are your thoughts harry

Feeling a dart of alarm at the idea of him finding out she hasn't been able to finish it yet, she goes to her bag to retrieve the damn book. The folded corner tells her she's up to page XX herself. She cracks the spine and curls into the sofa.

## *Blondie and Victim Selection*

You cannot become an accomplished serial killer overnight. However, if you have the patience, determination, and courage to couple with the teachings of this guide, then I can guarantee your success.

As you already know from my previous chapters, two of the things most likely to see you labelled a suspect in a police investigation are: killing people connected to you, and operating in your own locality. Almost 25 per cent of captures result from errors in judgement in these two areas.

### *Victim selection principles*

Superb victim selection practice is at the heart of my success. I made mistakes early on, with Jono and Sarah. Had I carried on the way I'd started my career, I'd almost certainly be writing this opus from behind bars. Thankfully, after my conversation with the police following Sarah's loss, I had the sense to develop some proper victim selection principles. Consistency in this domain is one of the main reasons I have been able to enjoy high kill rates and my freedom simultaneously.

The three core principles are:

1. Victims must be selected at random, with no characteristics in common that could lead to identification of a pattern or type.
2. Victims must not be known or connected to you, nor live near you.
3. Victims must not be children.

The final principle is, of course, a matter of personal taste. Be warned, though, that the public has an unnatural attachment to cases involving children/infants and this tends to result in a greater budget and effort-level from law enforcement. If your ambition is young ones, I advise that you achieve at least moderate competence levels first.

Alongside these core principles, I also tend to avoid particular types of potential victims who could be especially troublesome. These include: drug lords, mafia bosses or their families; people with elite MMA skills; anyone with a fighting dog in the home; HIV carriers; Vinnie Jones.

## What makes a good victim?

The answer to this question depends a lot on you. You may have a particular type of person that you intend to target. You may, for example, want to rid the world of lecherous men. I jest, of course – there'd be none of us left. As well as any agenda you may have, you also need to be guided by your own physicality and competence level. As your skills grow, you can select more challenging victims, but I'll give some general guidance here.

When considering your victims, their personality

is as important as their physicality. By far the best victims are those who are highly suggestible. This type of person is far more likely to enter a victim mindset, where they will basically do anything you tell them right up to the point they're sure you're going to kill them.

Compliant victims almost always guarantee a smooth kill.

You can identify more compliant personalities in a variety of ways. Look for people-pleasers and those with low self-esteem, who apologise often and seem to deem themselves unworthy of even existing. They'll try to blend in, to belong – which means dressing and acting like those in their immediate social groups.

Teddy Bundy was the absolute master at identifying the compliant victim. His strategy was to pretend to need help and to ask young women for assistance. Sometimes, he'd even wear fake arm or leg plaster casts, or carry crutches. Teddy could get those gals to walk miles at a time, lugging boxes and all sorts before they even whispered a complaint.

Teddy wasn't consistently great, though, and we can learn from that. For instance, he approached a young, pre-fame Debbie Harry in a public location, with witnesses, and had to practically beg her to get into his car. She even marched away from him at one point, forcing him to trail her – bad move, Ted – clear red flags. No wonder she fought back when she noticed that he'd removed the internal handles from his car. You already know that Debbie escaped and I confess I'm pleased that Teddy lost that one. Anyway – compliance. Look for it and reap the rewards.

Traits that make a good victim also include clear

weaknesses that you can exploit. Some examples: drug addicts, who'll do almost anything on a promise; people with mental illnesses; poor people and the homeless, obviously. Get to these people before the God-botherers pluck them from the street and buy them a Greggs in exchange for singing hosanna. Who even is Hosanna? I digress.

People who are motivated to disappear also make great victims – petty criminals and parolees, for example. People on bail. Look out for anything that limits the person's options or has conditioned them to be victims already.

In terms of the physical location of victims, a mid-sized city that is outside of your own police jurisdiction is best. Somewhere you can reach and return from within 6-8 hours. The rationale here is that optimum kill-time is around 3 a.m. in the still of the night. You can travel to the site two or three hours before, enjoy a comfortable kill-window, and be home in time to secure the alibi that your regular routine provides. It is my advice to never transport a victim – alive or dead – primarily because of the inevitable forensics trail that this will leave behind. Transporting a live victim also offers them a higher chance of escape, more opportunity for the public to spot you together, and an increased risk of creating circumstantial and digital evidence.

## Where and how to find your victims

In this day and age, finding your victims simply couldn't be easier. A plethora of options is open to you, and you really can have fun with this stage of the process.

Personally, I like to find my victims organically: a chance encounter on a train, a stroll along the beach, a pleasant wander in the park. But initially, a more distanced approach can be better for emerging talent.

There are the obvious places to find victims online: dating apps, social media and forums – and I would recommend those for beginners, but please ensure you read all my advice carefully before conducting any online recruitment. As your skills grow, however, you might enjoy thinking a little more outside of the box.

You can even have your victims find you.

One method that has delivered consistent results for me over the years is one I have affectionately dubbed the Samaritan Technique. Inspiration for the Samaritan came from a casual stroll I took one day when I was visiting my cousin at university. I visited as often as I could, despite finding the local accent thuggish-sounding.

During that visit, I had cause to cross a bridge close to Bobby's university. A truly stunning piece of Victorian architecture spanning the Big River. I was appalled to see that this feat of engineering had been littered with dozens of little laminated notes. These pastel-coloured placards had been secured with cable ties to every piece of metalwork as far as the eye could see. My initial thought was that it was another 'celebration' by people forcing their pride upon the world. I ripped several down, and only then did I notice that the notes had handwriting on them. *We are here for YOU*, one note proclaimed. The next read, *Suicide is never the answer – call St Martin's on 0800 968 968.*

As I continued my walk, I pictured people standing on the wrong side of the railings, looking down at the mangling murk below. Desperate people, ripe for death. Within six weeks, I'd covered four cities with new notes. Not long after that, Sean called me from that same beautiful bridge.

# 7

The dog shakes uncontrollably in the lift, and the moment the doors open, he drags Sam out on to the fourth floor. It's largely empty, save for a few tired-looking officers at desks, who Sam suspects have been here all night. They don't bat an eyelid as she fills the kettle and lifts the dog on to the sofa.

'Aw, who's this?' Chloe Spears comes over and pats him on the head.

'This is little . . . erm . . .' Sam stutters. 'The cleaners are in at home, and we have an appointment at the vet's in an hour, so I just thought . . .' Sam shrugs, takes a seat next to the little dog and checks her work emails as she waits for her tea to cool. There's one from HR, inviting her to 'Wellbeing Wednesday'. She rolls her eyes and archives it. Her heart skips a little when she sees a message from Claire, the linguist she'd worked with on a case years ago and who has agreed to help.

**Subject: Initial Thoughts**

Hi Sam,

I've done an initial read of *How to Get Away With Murder* and you'll have my report by end of next week. I wanted to send you my preliminary thoughts and let you know straight away that I believe we can tentatively conclude that Denver grew up in north-east England. This is because:

1. In his chapter about Jono, Denver claims he was wearing a black cats T-shirt. Most readers would take this to mean a top featuring black cats. However, the Black Cats is a nickname for Sunderland AFC.

2. Denver's uncle says 'nowt as queer as folk', which is common parlance in the North East. Other northern phrases such as 'dinner nanny' are also used.

3. When describing making a cup of tea, Denver uses the word 'mast' instead of 'brew.' This is an odd lexical variant I've not encountered before. I suspect it could be a mishearing of 'mash' (Yorkshire) that has grown in isolated usage within a tiny pocket of a northern county over generations.

4. I'm noticing a strange use of title case, too. For example: Big River and Still of the Night. I can't explain this yet, but I'm bringing it to your attention in case these words crop up elsewhere in your investigation.

More from me soon,
Claire

Sam quickly forwards Claire's email to Taylor and Tina, then sits, chewing her lip and thinking. Northumbria Police is the largest branch in the North East, both in terms of the population they serve and geographical area they cover – some two-thousand-plus square miles, including the city of Sunderland. Sam opens her *Who is Denver Brady?* list and reads down it. Then she opens a browser and types 'Where was Mary Ann Cotton from?' She scans the page and sees that Britain's most prolific female serial killer of all time worked as a nurse in Sunderland, although she lived in small villages all over Tyne and Wear and was born in County Durham. Could it be that Denver was so upset by the suggestion that Mary was innocent because she's the only serial killer from his hometown?

Sam checks the database. The victim searches have turned up nothing so far, and while she hasn't given up hope entirely, it wouldn't normally take this long. She decides to try things the old-fashioned way and types a quick message to Taylor telling him to call Durham, Cleveland and Northumbria and enlist their help identifying any potential real-life Denver victims.

She glances at her watch and gives the little dog a gentle stroke to wake him up – it's time for the vet's. He's modelling a perfect downward-dog stretch, almost ready to move, when Chloe suddenly hops out of her chair and grabs the remote for the communal television, turning the volume as loud as it will go. Sam freezes in place: the press conference is beginning.

On screen, Nigel Mathers cries deep, racking sobs.

'God, my heart just breaks for him,' Chloe groans. 'You know his wife was killed in a hit-and-run when Charlotte was a baby? And now she's gone, too.'

Sam steps towards the TV. Nigel looks even worse than he did on Monday, if that's possible. Sandwiched between Harry and Tina, his skin is ashen and his eyes hazed. As he appeals for witnesses to his daughter's murder, a map appears on the screen showing Charlotte's route the night she was killed. Actors appear, a reconstruction of Charlotte's final movements. There's a pretty, ginger-headed girl wearing a green school uniform and walking down a footpath towards Holland Park, Nigel speaking all the while – the most heartbreaking voice-over Sam has ever heard.

'I just want it to unhappen,' he says, 'but I . . . I know that can't be, so finding him . . . the monster who did this to my baby . . . my baby girl . . . is all I can do for her. Please. Just please, if you know anything at all. I have money. There will be an award . . . reward, I mean, reward. The police know about you, Denver—'

'Please,' Tina's voice cuts Nigel off mid-sentence, 'if you were in or around Holland Park at the time, call the Metropolitan Police.'

The reconstruction finishes and the camera zooms in on Tina giving out the number of the helpline for witnesses to call. Sam imagines she can hear the phones ringing on the civilian desks already. As Tina repeats the telephone number, Nigel's voice can still be heard but it's unclear what else he's trying to say. There's a commotion off-camera and suddenly the angle shifts back to Nigel, who appears to be pushing Harry out of his chair and trying to pull something from inside his own jacket. Does Nigel have a weapon? Alarm flashes through Sam as her godfather grabs at the tablecloth and sound equipment in an effort to maintain his balance. Then Harry falls backward, and a camera man steps into shot, trying to help him.

The camera pans wildly. Sometimes a flash of Tina, then Nigel, then a room full of startled journalists. Finally, it stabilizes. Nigel stands, shouting and waving something. It's not a gun but he points it like one – at Edris, who says, 'Please keep calm, Mr Mathers,' in her slow, considered way.

Harry is signalling to someone to end the broadcast but the camera keeps rolling. Nigel leans forward to speak into Tina's microphone but she quickly unplugs it.

Nigel's mouth moves, but his words are too quiet for Sam to catch. He turns and points the item in his hand at the gathered journalists, who are now on their feet, their questions flying through their own microphones. Harry manages to wrestle the item from Nigel's hand. A book. *Of course it's a book*, Sam thinks, feeling her stomach drop.

'Mr Mathers, do you think your daughter is the victim of a serial killer?' a journalist calls out.

'Mr Mathers, can you confirm that you're accusing the Metropolitan Police of covering up an active serial killer investigation?'

'DI Edris, DCI Blakelaw, how do you respond to these allegations?'

Uniformed officers flood into the room from the side door

but hover at the edge of the stage, looking to Harry. Before he is escorted away, Nigel Mathers makes a dive for Harry, snatches the book back and tosses it to the nearest journalist. The camera follows Nigel's grief-stricken face as he's manoeuvred off the stage and out of the room, yelling all the while. Nigel's words are inaudible to television viewers like Sam, but not to the room full of journalists who, she has no doubt, will print them on the front pages of the evening newspapers.

'Shit!' Sam mutters.

'Ma'am? Are you OK?' Taylor appears at her side. Sam is surprised to find her trainee's sudden presence reassuring, and her hand is steady as she points to the TV. Taylor watches, his brows knitted tightly. On the screen, the journalists are in a frenzy. Tina Edris is frozen in her seat, her hands in a surrender position, desperately trying to calm the room with her quiet voice. To the side of her, Harry is fumbling to plug his microphone back in.

'DCI Blakelaw,' calls a journalist, 'Craig Walton for the *Sun*. Is there any foundation in Nigel Mathers' accusations?'

'I know who you are, Craig,' snaps Harry. 'Let's not create unnecessary alarm here. Mr Mathers is under enormous stress. Please have some compassion for the family.'

'DCI Blakelaw,' another journalist says, 'for the record, is there an active serial killer in the UK right now? Today?'

'We have no reason to believe at present that the murder of Charlotte Mathers is connected to any other crimes. While this is something we never rule out, it is an ongoing investigation and I can't comment further,' Harry says. The journalist tries again, not satisfied.

'So there *might be* a serial killer?' he calls.

'This is an ongoing—' Harry begins but more voices join the call.

'Is there a serial killer?'

'The public have a right to know!'

'What is the Met hiding?'

'Who is Denver Brady?'

'What measures are you taking to protect the public from this killer?'

'For heaven's sake!' Harry spits, his face puce. 'There is *no* serial killer. Be reasonable!'

'Oh, God,' Sam says, her hands clapping to her cheeks. *Why would Harry say that?* How many times had he told her that you never say anything so unequivocal to the press? Especially when it's not true. Sam can't believe he's done something so stupid, with all his experience of handling the media, all of his years of service.

'DI Edris, can you confirm that no part of your investigation is exploring the possibility of a serial killer?' a second journalist asks. Tina Edris leans forward to speak into the microphone but Harry clasps his hand over the top of it.

'As I said, this is an ongoing investigation,' Harry says, uncovering the microphone so his own voice carries. 'We are here today to appeal for help from the public. We need witnesses who saw Charlotte that night, or any time in the days before, to come forward now. We are also appealing to anyone who thinks they know the killer. If you think you know the man who killed this young woman, please—'

'Child!' cries a journalist, but the word barely makes it through the hubbub.

'What about the book?' calls a journalist from the back of the room.

'Tell us about the book!' the journalists cry. Harry stands, followed by Tina, and they leave the stage. The television cuts back to a news anchor in the studio who looks stunned as she begins to tell the public what has occurred at the press conference.

'How did that happen?' Taylor asks, aghast.

'The Boss is in the shit now,' Chloe declares.

122

'Deep shit,' adds Sam, running her hands through her hair. 'The press is going to hit us like a hurricane in Kansas. I have a feeling you'll all spend the rest of today answering phone calls and emails instead of hunting for Charlotte's killer. And the last thing we needed was all eyes on Denver before we even know if he's actually for real or not.'

'Do you want some good news, ma'am?' Taylor asks. Sam's eyes snap to meet his, which are glinting. He's grinning. Something's happened.

'What, Taylor?' she asks, finding herself returning his smile. 'You've enrolled in tea-making classes and henceforth your brews will be passable?' He gives a genuine, heartfelt laugh. It's a pleasant sound that Sam realizes she's not heard before.

'Even better than that,' Taylor responds gamely. 'I found the place that printed Denver's book. It's a firm called Swinton's Printers, based in Brighton of all places.'

'Taylor, that's brilliant work,' she beams.

'I've been in touch with Sussex Police and they've been to the home of Rob Swinton, the owner. A bit of a one-man band, I think. Anyway, his neighbour claims that Rob left the country over a week ago. No idea where he's gone and they don't know yet whether it's just a holiday or if he's on the run.'

'Well done, Taylor,' Sam smiles, though she can't help but feel disappointed that they can't drive out and question this Rob Swinton immediately. 'This could be a real breakthrough.'

## A Gay Old Time

Sean was a 24-year-old mature student. About to qualify in music production or some equally useless subject. He called as I was making a cup of tea. When my little Nokia rang, I thought twice about picking up, to be honest. No one likes their cup of tea to be interrupted, even serial killers. But the last thing you do when someone calls a suicide hotline is leave them hanging. (Get it? Leave them hanging? My genius is wasted on you.)

In anticipation of the calls coming in, I'd rung the Samaritans a couple of times feigning various states of peril. I used a voice alteration device, of course. I'd made sure I was au fait with the Samaritans' use of language when dealing with these self-made mental-health-toting morons.

'This is the Samaritans, you're not alone. What's your name?' I said, and, I confess, a little vomit shot into my throat. Sean didn't speak for quite a while. I could hear the wind and I kept talking as I knew a Samaritan would.

'Take your time. There's no rush,' I cooed, easing myself into the role. Eventually, he told me his name and some dull facts about his life. He spoke with a thuggish accent so I tried to hurry it along.

'Where are you tonight, Sean?' I asked him.

'On the bridge . . . on the wrong side, like,' Sean said. The wrong side for him was the right side for me and, I confess, if I'd been of weaker character, I might have felt a little twitch in the pants when he said that. 'It's raining and I'm proper cold,' he whined.

'What's made you go to the bridge tonight, Sean?' I asked.

'I can't do it any more. My lass Jemma is pregnant. She's a nurse and she's nice enough, but a bairn? I can't raise a bairn!' he blubbed.

'Can't you provide for your family?' I asked, pouring the boiled water atop the teabags in my teapot and fitting its cosy. I absolutely adore the hiss a teabag makes when the water hits. It's called the *strike* – did you know that? Wonderful. I set my little timer and left it to mast.

'I can't provide for them,' he cried. 'I want to be a sound engineer and tour with bands. I can't do that with a bairn, can I?'

'No, definitely not, Sean. I'm sure you could find something else,' I encouraged. 'Supermarkets are always hiring.'

I listened to him crying for a while.

'I told her to get rid of it,' he whispered. 'Told her I'd leave her if she didn't.'

'Oh, Sean,' I said, 'That's not very respectful of a woman's right to choose, is it?'

'She refused,' he sniffed, 'so I told her I was leaving her anyway. That she'd be raising the bairn alone if she had it. I told her I'm in love with . . . with Steve.'

'Oh, poor, pregnant Jemma.'

'So now her family know and they've told the world that I'm in the closet. That I love cock.' I masked my laugh with a cough. This line of work really has its moments of comedy gold.

'They've put it on a thing called Facebook. It's a bit like MySpace,' he said. My little timer sounded and I poured my tea from the pot into my waiting cup.

'So everyone now knows that you're a homosexual? That you're what some feeble-minded people might call a poofter?'

'Well, not many people are on this Facebook thing. It might not take off.'

'But lots of people will have read that you're a raging homo,' I said. 'Word will surely spread. Let's be realistic here.'

'Maybe,' he sobbed.

'Everyone knows, Sean,' I insisted.

'But—'

'No buts, Sean, your secret is out.'

I added a splash-and-a-dash of milk. That's 11 millilitres, for you Neanderthals out there.

'Sean, this world is now a beautiful place where people like you and Steve can live happily ever after. In years to come, you might even be allowed to marry. Your parents will accept you, in time.'

'Ha!' Sean spat, 'you don't know my da.'

'You fear your father wouldn't accept your homosexuality?' I asked.

'Me dad and uncle took cricket bats to a *Brokeback Mountain* billboard outside the Odeon,' he wailed. 'Lit it up.'

'Sean, a leopard can change its spots. Would your own father really turn his back on you, shun you, cast you out of the family, humiliate you that way?' Your dad might just need some time to adjust to you and Steve cuddling on his sofa. I'm sure Dad and Steve will be heading to the working men's club together before you know it. The mother-to-be of your child will be delighted to have two men co-parenting with her. This is a modern time, Sean, people are starting to think differently about homosexuality.'

I suppose I'll never know at what point during my little speech Sean jumped. There was no scream. The line simply went dead, and that's how I knew that Sean was flotsam.

I had to remake my cup of tea, of course. But it was worth it.

Using this technique, I learned how to communicate with victims; how to manipulate their minds – what to say and what not to say. Remember, these were my first interactions with strangers and I was still a young man myself. I practised for a few months at a distance before I moved back to face-to-face interactions. I'm amazed at how often I still use the skills I developed during these early days. Never underestimate the power of practice and patience.

Soon enough, I felt ready to move on to more hands-on practice. Let me tell you about dear old Betty.

# 8

'We have a victim!' Taylor blurts without so much as a hello.

'Oh my God, he's killed again?' Sam sits bolt upright in bed and fumbles for the lamp. Her heart pounds and she sends the objects on her nightstand flying.

'Ah, no . . . Sorry, ma'am,' Taylor stammers. 'I'm talking about a real victim that matches one of Denver's in *How to Get Away With Murder*. A cold case.'

'Taylor,' Sam groans, finding the cable to her bedside lamp and flicking the switch on with shaking fingers before rubbing her eyes. 'It's past two in the morning. I really thought another girl was . . . Are you still at work right now? It's—'

'We need to go to Newcastle tomorrow, ma'am,' Taylor says, clearly running on pure adrenaline. 'Northumbria Police came up trumps. I've informed DI Edris and booked our train tickets already – we're on the six thirty-one out of Kings Cross. I'll meet you on the concourse.'

'Oh, God,' she whispers. She reaches for the lamp once again, then turns her pillow over, relishing the cool fabric against her cheek, and blinks into the darkness. Fear thrums in her stomach. Closing her eyes, she tries to count backwards from one hundred – a calming technique she learned in therapy – but her mind keeps conjuring images of Charlotte's pale skin against the rough bark of an oak tree.

*He might be real.*

The implications make Sam's skin prickle. If the victim Taylor has found matches one of Denver's and he is a real murderer, it's possible that Denver's telling the truth in *How to Get Away With Murder*. Of the three possibilities, this brings it down to two. Denver is a serial killer and he murdered Charlotte, or Denver is a killer but there's a separate, copycat person who murdered Charlotte. Which would be worse? All she knows for certain is that it's Charlotte's killer that she is determined to see behind bars. Sam squeezes her eyes shut and breathes in through her nose and out through her mouth.

One-hundred. Ninety-nine. Ninety-eight. Ninety-seven.

Sam hates early mornings. She walks the little dog quickly around the block, straining in the darkness to see if he is swaying less on his wonky leg, which might mean the painkillers the vet prescribed yesterday are working. He seems to be moving a little better. Once home, she fills the little scruff's kibble and water bowls to the brim and puts down three puppy pads. She pauses to look around the kitchen. The cleaners took eight hours and cost a small fortune, but goodness, they were worth it. The surfaces are clean, the lino floor three shades lighter, and the cooker is as close to sparkling as she's ever seen it. She says goodbye, closes the front door, and steps out into the beginnings of a grey sunrise.

Sam makes her way to Clapham North Tube station and runs aboard just as the train doors are beeping shut. Inside, the carriage is busier than she thought it would be this early in the day. There's a mingle of barely awake bodies, shuffling off to work while stuffing Costa croissants into their mouths. Sam inserts her headphones, presses play on an old Evanescence album and opens *How to Get Away With Murder*. Her progress is still painfully slow and she has to re-read the conversation between Sean and Denver several times. As the train jerks into the next stop, her cheeks are burning. The idea of Denver persuading someone at their most vulnerable to harm themselves makes her rage, and she slaps the button to open the train door.

King's Cross is heaving: travellers yawning underneath the departure boards, families with sleepy little ones riding their luggage, red-eyed tourists filtering through in search of Platform 9¾. Sam stands and punches out an email with shaking fingers as she waits for Taylor to arrive, alerting the police forces in all major cities to the possibility that someone is sabotaging the suicide prevention material attached to bridges. Even if Denver himself isn't behind any sabotage, there's a chance that some other sicko could be inspired by him. She hears the swoosh of it leaving her outbox and hopes it might do some good to someone, somewhere, even though the police are so stretched she's under no illusion as to where her request will fall in terms of priority.

'Ma'am.' She jumps as Taylor appears at her elbow, clammy-faced, two Pret cups in his hands. He looks like someone who's been awake all night, and when he smiles in greeting she sees the weariness in his eyes.

He moves through the crowd effortlessly, people stepping aside for the smartly dressed young man. He shows their tickets to the attendant, who blushes up at him and has to scan the ticket three times.

The tea is cool by the time they find their place on the train, but Sam slides into her seat and immediately swallows big gulps of the overly milky liquid. Taylor takes the time to hang his silk-lined high-sheen blazer on the hook, then arranges his laptop, mobile phone and cardboard document folders neatly on the table between them.

Before lowering into his seat, Taylor does that strange thing some men do with their trousers, grabbing them at the knees and tugging them upwards, which exposes his lemon-coloured silk socks. Sam's own father used to do this, but she's never seen it done by a twenty-something-year-old before. His socks make her smile.

'... Does that sound acceptable, ma'am?' Taylor interrupts her thoughts. He leans forward and sends a waft of designer musk into her nostrils. She clears her throat and nods, hoping to cover her lack of concentration. 'So, I'll tell you about the printer first and perhaps we can discuss our victim once I've, er, finished typing up my notes?' Taylor asks.

'If that's what you'd prefer,' she replies, noticing that Taylor is deferring his full explanation about why they're heading to Newcastle and who Denver's real-life victim is. Strange.

'There's been a development,' he begins, wincing at his tea. 'As you know, *How to Get Away With Murder* was printed in Brighton by a small firm called Swinton's Printers. Sussex Police emailed this morning and there was a fire at the printer's last night. The whole place went up.'

Sam feels the blood drain from her face. 'That cannot be a coincidence.'

'I wouldn't have thought so,' he agrees. 'Sussex Police are investigating and we should know more tomorrow. They managed to track down Rob Swinton, though. He's in Benidorm on holiday, not on the run. I spoke to him yesterday and he remembers taking the order for the book. It was for a three-thousand-copy print run, and paid for in cash.'

'Does Swinton have any connection to the Mathers family?' Sam asks.

'No,' Taylor confirms. 'Swinton had never heard of Charlotte.'

Sam nods, deflated. 'I suppose this Rob Swinton had no qualms about printing a how-to guide for serial killers?' she asks, not trying to hide the venom in her voice.

'I think Swinton's mainly prints leaflets,' Taylor answers levelly. 'Swinton said he wasn't hugely comfortable with the material, but the customer was friendly on the phone. Claimed to be a local man who'd written his first novel, and pushed an envelope of cash through the door, which Swinton had checked by his bank so—'

'Wait, Swinton actually spoke to Denver?' Sam interjects.

'Yes.' Taylor nods. 'He claims that the line was crackly and the customer had an unusual-sounding voice. No accent that he could remember. I'm guessing Denver used a voice distorter and burner-phone.'

'Does Swinton know where he delivered the books to? Surely, he can—'

'The books were collected. A white van showed up and took them.'

'And Swinton has no other details?' Sam rushes. 'By law, he's required to keep basic customer records.'

'Swinton kept company files on all customers and told me where to find them. This was before everything went up in flames. He had CCTV, too, but it was an old system and the server it was connected to is destroyed as well.'

'How convenient,' she snorts. 'It's like a bad soap storyline.'

'Is there a good soap storyline?' Taylor says, rubbing his already red-rimmed eyes.

Sam rolls her eyes. 'It can't be a coincidence the printers burned down the same night that Nigel Mathers went on TV and blamed Denver for killing his daughter. Arsonists use accelerants – petrol, usually. Petrol is very heavy, so they probably used a vehicle to transport it and parked somewhere fairly close to Swinton's. If we're lucky, they'll have been dumb enough to buy the fuel at a nearby service station. I want you to call Sussex and have them pull CCTV footage from all nearby garages, plus traffic footage within a one-mile radius of Swinton's for both the night of the fire and the day the books were collected. I'll let Tina know.'

'Yes, ma'am.' Taylor immediately begins typing on his phone.

Sam is too hot but doesn't have the energy to stand up and

remove her trench coat so she pulls back the material as far as she can. The landmarks drift by outside the window – giant tower blocks, Alexandra Palace and Emirates Stadium – before giving way to miles of fields and countryside as they tear through England, county by county. It's her first time leaving London in over a year. Last time had been with Phil Lowry, when they were investigating a connection between their case and one in Middlesbrough.

Sam's mouth tastes salty and she squeezes her eyes tight shut, focusing on nothing but her breath and the way it roars in her ears. *It's just one day*, she tells herself. *It'll be fine.* She takes out her phone and drafts an email to Dr Thomson as she should be seeing him today and obviously won't make it. Perhaps he'll be able to fit her in one lunchtime instead.

A response from the Glaswegian bank causes a swoop of adrenaline, and Sam clicks on the PDF. Her stomach drops. The student bank account that receives the money from Howtogetawaywithmurder.com is owned by a Mr Drew Mackay. The payments-in don't amount to much, but she'd expected that: sales of the book are low, and as soon as the press conference disaster had happened, Sam had asked DC Chen to take the website down. What's alarming Sam is that each week, the Glaswegian bank account automatically pays all monies into another account. She quickly googles the sort code. It's an account in Cardiff, and a suspicion forms at the back of her mind. *Shit.* The swaying of the train and looking down at her phone is making her nauseous so she quickly responds and, with as much charm as she can muster, asks her colleague to submit another disclosure request to the Cardiff bank account. She emails the Glasgow East police department, providing the details of the student account, and asks them to speak with Mr Mackay. He needs to explain why money from Howtogetawaywithmurder.com is landing in his account. Sam suspects she knows the answer.

She slides her phone away and closes her eyes for a second. When she next opens them, Taylor is watching her and she sits up and smooths her hair. He blushes lightly and turns his gaze to the window. There's a tense silence for a moment, and Taylor clicks and unclicks his pen. He looks strained; vulnerable somehow, in spite of his polished exterior.

'Have you heard the term "money mule" before, Taylor?' She pops some chewing gum in her mouth.

'Yes, ma'am.' He drops his pen. 'It's someone who lets criminals use their bank account to move money around. Often the cash goes from account to account and then out of the country, then back in, so that the criminal eventually gets it into their own account without police being able to track it.'

'Exactly. It's nasty,' Sam adds. 'Often the mules are vulnerable and poor, paid only a few quid. Exploited, basically.'

Taylor looks out of the window, the sunrise dazzling on his pallid skin. It's time for him to brief her on the victim, but he looks so strained that she decides to let him collect himself for a few more minutes. She orders them both a fresh tea using the train line's infuriating app, then takes *How to Get Away With Murder* from her bag and begins the next chapter. Glancing up at Taylor to make sure he's not looking, she uses her finger to trace and then retraces each sentence – it's slow, but it's the only thing she's found helps her still-skittish mind to maintain focus. She reads, sips tea and re-reads, until the conductor announces they're approaching York. That, to Sam, feels very far north. She's pleased to close the book, because Denver's words are bringing her close to tears.

'We're almost there, Taylor,' she swallows. 'It's time for you to tell me about the real victim.'

He wipes his hand over his face.

'OK,' he breathes. 'We have one real murder case that matches the details in Denver's book. The lady's name is Betty. Betty Brown.'

'I just read that chapter,' she gasps. 'I mean, re-read.'

'It's a tough one,' he sighs. 'The searches didn't show up because her name isn't actually Betty, it's Elizabeth. I should have thought to search for nicknames and contractions . . .' Taylor runs his hand through his pristine hair, clearly agitated. 'It was strange. When I called Northumbria Police, as soon as I mentioned the name Betty, I was put straight through to a DI Neil Duggan. He'll meet us when we arrive. He sounded harassed but sort of . . . overjoyed – that we were travelling up. He just kept thanking me.'

'Overjoyed?' Sam wonders. 'That's odd.'

Taylor nods. 'After Duggan, we'll meet with Dr Tweedy, the pathologist in Betty's murder . . . Oh shoot!' Taylor slaps his hand on the table. 'Dr Tweedy sent us a report to read. It completely slipped my mind. I'm so sorry.'

'It's OK,' she soothes. 'You're working crazy-long hours, Taylor. You're tired. It's not easy material we're handling. We can skim it quickly now.' She tries to sound assuring, but she knows they simply do not have time to review the report thoroughly, as the train is already slowing into Darlington. People begin to stand, only to flop back into their seats when an announcement informs them that they're being held outside of the station, pending a change of crew.

In a field, beyond the station, Sam can see a young girl cantering a pony around a small paddock. Her blonde ponytail bounces up and down as the little skewbald's legs hit the earth and take off again. Unbidden, Sam remembers the riding lessons her mother had taken her to as a child. She'd loved a little bay mare named Holly. When her father had accepted a job in the Met and she'd understood that London was a faraway place, she'd sobbed over the prospect of never seeing Holly again. A year later, when her mum died, Harry had asked her to name anything, anything in the world that would make her stop crying. She said, seeing Holly again. Harry had called the riding school, but Holly had gone to live somewhere else, he told her, with a kind family on a farm. Of course, Sam now understands exactly what he meant. *My lovely Mum*, Sam thinks then. She never really had a chance.

'Ma'am,' Taylor says quietly, 'are you OK?'

She rubs her cheek and nods, dismissing the concern etched into his pale face.

Sam stands and tugs off her coat, showering loose change, packs of pills, the netball keyring and two tampons into Taylor's lap. Taylor's face is the same colour as the pink wrapper as she gingerly retrieves her Super-Plus from his open palm. His Adam's apple bobs and he tugs at his collar, before wiping light perspiration off his upper lip. Something's really not right with Taylor and it's something more than her accidentally showering him with sanitary products. Past Sam would have shrugged off Taylor's emotions and ignored his mood until he was back to normal, so Sam is surprised to find that she genuinely wants to know what's troubling him. She sits back down and shifts in her seat, then steels herself and leans forward.

'What's up, Taylor?' she asks, softening her tone as much as she can.

He says nothing for a few moments, and she waits in silence.

'It's just Betty,' he says eventually, as if that explains things. He takes a silk handkerchief from his pocket and rubs his nose. 'She reminds me so much of my gran, who I just lost a few weeks ago. Of all the victims, I really hoped that Betty was just made up. Rotten luck that she's the one we found first.' He continues to stare out the window, but Sam can see tears in his eyes. He shifts uncomfortably and his knee rests against hers for a moment. Sam is surprised at the sudden heat she feels.

'Tell me about your gran, Taylor,' she says, and he smiles at her. She listens as he describes the woman, asking him questions that direct him away from the sadness of loss and firmly towards the joy of happy memories. She knows they should be reading the pathology report but instead she chooses to spend the final minutes of their journey smiling, as Taylor talks about a woman he clearly loved very much. By the time they reach Durham, it's heartbreakingly obvious to Sam why Betty reminds Taylor of his grandmother.

As the train crosses the bridge over the great River Tyne and they both pull on their coats, Sam finds herself praying that it's all made up, and Denver never really tested his prowess as a serial killer on an old lady called Betty.

## *Tea Time With Betty*

Sir Edmond Locard, a pioneer in criminology, gave the basic principle of forensic science to be that *every contact leaves a trace*. This is known as the exchange principle. Our response is simple: *fuck you, Locard*. While he may be technically right, it's perfectly possible just to leave no *meaningful* trace. In this chapter, I'll talk you through how to avoid leaving the police any useful clues or evidence.

You need to physically prepare yourself to ensure that your own body doesn't betray you and leave behind the evidence that will convict you. I recommend watching the opening scenes of Christian Bale in *American Psycho*. The shower routine is inspirational. You must exfoliate. Trim your nails. Ideally, remove all body hair. Hair is a big danger . . . and it's not just on your head. Wear a face mask (now widely available and socially acceptable in public – thank you, Covid-19). Glasses also distort your appearance. Wear no aftershave, perfume, moisturiser or lip balm – there should be nothing on your skin. If you intend to do any biting, wear dentures, and if you don't use a condom then I've no sympathy for you.

Come to think of it . . . I've no sympathy for anyone.

Only a small percentage of serial killers are identified using DNA or fingerprints, but these will be the things that convict you beyond a doubt. Use silicone (or superglue, for you cheapskates) on your fingertips, but for heaven's sake wear gloves. They need to be thin enough that your fingers can operate restraints etc. without impediment. I wear double latex gloves under a simple pair of Thinsulates, removing the latter during my experience. While you may be drawn to wearing animal skin, remember that leather is porous and your hands will sweat through it, so this is a bad idea. Interesting fact, on the subject of fingerprints: they can't be dated. Fingerprints made pre- or post-mortem are impossible to tell apart. This leaves some real opportunities open to you in terms of planting evidence at crime scenes and pressing the victim's prints on to it.

The correct clothing and footwear is vital. You should cash-purchase mainstream items, which should be in dark colours with no distinguishable features. Get into the habit of using cash for everything. Always purchase footwear a size or two larger than your own and simply wear two pairs of socks. If you're of short stature, or a woman, purchase much bigger footwear and add insoles to give you height – you need to aim to be around 5ft 10ins, or whatever is the average male height in your country of operation. Use clothing to conceal any distinguishing physical features such as breasts, a missing limb or skin colour. A fat suit is a great disguise, if a little sweaty. You can use walking aids such as a Zimmer frame, big glasses and a white cane, or even a wheelchair to make yourself invisible (what a cruel world we live in). The aim of any disguise is to make you appear vulnerable, weak or incapable of crime. You need to be entirely *forgettable*.

Disguise was important to me, as I enjoyed observing

my victims whenever I could. You can learn a lot about your victim in a very short space of time. What they wear, what's on their washing line or in their shopping trolley, the outside of their home, their socials – all ripe sources of information for us.

People-watching always makes me ravenous. I was hungry to graduate from the Samaritan Technique and enjoy face-to-face interactions once again. Sure, I'd killed Jono in the quarry at only twelve years old and I'd enjoyed Sarah in my sixth-form days, but I was wise enough to know that I was still a beginner. Sean and the others that I got with the Samaritan treatment were mere placeholders. When I decided it was time to put myself back out there, I did so with much caution and, without wanting to be overly generous to myself, much success. My scouting efforts paid off and several of these early conquests played out like a dream. Although I'd love to overcome my modesty and commit my neophyte achievements to paper, I can't share every detail of every victim with you. Alas, there really is only so much I can give away. Plus, I'm working to a word count, you know.

Because I was still developing my craft, I ensured that my one-to-one encounters were with low-risk victims, and you should do the same. In my younger days, I had some strange habits and practices that I've altered over time. Throughout this chapter, I'll be talking you through some of those early methodologies, and how I've changed my style as my experience has grown.

Let me begin with a little context.

As you can imagine, poor and forgotten senior citizens make perfect pickings for those of us starting out. In many towns and villages in the UK, one can generally locate the area most densely populated by the elderly: tiny estates made up of cubic bungalows. Handrails and ramps galore.

I met Betty one cold and wet November day. My arm was wrapped in a papier mâché plaster cast *à la* Teddy Bundy. (What can I say? I was a young fanboy. It was a phase.) Tony wasn't with me that day, but I had walked the area a few times ahead of selecting Betty for a house call.

I had to ring the doorbell lots of times before her watery eyes peered out through the tiniest crack. Several chains held the door in place. I explained that my car had broken down and I needed help. If I could just come in and call the AA?

The teapot wore a floral jacket. A tea-cosy that had been passed down through her late husband Albert's family. Albert had always said that he could tell instantly if tea had come from a pot without a cosy on it. It wouldn't mast the same, according to him. I agreed.

Betty wore a white blouse with faded flowers, and a pale pink skirt. Despite the chill temperature inside the bungalow, she'd also donned thin tights and beige Jesus sandals. There were photographs on every surface, including one of Jimmy Nail. A Wedgwood collection and dozens of china dogs. A cabinet full of Albert's war medals. Everything blanketed in a thick layer of dust.

I spent a good couple of hours with Betty. The old gal could really chat. She told me about rationing during the war. How she and her sister used to go to school on alternate days because they had only one pair of shoes between them. How her mother was left with nothing when her father died with his lungs full of coal dust. How they'd been saved from the workhouse by the Salvation Army.

'There won't be much when I go,' Betty said, completely out of the blue, 'but what there is will go to them.'

Betty told me about her and Albert's shotgun wedding. Spicy stuff. A son born six months later. How their boy graduated from university, only to fall in a river on his way home from the ceremony. She began to weep and I felt the time had come, so I removed my plaster cast. Betty looked confused, but not for long. I used her favourite Wedgwood clock. It's what she would have wanted. The distinctive design was soon invisible beneath the blood and the fragments of skull.

Afterwards, I went to the kitchen and pulled on Betty's rubber gloves. I located her black bin bags and put the now rather bloody clock inside one, and the outer layer of my clothing in another. Then I made my way around the bungalow, rifling soundlessly through drawers and placing small items of value in another bin bag. I did fret for an instant over the amount of plastic I was using, but sometimes needs must.

I slid Betty's wedding band from her finger, along with a beautiful blue ring. The big star sapphire gemstone must have been worth a fortune, and the light danced around it so that it looked like it was glowing. Her hands were desperately arthritic and I had to exert a little more force than I'd envisaged. I confess, it's possible I broke a finger in my quest for a trophy.

I put Albert's medals and some photographs inside a tea-towel and stamped on it quietly. Then I scattered the broken pieces around the room. The towel went in a bin bag, too. I'm sure you've deduced my aim by now: I was attempting to present the scene as a robbery gone wrong. Hooligans after a quick buck to feed a heroin addiction.

Once the stage was set, I turned the heating on and the thermostat up. A brilliant method to widen the possible-time-of-death window that the pathologist would eventually give to the police. A warmer body decomposes faster and decomposition is our friend as it makes precise conclusions about the death far less likely at the post-mortem. Also, I was freezing cold in that bungalow. Betty was clearly a tough old bird.

Upstairs, I found all of Albert's clothes still neatly arranged in the wardrobe. His glasses atop a book on the bedside table. His flat cap on a hook as if he'd just come back from to the shops. By the door was a beige overcoat, scarf, walking stick and a tartan shopper. I put it all on, turned the coat collar up, pulled the scarf tight, and hunched myself over.

Outside, I cleaned the doorbell with a Dettol wipe (I dip my fingers in silicone on a weekly basis but you can never be too careful), then I shuffled down the ramp, pretending to hold the rail. I remained in character until I was beyond the little village. It was dark by the time I reached my bicycle, which I'd concealed behind some trees. I peeled off all the clothing, revealing my cycling suit beneath. I detached the bag from the shopper's frame and stuffed everything into my backpack. I cycled the thirty miles to my car in no time. I adore the bicycle: you wear so much gear that it's impossible to identify you, or even discern your gender; plus, you travel five times faster than on foot, so camera footage of you will be blurry.

My backpack and its contents, the shoes I'd worn –

it all went into the river. The clothes, the clock, everything. It's a misconception that burning evidence is the best disposal method; a deep body of moving water is superior. While both fire and water corrupt evidence, water has the added advantage of taking it away and hiding it for you, making it incredibly difficult and very costly to find. Fire, on the other hand, is confined to a location that is known to you, and house fires in particular attract a lot of attention. Imagine if I'd set Betty's place on fire. The authorities would have been there within minutes. After my stroll along the river, I boil-washed my cycle suit with oxygen-based detergent, three times. Bleached my bike. Then celebrated with a nice Chablis from Marks and Spencer and a share-pack of Maltesers.

No one found Betty for weeks. According to the newspapers, her nephew turned up for a rare visit and noticed a smell coming from the letterbox.

Over the coming months, I enjoyed the company of several other old-timers. I learned an awful lot about bingo, snooker and Blackpool hotels. I have never drunk such good tea before or since.

# 9

The second Taylor opens the door to the headquarters of Northumbria Police and Sam enters, a man of indiscernible age steps forward and introduces himself as DI Neil Duggan. He looks windswept, despite being indoors, and his shirt is hanging out on one side. His accent is broad, and somewhat soothing, although she has to concentrate to understand him fully. Sam apologizes for their lateness, explaining that the train was delayed.

'Aye, the trains are chaos,' Duggan says as they sign in and follow him through the building. 'Beeching's Axe swung hard in the North,' he adds, but Taylor only shrugs when Sam sends him a questioning glance. She decides not to seek clarification.

They sit in a small but clean and modern meeting room and Duggan brings them each a frothy coffee from a machine in the corridor.

'We've only five minutes,' Duggan says, slurping his own drink. 'Then Tweedy will be here and he waits for no man, or woman, so I'll have to catch you afterwards. I canna tell you how Betty has haunted me. I spent hours on the application to reopen the case. I spent days on the forms. Went down to London and did the presentation to the board. All in my own time and at my own expense, too. The DCI isn't very ... er ... supportive of going over old ground. Especially given that Betty is Durham's case, and I transferred here a decade back. All DCIs care about these days is improving on last year's statistics.' Duggan shakes his head but then smiles, his entire face lifting. 'But now, you're here. I can't believe I did it. Betty's case. Reopened.'

Taylor clears his throat awkwardly and Sam takes a sip of her coffee before asking, 'To reopen Betty's case?'

'Aye,' Duggan's brow wrinkles. 'You lot are from the cold-case review team, aren't you? The new team of . . .' He lets his words die as Sam shakes her head. 'Well, what then?'

'We're part of the Charlotte Mathers investigation,' Sam says. 'A child who was—'

'Aye, I watch the news.' He leans forward: 'But, how's that . . . ? So, is Betty's case reopened or not?'

'DI Duggan,' Sam says, 'I'm sorry, but we're investigating a possible connection to Charlotte's murder. A book by a man named Denver Brady, *How to Get Away With Murder*, describes Betty's murder and has another murder in it that is incredibly similar to Charlotte's. A copy of that book was also found among Charlotte's possessions at the crime scene.'

Duggan just stares, unblinking. Sam shifts in her seat and Taylor clicks his pen.

'I did send over all of the . . .' Taylor begins, but Sam shakes her head sadly. It won't comfort the man to know that the full outline of their visit was in the late-night email he'd clearly not read in full.

'So, Betty's case,' Duggan folds forward, rubbing his hands through his hair, making it stick up even more than it was. 'You're kind of looking at it because it's in that serial killer book that was on the telly. But you're not really investigating—'

A sharp rap on the door and the entry of a young woman in civilian attire ends the conversation. They're bustled down corridors towards another meeting room, where they're told the pathologist is waiting for them. Duggan mumbles something and disappears. Sam's head begins to throb and she swallows two ibuprofen. She glances at Taylor, who looks ghostly pale.

'Taylor,' she whispers, as they follow the young woman down some stairs, 'you can sit this one out if you want to. It might not be good for you to hear the grim—'

He shakes his head and she sees the determination in the set of his jaw. She understands it. Every police officer does. The need to see the case through, in spite of the personal toll.

Dr Tweedy is everything the name suggests and is even wearing a green tweed jacket. If Sam wasn't feeling drained already, she might smile at that. They each introduce themselves and she slurps her coffee, which tastes good but is doing very little to combat her exhaustion.

'I've read the chapter of *How to Get Away With Murder* that you emailed me, TDC Taylor,' Tweedy launches straight in. 'I need to tell you both up front that I am hugely concerned about this situation. Especially given what I saw on the news. That's the only reason I agreed to such a last-minute meeting. I will be writing to the Commissioner to voice my alarm.'

'Why is that?' Sam asks, rubbing her brow.

'Haven't you read my pathology report on Elizabeth Brown, DI Hansen?' Tweedy demands. 'I emailed that first thing this morning. Ample time, considering the three hours you've just spent on a train.'

Sam feels her cheeks burn. Taylor tenses and leans forward, and she knows he's about to take the blame and apologize.

'We've given your report a cursory review, Dr Tweedy,' Sam jumps in, 'but we'd prefer to hear it directly from you.'

'Very well,' Tweedy replies, clearly unconvinced. 'In the case of Betty Brown, there was no forensic evidence linking the scene to a third party. Some fibres, but without clothing to compare them to, they were meaningless as they came from widely available items.'

'That's very similar to Charlotte's case,' Sam begins. 'Our pathologist has found nothing useful that—'

'I'll talk you through the facts of *my* case,' Tweedy interrupts, 'and then I'm sure the reason that I'm so concerned will become obvious. Betty Brown. Aged eighty-four years. Cause of death was blunt-force trauma to the skull. The exact date and time of death are unclear but we believe Mrs Brown was killed between 24 and 26 November 2007, in her own home. As described in *How to Get Away With Murder*, the central heating in the home was turned up and the body wasn't discovered for weeks, by which time decomposition was advanced and only an approximate time of death could be given. The murder weapon was a heavy object of forget-me-not blue, unglazed ceramic, consistent with—'

'Betty's Wedgwood clock. Just like in the book,' Taylor mutters.

'Yes. But that is where the accuracy ends, officers, and this is the reason I am so concerned.'

'How so?' Sam asks.

'According to Denver Brady's book, Mrs Brown was surprised when he removed a Bundy-esque papier mâché arm cast, then he immediately killed the victim by a beating her skull with the aforementioned weapon – but that's not what happened.'

'So what did happen?'

'Detectives, when you actually read the documentation that I've already sent to you, you'll see that the accounts are contradictory on one important point. It is this single point that means I have never forgotten Betty Brown, nor has DI Duggan, and nor will you once you understand what went on.'

'That being . . . ?' Sam presses, barely concealing her frustration. She pinches the top of her nose, focusing hard.

'Brady claims the victim died quickly, and was surprised by her attacker. He further claims that he removed Mrs Brown's rings post-mortem and may have accidentally broken the phalanges – the fingers. The reality was, sadly for Mrs Brown, rather different.'

'Spit it out,' Sam hisses, her head now throbbing too much for her to care about manners.

'Betty was tortured,' Dr Tweedy says baldly.

'Tortured?' Taylor gasps, his pale face turning green about the edges. Sam looks quickly around the room for a bin, in case he vomits, then passes him a cup of water. '*Tortured*,' Taylor whispers again, his hands gripping his thighs under the table.

'Tortured,' Tweedy repeats. 'Badly.'

Taylor leans forward, his hand brushing against Sam's. She doesn't pull away, but leaves the back of her hand resting against the side of his.

'I've never seen anything like it in all my years as a pathologist. An old lady. Tied to a chair and . . .' There's a roaring in her ears and Sam feels Taylor's hand pressing hard against hers. He's shaking. Their eyes meet and they interlace their fingers, holding tight as Tweedy goes on. 'Tortured. For at least an hour. Probably longer. All ten of Betty's fingers were broken while she was alive – I could tell that from the haemorrhaging. Each finger was bent back until it snapped. She had strong bones for her age – mild osteoarthritis, but the fingers wouldn't have broken easily. Tearing to the vocal chords suggest that Betty screamed for—'

'Stop,' Sam says, as Taylor folds forward. She keeps a firm hold of his hand as he takes long, deep breaths.

The implication of what Tweedy has just said becomes clear to Sam as they sit in silence: Denver Brady is a liar. He lied about breaking Betty's fingers accidentally. He lied about how many he broke. So, what else is he lying about?

'You'll need to speak to DI Duggan,' Dr Tweedy carries on, 'but I believe he found family photographs of Betty that showed that she only ever wore two rings: a wedding band and an impressive star sapphire ring that had come down through her husband's family. In which case, why would . . .'

'. . . Denver break *all* her fingers?' Taylor finishes, turning to Sam. Sweat coats his upper lip, and a strand of his sculpted hair has come loose and dangles over his face.

'For pleasure, Taylor. He broke her fingers because he enjoyed it,' she says, her voice a sad whisper. Taylor's eyes widen. 'I'm so sorry,' she says.

'A pathologist cannot speak as to motive. And I'm afraid you may be missing the *bigger point* here, Detectives,' Tweedy says.

Sam rolls her eyes. 'And that is . . . ?'

'How did Denver Brady know that any of Betty's fingers were definitely broken?' Tweedy sits back in his chair. 'That information was not revealed to the family or the press.'

'*How could Denver know?*' Taylor wonders aloud to himself, wiping his face with his free hand.

'Denver Brady has some unique knowledge of the Elizabeth Brown murder that could only be known by the perpetrator, or someone directly involved in the case,' Tweedy states.

'Shit,' Sam says.

'Shit indeed, Detective Hansen,' Tweedy affirms. 'I've read only Betty's chapter in *How to Get Away With Murder*, but I can imagine the nature of the book, and the claims of the author. I also saw the press conference that aired yesterday, in which your DCI denied that any serial killer is being investigated. But if Denver Brady killed Betty Brown, which seems probable to me, that means there has been a serial killer operating unimpeded in the UK for almost twenty years.'

'Rest assured, Dr Tweedy,' Taylor says, his chin up, 'if that is the case, the Metropolitan Police will find him and see him behind bars.'

'From what I've heard,' the pathologist says, 'the Met are still in special measures and—'

He breaks off at a knock on the door, followed by the entry of DI Duggan.

'Tweedy,' he says in greeting, before turning to Sam. 'Detective Hansen, please may I borrow you for a moment?' Sam drops

Taylor's hand, stands up as smoothly as she can, given her pounding head, and follows him into the corridor.

'I'm sorry to do this, DI Hansen,' Duggan begins, 'but I've been called away to an emergency. A multiple-casualty pile-up around Haymarket. I didn't want to leave without speaking—'

Sam's eyebrows raise in surprise, 'A traffic incident?'

'I'm afraid so.' Duggan reddens through his three-day stubble. 'We're a little short-staffed here at the moment. Cutbacks – Northern policing has been badly hit. And it's a bit of an all-hands-on-deck situation.'

'Sir.' A red-faced PC jogs up to them. 'We're leaving now.'

'One minute, Constable.' Duggan turns back to Sam and rubs his forehead as if trying to push his brain back on track. Sam wonders how many shifts this man is working, and on how many hours' sleep he's currently functioning. 'I had very little to go on for Betty's murder. No witnesses. No evidence. No third-party DNA, only Betty's and her nephew's – he found the body. Betty's neighbour's DNA was also present, but he was old and ailing. Betty and Albert didn't have any other family who visited. Their only son died young – drowning. Very sad story. The boy had only just graduated and—'

'Sir,' the PC interrupts again, 'it's just that—'

'One minute, Constable!' Duggan snaps, running a hand through his hair. 'Look, Hansen, like I said earlier, when looking into Betty's murder again in my own time, I discovered that Betty did a strange thing not long before she died and I think it's enough to get the case reopened. That's why I want the cold-case team to—'

'Sir, please—'

'What did you find?' Sam asks.

'Betty and Albert were from mining stock. Coal miners, just like my family. Back then, the pit houses came with the job and if the bloke was killed, well, the wife and kids were thrown out, sometimes the same day. Betty and her mam were chucked out their house and saved from poverty by the Sally Bash, and that's—'

'Sally who?' Sam interjects, wishing that he'd get to the point without a Catherine Cookson-style back story.

'Sally Army. You know, the Salvation—'

'Duggan! Get your arse up here now!' someone bellows from around the corner and both the DI and the PC jolt as if they've been tasered. Duggan rubs his brow again, clearly fighting to remember something else he had hoped to say. After a few seconds he shakes his head, then shakes Sam's hand and scuttles away.

Sam leans up against the wall to process everything she's learned. The Betty Brown case sounds completely unlike Charlotte Mathers' murder. A different victim-type. A different MO. Yet both victims seem linked to DB – Denver Brady. But then, Denver does advocate selecting victims at random – in fact, it's one of his victim selection 'principles', so perhaps the seeming randomness of location and victim actually points *towards* Denver. Yet Denver simultaneously claims not to murder children.

Sam lingers in the corridor, letting her thoughts brew. There's a growing tightness in her chest, like an elastic band has been wrapped around her and is slowly cutting her in two. She inhales deeply through her nose, then closes her eyes and focuses on the exhale. It's so long since she last left London and everything's feeling incredibly intense. Perhaps she shouldn't have agreed to give up her rest day and skip her session with Dr Thomson, after all. But acknowledging this only makes her feel less in-control. She pulls in air, concentrating hard on clearing her mind. She can't let herself have a panic—

A door clicks open.

Sam opens her eyes as a young woman steps out, followed by a police officer. The woman holds her bandaged arm across her chest, and Sam sees a tiny split in her lip. The way she walks down the corridor, as if concussed, is so familiar to Sam that she has to resist the urge to call out to the woman. She's wearing a polo neck that she pulls up under her chin and Sam knows, can picture precisely, the thumb marks on the throat beneath. As they turn the corner, the woman moves her fingers to her hair, smoothing it forward to cover her ears and the sides of her face. Ears, Sam suspects, that are black and swollen, hidden from view, but ringing loudly. Sam wonders if this woman has a little girl at home and who the child might think her mother is fighting with to get the marks she shouldn't see, but does.

Sam's chest tightens even more. The salty taste floods her mouth and the smell of seawater fills her nostrils. Her ears begin to roar. She's losing her grip. She tries deep-breathing again. *In for four, hold for two, out for four. Repeat. And again.* After a few minutes, though, she can't keep up the pattern. Her breaths turn into short sucks, like panting. She battles to restore a rhythm, but her vision begins to spot. The tightness in her chest increases until it's overwhelming. The air is void of oxygen. Her armpits prickle with hot sweat. Her stomach churns. Heart pounding. Chest in agony. Her head feels like it's floating. She's going to die, she's sure of it.

Sam doesn't hear the meeting-room door open, but suddenly Taylor's piercing blue eyes are in front of hers. He is speaking but she hears only echoes of his voice through the whooshing that crashing in her ears. She sees her own hands reaching for him as she begins to slide down the wall.

'Out . . . side,' she gasps, the panic attack now so advanced that she can barely draw breath. Then her feet leave the floor. Her body is moving through the air, surrounded by warmth and Taylor's musk. Her head flops on to his shoulder as he carries her towards the emergency exit, and everything turns black.

## *The Truth Won't Set You Free*

By far my favourite thing to do is to frame someone else for my crimes. While false confessors can be useful, there's nothing more satisfying than seeing someone else protest their innocence as the cuffs are tightened and down they go. I can't wait to tell you about Melanie and her charming boyfriend. But before I do, let's discuss Point 6. You've probably forgotten that we're working through the list of reasons you'll become a suspect, so here I am, kindly jogging your memory. Point 6 is: You confess.

A whopping 5 per cent of you will march into a police station of your own free will and confess.

Very few budding serial killers will believe it's possible that you'll have the urge to confess your crimes. But trust me, you'll find it more difficult than you anticipate to keep your mouth closed. You will want to tell someone. Or, like me, everyone. However, you must resist for a long, long time. As I have.

In order to achieve true greatness, you need to aim for a high victim count before the police are aware you even exist. This has been my recipe for success. Now that I'm at the top of my game, I can declare myself to the world and satisfy my ego. The sooner you discuss your activity, the less notoriety and respect you will ultimately achieve, as talking will inevitably lead to your capture. You have no idea the lengths I've gone to in order to protect myself ahead of this, my debut. Once you're famous, things only get harder, because false confessors will flock to the police stations in their droves, claiming to be you. That's unlikely to be an issue until you're in the front-page headlines, though.

The most likely reason you'll talk before you're ready to go to prison is that you'll hear others talking about your or similar crimes and feel the need to correct their stupid assertions. This includes the press, online sleuths, the general public and your nearest and dearest. Should your crime make the news, it's best that you don't watch any of the footage. The police will try to appeal to you and they'll try to goad you. They'll try to convince your loved ones to dob you in by telling them that you need medical help. As the police fail to catch you, their appeals will turn into attacks, aimed at angering you so that you'll slip up. Hence my advice to avoid all coverage about your crimes. Don't even google it until at least a year later. Don't talk with those around you about crime, either. They'll have made incorrect assumptions and it'll be almost impossible not to correct them.

No one is perfect. I gave in to the urge to talk one night when I was visiting my cousin Bobby at university. I'm taking you back to my youth again here, and I apologize for hopping about in time, but I hope you're not too stupid to cope. I acknowledge the structure is less formulaic than you're accustomed to, but why can't a serial killer push genre boundaries?

Bobby and I were both drunk in a waterside bar, watching girls walk by the window in dresses that barely covered their bottoms, despite the fact that it was snowing.

This was around the time that Harold Shipman, aka Doctor Death, was on trial. The case was all over the news, especially up there because the doc had studied and lived so nearby. That night, Bobby brought Shipman up in conversation and made some unflattering assertions about the base instincts of serial killers.

'I think it's biology what makes monsters like that,' Bobby said, slurping from his third bottle of ale. I just shrugged, not wanting to be drawn in. 'They're wired up wrong. Shipman wasn't abused, so no one can blame trauma or his mammy. They all blame their mams. Like—'

'Let's talk about something else,' I tried, but Bobby was like a dog with a bone.

'Maybe Shipman got a head injury as a kid. I read that can be linked with psychotic tendencies in adulthood. What do you reckon?'

'Another round?' I tried again.

'Come on, Denver,' Bobby said. 'You did psychology, and you read all them books. What made him—'

'He did it because he wanted to, OK?' I said to Bobby, somewhat shortly. 'His motives were pure.'

Something about what I'd said or the way I'd said it silenced my cousin and he simply stared at me for a long while. For the rest of the night he was subdued and we went home early, despite previous promises of dancing the night away in a multi-level club filled with women.

I slept badly that night, which is rare for me. Bobby had rattled me and I'd said more than I should have. The next morning, before I left to walk to the train station, Bobby hugged me. I don't think Bobby had ever done that before. I stood rather stiffly at first, but then I reached around and patted my cousin's back, just like they do in movies.

'You know, I . . . you know I love you, right, mate?' Bobby said to me.

'I love you too, Bobby,' I said, without hesitation or awkwardness, and waved him goodbye.

We lost Bobby under tragic circumstances the following July and I was so pleased we'd had that moment together. I also learned a great deal from it. Mainly that a murderer should never, ever, discuss murder with others. The outcomes are almost always undesirable.

With longevity and a high victim count comes that other risk: the possibility that someone else will confess to your crimes. It's happened to dozens of us. While this sounds like a blessing, seeing another person on Netflix, taking credit for your work, is enough to drive even the most stable among us to madness. It's a position I've not yet been in myself, but I anticipate that changing should this book gain me the notoriety that I crave.

People who falsely confess usually have something to gain by plagiarizing your work. Often it's about bringing meaning or notoriety to their lives, but not always. One woman – you've probably heard of her if you're well read – confessed to murder and named her ex-boyfriend as her accomplice. She was a smart lady – a teacher, I think. She used facts gathered from newspapers and her knowledge of the local area to ensure that they were both jailed for life. Her boyfriend pleaded guilty to avoid death row. The murder was in fact committed by a serial killer known as Happy Face. He was offended by the false confessor and sent little notes to officers and later newspapers, with a smiley emoji in the corner. I think of him every time I see a :)

The more intelligent among you may have considered turning others' desire to falsely confess to your advantage. You can reclaim your crimes as your own, should you wish, in the future. But you may want to buy yourself time by using a proxy. Especially if the police are beginning to show an interest in you, in which case a confessor can really come in handy.

You can induce someone to confess in a number of ways. The easiest way is to achieve fame and then the confessors will line up, hoping some ambitious cop with a questionable sense of morality will accept the confession as a way to boost their own career. Other incentives, such as money, for themselves or the family left behind, can induce potential confessors.

It's actually easier than one might think to induce another to confess, as the life of a famous serial killer can be appealing. Perhaps the confessor anticipates a life of fame and notoriety. They may desire three guaranteed meals a day, a warm bed at night on His Majesty's dime. Just a couple of years ago, an elderly man walked into a police station and confessed to a murder committed in the 1980s. Police investigated and found that the pensioner was facing homelessness and poverty, and relied on foodbanks for his meals. Police released the man, surmising that he just wanted a night in the custody suite instead of in a shop doorway. They rearrested him two days later when DNA proved that he had in fact committed the murder. When interviewed, the man said that he'd confessed because he was in his eighties and he thought that the prison's routine, hot food and clean sheets would do him good.

False confessors may also be enticed by the flocking women (or men – let's not discriminate here). They may fancy a wedding in the prison chapel and conjugal visits without the arduous 'Do you love me?' shit after the dirty deed is done. Charles Manson was eighty years old when he got a licence to marry a 26-year-old hottie. Apparently, it's hybristophilia – the condition of being turned on by someone who commits violent crime – that brings the bright young things to the prison door, hoping for a visit. The badder the serial killer is, the hotter they get.

Then there's the fan mail. There's tonnes of it for your false confessor. Letters from all around the world, telling them how sexy their mug shot is. The fame brings with it a new voice and image for your confessor. Louis Theroux will be popping around for a chat. Maybe Oprah will call. There's the chance an A-lister will play them in the movie.

It can be a fun life, so I'm told. Enough to elicit even sane people to confess to your crimes. Personally, I'd rather stay this side of the prison walls. Just thinking about those chilly steel toilet seats is enough to make me constipated.

To equip your confessor, they'll need a few facts about the crimes that aren't known to the public. This is a risk, of course, but one you might feel is worth taking. The more famous you are, the more readily the police will gobble up your confessor's revelation. Let your confessor know one or two minor details and then stick to information in the public domain. If possible, supply them with a small piece of physical evidence: the dentures you wore or a trophy you took. If you think your confessor might back out at the last moment, it may be better to conceal the physical evidence at their home ahead of time. There is simply no coming back from a confession, no matter how ropey or vehemently retracted, when it's accompanied by physical evidence.

We've all seen the series *Making a Murderer*, right?

That's exactly what you're doing here: making your own murderer.

# 10

'*Thirteen!*' Harry bellows across the Holmes Room on Monday morning. 'Thirteen Denver-bloody-Bradys. The custody suite is *full* of them. We've had news crews lining the street outside all weekend and there's more of them arriving by the hour!'

Sam's head rattles inside her skull. She's spent the entire weekend trying to banish the memory of her panic attack and the associated migraine and sickness. She's only just feeling human again and now Harry's yelling brings her out in a cold sweat.

'Earth to Sam?' Harry yells.

'Sorry, sir,' she says, looking up from her half-written email response to HR. 'What was that?'

'I said,' Harry says through gritted teeth, 'I want you and Edris in my office. Now.'

She glances across the fourth floor at Taylor. She really shouldn't have persuaded him to head to a Newcastle pub on Friday afternoon. She'd become the cliché she hates so much: a detective who washes away their mental health issues with a bottle of wine.

First, she'd vomited all over the cobblestones the moment she regained consciousness, then she'd told him she couldn't go back inside the police station and she needed a drink, and they'd walked to the nearest pub – which, in Newcastle, took thirty seconds. The Dog and Parrot was everything Sam had thought a Tyneside pub would be: worn wooden bar, sticky damask carpets, old men sitting around playing dominoes, the clacking sound of snooker balls colliding. She ordered a glass of Pinot, then a bottle.

Taylor had been unable to drink his bottle of Newcastle Brown Ale, his delicate Home Counties palate wincing at the authentic bitter. She'd bought him a Smirnoff Ice with a pink straw instead, much to the bartender's amusement. Sam can't remember if he drank the alcopop or not. Come to think of it, she can't remember much of anything after she'd dragged him on to the pub's tiny dance floor and sang 'Teenage Dirtbag' at the top of her lungs. She can't remember the train journey home or the taxi ride from King's Cross. She can't remember feeding the dog when she got home, but there were fresh puppy pads and kibble in his bowl the next morning. She herself woke up on her sofa under a blanket, with a large bucket and a glass of water left beside her.

No wonder he won't meet her eye now.

The women follow their DCI into his corner office and close the door.

'Sir—' Tina begins, but he cuts her off.

'This is on you, Edris!' he barks. 'You're SIO. You put a drugged-up father in front of a room full of journalists and didn't think to frisk him or brief him about what not to say? Take a look out there!'

Harry points to the office beyond his glass window, where the floor is a hive of activity. The civilians are all typing furiously and talking into headsets. The police officers are huddled around the lift, waiting their turn to ride down to the custody suite.

Tina looks at the chaos as directed, her back straight, hands clasped neatly in the front.

'We're buried in phone calls, emails and confessions,' Harry continues. 'I warned you both about what a shit show this would become if the existence of that bloody book leaked to the press.'

'Sir, Nigel Mathers concealed the book from both of us at the press conference. How could I have known he'd jeopardize the investigation like that?' Edris tries. Sam can see light sweat forming along her colleague's hairline, but her voice is controlled.

Sam wonders if Nigel Mathers realizes how much his actions will take away precious time and effort from solving his daughter's murder; work now diverted to managing the thousands of phone calls from the public and following up on dozens of leads, most of which will meet a dead end.

Sam begins, 'Sir, Nigel Mathers—'

'Nigel Mathers is almost as much of a corpse as his daughter is,' Harry says, coldly. Sam's mouth drops open at her godfather's callousness. 'I mean, Nigel Mathers is a grief-stricken father,' Harry corrects himself. 'You were supposed to manage him, Edris. You failed. For the love of God, tell me that you've found Denver, Sam.'

'Sir, we've not got anything solid to connect Denver to Charlotte yet,' she replies, determined to stick to the facts. 'However, there is a strong probability that Denver does exist and he definitely has unique knowledge of the Betty Brown murder and perhaps others. Either Denver is a serial killer and he murdered Charlotte, or we could be looking at two killers: Denver and a copycat.'

'DI Hansen,' Tina chimes in. 'Did you follow the money trail, as I suggested?'

'The money from the website is landing in a Glaswegian student account in the name of Drew McKay, then moving into a Welsh account in Cardiff. Details pending, but I suspect Denver is using money mules. We do have one good lead: the printers where the book was pressed was subjected to an arson attack. Sussex Police are investigating. If they find the arsonist—'

'We find Denver,' Harry finishes. 'I'll call the right people at Sussex and speed that up. But it's not enough. We'll have to respond tangibly here. It's not just about what we do, it's about what we are *seen* to do.'

'We can't let media pressure dictate our—' Tina begins, but Harry cuts her off again.

'Sam, I'm making you joint SIO,' he declares, and Tina gasps.

'We'll have to quadruple the size of the team on the Brady side of the investigation and you'll need to work more closely with Edris to understand all the details of Charlotte's case, to speed up the search for further connections. It'll be a joint taskforce, with you two leading together. Sam, you'll remain focused on finding Denver and I'm sorry, but I need you on that full time. I can't bring someone else in now – you're already well on your way to finding him and Edris can't handle both sides of the case.'

'Sir, no!' Edris raises her voice. 'Detective Chief Inspector Blakelaw, this is my case. I am Senior Investigating Officer. I have progressed the case well, under the circumstances. We have no physical evidence, no witnesses. I simply need a little more time—'

'Time?' Harry yells, 'The word "serial killer" is on the front page of every newspaper from here to John O'Groats, and you're asking for *time*?'

'Sir,' Tina tries again, her voice now containing a small tremor. 'Detective Inspector Hansen is on phased return. More pressure and workload could be really damaging for her. We need to speak to HR about—'

'Sam will handle it,' Harry says, staring out of his window as another news van pulls up. 'I'll handle HR. Can't you see that all our careers, our reputations, are on the line here?' he says, not looking at either woman.

Sam stares at him, her mind whirring. His decision baffles her – why on earth would he make her joint SIO? But she tells herself there's no way Harry would risk her health unless he believed she could manage it. He's always done what's best for her, ever since she was a kid. Even when—

A new sound pulls Sam from her thoughts, and she moves to stand behind Harry at the window. Crossing the road is a small group with placards. They come to a stop beneath the iconic rotating New Scotland Yard sign. Muffled chants rise and a woman pulls out a megaphone. Sam pinches the top of her nose. She's already struggling to keep it together, as the trip to Newcastle showed. How can Harry think she is ready for this amount of pressure and responsibility?

Sam sighs, torn. She wants to tell Harry about Friday's panic attack. About needing time to catch up with Dr Thomson. That she hasn't yet been able to bring herself to look at the crime scene photographs. But she doesn't want to let him down. She doesn't want to let Charlotte down . . .

'Sir,' Tina Edris says, 'I must object in the strongest terms—'

'Noted, Edris,' Harry says, then waves them out as he picks up the ringing phone. 'Ah, Commissioner, I was just about to call you.'

Sam walks out of Harry's office feeling lightheaded. She tries to catch Tina's eye, but DC Chen is hovering and insists he has something Tina needs to look at urgently. Sam makes her way through the hubbub, towards the communal TV and seating area. She's desperate for a cup of tea and sits on the sofa as the kettle boils.

Joint SIO. Harry has made her joint SIO. That means she is now in shared command of investigating a child's murder and a potential serial killer. It was what she thought she wanted, but now she knows it's just too much. Sam sucks in a deep breath. The TV screen next to the sofa is filled with news headlines, the words *FEAR MOUNTS OVER UK SERIAL KILLER ALLEGATIONS* scrolling across it. Sam switches the channel, but it's worse: *MET DENIES SERIAL KILLER INVESTIGATION*. Sam closes her eyes.

When she opens them a few moments later, a steaming mug of tea is on the table in front of her. Sam looks around and sees Adam Taylor across the room. She smiles at him and mouths 'Thank you'. He nods gravely, holding her gaze until she looks away. It's progress. Not an hour ago she thought he was avoiding her. The relief it brings, knowing Taylor's still got her back, is stronger than she cares to acknowledge.

'DI Hansen,' a civilian colleague says, making her start. 'Your brother called for you. He said it was urgent.' The woman holds out a Post-it note with a telephone number on it.

'I don't have a brother,' Sam says and the woman looks at her blankly.

'Are you sure?' The woman shakes her head at her own silly question. 'I'm certain he said he's your brother. I'm sorry, I'm new here.'

'It'll be a journalist,' Sam says. 'They do it all the time. Claim to be family.'

'The little ... scallywags.' The woman scowls and Sam smiles. 'By the way, that bank in Cardiff came back. I've forwarded you the email. And, er, DC Chen asked me to tell you that Howtogetawaywithmurder.com was cloned within hours of him taking down the original site. It's live and selling again. Sorry.'

'Oh God, no.' Sam pulls up the website on her phone. There's a huge *SOLD OUT* label across the button to add the physical book to the basket, and the e-book has tripled in price. Denver has even added 'As Seen On TV' and a screenshot of the press conference. His audacity takes Sam's breath away.

'Chen said it's now being hosted abroad and it'll take him at least a week—'

'Ugh,' Sam groans, resting her forehead in her hands. When she looks up again, the woman has decided to deploy that quintessentially British strategy universally implemented during times of crisis: she's put the kettle on for more tea.

Sam smiles her thanks, then opens her email. There are more new messages than she can count, and she scans down until she spots the one she's looking for. As the Cardiff bank statement loads, she twirls the little netball in her hand and sips the tea. It's not good – far too much milk, and the cup is chipped beyond salvation. She takes another sip anyway.

As soon as the document comes into view, she knows it's

another mule account, this time owned by a Mrs Gladys Bryn. It receives the money each Monday from Drew Mackay's Scottish student account and empties every Tuesday into a third. Sam winces when she sees how the revenue from the website has shot up to five figures since the press conference. She takes a long drink.

'Oh no,' she moans to no one, as she spots that the money going out of Gladys Bryn's account is being sent to a 'KY' international bank. A quick internet search confirms her suspicion – it's an offshore account in the Cayman Islands. A dead end, unless they can identify the UK bank account receiving the sums back from offshore, which would be like finding a needle in an ocean-sized haystack. Sam rubs her forehead and emails South Wales Police, asking them to visit Gladys Bryn. It's slim, but there's a chance the woman could know something useful.

Sighing, Sam pulls the book that's causing this whole nightmare from her bag, trying to find the place she left off. Just as she picks up from the sentence she last read, she sees Tina Edris marching straight for her. Sam tenses and rises to her feet. She looks around for Taylor, but he's left the room, probably to interview another Denver wannabe.

Tina barely comes up to Sam's neck, but she's formidable and she's not happy. The upshot of her long rant is that she's deduced that Sam has not yet looked at the crime scene photographs nor finished reading the book at the centre of their now-joint case, and is demanding that Sam marches upstairs to HR and tells them she can't handle being SIO.

So much of Sam knows that Tina is right – wasn't she just thinking the same? – but, hearing it from someone else, her old defiance stirs. 'I think Harry really believes I can do this,' she replies, with much more conviction than she feels.

Tina stares at her. 'I'm sorry, Detective Inspector Hansen, but DCI Blakelaw has only made you joint SIO because he needs plenty of heads in line to roll before his own. He's lining us up like Henry the Eighth did with his wives. I bet this isn't the first time he's—'

Before Sam has time to process her thoughts, anger spews from her mouth. 'You're lucky I only joined you as SIO and didn't replace you, Tina. You've made no progress for Charlotte. No suspects. Maybe your head *should* roll!' she hisses.

Tina's nostrils flare. 'Seeing and saying the truth requires courage, which is what I – at least – have,' she growls. 'This DCI isn't on our side, or Charlotte's. He's only out for himself, whether you're brave enough to face it or not.' She turns on her heel and storms away.

Sam curses under her breath, moving to stand by the window. She watches as the brown water of the Thames churns, the London Eye turns and the red double-decker buses shuttle tourists around the city. On the pavement below, the journalists swarm as Tina Edris rushes past and into a waiting car – Sam knows they'll stop at nothing to get a quote or a photo. She scans the faces in the crowd, wondering if the killer could be among them. Watching. Waiting. Getting some sick thrill from the chaos he's caused. Just biding his time until the urge takes him once again. Sam shudders and steps away, pulling out her phone and texting Tina to apologize for her harsh words. What Tina said about Harry has struck a nerve, hard. Could she be right about him? Could he really care more about himself than Tina, Sam and Charlotte combined? She doesn't want to believe it, but she's never been one to bury her head in the sand. Is it possible that she doesn't have the courage to face reality? Harry's all the family she has left and she's needed to believe in him. Has that blinded her to who he truly is?

She walks to her desk and flops into her seat, holding her head in her hands. Her phone pings and she hopes it might be Tina, but it's a message from the shelter saying that they can take the dog off her hands next Wednesday. Sam smacks her phone down on the desk. A second later it pings again, this time with an email from Glasgow police. They have spoken to Drew Mackay, the owner of the first account that the website revenue lands in. He's admitted to money-muling to pay off his student debt. A man had approached him at a local foodbank, and he'd not thought twice. Glasgow Police won't be taking further action. There's also an email from Neil Duggan with the subject '*Jono?*':

DI Hansen,

Good to meet you the other day. Sorry for running out like I did. Needs must.

I'm reading *How to Get Away With Murder* and the first murder, Jono (in the quarry), jogged a memory.

Betty kept a scrapbook and in it there were lots of newspaper clippings. I've attached a photograph of the one I'm referring to, but basically it's about a young lad (Jonathan 'Jono' Glenholme) who drowned in Stanhope quarry in the early nineties. Tragic.

The story loosely matches Denver's but the strange thing is this: the boy who drowned was a local swimming champion who used the quarry for practice, as the council closed his nearest pool (typical story in the North, I'm afraid.) Jono's death was definitely an accident. No one else was involved.

Seems odd that Betty has this newspaper article and Denver's story is quite similar?

Anyhow, I'm still hoping that we can get justice for the old girl.

Keep in touch.

Duggan

DI Neil Duggan

Northumbria Police

Sam's first feeling is irritation that neither she nor Taylor had found the article themselves during the course of their research into the named killings in Denver's book. But, she reasons, they're focusing on crimes rather than accidents. Sam clicks on the attachment and finds a blurry photograph of a newspaper clipping. Duggan's thumb is partly covering the main photograph but Sam can make out a smiling young boy with pale skin and chubby cheeks. '*Milky, doughy creature*', Sam recalls Denver writing. *Very interesting*, she thinks. Could Denver simply have been inspired by this story and morphed it into something sick? They already know Denver lies, so it's perfectly possible Jono is just a disturbed fantasy. Sam immediately dials Duggan's number. They need to discuss this idea more fully. Maybe there's something here and—

'Sam,' Harry's voice cuts into her thoughts, and she cancels her call at once. 'Detective Sam Hansen, SIO in the case we've just been discussing. Let me introduce Cecil Taylor. He's kindly stopped by to offer his support. Mr Taylor is MP for Runnymede and Weybridge, that's over in—'

'Surrey,' Sam finishes for him.

'Please, call me Cecil.'

She stands and reaches out her hand to the tall, finely dressed man with fiercely blue eyes and a familiar jawline. 'Have we met before?' Sam asks, but before Cecil has time to answer there's a loud smashing of ceramic from immediately behind him. Everyone turns to see Trainee DC Adam Taylor drop to his knees and begin to pick up pieces of mug, the tea-soaked carpet steaming around him. Taylor's cheeks are bright red and when he speaks; he doesn't look up.

'What are you doing here?' Taylor asks, his voice deep and quietly angry.

'Ah, some things never change,' Cecil says to Harry, ignoring Taylor. 'Adam's always been a bit of a klutz. I hope he's not too much of a nuisance for you, old chap?'

'Not at all, not at all.' Harry wobbles his head. She realizes then that Cecil is Adam Taylor's 'rich daddy MP' that Harry mentioned on her first day back at work. Sam looks down at Taylor, who is still fishing pieces of the former mugs from under desks. The back of Taylor's neck is bright pink and Sam immediately feels protective of the young TDC, who took such care of her when she was at her most vulnerable.

'Actually,' Sam says, making her voice loud and clear, 'Trainee Detective Constable Taylor is an excellent member of my team and is playing an invaluable role in solving a child homicide and potential serial-killer case.'

'If he was so invaluable, sweetheart,' Cecil scoffs, 'he wouldn't be earning less money than my man Barney who I pay to remove dog turds from my lawn.'

Sam just about manages to keep her cool. 'Yes, police officers are significantly underpaid. I'm so pleased MPs recognize that, as you're the ones with the power to change it.'

Cecil reddens, pointing at Taylor. 'That boy has a first-class law degree from Royal College. His grandfather was Deputy Prime Minister. Adam is from excellent stock and should have followed the family line. We're politicians, change-makers, ambassadors. Not street bobbies.'

'Sam's father was an excellent detective,' Harry says, clearly trying to break the tension and missing the mark entirely. 'A good friend of mine. Sam followed in her father's footsteps and now she has the highest solve-rate on the fourth floor. The apple doesn't fall far from the tree.'

'Thankfully, sir,' Sam says, holding Cecil's eye, 'in some cases, the apple falls miles from the tree. Let's go, Taylor. We have a murderer to find.' Sam spins on her heel, turning her back on the MP and striding away from him and Harry without a backward glance. Behind her, she hears Harry begin to waffle an apology and then the DCI drops his voice to a whisper. Sam doesn't care what her godfather is saying about her; she's proud of herself for standing up for Taylor only minutes after failing to support another colleague.

Watching Harry toadying to that arsehole makes her see him in a distinctly unflattering light. Perhaps Tina was right, and Harry is motivated purely by self-interest – and maybe this isn't the first time he's put himself first when he should have looked out for her. She remembers, all those months ago, his warm hand on her shoulder and his whispered words of advice: *Making a formal complaint could damage your career, Sam. Let me deal with this quietly. I only want what's best for you.* She pushes the thought away. She needs to focus on what's happening here and now. Here and now, Charlotte is the most important person, not her, not Tina, and certainly not Harry. She shouldn't be SIO, but she is, and she'll give it everything she has left to give.

'That was brilliant,' Taylor hisses, matching Sam's stride, his hands full of broken crockery. 'No one ever stands up to him like—'

'Nothing's harder than standing up to your own father, Taylor.'

'Thank you, Sam,' Taylor says, a little breathless.

Taylor deposits the broken mugs in the bin and refills the kettle, before taking new mugs from the cupboard and dropping a teabag into each. Sam looks over to Harry and Cecil, now seated in the DCI's office, chatting amicably. Both men look like they haven't a care in the world. Oh, to have a—

'Ma'am,' says Taylor, interrupting her dark thoughts. 'I was hoping we could, er, talk about what happened after we got back from Newcastle on Friday?' He steps from foot to foot, examining his shoes.

Sam runs her hand through her hair. 'I hope you don't mind, but I can't talk about that right now,' she says. 'I'm truly sorry, and really appreciate you getting me home safely. It was so unprofessional of me, but I can assure you, I have never done anything like that before and never will again. Please can we leave it?'

'No, of course, I know that,' he begins. 'It's just—'

Suddenly the space between them is filled with a song that Sam recognizes. Is that 'Anti-Hero'? She can't help but laugh. Taylor blushes and pulls out his phone, sliding to answer. After a series of mm-hmms, his face grows white. He starts to pace the room.

'There's another real Denver victim,' Taylor says a moment later, his jaw twitching. 'Melanie Davison. Apparently, someone else went to prison for her murder. That was his lawyer on the phone. The chap Denver claims to have framed for killing Melanie wants to meet us. I think we should interview him as a priority.'

Sam racks her brains. She can't remember a Melanie, but it's entirely possible she hasn't managed to get to that chapter yet.

'It was the most compelling murder, for me,' Taylor says. 'Reads just like a real whodunnit.'

## *Brutes*

The kill itself is very personal, and how you perform it is up to you. For beginners, I'd recommend having the victim restrain themselves by self-fastening to a solid object such as a bed frame or radiator. This obviously isn't necessary with victims who are significantly physically inferior, but it's a good habit to get into. Even the best serial killers have had victims escape. Jeff Dahmer was particularly careless, but the cops brought his boys back for him – you will almost certainly not be so lucky. Remember that in 15 per cent of cases victims survive or escape, and in 1 per cent of cases victims kill the killer. So take extra care.

Men are far more likely to fight you, but women are noisier, so plan accordingly and gauge your level of expertise against the prospective victim. I'd recommend using a gag. I also put socks over my victim's hands. This prevents scratching, which can lead to your DNA being collected by the victim. Too many people are forensically aware nowadays (fucking *CSI*) so vics will sometimes try to scratch you for this reason alone. I've even had one try to write a message in their own blood, so I now take care to minimize blood splatter, too. You can do that in a variety of ways; cling film (shout-out to my boy Dexter) and plastic bags work well.

Don't use the victim's bathroom. If you need to, pee

in the sink and then run the hot tap for at least ten minutes. Definitely don't take a dump, but if the worst happens, flush the toilet multiple times and use a lot of bleach. Don't drink from the victim's crockery or eat their food. A woman was recently captured by police after her DNA was found on a Krispy Kreme doughnut left at the crime scene. (I can't blame her, really – who can resist a Krispy Kreme?) Don't vomit. It's almost always smell that makes one sick, so avoid rupturing the stomach and intestines where possible – the odour is overwhelming. Pin your nose in your early days; a simple swimmer's nose clip does the job.

You might be tempted, as I was with Betty, to take a souvenir. This can be very risky, but I confess to having magpie-like tendencies and I admit that I found my favourite pair of earrings under the most unusual circumstances.

All across England there are affluent spa towns, inhabited mainly by the wealthy. In Victorian times, the gentry would retreat to these places to take the air and recover from the demands of the social season. I've always enjoyed British tradition, so whenever the stresses of life become too much, I find myself gravitating to these places and taking some time for myself. Who doesn't love a firm-fingered massage?

Tony and I were enjoying a weekend of self-care, complete with riverside strolls. I spotted Mel crying on a bench by the river, her fake eyelashes hanging askew. Tears rolled down her orange cheeks. A cigarette dangled between two bronze fingers, tipped with neon-pink plastic. An ugly dog, some kind of bull-jawed fighting thing, was at her feet, straining on its studded diamante collar.

'Don't worry. She's soft,' Mel said through a smoky exhale, as I approached.

I'd heard many an owner of these beasts say similar things to rightfully wary passers-by. A week later the brute eats their baby. I had Tony on the lead and he whimpered as I sat at the far end of Mel's bench.

'Is something wrong, my dear?' I asked, feigning a Home Counties accent to match my old-man disguise. Mel shook her head and wiped her nose on the sleeve of her polo neck.

I was tempted to leave it there; I rarely engage in conversation with victims beforehand, especially in public. It's highly risky. But I was seeking a new level of challenge, and something about her person had set an idea germinating at the back of my mind. So I pushed a little.

'You can tell me, dear. I've seen it all already. I don't judge.'

'It's my bloke and his raging,' she said after another drag on her cigarette. 'He never means it. He feels awful for it. But sometimes I piss him off so much he just loses the plot. Jealous, see.'

'Why is he jealous?'

'Not him. Me. I'm jealous. I seen another girl on his Facebook and started mouthing off again.' She shrugged, then winced with the motion.

'Oh dear. Jealousy is never good in a relationship. What happened next?'

Melanie took another long draw on the cigarette, forcing smoke out of the corner of her mouth and revealing a cracked incisor.

'Lashes out, don't he? Gives me a slap round the head . . .' Mel lifted up her peroxide-blonde hair to reveal a swollen and blackened lump of an ear, her fingertips tracing out more bumps across her skull. Then she pulled down the collar of her polo neck, revealing thumb-shaped bruises around her neck. I noticed tiny scars on her cheekbones and one on the tip of her nose, with faded stitch marks around it. A little diamond stud twinkled in the daylight; I remember thinking that the tiny rhinestone was the classiest thing about our Mel. Poor bitch.

'Lovely earrings, dear,' I said.

'Ta. Me mam got them. Real diamonds. My fella – Richie, he's called – wants me to take them down Ramsdens and get a new TV.'

It was clear to me that this Richie fellow was a low-level predator. Barely bobcat-level. Beating his tiny girlfriend around the skull was smart: no visible bruises meant no proof. Fair enough – he might occasionally mishit and blacken an ear. But scarring her face? That was plain stupid. His stupidity pissed me off. Men like him give men like me a bad name. Driven by base instincts. No control. Unoriginal.

'Excuse my ignorance, dear,' I said, readying to ask the most obvious question in the world, the one dumb women like this one never want to hear, 'but why don't you just leave him?'

Melanie chuckled slightly, rubbing her rugby-player ear.

'I have,' she said. 'I've left him five times. He tracks me down, don't he? Them restraining orders do nothing. Last time I ran, I hid at my mate's house but Richie'd put this tracking software on my phone. He broke in and beat the shit out of me – and my mate, too. She pressed charges but he scared her out of coming to court because Richie knew she was dealing on the side and . . . well, everything was dropped. Anyone who tries to help me is putting themselves right in danger. Richie would kill them, and me too.'

'That's a very sad story,' I said. 'I hope it all ends for you soon.'

Mel never saw me again after that. But we saw her a lot, Tony and I. We saw her and her gentleman head to their local the following Friday. Mel in a dress shorter than her eyelashes, tottering on narrow heels; him in a muscle top, revealing an enormous chest and bulging neck that was home to a Union Jack and several Chinese symbols.

The couple followed a fairly regular routine and I soon knew who'd be where, and when. Their Asda shopping arrived every Friday and the driver left it in their porch. It was too easy for me to slip an extra bag in amongst the next delivery: three bottles of fine wine (cork tops of course), some king prawns and two large steaks.

That evening, I knocked on their door, holding Tony's lead in my hand. As I'd planned, they were enjoying my gifts – without knowing they were from me, of course – and as Mel swayed against the door jamb, I could see her boyfriend slumped in a chair at the kitchen table. I told her that Tony was missing and I was searching people's gardens for him. Mel let me in without question, walking me through the small home to the back door. I searched the garden thoroughly and by the time I let myself back inside, Mel was nodding off on the sofa.

I ensured the boyfriend was well and truly unconscious before I slipped on my rain mac and a pair of his fake Nike trainers that were by the door.

Then I beat Mel to death with my gloved hands.

It took a lot longer than one might expect! And considerable strength and stamina. I'd placed an Asda bag for life over her head to minimize blood splatter, but removed it afterwards so that I could fully admire my artwork.

When it was done, I took one of the chap's muscle T-shirts from the laundry basket, soaked it in Mel's blood and then put it in the washing machine – the logical next step for a really stupid murderer. Where should we dispose of our clothing? I really hope you remember. I smudged blood under his fingernails and around his neckline. I even rubbed a little inside his nostrils; I thought this was a particularly adroit move as the brute might shower before the police arrived. Then I stuffed the bag for life in his coat pocket. I doubted the forensics team would look too far beyond these efforts, given the likely long paper trail of police reports following phone calls from concerned neighbours. There were probably hospital records of injuries the boyfriend had inflicted on Mel over the years, too. If I was really lucky, the restraining order would be the final nail in his coffin. Everyone knows restraining orders are of no use when the woman is alive, but their evidential value would serve me well.

Finally, I picked up the dog lead, ready to leave, and took a moment to admire my masterpiece. I've debated whether or not to include this next detail in my book. I know it could go against me in later life and my advice is to never remove anything from the crime scene. But . . .

Mel's face was, for the most part, obliterated. However, her lovely little blackened ears were still intact. Her diamond earrings twinkled through the congealing blood, which was turning a stunning deep scarlet. Blood that's partially dry takes on a delicious hue; it's the most moving colour in the world. I've written to Dulux several times but they're unable to match it. What a feature wall it would make.

I digress.

I wanted to remember Mel. Not as she was, but as I'd made her. So, I took her earrings as a small souvenir. I keep them in a drawer with Betty's rings and other precious things. Sometimes, when there's a long stretch of normal life to power through, I put one of them in my pocket and it gets me through a dull day. I figured the police would assume the boyfriend had stolen the earrings, either after killing her or at some point earlier. Witnesses could come forward to say that he thought the diamonds were valuable and should be sold. Heck, it might even harm his defence, as such calculating thoughts about selling diamonds would surely convince a jury that he didn't kill Mel in the heat of the moment. Glorious. As I type this, I am reaching down occasionally and caressing all that's left of little Mel.

In a tragic turn of events, I really did lose Tony. It happened not long after Melanie's boyfriend, Richie, was convicted of her murder. On finding his little body cold and stiff one morning, I bought a small wicker basket from Home Bargains, dug a large hole beneath an oak in a park and carved his name into the tree trunk. I couldn't stop crying. I probably should have had counselling, but for obvious reasons I had to suffer alone. I never returned to that town again.

What I did do, however, was research the location of

women's shelters in towns and cities I wanted to visit. I'd realized that a predator already existing in a victim's life made it far easier for me to avoid any kind of in-depth investigation. In reality, it's always the husband 'what dunnit', so why not turn that to my advantage?

I repeated this winning formula several more times. Thanks to me, a not insignificant number of domestic abusers are now wallowing in prisons around the United Kingdom.

That's more than any police officer can honestly say.

# 11

Sam and Taylor head northwest along the M4. She reads as he drives, comparing the case file to Denver's chapter about Melanie and her Richie. She keeps her notebook open on the centre console and occasionally scribbles in it.

Sam's phone vibrates in her pocket, and she cancels the call from Dr Thomson. She'd had to email him earlier that morning to reschedule her already rescheduled session. She's done her best to explain that the prison they're travelling to has limited availability for visiting slots owing to an already stretched prisoner-to-guard ratio, coupled with the fact that many of the meeting rooms have been repurposed as cells for the burgeoning incarcerated population. What choice did she have? Still, rather not talk to him directly, if she can avoid it.

By now, Sam is fairly certain that Denver is a murderer and that he tortured and killed Betty. Perhaps a woman called Melanie, too. But no matter how hard she tries, she still sees no clear link to Charlotte. She believes that the presence of Denver's book at Charlotte's murder, plus the similarities to Sarah's murder, are more suggestive of a copycat, which means that she's hunting a killer, but it might not be *the* killer – the man who murdered Charlotte, the man she is determined to catch. Denver strongly advises against repeating MOs, and leaving his own book at a murder that he himself committed seems a bridge too far. She's even contemplated the possibility that, owing to his explicitly stated craving for notoriety, Denver could have somehow persuaded another killer to plant his how-to guide at Charlotte's murder scene in the hope of sending the book viral.

She takes a sip of coffee from her travel mug and focuses on her task. Sam knows right from page one of the ten in Richie Scott's case file that he's a monster. Melanie's neighbours and family called the police no fewer than thirteen times. Some action had been taken; a Domestic Violence Protection Order was granted by the magistrate's court, although Melanie herself was too afraid to testify, even with a screen around the witness box. Sam knows all too well that most victims of domestic violence are simply petrified of voicing what's happened to them. *We need to do so much more to protect these women*, she thinks. She looks at Melanie's photograph. She has high cheek bones and big doe eyes. A primary school teacher who volunteered at her local foodbank and went wild-swimming at weekends. Details that Denver didn't bother to find out, preferring to lean into a stereotype instead.

Sam pulls out a hospital report detailing facial injuries Melanie sustained after Richie Scott pinned her down and piled spaghetti Bolognese on to her face. The brute had sat on her small body as their dog ate its dinner off his girlfriend. Mel needed ten stitches that time, to her cheeks and the tip of her nose.

'Were your dad and DCI Blakelaw in the same police cohort?' Taylor asks.

Sam nods. 'They were both recruited to the Met at the same time. In the eighties, it was all about gun crime and they worked as part of an operation to get weapons off the streets. Dad loved guns – collected pistols from the wars – so when he got the offer of joining the gun squad, he moved the family to London.'

'How about your mum? What did she do?'

'She struggled. Even though she wasn't close to her parents and didn't have tons of friends, the move to London isolated her completely. She only had me, and I was in school all day.'

'Oh.'

'Then one day, when I was nearly ten, not long after we moved to our place in Clapham, I found Mum at the bottom of the stairs. Her death was ruled accidental . . .' She trails off, caught off-guard by how open she's being with him. Past Sam would never have let someone in like this. She smiles, pleased to have found at least one element of Present Sam that's an improvement.

Taylor turns to Sam, his face filled with concern, she gives him a shrug and then returns her eyes to the page. 'Was your mum's death ever investigated?' he asks a little warily.

'It was – not that I knew it at the time.' She looks up again. 'But I found the file in the archive once I joined up. My dad was only the suspect, but he had a watertight alibi. He was drinking at the pub down the road from our house. At least a dozen other officers confirmed it.'

'Mmm,' Taylor says, and Sam can tell he's tempted to speculate that her father might have left the pub and returned, unnoticed. 'Was DCI Blakelaw in the pub that—'

'The man's a monster,' Sam cuts in.

'Your dad?' he asks, and Sam gives him a confused look.

'Richie Scott. A monster. A beast,' Sam clarifies. 'Such a short prison sentence for all this abuse, and then murder reduced to manslaughter. Where's the justice?'

Taylor's eyes flick from the road to Sam's face, still searching for some trace of emotion, so she smiles at him reassuringly.

'Old wounds, well healed, Taylor,' she says, and means it. She'd found her own ways to cope after her mother's death left her in her father's sole care. She'd learned to get herself to school on time, to use the washing machine and to keep out of his way when his temper got the better of him. She'd read a lot. True crime, mainly. She could relate when Denver said the librarian gave him a funny look for his book choices.

'I'm sorry, Sam,' Taylor says.

'Really, don't worry,' she assures him. 'It was a long time ago.

My dad died when I was nineteen and I inherited the house and joined the police with Harry's support. The rest, as they say, is history.'

Sam returns her focus to the case file, and Taylor taps the steering wheel in time to a song on the radio. They cruise like this for close to an hour before he speaks again.

'You probably don't want to hear this,' he says, 'but Richie Scott's new lawyer filed for his release after the Denver Brady publicity, on the basis that another person has confessed to the crime.' Taylor fiddles with the radio, flicking buttons on the steering wheel in search of a song he likes.

Sam's eyebrows shoot up. 'Jeez, that was quick. It'll never stick. Well, not unless we catch Denver and he legally confesses and is actually convicted of murdering Melanie.'

They travel in silence for a few more minutes before Taylor says, 'Actually, I was hoping to talk . . . we never got the chance to . . . talk about Newcastle?' His voice is small, gentle.

Sam takes a long, slow breath in. 'Don't worry, Taylor,' she says, reaching inside her bag for a paracetamol. 'I get headaches and stuff for reasons unrelated to alcohol. I promise that time in Newcastle is the only drink I've had for months. So, can we park it, please? I swear it'll never happen again.'

'Erm . . .' Taylor changes lanes and passes a lorry.

'Please leave it, Taylor,' she says. 'All I have space for right now is Charlotte.'

He frowns, hands tight on the wheel, gaze fixed on the road ahead, seemingly trapped in thought – whether about Newcastle or something else entirely, Sam has no idea. More of the southern England flashes past their window.

Gradually, Taylor relaxes again and begins humming along with 'Denis, Denis . . .'. After the song has ended, he says, 'Hey, did you know about Blondie and Bundy?'

'No. That was a new one for me,' she admits. 'I googled it. Some sources suggest it wasn't Bundy. They claim he was elsewhere when Debbie was abducted. Which is even scarier.'

'What's scarier than Ted Bundy?' Taylor asks.

'If it wasn't Bundy who abducted Debbie Harry, it means there was a copycat in New York that summer that was never identified or caught. That's scarier than Bundy.'

'Yeah,' he agrees. 'It is.'

A text pings from Dr Thomson with a new appointment date. Sam sends a thumbs-up emoji but doesn't add it to her calendar. When she looks back up, HMP Bath looms before them.

They wait with the other visitors – mainly women and children – and Sam can see that Taylor is discomforted by the place. She tries to see the prison through first-time eyes. The absence of bars, the relaxed atmosphere, children's pictures all over the walls, books and whiteboards: it's nothing like TV, and all the more disturbing for it. They're shown to a small meeting room and Taylor sets up the recorder, which they'd had to bring along as the prison doesn't have its own interview equipment.

Richie Scott is far smaller than Sam supposed he would be, although he tries to walk like a much bigger man; around 5ft 5, with greasy hair that's receding. There's a faded Union Jack tattoo on his neck, the red more clementine than crimson, the outline pixelated by time. He adjusts his balls and lets his eyes creep over Sam, whispering something to the guard who walks beside him.

Taylor had shown Sam the online petition that Richie Scott's lawyer had launched on his client's behalf. This man already has over 200,000 signatures demanding his freedom and exoneration of the murder of the girlfriend that he's on record as having beaten up numerous times.

The guard leaves and Richie sits down, swinging the chair the wrong way around and straddling it like a cowboy on a horse. The man is clearly high on ego and expectation, believing he will soon leave this place and be greeted on the outside by scores of cameras. She has to fight not to curl her lip at him.

'Mr Scott,' Taylor begins, sliding their business cards across the table towards him. 'I'm TDC Adam Taylor and this is DI Sam Hansen. We're here to talk to you about the night of 10 June.'

Richie Scott pockets the cards. Sam's surprised when he produces a creamy card with a black logo on it and slides it to her in return, giving her a little wink. It must be his lawyer's card, and she leaves it where it lies.

'We're lead investigators in the Denver Brady case,' Taylor says, 'and any information you can give us relating to *How to Get Away With Murder* will be much appreciated by—'

Richie scoffs and inserts a fingernail between his back teeth, fishing for some food that's apparently lodged there. He removes the finger and examines the retrieved morsel that's now under his nail. The convict's colourless eyes meet Sam's gaze and hold it. Without blinking, Richie runs his tongue up his finger, collecting the moist lump on the tip and pulling it slowly back into his mouth. Sam keeps her face neutral. Taylor shifts uncomfortably at her side.

'Already told you lot exactly what Denver says in his book,' says Scott. 'Which, by the way, everyone got to read before me, even though it's *about* me. Wasn't until my new lawyer printed it off on paper and it was classed as legal documents that I got to read it. No point asking me questions, pretty boy. *How to Get Away With Murder* is spot on.'

'What makes you think Denver killed Melanie?' Sam asks. Her trainee's confident handling of the man she knew she hated even before she walked in the room bolsters her resolve. Her heart rate is steady, her mouth free from the salty taste that she's become so used to.

'You thick or just stupid?' Scott hisses. 'Like what Denver says: he fucked with our shopping then came in and killed her. Denver did it. So my question to you lot is when you gonna let me outta here?'

'Can you tell me, precisely, what was strange about your shopping?' Taylor asks.

With an eye roll, Scott replies, 'Just like what Denver says: he sent us steak, wine and prawns. We cooked the steaks right up. I never knew what to do with a prawn. Weird-looking things – still have their eyes in. Our Bella – that's the dog – we gave her the prawns. The posh wine tasted like shite. Gimme a cold tin of Fosters any day. That's what I'll have for my first free drink: a cold tin and Bristol City on the telly. Wanna join me, love?' Scott winks at Sam.

She ignores him, but she feels an uncomfortable heat bloom across her chest as the creep's eyes roam her body. Taylor sits up straighter, clenching his fingers around his pen. Sam refuses to allow Richie's lechery to put her off her stride.

'Mr Scott, does the name Charlotte Mathers mean anything to you? . . . Nigel Mathers? . . . Jack Mathers?' she asks. Her words are calm, controlled.

'Never heard of 'em,' Richie says. 'Are they Denver victims too? I only read my chapter – that's all my lawyer was allowed to give me. To be honest, I'm not a big reader anyway.'

'Mr Scott,' Taylor replies, 'almost every detail that Denver mentions in *How to Get Away With Murder* is information that's in the public domain. The evidence brought forward at your trial was compelling, the jury's verdict unanimous. Denver's account doesn't explain a lot of details that speak to your guilt. For example, your bloody fingerprints on the washing machine, your footprints around Melanie's body, and the fact that you fled the scene and were apprehended at a friend's house, hiding under the bed—'

'I'm done talking to you, you fuckin' toff.' Scott takes a long sniff and then spits a glob of phlegm on to Taylor's shiny shoe.

Sam hears Taylor's pen crack in his hand, and leans forward. 'Mr Scott. Richie – may I call you Richie? As my colleague said, *almost* every detail in *How to Get Away With Murder* is in the public domain. It's in your best interest to tell us how Denver might know things that only the perpetrator and the police should know.'

'You mean the earrings. The papers never mentioned Mel's earrings. No one knew about those except the killer and that just proves it wasn't me,' Scott says, letting his eyes rest unashamedly on Sam's breasts. *I should have worn my Nordic sweater*, she thinks, then almost smiles at the thought. Since when has chunky, oversized clothing kept women safe? Beside her, Taylor tenses.

'It could be argued that you took Melanie's earrings. They were portable items of value that you could sell to support yourself while on the run from police,' Sam says.

'There weren't any earrings on me when I was arrested,' Scott says, in a way that indicates to Sam that he's been coached by his legal representative.

'Perhaps you hid the earrings before your arrest. You had days to do that. Or you sold them,' she challenges.

'Whatever, bitch.' Richie leans back in his chair, letting his eyes wander the room, clearly unbothered. The thought of this man walking free makes her skin prickle, but she needs to keep her mind in the room, so she pushes on.

'Just tell us who you told about the earrings, and if that leads us to Denver Brady, we're all better off,' Sam says.

'I'm innocent. You know it. Pretty Boy there knows it. The whole world knows it. Fuckin' outrageous keeping me in here. We're gonna sue for millions. Wrongful imprisonment, reputational damage – the lot!'

'I'd say the reputational damage was taken care of by you, Mr Scott, when you beat up your girlfriend,' Taylor says.

Richie fires up immediately. 'She was a fuckin' nut job, Mel. She gave as good as she got. I had scratch marks all up my arms all the fuckin' time. She knew what buttons to push. Read the book. Denver says that Mel confessed to starting our fights.'

'Yes, I know there are women like that. Psychos.' Sam lets her comment hang, avoiding Taylor's outraged glare. 'We have a common goal here. For you to get out of prison, we need to find Denver. Help me to help you. Tell me everything.'

'My lawyer told me to tell you what I remembered.' Richie scratches his head, then cleans his fingernails on his bottom teeth.

'Your lawyer is right, Richie,' Sam says.

'He's a clever bloke,' Richie says, and Sam wonders if that's true, given that no lawyer worth his salt would allow a client to speak to the police unrepresented.

Richie leans forward, inches from Sam's face, and she automatically switches to breathing through her mouth. Taylor's knee presses up against hers under the table, as if promising to keep her safe.

'I've been having these memories since I read my chapter,' Richie says. 'Flashbacks. Of a voice with an accent talking to Melanie in our house.'

'What kind of accent?' Taylor asks.

'Romanian, maybe, like my cellmate. All sound the same don't they, foreigners?' Scott says. 'But, yeah ... I think Denver is a foreigner. Probably come 'ere illegally on a dingy.' Richie sniffs loudly.

'Go on,' Sam says.

'I remember a man knocking on the door. Saying something about his dog, Tony. Stupid name for a dog. I was well out of it, but I remember the geezer was lanky. Like, really tall. With black hair.'

'Anything else?' Taylor asks, scribbling wildly in his notebook.

'No. I've told you everything now. But this is the most important thing, son: I didn't kill my Mel. I knocked her about a bit but a saint woulda knocked Mel about. Catch the fucker what killed my girl. Do ya fuckin' jobs.' Then, without another word, he stands up and the guard escorts him from the room.

As they drive back towards London, Taylor hums along to the Libertines' 'Time for Heroes' and Sam marvels at the young man's diverse taste in music. He sings along quietly to Northern Soul, hard rock and country on the radio, skipping channels to avoid the overplayed rubbish that she hates too – 'Viva La Vida' makes her soul die a little each time she hears it and Taylor's thumb changes the station before the vocals have time to kick in. She remembers the songs her mother used to sing as they drove together to school. Once the family moved to Clapham, the singing stopped. Not just because her mother no longer drove anywhere – her father sold the car immediately – but because her dad's new role in the Met came with strains and stresses he didn't know how to handle. His moods became more frequent, his frustrations and fear bursting through without warning. Sam and her mother trod on eggshells around him, but soon enough, one cracked. From then on, whenever her mother sang, the words were slurred and Sam turned up her own music to drown out the sound. That was when Sam discovered that heavy metal and hard rock were the perfect way to shut out the world around her. Disturbed, In Flames, Audioslave – their angry voices, their pain-soaked lyrics somehow soothed her.

Taylor taps the break as the slow line of traffic halts once again, jolting Sam out of her memories.

'What were you saying, Taylor?' Sam asks. 'I was in my own world there.'

'Yes, ma'am, I know the look by now.' He smiles, and she returns it. 'I was just saying that we need to tell DCI Blakelaw and DI Edris what we've learned about Denver potentially being a tall, dark-haired man with a foreign accent. God, I'm loath to help Richie Scott out of jail. But it's potential evidence that Denver may have murdered Betty *and* Melanie.'

'It's not evidence at all,' Sam says stoutly. 'Scott could have made it all up. We'll not mention anything he said today. Not to Harry, not to Tina, not to anyone. This is completely irrelevant to the case unless it's connected to Charlotte Mathers – which it isn't. Yet. So, we say nothing.'

Taylor peers at her, uncertain. 'Aren't we obliged to share our findings, boss?'

'We say nothing,' she insists.

'There's a chance Richie Scott is innocent of Melanie's murder, though,' Taylor argues. 'If that's true, Denver now has two victims that we know of. It's looking like Denver really is a serial killer.'

'There's also a chance Denver killed Mel before Richie got to deal the final blow,' Sam says, 'but otherwise Richie Scott would eventually have killed Mel himself. He *almost* killed her more than a dozen times. Richie Scott belongs in prison. Do you know that in 2021, of the eighty-one thousand women in the world who were murdered, forty-five thousand died at the hands of an intimate partner or family member? Forty-five *thousand*, Taylor.'

'That doesn't sound right, boss,' Taylor says tentatively.

'It's not right,' Sam replies. 'It's appallingly wrong.'

Sam's stomach churns as she imagines that man on the loose again. Free to find a new woman to prey on. To coerce. To abuse. To kill.

Taylor Swift's voice fills the car and Sam notices that Taylor is trying his hardest not to sing along like the closet Swifty she knows he is. When the verse arrives at the point where Romeo kneels to the ground and pulls out a ring, Sam takes a deep breath and launches into tuneless but powerful singing. Taylor laughs then joins in, both knowing every word and bellowing each one at the top of their lungs. As the song finishes, Sam and Taylor grin at each other.

'Charlotte Mathers loved Taylor Swift too,' Sam says, and the joy of the moment drains away as their minds turn back to the dead child. 'We need to push that arson lead again, Taylor – surely Sussex Police have found *something*.'

'And if the person who burned down the place where *How to Get Away With Murder* was printed turns out to be a tall man with a foreign accent, like Richie Scott said?' Taylor asks, and an unexpected sense of foreboding begins to brew deep in Sam's stomach.

Now that *would* be too much of a coincidence.

## *Timing and Alibis*

The best time to kill is usually in the early hours of the morning, between 3 and 5 a.m., when the fewest police officers are on duty. It also means that you can maintain alibis, as you can be present when your alibi (spouse, pal, mother) falls asleep, and you're there when they wake up. Using your regular routine and cover-life in this way should not only eliminate you from any police enquiries early on, but also greatly reduce the chance of you ever being convicted, as it raises reasonable doubt in the minds of jurors.

Alibis matter. Let me teach you how to build one.

I spotted this heavenly creature in a coffee shop. Daisy's name-badge was pinned to a T-shirt with the words *Swift-Tea* on it. I couldn't not look, with a top that tight. Our fingers brushed against each other's as she passed me the steamy macchiato. (Don't believe everything you read about serial killers – black coffee isn't our go-to. But I digress.) As I sipped, I noticed a little smiley face next to where my name was scrawled (and incorrectly spelled) on the takeaway cup. I was desperate to touch that soft, young skin. I rarely feel that kind of urge. I came up with some chit-chat about how hard baristas work and managed to discover what time Daisy's shift finished. I knew I wouldn't be able to stop myself from being there to walk her home.

I was in the city for a conference. It was a huge, all-day networking event and I didn't really know anyone there. I was confident in my own killing skills by this point, but I decided that an alibi could only be a good thing. I mingled my little heart out that day. I was sure to introduce myself and say my name clearly and loudly to as many people as I could. The event stretched well into the evening, but when the time came, I visited the lavatory and secreted my mobile phone underneath the pot plant in the corner of the bathroom. It was one of those strange, mixed-gender affairs – a large room and cubicles within it that anyone can use – and I noticed that a boxed pregnancy test had been left on the top of the wastepaper basket. It had *Twin Pack* written on it and I quickly surmised that one test had been used and the other discarded. *Interesting*, I thought, and, using a piece of tissue, I took the unwanted pregnancy test with me, a little idea flitting about in the back of mind as to how I might use it.

I pulled on my waterproof jacket, hat and glasses, and left.

The event wasn't far from the coffee shop and I waited patiently outside for my date. I followed her for a while. She took a route that led down through a picturesque hamlet and along a riverbank.

Daisy hummed as she walked – I think it was Coldplay. Music for people who don't like music, in my opinion. Never mind yellow, they're beige. Haha. Occasionally, Daisy turned, looking over her shoulder towards me. I was alone, without Tony, and I sensed that she was immediately uncomfortable about my presence. The humming stopped. The looks over the shoulder grew more frequent. I knew I was in trouble but I also have come to understand that women rarely act on their instincts, favouring politeness over their own survival.

'Excuse me,' I called out, 'Excuse me!' Daisy hesitated, looked around for other people (there were none), then stopped. Slowly I approached, a smile on my face. 'I'm a little lost,' I said. 'Could you point me towards Notown?'

'Oh, sorry, I just moved here and . . . ,' Daisy said. 'Wait, didn't I serve you . . . ?' She didn't finish the sentence. She'd recognized me. The game was up. I smiled at her reassuringly but she turned on her heels and ran. Ah, Daisy, if only you'd done that earlier.

I caught her easily, of course. She was carrying a satchel that slowed her down and wore flat pumps that simply weren't suitable for cross-country. I pushed her shoulder and she fell down the river embankment, landing in the ferns and brambles at the bottom. I climbed down after her to be sure she was OK.

I spent a little time with my barista in the undergrowth. I suspect that she had a weak heart, because we really didn't get much time together before she expired. Not a bad thing, I supposed, because I didn't want to be gone for too long. I confess, I was once again tempted into taking a shiny dragonfly necklace from her neck as a wee keepsake.

I retrieved Daisy's satchel, which she'd dropped nearby. Taking the pregnancy test from my pocket, I pressed her fingers all over it. Remember, folks: fingerprints made immediately after death cannot be discerned from those made while alive.

On the return journey, I left my outer jacket in the doorway of a British Heart Foundation charity shop – I like to give back when I can. I wiped my shoes down and arrived back at my networking event. No one had noticed my absence, of course. I collected my phone and enjoyed a few whiskies in celebration. When the night was drawing to a close, I cajoled one or two fellow guests to share a taxi with me. I got dropped off first, and when I entered the hotel, I made a pointless enquiry at the front desk to ensure that the receptionist noted my arrival and thus added more weight to my alibi. In my room I ordered a paid-for movie, to prove that I was indeed present in the hotel.

Creating alibis in this way ensured that I was unlikely to be labelled a suspect in Daisy's murder and introduced reasonable doubt, should I have had the misfortune of ending up on trial. I took a little pride in the pregnancy-test red herring, imagining police officers and profilers looking closely at the men in her life. As long as Daisy wasn't some rainbow-flaunting rug-muncher – and based on her haircut and fingernails, I didn't believe she was – there was bound to be a man somewhere in her periphery upon whom suspicion would land.

I didn't receive so much as a phone call about the whole thing. Daisy's ex-boyfriend was arrested for the crime. Unluckily for him, he was working in the same city that very weekend. I couldn't have planned it better. The boyfriend was charged but the jury found the case not proven and he went right back to his life. I doubt he ever thinks about poor little Daisy.

I do.

I think about her every day, as I sip my macchiato.

# 12

Sam watches the man on her bus. He's reading. The book is curled painfully back on itself so she can't see the cover, but she knows what it is from the size, shape, even the font. She's re-read the Betty Brown chapter so many times that she can even guess what sentence the man's eyes are on. He has a coffee in his free hand, and she wonders if it's a macchiato. He takes a sip and licks his lips. Smiles at something on the page, then casts a guilty glance around. *It's not about Denver-bloody-Brady*, she wants to yell. To scream. *What about Charlotte?* Everyone needs to remember her name, not her killer's and not Denver's. She sighs, knowing that her day will be filled with more searching for the man behind the book, and while Sam believes that Denver is a killer, she doesn't believe that he is *the* killer. Charlotte's killer is the man she wants and Sam is convinced he's a copycat.

Sam yawns and takes Taylor's timeline from her handbag. She unfolds and scrutinizes it as the bus sways towards New Scotland Yard. The piece of A3 paper has grown messy since the first day they'd looked at it together and the bottom few items on their list are curled underneath, out of sight:

*How to Get Away with Murder – Timeline*
- *Denver is born – approx. 1981.*
- *Denver kills Jono (Quarry. DB age 12) – 1993.*
- *Denver kills Sarah (Convent. Physical evidence: letters) – 1997.*

- *Denver becomes a serial killer by age 20 (Missing victim?) – 2001.*
- *Denver kills Sean (Samaritan Technique) – 2006.*
- *Denver kills Betty (Physical evidence: blue star-sapphire ring) – 2007.*
- *Denver kills Melanie (Physical evidence: diamond earrings) – 2019.*
- *Richie Scott is convicted of killing Melanie – 2019.*
- *Denver kills Daisy (Barista. Physical evidence: dragonfly necklace) – 2020.*

The bus jerks to a halt at her stop. Outside New Scotland Yard, the street is entirely blocked. There are uniformed traffic cops trying to get the road cleared, but the number of press vans, journalists and protestors is insurmountable. Thankfully, there's a back entrance that officers can use, and as she walks towards it she hears journalists broadcasting live in various languages. Sam walks a little faster, eager to pass by the news crews unnoticed and even more eager to solve the case they're all talking about. She doesn't speak any foreign languages, but she doesn't need to. A phrase that needs no translation is spoken time and again:

Denver Brady tueur en série.

Denver Brady asesino en serie.

Denver Brady serienmörder.

You don't need a language degree to work that out: the UK has a serial killer on the loose and his name is Denver Brady. Not a single reporter mentions Charlotte's name.

When Sam steps on to the fourth floor, Taylor immediately waves her over, a cup of tea in his hand.

'Thanks, Adam,' she says and he blinks.

'Er, you're welcome,' he replies, then adds, '. . . ma'am.' She smiles at him, enjoying her confidence that he's one of the good guys, when only a few weeks ago she hadn't believed they existed. Progress.

'Detective Chief Inspector Blakelaw would like us all to assemble in the briefing room,' Tina Edris says as she walks briskly past and clicks the kettle on. 'The DCI has brought in an offender profiler.' It's the first time she's seen Tina since she said those awful things she deeply regrets. Sam tries to meet Tina's eye but the other woman only has eyes for the task at hand.

'We can't make it, ma'am,' Taylor responds. 'I know you'll be sad to miss it, what with how effective you believe profilers to be . . .'

'We need a damn good reason to miss it,' she says, looking at him hopefully, noting the glint in his eye.

'Sean is in the interview room downstairs, ma'am,' Taylor says to both Sam and Tina.

'The guy who jumped off the bridge?' Sam clarifies, and Taylor nods. 'But he died in 2006.' She pulls the timeline from her bag, waves it at Taylor.

'Not like you to be wrong,' Tina says sarcastically, blowing on her herbal tea. *Fair*, Sam thinks. Tina is still cross with her, and she deserves it.

'But, Denver—'

'Lied to us,' Taylor says. 'Again.'

Sean Lister doesn't smell good – and not because he's dead. He's very much alive but still reeks as though he's just washed up out of the river. He wears a Harrington jacket and a flat cap, and carries a plastic folder under his arm.

As they take their seats in the empty interview room, Sean removes his cap and reveals a truly dreadful mod haircut. Taylor starts the digital recorder and makes the introductions.

'I want to do this quick,' Sean says in a Geordie-cockney hybrid. 'I'm not dead and, more importantly, I'm definitely not gay. I've brought a statement from my girlfriend Lucy saying I'm as straight as they come. I *am* the Sean from *How to Get Away*

*With Murder,* and I'm alive and straight.' He says all this a little breathlessly, pushing his folder across the small steel desk.

'Does the name Charlotte Mathers ring any bells?' Sam asks.

'No,' Sean says.

Sam takes the folder and begins leafing through it. It's all colour-coded, precisely labelled and arranged chronologically. *This took a lot of work*, she thinks, feeling her old instincts kicking in. She'd grown up watching *Judge Judy*, whose motto was *If something doesn't make sense, it isn't true.* Sean's level of effort, and his timing, isn't making sense to Sam and that makes her very wary.

'Describe for me, in detail, how you know that you're the Sean in *How to Get Away With Murder*?' Taylor asks.

'My name for starters. Plus, everything about my life. My music production course. My ex was a nurse called Jemma who got herself pregnant. My dad and uncle torched that *Brokeback Mountain* billboard. All of that's true,' Sean says. 'Except the gay shit. I'm *not* gay. Read the statement from my girl—'

'Why are you here, Mr Lister?' Sam says, gesturing to the folder. 'You've put a lot of work into this and you don't strike me as the altruistic type. You're not here to help. What's really going—'

'To set the record straight,' Sean says, folding his arms. 'And to tell you lot who Denver Brady really is. I'm here to solve your case.' He puffs out his chest.

'You know who Denver is?' Sam raises an incredulous eyebrow. 'Let's have it then.'

'I knew him. Jemma was in digs with his mate. Up in Wallsend. Sometimes Denver came and visited. He was well weird. Weird music. Weird books. Wouldn't shut up about Ted Bundy – called him Teddy like they were pals. Real bee in his bonnet about Mary Ann Cotton letting him and the North East down. Had a proper crush on Jemma. Once I caught him sniffing her coat what was hanging up.' Sean Lister falls silent, sitting up straighter as if he's just won a court case.

'So, what's Denver's real name?' Taylor asks, and despite herself, Sam finds herself leaning forward, holding her breath.

'Well, I can't remember his name.' Sam rolls her eyes and slumps back in the chair. 'We're going back twenty years or more. He was just a lad that visited sometimes. But it's him. He's definitely Denver.'

'Right,' Sam sighs. 'Can you at least describe his appearance?'

'Aye . . .' Sean thinks, then offers, 'Good few inches shorter than me. Pale as milk. Sandy hair. Scrawny.' Taylor catches Sam's eye and she knows what he's trying to convey: Richie Scott described Denver as tall and dark-haired. Someone – other than Denver – is lying.

'But you don't remember his name?' she asks. 'Not even a first name. Think, Mr Lister.'

'I have. I can't remember. But I never forget a face. I'll ID him no problem and testify against him, too, when you catch him. The little weed put me in his book to get back at me for . . . well . . .'

'Bullying him?' Sam suggests.

Sean shrugs. 'I wasn't a bully. It was different times back then. I might have put it about that he was gay. I put a few bits on Facebook.'

'You called Denver homophobic names?' Sam asks.

'But that's just more proof, innit?' Sean argues. 'Proof that it's revenge against me. That I'm a victim.'

'Can you remember the name of the student he visited?' Taylor probes.

'No,' Sean says.

'Does the name Betty Brown mean anything to you?' Sam tries.

'Brown rings a bell . . .' Sean rubs his chin. 'I think the lad Jem lived with was called Brown. Or maybe Smith. Or could it have been Jones? But maybe I'm just remembering Brown from Denver's book. I skimmed the chapters after mine to be—'

'Does Jemma remember?' Taylor asks, and she hears the undertone of frustration in his voice.

'We aren't in touch. I don't want her to know where I am, right? That's confidential.' Sean shoves his chin out to emphasize his point.

'So she didn't have the baby?'

'She had it, aye.'

Then it falls into place. Sean's evasiveness and odd word-choices; the way he described Jemma as 'getting herself pregnant' and just now referred to his child as an 'it'. This man ran away, as many unwilling fathers have before and many will again. Sean didn't want to be a dad. The baby wasn't in his belly, so he had choices. He chose freedom. He's not a victim, just another absent father.

'What's Jemma's surname?' Sam asks.

'Hammond,' Sean says, then adds, 'Why do you need to know that?'

Sam ignores the question and pulls from Sean's folder a driving licence and a utility bill with his current address on. Sam photographs the documents using her phone.

'So you believe me?' Sean asks. 'You believe that I'm one of Denver's victims?' Sam fishes through the rest of the paperwork. It certainly looks like Sean was a 24-year-old music student at around the right time, although he didn't complete the course. There's a photograph of a man posing next to a burned-up billboard, Jake Gyllenhaal's face charred and flapping in the wind. Some song lyrics and various letters and bills. The details are exact matches for those Denver supplies in his book.

'We'll speak to Jemma to see if she remembers the name of the man you think might be Denver,' Taylor says.

'Right, but my details stay confidential,' Sean demands.

'What university did Denver's friend attend?' Taylor presses, pen poised.

He thought a moment. 'Newcastle,' he says. 'Or maybe Northumbria.'

'Let's wrap this up,' Sam says. 'Taylor, get on to those unis for a list of students that fit our time frame. I'll have DI Duggan speak with Jemma personally. He's keen to help.'

'Wait. I need a receipt,' Sean says. 'For my visit. Something to prove that I came here today and you agree I'm a victim.'

'This is New Scotland Yard, not Primark,' Sam scoffs. 'We don't do receipts.'

'Well then, I need you to sign something to say that I am *the* Sean from *How to Get Away With Murder*.' He takes his folder back from Sam and extracts a few sheets of typed paper from it, placing them on the desk. She glances at the top sheet – an incredibly basic form stating exactly what Sean has just described. At the very bottom she spots the name of a company – a plc she's never heard of, but her mind connects the dots.

'You're trying to sell your story,' Sam declares, her understanding dawning. 'And the newspaper, or media group – whoever is interested – won't publish without some kind of proof.'

'Look, this story is worth more money than—'

'Get out,' Sam snaps.

'I'll split it with you,' Sean begs.

'Cut this homophobic loser loose, Taylor.' Sam stands to leave the room then turns back, loathing suffusing her face. 'We have a dead child and at least one killer on the loose. A killer who could strike again any moment. And your only concern is—'

Sean slams his fists on the table. 'It's just a signature!'

'Pay your child support, you spineless fraction of a man!' she spits.

'You fuckin'—'

'See him out, Taylor,' Sam says dismissively, pulling her phone from her pocket and noticing several missed calls from Dr Thomson and DI Neil Duggan.

'Listen to me, you cunt!' Lister yells, jumping to his feet and grabbing at her over the table. 'Denver has the world thinking I'm a faggot—'

Before Sam knows what's happening, there's a crunchy pop and Lister is clutching his nose as blood immediately starts to run between his fingers. She gasps, then turns to Taylor, who's nursing his right fist. *Shit*, she thinks, watching her trainee turn pale. Sean begins to whimper and mumble about police brutality. Sam grabs some tissues from the box on the table and hands them to Sean. They all stand frozen for a second, looking at one another. Sean tips his head back and holds the top of his nose. Taylor flops forward in his chair, head in hands.

'What have I done,' he moans. 'I—'

'Stay here,' she barks at Taylor, then points towards Sean. 'And clean him up.'

Sam quickly turns off the digital recorder, then leaves the interview room, closing the door behind her before entering the adjacent room, the one where she'd hidden to watch Tina and Harry interview the Mathers men. Sitting at the desk, Sam logs on to the server and navigates to the recording of the interview they've just done with Sean Lister. She hesitates for a second, then deletes it. A pop-up warns her that the recording has not yet been uploaded to cloud storage. She swears under her breath, then hits 'Permanently delete'. Next, just to be sure, she reaches for the jug of water on the desk. The backup to the server runs every night, so if she destroys this drive, it'll mean at least twelve hours' worth of missing evidence. Entire cases could fall apart. The whole building shares interview rooms, so this server contains recording from all kinds of investigations. Sam looks up and through the one-way mirror. Taylor is wiping blood from Sean's jacket, his hands shaking. This will end his career before it's even really begun. She braces herself and pours all the water over the drive. The machine flickers, hisses, then all its lights turn off.

Sam strides back to the closed interview room door. She takes a few deep breaths, wipes sweat from her upper lip and enters. Sean Lister has reseated himself and has twisted tissues sticking out of each nostril. Taylor is pacing back and forth, his hands in his hair.

'Mr Lister,' Sam tries, but her voice doesn't work. She swallows, clears her throat and tries again. 'Mr Lister. As, er, a result of your use of homophobic words and your behaviour . . .' She pauses, thinks for a second, straightens and begins once more. 'Mr Sean Lister, I am arresting you under Section 4 of the Public Order Act 1986. You do not have to say anything, but it may harm your defence—'

'Wait, what?!'

'. . . if you do not mention when questioned—'

'He hit *me*!'

'. . . something which you later rely on—'

'Don't you dare!' Sean seethes.

'It is a Public Order Offence to—'

'But *he* hit *me*!'

'And Officer Smith here will be disciplined for his actions and likely fired. But you will be charged for—'

'All right! Stop!' Sean yells. 'Let's work something out.'

Sam sighs dramatically and sits down. Taylor is frozen to the spot. She leans forward and holds Sean Lister's eyes.

'OK, Mr Lister,' she says calmly, 'I can drop the charges against you. I would simply ask that, in return, you consider saying nothing about what my colleague, PC Smith here, has just accidentally done.'

Sean's nodding before Sam has even finished her sentence. She gives him more tissues and he carefully removes the ones sticking out of his nose, dabbing to see if the bleeding has stopped. She escorts him to the custody suite's fire exit to leave unnoticed, then makes her way back to the interview room. Taylor has sat down at the desk and is sobbing like a child. Silently, she places her hand on his shoulder and feels the damp of his shirt.

'I screwed up,' Taylor whispers. She barely hears him over the pounding of her own pulse in her ears.

'It's OK.' She tries to smile, tries to sound calm. 'That homophobic loser would tip anyone over the edge. I understand why—'

'It wasn't the homophobia that did it,' Taylor says, but Sam isn't listening as she pulls him gently upright, so that they're standing squarely, facing each other.

She drops her voice low. 'Look, Taylor, I doubt Sean Lister will come back. I've deleted the interview recording and destroyed the hard drive, but—'

'Wait, ma'am,' Taylor objects. 'We need to report this.'

'No, Taylor,' she soothes. 'You fucked up, but you're a good person. A good officer. Now, we just need a backup story in case that prick does shout his mouth off or tries to press charges against you.'

'Backup story?'

'Yes, we're going to say that he punched me and you were forced to restrain him, and accidentally burst his nose in the process.'

'Punched *you*?'

'Yes. So, I need you to . . . I need a bruise . . .' Taylor's face whitens as he understands her meaning, and he shakes his head. Sam nods, gently pulling his right arm out of his hair and closing her hand over his to make it form a fist. 'I need you to hit me, just hard enough. Right here . . .' She points to her cheekbone. 'I bruise like a peach.'

'No. I will not.'

'Taylor, your career is on the line here, you have to—'

'Absolutely not,' Taylor snaps. 'I'll take my chances.'

'We need a plausible story, Adam. I'll go back upstairs and we'll have countless witnesses to Sean's assault on me. I just need a bruise,' Sam says. 'It looks better if it's me that got hurt. We can play the old chivalry card – God knows it's good for nothing else.'

'No!' Taylor barks. 'This has already gone too far. I've hit a man and you've tampered with evidence and destroyed police property. We should just go to the DCI and confess.'

'You do that and we'll *both* be fired,' Sam retorts.

'Maybe that's exactly what we deserve,' Taylor hisses, and he storms out, slamming the door.

Sam groans, and looks around the empty room. She kneels down next to the steel table and wraps her hands around its leg. She takes a deep breath, moves her head back and then thrusts her face hard towards the cold metal. The pain makes her ears roar. Somehow she's caught the high eyebrow bone and her eyes flood with tears. The skin is already throbbing.

It'll be a perfect bruise by tomorrow.

Sam quickly ends the call with DI Duggan and emerges from the lift as dramatically as she can, crying and folding herself on to the fourth-floor sofa. Chloe Spears and another woman jog over and together they administer a cold compress to Sam's eye as she explains how the interview with Sean Lister went very wrong.

'He smacked me right on the eye,' Sam whimpers to Chloe. 'Bastard. Taylor had a right job restraining him.'

'Want me to write up the report for you? Can you see OK?' Chloe asks.

'I'll manage the report,' Sam says – though, of course, she won't. Several people come over to ask if she's OK, and once she has enough witnesses to her injuries, she makes her way back to her desk and pops two paracetamol. Taylor is sitting at his desk, holding his head in his hands and watching her out of the corner of his eye. Chloe hovers in the background.

Sam refuses to let Sean Lister waste another second of time they could be spending working on Charlotte's case. She pours herself a cup of water, downs it and speaks with as much authority as she can muster.

'DC Spears . . .' She waves Chloe closer. 'I assume you've been told you're joining our team?'

'Yes, ma'am,' Spears confirms. 'And congratulations on being made joint SIO. Also, your sister called for you, ma'am. She said it's urgent.'

'SIO?' Taylor spins in his chair, sounding hurt. 'You didn't tell me.' Sam shrugs and smiles at him, wincing as the expression reaches her throbbing bruise. 'Ma'am, there's something I need to—'

'Look, I have a theory I want to run by you both,' Sam cuts in. Can you come with me, please?' As she stands, the throbbing over her eye increases and she adjusts the cool-pack she's holding there.

The tiny meeting room in the corner opposite Harry's office is vacant and they sit toe-to-toe. Spears's perfume is light and floral, and reminds Sam of her mother, which she finds soothing. She sits back in her seat and waits until everyone is comfortable and paying attention.

'Even before Sean Lister came forward, something was really bothering me about Bobby – Denver's cousin,' Sam begins. 'I felt like he was in Denver's book twice. Sure, Denver talks about him a lot, but I thought Bobby had popped up somewhere he shouldn't. It took me a while to spot the clue. I'd focused only on the murder we know Denver really might have committed—'

'Betty Brown,' Taylor says, his eyes flicking to the pack on her face. The concern in his gaze makes her cheeks hot.

'Exactly. The detail about Betty's broken fingers was not in the public domain and the family were never told.' Sam adjusts the ice pack. 'We haven't been able to find anything on Daisy. Jono died in an accident. Sean is alive and Richie Scott could be lying, as he was convicted of murdering Melanie and stands to gain significantly if—'

'And Denver himself says Basil survived,' Taylor bursts in. 'I've searched high and low for him and I'm certain nothing was reported to the police. The old man must have kept it quiet.'

'Mmm . . .' Sam feels more heat in her cheeks at another mention of this victim whose chapter she's not yet reached. She decides to plough ahead. 'We also know that Denver lied about torturing Betty, actually minimizing the harm he did to her in his version of events, which is odd for a man who's boasting about being a serial killer. I read Betty's chapter again and again. Then I read the bit about Bobby again and again. That's why I've come to believe that Betty Brown was Bobby's mother. Betty is Denver's aunt.'

Taylor and Chloe stare at Sam, stunned into silence. Sam sips some water, enjoying a flush of pride at having solved the mystery of the missing victim. After a moment, she can see that her conclusion may take some more explaining. She strokes the little netball in her pocket, soothed by its smooth roundness.

'Bobby died, right?' Chloe checks.

'Yes,' Taylor confirms. 'But Denver doesn't tell us how.'

'But he does tell us when,' Sam says, 'and that's the clue we needed to spot.'

'I spotted it,' Taylor says. 'Bobby died in July.'

'And what happens in July?' Sam asks them both.

'Glastonbury,' Chloe guesses. Sam smiles but shakes her head, then opens *How to Get Away with Murder*. She turns to a page with a folded-down corner and points to a highlighted paragraph:

'. . . *their boy graduated from university, only to fall in a river on his way home from the ceremony.*'

'Graduation,' Taylor declares, his mouth open. 'Betty's son died after graduation, which is in July – the same month Bobby died.'

'Now, here's the paragraph about Bobby's death,' Sam says, flicking to the relevant chapter.

'*We lost Bobby under tragic circumstances the following July and I was so pleased we'd had that moment together.*'

'I think that what Denver tells us about his family is true. But he's slipped up – he's also included Bobby's death in Betty's chapter, and that was the connection we needed to make,' Sam says.

'And Lister just told us . . .' Taylor begins, but hesitates.

'Lister just told us that Denver used to visit another boy, possibly called Brown, at a Newcastle university in the early noughties,' Sam says. 'Betty lived in the North East. DI Duggan will ask Jemma Hammond if she remembers anything and is willing to make a statement. He'll give her Sean Lister's address as well, and tell her to sue him for backdated child support.'

'If you're right, ma'am,' Chloe announces, 'then you've solved Betty Brown's murder and led us straight to Denver.'

Sam nods. She's keen to know what Taylor thinks of her theory, but he seems a little dazed and is staring absently out at the busy fourth floor.

'Perhaps Denver killed Bobby and Betty suspected it, so Denver killed her too,' Taylor ventures. 'Maybe,' Chloe says. 'But if Betty suspected it strongly enough, she'd have gone to the police – and she didn't.'

'But she did do one thing,' Sam says. 'She changed her will. DI Duggan half told me when we visited Newcastle but he got dragged away. I called him earlier this morning and he confirmed it. A few months after her son died, Betty changed her will and left all of her money to the Salvation Army. Effectively disinheriting her nephew. Her only remaining family. Why would Betty do that unless—'

'Shit,' Taylor says, and Sam is surprised to hear the word on his lips. 'You've cracked it. All we need to do is search the general register office for Betty and Albert Brown's nephew and we have Denver. You're a genius, Sam—I mean ma'am.' Taylor flushes. 'All the clues were right there, in *How to Get Away with Murder*,' he says, smiling.

'I hate to mention it, ma'am,' Chloe ventures. 'Your theory is great but very, erm, loose.'

'You're right, Chloe,' she sighs. 'There's no way I'd get a warrant to arrest Betty's nephew based on what I have right now. Even when we find him, we're nowhere near meeting the burden of proof that he is Denver or that he hurt Betty.'

'Tell us what we need to find, ma'am,' says Taylor, leaning forward with pen poised.

'Cold cases are almost always solved by forensic breakthroughs or new physical evidence – or by circumstantial evidence that is so strong that a jury believes without doubt that no one else could have committed the crime.'

'Betty was cremated and the crime scene is long gone,' Chloe wrinkles her brow. 'But we might be able to find some physical evidence that connects Betty's nephew to the book. A notepad with an early draft of the novel on, for example. Or the profits from the book sales.'

'Yes,' Sam responds, 'or a physical connection to another person mentioned in the book – that would work, too. Denver claims to have taken Betty's sapphire ring, Melanie's earrings and Daisy's dragonfly necklace – so, that kind of thing.'

Taylor butts in: 'Can't we just arrest the nephew and—'

'That's not how it works, Taylor,' she responds. 'We need some physical connection.'

'But at least we have a solid idea who Denver is,' Chloe says.

'Maybe,' Sam sighs, 'but Charlotte's case isn't.'

'Sam! Sam Hansen!' Harry yells from across the room, causing a temporary lull in chatter as heads turn Sam's way. She moves to the doorway of the tiny glass meeting room. 'I've got him!' Harry bellows. 'The man who burned down the printers. He's here in London. I've got Denver-bloody-Brady's address.'

Less than an hour's drive from New Scotland Yard is the east London neighbourhood of Barking. Once a thriving community, many residents now struggle to pay extortionate rents to corporate landlords who fail to maintain their properties. Tower blocks of rotting flats are filled with mould that kills the people that live there almost as quickly as the drugs and guns wielded by the gangs that have grown in number and strength as the area has gone downhill.

While Taylor drives, Sam scribbles in her notebook.

'Are we still developing our *Who is Denver Brady?* list, ma'am?' Taylor asks. 'Given that we now know he's a liar? Or at least, he lied about Jono. Plus, he downplayed what he did to Betty and now we know Sean is alive.'

'I'll keep it going in the background,' she says. 'If I spot any significant connection, I'll flag it, but there's so much going on here that I think all eyes have to be on the main story in case a clue slips by.'

Sam slides her notebook away and takes out her phone. She's beginning to feel travel sick, but she still rewatches the CCTV footage that Sussex Police sent to Harry. It clearly shows a man entering a petrol station and paying at the counter. A simple facial recognition search identified the man as Andrei Albescu, a petty criminal of Romanian origin now living in Barking.

To quell the motion sickness in her stomach, she puts her phone away and stares out of the window. She scours the streets of Barking, as if she might spot Charlotte's killer, somehow knowing who he is on sight. He could be out there right now, watching someone, waiting. Ready to kill again. Sam opens a pack of Polos and palms one into her mouth. She returns her eyes to the face of each passing man. She sees a group of teenagers and does a double take. One of them is wearing a T-shirt that says *I Love Denver* and is holding hands with another, whose top reads *I AM Denver*.

'My God,' she whispers. Taylor doesn't respond, but flicks through the radio stations. A Bring Me the Horizon song fills the car and Sam feels her shoulders immediately relax. Still, she keeps her eyes fixed on the pedestrians as London whizzes by.

They're not far from their destination when her phone vibrates. Even though her stomach has only just calmed, she can't resist reading the email from DI Duggan.

Hansen,

I've just spoken to Jemma Hammond's mother. It's not good news. Jemma was killed last year in car crash. Bloke in a truck on his phone drove right through her car. Her son survived so I've passed on Lister's details to him, but the lad says he wants nothing to do with his dad. Jemma's mam can't remember the names of her uni friends but I'll keep pursuing it.

I'm up to the chapter 'Timing and Alibis' and I think Denver's made this one up, too.

I believe Daisy the barista was actually Marguerite Moreau. I didn't realize that the name Daisy is used for Marguerite, but apparently it used to be very common. Who knew? Well, Denver apparently.

I'm sure you remember the Moreau case? It was all over the news at the time. French girl studying medicine in Edinburgh. No one was ever convicted but Moreau was in an on-off relationship with a personal trainer who had previous convictions for domestic violence and he was charged. The verdict the jury returned was 'not proven', a verdict that only the Scottish legal system allows, whereby the jury aren't happy to say he's innocent, but the Crown Prosecution Service haven't enough evidence to prove guilt.

I've attached the case file. Looks to me like the PT did it. He's currently serving a separate rape charge in HMP Edinburgh.

Is Denver just twisting real stories into something else? If so, how does Betty fit in?

Neil

DI Neil Duggan

Northumbria Police

*Good question*, Sam thinks, but more important to her is the question *How does Charlotte fit in?* Denver's stories are unravelling one by one, and it's becoming impossible to keep up with his truths and lies. Denver has potentially lied about Daisy the barista and yet he knows details about Betty's murder that only the perpetrator and police should know. Still, she reminds herself, there is no clear link to Charlotte. Nothing at all that a copycat couldn't have lifted from *How to Get Away with Murder*.

Sam replies to Duggan, telling him they now believe Denver may be Betty's nephew, and to send all information he's gathered on the nephew's whereabouts. She searches the name Marguerite Moreau and a photo of a smiling woman with a roman nose and long, straight eyelashes fills her screen. Sam traces her fingers over the woman's dragonfly necklace, her blood bubbling. Betty's nephew chose to twist and retell Marguerite's tragic story for his own gain. Even death didn't stop her being used and abused by awful men.

'We're here, ma'am.'

She looks about them as Taylor slowly drives past the tower blocks that contain their target location, then loops around and does the same again. They see nothing suspicious, no one hanging around. No vehicle is registered at the address, so they have no idea if the person they're looking for is likely to be home or not.

They leave the car in a parking space and Taylor's eyes linger on their Mercedes as he pushes the button to lock the doors and activate the alarm.

'We'll walk around the building, see what we can see,' Sam says.

'And if he's in there?'

'I'll make an arrest,' she says. 'Andrei Albescu has a string of petty convictions on his record and the CCTV Sussex Police sent over is clear: Albescu bought two cans of petrol from the garage next to Swinton's only a couple of hours before someone set the printers ablaze. Albescu might not be Denver, but he might be able to tell us something useful.'

'According to google,' Taylor adds a little apprehensively, 'Albescu is a popular surname in Romania. He'll likely have an eastern European accent, just like Richie Scott suggested. And the guy in the CCTV footage looks pretty tall . . .'

Sam loosens the top button of her shirt and takes a deep breath.

'I still think Denver is Betty's nephew. This Albescu is perhaps hired help,' she says. 'Is your body-cam on?'

Taylor nods. They look at each other, share a tight-lipped smile and walk towards the lobby of the nearest building.

Predictably, the lift doesn't work and Sam and Taylor begin the arduous climb to the tenth floor. They each cover their noses; Taylor with his silk handkerchief, Sam with her sleeve. There are yellow stains in the corners of the landings and the stairs are littered with debris – needles, condoms, babies' pacifiers. The long corridor of the tenth floor is filled with garbage bags and the occasional faded plastic toy. Where once there had been CCTV cameras, now there is only melted plastic or dangling wires.

Outside flat number 1064, they pause. There's a storage box with a broken lid, from which the rusted frame of doll's pram sticks out. Sam presses her ear to the door. She hears a woman's voice, singing or perhaps pacifying a child. Sam nods to Taylor, then raises her fist and bangs on the door.

For a minute, it doesn't open, but they hear movement inside. A woman talks in a language that isn't English. A baby cries. Eventually, the door is edged ajar on a chain.

'Mrs Nadja Albescu?' Sam begins, 'I'm DI Sam Hansen. Is Andrei at home?' The woman shakes her head. 'May we come in, please?' Sam asks. Nadja's eyes flick to the bruise over her eye.

'Come,' Nadja says, calmly opening the door. Sam glances at Taylor, wondering if he's picked up on what she's noticed: usually, police officers aren't just admitted by an unexpecting homeowner without a few questions being asked first. Nadja hasn't even enquired as to why they are there. Sam doesn't know what to make of it, but it's definitely odd.

They follow her down a dingy hallway towards a dark lounge. There are two rooms off the corridor and Sam checks each in turn. Empty, save for mattresses and the odd piece of old furniture. The lounge is swelteringly hot, but then the windows are all shut. Two toddlers sit in front of a television that's showing *PAW Patrol* without any sound. A baby wails in another room. Nadja stands silently as Sam calmly checks the kitchen and a large storage cupboard for anyone else in the home.

'Can you tell me where Andrei is, Mrs Albescu?' Sam asks, once she's confident he isn't here.

'Andrei, he is work. I bring you drink?'

'Yes, thank you,' says Sam. She isn't thirsty but one of the first things you learn on the job is to always accept an drink offered by a potential witness. It buys time in their home, and makes the meeting feel more relaxed; a friend popping around for a cuppa. As Nadja turns to leave the room, Sam notices her swollen abdomen under her dress. They hear her cooing, and the baby in the other room stops crying. Then there's the sound of cups and cupboard doors from the adjacent kitchen. Sam squeezes past Taylor to take a seat on the haggard sofa between two children. Taylor quietly updates their backup team: suspect not in abode.

'Hello, you two,' Sam says softly to the children. 'What are you watching?'

'Chase! Look!' says the older child, pointing at a dog on the screen. Sam supposes the child is around three years old. Both little ones wear vests and nappies; the place is too hot for anything more. The vests are well worn and greying, but clean. Sam feels a bead of sweat slip down the back of her collar. Nadja re-enters, a baby balanced on one hip, and hands Sam a chipped mug. She takes a sip. Lukewarm water.

'Thank you, Nadja,' Sam says. The woman nods and lowers herself awkwardly into an ancient armchair in the corner.

'You said your husband's at work, Mrs Albescu. Who does Andrei work for?' Taylor asks.

Nadja shrugs. 'My husband had good job as bricklayer. Then he got fired and now he just have sometimes job.'

'Your children are beautiful, Nadja,' Sam says, honestly. 'How many do you have?'

'Three . . . for now.' Nadja smiles down at her stomach.

'A real handful,' Sam says.

Nadja strokes her abdomen and smiles at the children, who babble their own words to the canine characters on the screen.

'TV broke. No sound,' Nadja says. 'But my babies smart. They make their own sound.'

'We're keen to speak to your husband today, Mrs Albescu. What time will he be home?' Taylor asks.

Nadja shrugs.

'Can you call him please, Nadja?' Sam presses.

'No phone,' Nadja says.

'Does the name Charlotte Mathers mean anything to you, Nadja? Or Jack Mathers? Nigel Mathers?' Sam asks. The woman shakes her head to each. 'How about Denver Brady?' Another shake.

Sam decides to try a different tack. 'When are you due?'

'Next month,' Nadja says, then rubs her forehead. 'Brian start nursery this year,' – Nadja points to the larger child – 'so I have more space for baby. All baby is blessing from God, but this one is not plan.'

'I can see that you are working very hard,' Sam says, in a tone she hoped would sound kind but instead came out as condescending. She sips her water and peers around the room again. She can tell that every effort has been made to make the place pleasant. There's a *Frozen* blanket spread out like a playmat for the children, concealing the thin brown carpet beneath. The sofa and armchair are clearly second, third or fourth hand, but the leather has been wiped down and is soft to the touch. There's an apple sliced in a bowl for the toddlers. An overwhelming sadness swallows Sam.

'He's called Brian?' Taylor says, staring at the child.

'I choose good English names for my babies. That Brian. Her Edith. Baby Charles, like King. In my family, we think a name says a lot.'

'Do you have a photograph of Andrei?' Sam asks. Nadja nods and points to the only picture frame on the wall. It's small, around A5 size, and very old. In it, Nadja wears a wedding dress, the man next to her a suit. Taylor examines it, then passes it to Sam. The man is definitely the same person Sam just saw in the CCTV footage. He has dark hair, brown eyes and deeply tanned skin.

'He's tall,' Taylor notes, discreetly.

'Does Andrei have a computer, Nadja?' Sam asks.

'He used to have computer. Spent long time on it. Made some friends on it, I think. But then we sell when he lost job.' Taylor tries, unsuccessfully, to find out who the machine went to.

'Nadja, we'll get out of your hair now, but I need Andrei to call me today.' Sam hands the woman her business card. Nadja takes it, nodding, and Sam notices that Nadja's eyes are filled with tears. Instinctively whispering, even though there's little point in such a small room, she adds: 'Nadja, if there's anything you want me to know, now is the time. I promise to try to help you.' Nadja grasps Sam's hand, a tear trickling down her cheek. 'You can trust me, Nadja.' Sam says. 'Woman to woman, I promise to . . .'

Nadja releases Sam's hand and walks over to her purse, on the floor beside the sofa. She rifles through it and pulls out a small, oblong card similar to the one that Sam handed over only a moment before, but this one is tattered and worn. There's a symbol of some sort on it and Sam feels a tug at her memories, but nothing clicks. She reaches out to take it—

'Enforcement Officer!' A loud voice suddenly booms behind them.

Everyone jumps. A man has entered the room and stands behind Taylor, who spins to face him, drawing his baton.

'Police!' Taylor shouts. 'Freeze! Identify yourself!' The man holds up his hands in surrender. He's smartly dressed, with a neatly trimmed black beard and a clipboard.

'Officer,' he says, in a deep baritone. Sam feels Nadja standing behind her, as if for protection. 'The door was open. I have the right to enter these premises. I'm here under the Repossession of Property clause in—'

Sam releases a held breath. 'He's just a bailiff, Taylor. Stand down.'

'Please, sir, step outside,' says Taylor, straightening his 6ft 2 frame. 'This is a police matter. I respectfully request that you come back another time.' The man's mouth moves, as if he's considering objecting, but then he nods and leaves.

Taylor and Sam turn back to Nadja, who's picked up her daughter, straddling both her baby and her little girl across her bump. Sam looks at her but Nadja is already shaking her head.

'I like you leave now,' Nadja says.

'I—' Sam tries.

'Please,' Nadja begs, and Taylor nods towards the hallway, indicating that they should go.

'Andrei *must* call me today,' Sam insists. 'It'll be so much better if he finds me, rather than the other way around.'

Outside, the bailiff is knocking again, this time three doors down. Sam tells their backup team that they won't be needed, and she and Taylor walk silently back to the car. Once inside, Taylor exhales loudly and rubs his face. Sam is reminded just how new this still is for him.

'My God,' he says, 'I felt so uncomfortable in there. What a life. It was so hot.' Taylor starts the car but instead of turning on the indicator to signal his manoeuvre, he sets off the windscreen wipers. Sam tells him to turn off the ignition; it's clear he needs a minute. She suspects there's something deeper troubling him, too, as his reaction to Nadja's sad situation seems disproportionate.

'Is there something else bothering you, Taylor?' she asks, and he looks at her, reddening a little. He shakes his head, looking at her again in a way that makes Sam feel like she should already know what's bothering him, but doesn't.

'Sam . . .' The way he says her name makes her stomach lurch.

'We can sit here for as long as you need,' she assures him, then connects her phone to the car's Bluetooth and selects the playlist *This is Taylor Swift*. A few songs later, he still seems tense, his fingers playing with car keys. 'Taylor,' Sam says, more firmly now. 'What's going on?'

He sighs. 'There's something you need to know. It's about the day we went to Newcastle.'

Sam is suddenly tingling with concern. What had she done? What had she said? She pushes her mind back, but she can't get beyond the Dog and Parrot pub and then waking up on her sofa, under a blanket and still in her work clothes.

Suddenly there's a sharp rapping on Sam's window, and Sam and Taylor both jump. The car has steamed up and they can barely make out the figure outside. There's an uncomfortable delay as Taylor fumbles to start the car so Sam can wind the window down.

'Well, that's bloody frustrating,' Harry says. 'We need this Romanian bringing in pronto. I've issued a Force-wide alert. We'll engage the press, too.'

'Harry . . . ?' Sam says, bewildered. 'What are you doing here?'

'You didn't think I'd miss the arrest, did you? I was waiting in the backup vehicle.'

He was waiting to escort Andrei Albescu into New Scotland

Yard in handcuffs, Sam thinks, in front of all the cameras. To claim the credit.

'You get anything useful from the wife?' he asks. 'Maybe we should bring her in for questioning?'

'Sir,' Sam begins, 'Nadja didn't seem surprised to see us. Something more is going on here. I'm sure she was trying to tell me something before we got interrupted. Plus, there's no way someone living like that has cash to spend on printing *How to Get Away with Murder*. I accept Albescu is our arsonist but something doesn't feel right to me. I think we leave Nadja where she is – she's not going anywhere, and we might get more from her next time if we keep her on side. I'm convinced Andrei Albescu isn't Denver Brady. In fact, we had a promising breakthrough just before—'

'Nonsense,' Harry scoffs. 'It was the Romanian who burned the printers down, and I reckon that now we have a warrant and can do some proper digging, the evidence will mount. He's our man. Follow the facts, Sam, not . . .' – Harry waves his hand around in the air – 'intuition.'

Sam sits back in her seat, feeling like her godfather's words have just slapped her in the face. He'd always told her to trust her instincts, follow her intuition. Why, when it doesn't suit his agenda, is he so—

'With all due respect, sir,' Taylor speaks up, 'DI Hansen has a superb theory about Betty's nephew, who is likely responsible for her murder and is most probably Denver Brady.'

'Young man,' Harry spits, 'we follow evidence. Means, motive, opportunity. The arson led us here. A solid lead. One that would hold up in a courtroom. Bring in the Romanian and do it quickly so we can rule him in or out of Charlotte's murder.' Harry turns and walks away, climbing into a waiting black van.

Sam runs her thumb over the soothingly smooth surface of Charlotte's netball keyring as they watch the other vehicle drive away. Taylor starts the car, but doesn't put it in gear, sitting still instead, gripping the steering wheel.

'I have a really bad feeling that we're doing exactly what Denver Brady *and* Charlotte's killer want us to do, assuming I'm right and Charlotte's is a copycat,' Sam says. 'We're following the breadcrumbs they've left us, but they're leading us away from the killers, not towards them. In the meantime, they're both still out there, free to kill again.'

## Technology for Modern Murderers

You do not have to be a tech genius to understand the world of digital forensics. Even aspiring serial killers of the third age, or those who do not speak great English, can excel at utilizing modern technology. I know – the prospect of having your devices monitored and your online actions recorded can be intimidating. But approach this chapter with an open mind and you'll find most of it is common sense.

First off, you need to remember that every internet-enabled device, both yours and your victim's, is trackable at all times. This includes your car satnav, the little fobs that are part of your car keys, and even your trusty Kindle. Cameras and microphones are everywhere. Our laptops, computers and phones are as effective as semen in fertilizing forensics reports. We all use these devices, and many of you will be addicted to a variety of apps that mean you already have a digital persona. Your Instagram profile, for example, is a digital version of you living your best life. You need to take as much care over your digital self as you do your physical self. If you are arrested in the metaverse, you're equally likely to be holding on tight to your soap in the real world.

While your digital activity, and that of your victims, can pose a risk, there is also the opportunity to use it to your advantage. Take tracking, for instance. Even the simplest of mobile phones have tracking features. You can pop a tracking device into your intended victim's satchel and discover their regular routes; people rarely deviate from their usual journeys and routines. Perhaps you could be really creative and use a tracked phone to lure a victim to where you want them to be by posing as someone else. Tracking can be very useful when properly understood.

As well as technology to track your physical movements, there's also tracking to follow your activity on your electronic device. This means that every stroke of your keyboard or tap of your phone screen can be tracked from elsewhere. However, the ability of law enforcement to perform activity tracking is significantly exaggerated in the movies. The average murder investigation in the UK, Europe or even the U, is far more mundane, and officers will instead physically search through your phone or laptop. It will then be sent to a lab for more in-depth analysis and the recovery of deleted files, etc. This takes time and can only be done when your device is physically present and the hard drive is in good condition. I recommend using so-called burner phones, bought using cash, which have none any of your real data on them. There are countless YouTube videos to help you get going with burner phones. Keep one 'real' phone that you use for family activity, and never use it for research or communication related to killing.

Never take your phone with you when you're out enjoying yourself. Your phone randomly being turned off (to avoid being tracked) when you enter the victim's proximity is very damning. Several cases have been won in recent times using a mountain of circumstantial evidence of this sort, one of which hinged on the fact that the killer's phone had not been switched off for more than three months, then suddenly there was a three-hour window of nothingness. So, take care. Leave your phone wherever you're going to claim to have been, should you need an alibi. If this is a public venue, simply secrete your phone somewhere safe and leave it connected to the venue's Wi-Fi across your murder window.

Remember that your victim will have a phone on them, too. You might want to use this to your advantage and leverage the phone to incriminate someone else. For example, you could attach your victim's phone to a power bank and plant it in someone else's house or car. This will mean that the phone is active for days after your victim is dead, thus reducing the accuracy of the police's timeline and implying that someone else was involved.

If you're keen on harnessing the power of technology, you can even learn to use the dark web. Honestly, it's far more user-friendly than you might imagine.

The internet is made up of three parts. Currently, you use only two of these. The first layer includes websites carefully curated by search engines such as Google and browsers like Safari. Maybe you're even old enough to remember Ask Jeeves. (I miss Jeeves – whatever happened to him?)

The second layer is known as the deep web. This is where all the websites exist that are not accessible to the public via search engines – for example, private company databases, banks and paywalled sites. Our emails live on the deep web, as does the private content of our social media (or so we are told).

These two upper layers account for 99 per cent of the

internet that we use. However, hidden at the bottom is the dark web. It sounds sinister because of its name, but a lot of it is pretty legit. The BBC is on the dark web. Their mirror site was launched there so that people in countries where democratic content is blocked can access it. Not that I'm pushing the old Beeb. ProPublica is the only outlet I trust for news, personally.

There is a darker part of the dark web, of course. You can find some stunning artwork in this area of the internet. You can also find some sites and sights that are enough to trouble even the most troubled mind. It's a surprisingly friendly place. You can join forums and social networks for like-minded people with similar interests to yours. I've met many a chum in these forums. Some of them have gone on to become lifelong friends. Others are nuts.

I met Gerry in a dark-web chat room and we became friends. Actually, I started out as his client because, despite my best efforts, I'd been unable to snap out of my grief following the loss of my dear Tony, shortly after Richie was convicted of the lovely Mel's murder. I had acquired a fresh pet from a shelter a few days after Tony's demise but I found that I could not love Tony the Second as I had his predecessor. In all honesty, I was contemplating tying the usurper to a lamp-post and commending him to his fate.

I found Gerry through an advert he'd placed in a forum. He offers counselling services to individuals of various tastes, in the secure, anonymous chat rooms of the dark web. You see, Gerry used to be a doctor, but he vacated that role when the morgue assistant began wrestling with apprehensions about the private arrangement that he and Gerry had made.

Gerry had come to believe that people, his own parents included, used a condition known as PTSD as an excuse for wallowing, drinking and generally failing in life. To prove this hypothesis, he needed to conduct some under-the-radar medical tests. He came across a dark site called *Human Experiments*, a group made up of people wishing to prove controversial ideas by necessary but occasionally fatal experiments. They're a bit like Flat Earthers, but much more rational.

Dr Gerry recruited a number of PTSD sufferers, mainly veterans from the homeless population. He secured the participants to an electrified dentist chair with a small TV screen above it, and monitored their brains and physical reactions while they were bombarded with war footage, complete with soundtrack, and exposed to the smells of barbequing meat and rotting fruit. If they reacted, they were given an electric shock. Gerry theorized that reverse conditioning would swiftly occur and their PTSD would vanish. However, it did not. He turned up the electric shock each time until he was Liam-Neesoming the shit out of them. Still, no results. It was a hard lesson for Gerry and he took to his bed for several months after the trials failed. I digress.

As well as meeting interesting people like Gerry on the dark web, you can also conduct private transactions, message anonymously, and secretly recruit people to do illegal things for you. There are marketplaces, too – just like Amazon and eBay, but without any rules. These are truly liberating. You can buy anything your heart (or other parts of your body) desires. Check out my favourite store – Humanleather.com. It's vegan.

As a serial killer, the dark web has so much to offer. You can purchase all kinds of drugs, from sedatives that don't show on tox reports to recreational substances and serums. Specialist equipment can be found, should your tastes be more niche, or perhaps you're a collector and would like to procure a swatch of Aileen Wournos's knickers. The usual items are available, too: untraceable phones, phoney preloaded debit cards, mule bank accounts, dropboxes and so on. I know that technology can be really frustrating, but I promise the dark web is worth the effort.

I realize I'm pushing this hard, but the dark web has a particularly special place in my heart. You see, I'm a bit of a wallflower and the internet has helped me to make friends globally who have similar interests. I confess, I haven't travelled much in my life, although I hope to take some Saga tours in my older years.

But let me tell you about the one holiday I did take, during which I met Amy, the love of my life.

# 13

Dr Pete Thomson is the last person Sam expects to see when she arrives at work on Thursday morning, yet he's standing in the doorway to Harry's office, smiling at her and holding a box of Lindt chocolate balls. Behind him, Harry is busy trying to organize a press conference so that he can plaster Andrei Albescu's face all over the news.

'Who's he?' Taylor asks when Sam freezes as they step off the elevator to the fourth floor. Sam doesn't respond. She doesn't want Taylor to know that her therapist has tracked her down because she's skipped every appointment he's offered her over the past couple of weeks and shouldn't be at work today. A dark shadow falls over Taylor's face, and she wonders fleetingly if he could be thinking that the doctor is her boyfriend. His eyes darken and he steps closer to her as Pete comes towards them, leaving Harry to his phone call. Her neck prickles at Taylor's proximity. Most of her wants to lean into the heat of him, but she does the opposite, for both their sakes.

'Samantha,' Dr Thomson says, from a few paces away. 'Ouch, that's a shiner,' he adds as he gets closer. 'What happened to your eye?'

'*Samantha?*' Taylor mutters. 'No one calls you that.'

'Taylor,' Sam replies, more sharply than she means to. 'Claire, the linguist I sent *How to Get Away With Murder* to, has sent me her report. Can you take a look and summarize it? . . . Now, please?'

He looks at her, something like anger bubbling in his expression. She wants to ask him to say it aloud, whatever is bothering him, but now isn't the time. She's suddenly very aware of his scent – sweat and expensive musk – and of the hot moisture on her skin. She turns away from him and ushers the doctor towards the small meeting room.

'You missed last week's session,' Dr Thomson says, 'and the one before that, and—'

'Do you normally do house calls, Doc?' Sam asks. 'Or *work* calls? Look, I'm sorry I missed my sessions but there is a killer in this city and it's only a matter of time before he strikes—'

'I saw the press conference,' he says. For her, it feels like months ago that Nigel Mathers had thrown *How to Get Away With Murder* to the press, but it was only the week before last. 'Harry's just told me he's made you SIO in a combined child-homicide and serial-killer investigation. I've told him what I'll tell you now, Samantha: it's too soon.'

'Joint SIO,' Sam says, sounding pedantic even to her own ears.

'Harry isn't doing right by you here, Samantha,' the doctor says. Then he lowers his voice to a whisper and adds, 'He's doing what's best for the Met . . . for himself. I have to say it as I see it, Samantha. Harry is putting you at serious risk of—'

'Stop,' Sam whispers. 'Please.' She stares out through the room's glass walls. The room beyond is as frenetic as a beehive but less well organized. On the whiteboard in the middle of the room, a child with green eyes stares back. 'Look out there, Doc. See her face? That's Charlotte Mathers. Fourteen and dead. Tomorrow, we could have another one just like her. I can't think about Harry now.'

'I brought you these.' Dr Thomson sighs sadly, placing the chocolates on the table between them. Sam wipes her eyes and reaches for a chocolate, pulling both ends of the wrapper and watching the red ball spin, the foil peeling back to reveal the confection beneath. She pops it in her mouth. It's warm, but all the better for it. Sam doesn't thank the doctor, though. She resents him for knowing how much she enjoys these chocolates. Resents him for knowing everything about her. Even resents him for suggesting that Harry isn't doing the right thing by her now. Because the leap she doesn't want to make is simple: Harry hasn't done what's best for her for a long time – not now, and not in the past, when it really mattered. It's easy to treat people well when it costs you nothing, but Harry will always put his best interests first. The weight of it is too much to bear, even though she knows in her own bones that it's the truth. Harry's been part of her family for as long as she can remember, and since the death of her father he's been the only family she has left. The dawning understanding that he's failing her feels like too much to shoulder. She sags in the chair, as if the pressure of it is bearing down on her body.

They sit in silence for a few minutes, until Dr Thomson asks, 'How are you coping really, Samantha?'

She shrugs and reaches for the jug of water that no one ever seems to change. It tastes of plastic, but she downs it and pours herself another cup. 'I think I might have figured out who Denver Brady is,' she says. 'It's more of a theory, really. We just need some physical evidence. I'm fairly confident Denver didn't kill Charlotte, and that the person who did is a copycat.'

'OK,' the doctor says. Then he waits, letting the silence stretch so she feels the urge to fill it.

'I got a dog,' she volunteers.

'That's great,' he smiles. 'What's it called?'

'Toni, I've called him.'

'Strange name for a dog?' He raises an eyebrow.

'I don't know why I've called him that. I think my head is so full of Denver . . . I was calling the dog Little Scruff and then "Toni" just slipped out. When I registered him at the vet, I made it Toni with an 'i', not Tony with a 'y', so . . .'

The doctor says nothing.

'He's got a wonky leg,' she adds. 'Bad breath. A snaggle tooth. He's honestly a bit of a wreck. But I love him all the more for it. Sometimes, what is healed mends stronger than something never broken.' No response. She sees him notice the little netball she's clasping in her hand. 'It's Charlotte's,' she says, without waiting for him to ask. 'A netball. Her friend gave it to me. Asked me to carry it with me until I find the killer.'

'How does carrying a dead child's token around with you make you feel, Sam?'

She doesn't respond. She's not even sure she knows the answer, but the word *pressured* rumbles around her brain. She curls forward in the chair, resting her head in her hands. Closes her eyes. The silence in the room is so loud. She hears Dr Thomson swallow, the creak of faux leather as he shifts in the cheap chair. She opens her eyes. The doctor is sitting, still and calm, waiting. She sighs.

She's going to have to tell the doctor something meaningful, or he won't leave. She can't tell him about the full-blown panic attack she had in Newcastle. A panic attack triggered by seeing an abused woman who reminded her of her mother. Or that the panic attack had left her unconscious in Taylor's arms, then vomiting on to Newcastle's cobbles. She's also keenly aware that her drinking on the job, even if she's only done it once in her life, needs to stay between her and Taylor. If that gets out, she can kiss goodbye to her career. The very thought of him knowing this about her, on top of every detail he's already privy to, makes her temples throb. So, she'd better say something else.

'I cope with it,' she says. 'But I can't cope with . . . I can't look at the crime-scene photos from Charlotte Mathers' murder. Now I'm joint SIO, I'm meant to look at them. I *need* to look at them. But I can't.'

'Thanks for telling me, Samantha,' Dr Thomson says. 'You know that avoidance behaviour is a classic response to the trauma cascade. Remember the story I told you about the woman who was mugged outside a reggae club and now can't hear that music without having a panic attack? She avoids the radio, TV, even restaurants for fear of encountering that trigger.'

'There's no reason why I should avoid the crime scene photographs of Charlotte's murder, though. It's not linked in any way to my own problems.'

'Not directly, no,' Dr Thomson concedes, 'but your original trauma is from childhood, Sam. Finding both your parents dead – your mother when you were nine, your father when you were nineteen. It's all linked. The reason the encounter with DS Lowry caused your breakdown months ago was because his actions triggered your trauma response. It doesn't matter how different those events are; it's still—'

A knock on the glass cuts the doctor short. Taylor gestures for Sam to come out, but she shakes her head, surprised to find that she wants to hear the rest of what Dr Thomson has to say. Taylor reddens slightly, then tries the door. Locked. Taylor tries mouthing something to her but Sam turns away.

'On a completely different note, Samantha,' Dr Thomson says, watching Taylor walk away. 'You do know that that young man . . . how do I say it? Looks at you in a certain way that—'

'There's nothing going on,' she snaps. She gulps down more of the stale water, wincing at the unpleasant tang.

'Are you still tasting flavours that aren't really there?' the doctor asks. She nods, sneaking a glance at Taylor, who's gone back to his desk. What could it mean, how he looks at her and how he behaved just now when he saw Dr Thomson? There's more than ten years between them and Taylor could choose any woman he wanted.

'Sam, I asked how you're managing your symptoms? The phantom tastes; the concentration, energy levels and headaches were all troubling—'

'Fine. I take paracetamol. My trainee makes me tea constantly,' she says. 'I use mints, too. My energy has been OK, but my concentration and focus ... I'm trying to read this book for the case and to be honest it's gruelling. I have to read every sentence twice, and I can only manage a chapter at a time. It's taking me ages. But I've never told you about tasting anything. How could you know?'

'The chocolates. You hold them in your mouth. I've seen it in other patients, too. Chewing gum, boiled sweets ... Samantha, tasting things that aren't there, hearing things, even seeing things: these are common symptoms of—'

'I know, Doc.' She sighs. 'I'm sorry I wasn't open with you before.'

'Don't worry,' he reassures her. 'You're obviously making progress, Samantha, but you really need to stick to your reduced hours and please don't skip any more sessions. And over the next few weeks, we can build up to looking at those crime-scene photos.'

'I haven't got a few weeks, Doc,' Sam protests. 'He's out there now. A killer. He could murder someone tonight.'

'And you really think that by looking at some photographs you could stop him?' the doctor asks. 'You're taking on too much personal responsibility for ...'

... Dr Thomson keeps talking but his words make Sam's heart race. *You could stop him.* She thinks of Past Sam, of the clues she'd gleaned from photographs or the crime scenes themselves. Clues that had seen a suspect identified and locked up within just a day or two. *He could murder someone tonight.*

Sam bolts to her feet. 'I need to look at the crime scene photos straight away!' she blurts. 'You're right – I could stop him. I could save a girl's life just by—'

'That's not what I said, Samantha – quite the opposite. You're twisting—'

'I'm going to do it right now,' she says, moving to the door. 'Doc, you should leave.'

'Why not come by for a proper session tomorrow?' Dr Thomson offers. 'We could tackle the photos then if—'

'No,' she says, opening the door. She walks directly to her desk and finds the brown envelope, before quickly re-entering the meeting room and locking the door once again. She slams it down on the table with more force than she'd intended. 'You really should leave, Doc.'

Sam takes a couple of deep breaths. Wipes her palms on her trousers. *I can do this*, she tells herself, running her hand over the coarse cardboard of the envelope. Her fingers tremble as she opens the gummy flap and slides the photographs out. Mercifully, they're face down, but Dr Thomson still takes a sharp breath in.

'It's okay, Doc,' Sam assures him, 'I can do this. You should go, and I'll see you tomorrow – I promise.'

He swallows, straightening in his chair. 'No, if you're really doing this now, it's best I'm here. I'll close my eyes.' He briefly drops his head into his hands and mutters, 'Jesus Christ.'

'Sure?' she checks. He nods. 'OK. Look away now, Doc.'

Charlotte's skin is pale. The contrast with the bright green of her school uniform is striking. The girl looks almost translucent. She's curled up beneath an oak tree, her head resting against its giant trunk. Rough bark against such a delicate cheek. Her red hair is free from debris and a few strands fall gently over her face. Her eyes are closed. Her hands rest on her lap. On the grass in front of her, her school bag and various possessions are strewn about. The messiness of the everyday objects is jarring next to the almost saintly serenity of the dead child. Sam breathes. She knows there's nothing serene about this, not at all. This death wasn't holy, it was violent and ugly. Too quick and too slow, agony and the obliteration of a soul.

Sam's breath comes in erratic bursts. She tries to pour herself more water from the jug, but it slops on to the carpet. Dr Thomson opens his eyes, gently takes the jug and fills her cup. She gulps the water. She looks up at the doctor, thanks him. His eyes are skyward, roaming above her head, deliberately avoiding glimpsing the pictures in her hands. He really doesn't want to see these photographs. *Police officers deal with more trauma every day than most people will in a whole year*, Sam remembers Harry saying to her on the very first day of her induction. Seeing the fear in the doctor's eyes strengthens her resolve. *This is my job*, she thinks. *I can put this man behind bars.* Her breathing eases slightly.

Still on the first photograph, Sam holds it closer to her face, examining each of the objects in turn. There are a couple of school books – *Blood Brothers* and *GCSE PE*, books for exams Charlotte will never take – and, of course, *How to Get Away With Murder*. There's also a foldable hairbrush, various lip glosses, vanilla body spray, a compact mirror, concealer, sanitary pads, and pens. Plus a Squishmallow soft toy, a plastic Troll doll with pink hair, and a Boost chocolate bar.

'Take a break if you need to,' Dr Thomson says. Sam declines, holds her breath and turns to the next photograph. It's a close-up of a tree trunk. She exhales. Some of the bark has been hacked away, exposing the lighter, softer fibres beneath. In an asymmetrical heart shape, she sees the initials: *CM + DB*. Sam rotates the photograph and examines it from a different angle. The carving is precise. Not at all rushed. It clearly took time – at least half an hour, the expert they consulted had told them, and that was the minimum time needed. Not to mention the preparation. Tools were used. Tools and time. Very risky, to linger in a public park with a dead body, just to carve a tree. Unless the killer carved this before the murder. But not even Charlotte herself knew she would be in the park that night. Perhaps he carved some of it earlier and left the centre space blank for his victim's initials. Sam squints at the 'CB', holding the image at the end of her nose. The letters don't appear to have been hastily added – they're equally well crafted.

'"Mobile phones have tracking features",' Sam says aloud. '"You can pop a tracking device into your intended victim's satchel and find out their regular routes; people rarely deviate from their usual journeys . . . Perhaps you could be really creative and use a tracked phone to lure a victim to where you want them to be . . . Tracking can be very useful when properly understood."' She's amazed at the accuracy of her recall. She'd read Denver's chapter about the dark web several times in a row, even taking it into the shower with her and propping it up on the soap shelf so she could read it again, but even so.

'Pardon?' says Dr Thomson, his eyes still squeezed closed.

'Thanks, Doc,' Sam says, standing up and sliding the rest of the photographs back inside the envelope without looking at them. 'You can relax now. They're gone. It's over.' Dr Thomson lets out a breath of relief and opens his eyes, blinking rapidly. His face is pale and his skin clammy.

Sam struggles to keep calm as she walks the doctor to the elevator. Her mind races with her discovery and she presses the button for the ground floor over and over again until the lift finally chimes and the doctor steps in. Even before the doors have closed, Sam spins on her heel.

'Taylor!' she calls. 'Adam Taylor!'

'Here,' he says from behind her. He's standing at the small kitchenette, three cups lined up and the kettle in his hands. Taylor looks over her shoulder to where Dr Thomson has just disappeared behind the lift's closing doors. 'Taylor, find Tina, bring Chloe too, and meet me in the briefing room,' she says. 'I think I've found a clue.'

Taylor places mugs of tea down in front of Tina, Chloe and Sam. He doesn't meet Sam's eye and the distance this creates unnerves her, but she can't deal with that now so she takes her tea gratefully, then puts the two crime-scene photographs she was looking at in the middle of the table. They're sitting in the large briefing room, around one end of the table. On the whiteboard behind them are the case notes and Charlotte Mathers' photograph. Sam's phone buzzes: another email from DI Duggan.

'Aw, cute,' Chloe coos, catching a glimpse of Sam's phone screen. 'Is that your dog?'

'Ma'am,' Taylor says, 'I didn't mean to interrupt your meeting with that gentleman. But I wanted to tell you immediately that I've received a call from DI Neil Duggan at Northumbria Police. Duggan confirmed that Betty's son Robert Brown attended Northumbria University. Bobby's death certificate says . . .' Taylor pauses and pulls out his phone. 'Robert Albert Brown. Aged 22. Cause of death: Accidental. 1A – drowning. 1B – Fall into a river. Location: Tynemouth.' So, your theory about Bobby potentially being both Denver's cousin and Betty's son seems to be adding up. Duggan has been working to track down a current address for Betty and Albert Brown's nephew for some time and he's proving very difficult to locate. Apparently Duggan put a lot of effort into finding him when he tried to get Betty's case reopened – sent letters to all known addresses, social media, DVLA, the usual – but got no response. In all likelihood, the nephew has concealed his identity.'

'Congratulations, Detective Hansen,' Edris says, her voice laced with resentment. 'I'm not sure why I'm in this meeting, though. I still stand by what I said to the DCI about us sharing the SIO—'

'And I agree with you,' Sam says, genuinely. 'I'm not ready to be SIO. Look, Tina, I'm sorry – OK? You said that Harry wasn't doing the right thing by us and you're right. Harry has failed me before, when I needed him most. But at other times in my life, he's been more than a godfather to me. It's difficult to reconcile, and I lashed out. I'm sorry about what I said to you.'

'Mmm,' Tina says. 'All right. I suggest that we approach DCI Blakelaw again and attempt to—'

'My therapist, who you all just saw out there, has told Harry himself that I shouldn't be SIO. But I know Harry better than any of you, and no one will change his mind once it's made up.'

Tina opens her mouth to respond, but instead she turns her eyes to the crime-scene photographs and stares at them as though she hasn't seen them a thousand times before.

'Your *therapist*?' Taylor asks, and Sam tries not to hear the relief in his voice. She can't look at him right now, not given what Dr Thomson has just said about how Taylor looks at her. The idea that there's something between them makes her cheeks burn. It's not something she has space to process at the moment, so she returns her attention to the matter at hand.

'I have another theory,' Sam begins—

'Exciting,' chirps Chloe, smiling and leaning forward.

Sam points to the photograph showing Charlotte positioned as if asleep against the tree trunk. With her finger, she gently circles first the girl's body, then the items scattered on the ground.

'Notice the contrast between the precise positioning of Charlotte's body and the disorganized scattering of her possessions?'

They all nod.

'I don't think this is a coincidence; I think the killer scattered the belongings in a great rush, after the murder and the positioning of Charlotte's body, and having carved the initials into the tree. That's when he tipped out her school bag. It was dark and he was probably in a frenzy. But why would he have been composed about the murder, then so panicked at this point?' Sam taps her fingers on the photograph showing Charlotte's things.

'It's a good question,' Chloe says. 'The profiler suggested that the killer was searching for a trophy and possibly took one, though Nigel Mathers couldn't say precisely what possessions his daughter was carrying that day.'

'He was searching for something, all right,' Sam says.

'What's your theory, ma'am?' Taylor asks.

'No money was found in the bag. Could be simple robbery,'

Chloe offers, although her tone suggests she doesn't believe theft to be the reason at all.

'I don't think he was looking for money,' Sam says. 'Charlotte's Rolex wasn't taken. I think Charlotte's killer had hidden a tracker in her satchel and used it to follow her route home that night. Just like Denver describes in the chapter about how killers can use technology to their advantage.'

'The one about the dark web?' asks Chloe. 'That all seemed implausible to me. Human experiments in bunkers? Surely—'

'I will refer you to some cases later, Detective Constable Spears,' Tina cuts in, 'but we have a murderer at large and now is not the time.' Tina gestures at Sam to continue.

'So far, we've been working on the understanding that no one knew Charlotte would be in the park that night, because Charlotte herself didn't know she'd be walking home,' Sam says, her voice feverish. 'Only Jessica and Jamil Patel knew that she had left their house on foot. Possibly Nigel Mathers, too, although he claimed to be asleep. So, we've assumed Charlotte was either chosen at random or followed by one of those three people. *But* . . . what if I'm right about the tracker? That blows our suspect pool wide open. It could be anyone who had access to her bag. Someone at school, on the bus, in her home – there's a housekeeper, a gardener, probably other staff, too. Charlotte had walked home from Jessica's on other occasions when Nigel had fallen asleep. Someone could have been tracking her and known in advance that she sometimes took that route.'

'Denver says that people rarely alter their routes,' Chloe offers.

'The case has indeed been based on the assumption that very few people knew Charlotte's whereabouts on the night she died,' Tina says, brow puckered. 'If someone had placed a tracker in Charlotte's bag on an earlier occasion, that would change things considerably.'

'Exactly,' Sam says. 'I think we should look again at the people close to Charlotte. Her dad, uncle, friends, teachers, and so on – anyone who could have slipped a tracker into her bag. That's how we catch Charlotte's killer.'

Everyone is frozen for a moment, then one by one they look at one another, nodding. Taylor begins to pace the room. Chloe pulls out her notebook as if wanting to review her notes through this new lens.

Tina purses her lips, evaluating the information. 'An interesting theory, Detective,' she says, breaking the silence. 'May I suggest that I run with it and you concentrate on Denver Brady and Andrei Albescu? Otherwise, it is like a giant jigsaw, and you're trying to manage too many pieces.'

Sam hesitates. She would give up chasing Denver in a heartbeat if it meant she could be the one to arrest Charlotte's killer. It's all that really matters to her. But she can see that Tina's suggestion is her colleague offering an olive branch after her angry words.

'OK, Tina,' Sam nods, 'let's do that.'

'Where are you with Denver?' Tina asks.

'I think Betty's nephew is our Denver Brady,' Sam says, without preamble, 'and that there's some other explanation as to why Andrei Albescu burned down Swinton's Printers. Perhaps Betty's nephew knows Albescu—'

'You should know, ma'am,' Taylor says to Sam, sitting down and leaning back as if keeping himself away from the bomb he's about to drop. 'While I think your theory on Denver being Betty's nephew is solid, the evidence that Denver is in fact a Romanian named Andrei Albescu is mounting.'

'Mounting how?'

'DC Chen submitted a warrant and has accessed Albescu's bank accounts,' Taylor continues. 'Andrei Albescu receives weekly payments from an account in the Cayman Islands. He had more than ten thousand pounds in a separate savings—'

'Ten grand?' Sam almost spits out her tea. 'He has money and his family live like—'

'I know, ma'am.' Taylor looks down at the floor.

'Did you say *had* ten grand?' Sam asks.

Taylor nods sullenly. 'It was withdrawn yesterday, and Nadja and the children have vanished.'

'Ugh.' Sam holds her face in her hands. 'Ten grand is a lot,' she says through her fingers, 'but . . .' She lets the thought drift into silence.

'That's pretty damning evidence against this Albescu guy,' Chloe says. 'He burned down the place that printed the how-to guide and received the profit from book sales. It's not much of a stretch to conclude that Andrei wrote the book, too. I still don't see how *How to Get Away With Murder* links to Charlotte, though.'

'I'm not sure it does,' Sam says, rubbing her tired face. 'We've never been sure there's a concrete link between the book and Charlotte Mathers.'

'Then why did someone carve Denver's initials into the tree next to Charlotte's body?' Chloe persists.

'We've known from the start that there are three possibilities,' Sam says. 'Either Denver is a serial killer and he murdered Charlotte; or Denver is a real killer but a copycat murdered Charlotte; or, finally – and it's the option I'm most confident about ruling out – Denver is an innocent fantasist who made the whole book up. The copycat carved Denver's initials in the tree and left his book there to misdirect the investigation.'

'Two killers,' Chloe breathes. 'The copycat who killed Charlotte and—'

'Denver himself. And he's the one who killed Betty.'

'DI Hansen?' A civilian colleague stands in the doorway. 'We've got a woman downstairs. Apparently, she's met Denver.'

## *It's A Love Story*

I met her at Venice Beach, next to the skatepark near the Muscle Beach gym. I'd spent a sunny morning watching the skateboarders fly around the kidney-shaped bowl while tourists milled about and locals in Lycra jogged or roller-bladed by. Gaggles of nomads with van-life or similarly incomprehensible aspirations lingered beneath the palms and entertainers of various types performed mini 'shows' – 'entertainers' being a stretch here; they were vagrants with juggling pins and the like.

I digress. Back to Amy. I've never seen a dirtier woman in all my days. Hair in black-and-pink clumps that weren't far from dreadlocks. Long fingernails rimmed with grime. Brown teeth and a scrawny frame that spoke of years of poor choices. A single gold front tooth – an incisor, I believe – that reminded me Joe Pesci's burglar character in *Home Alone*.

One of the 'shows' on offer was a hanging-bar competition. Quite simply, two pull-up bars were positioned side by side and people took turns to dangle in pairs for as long as they could. Passers-by placed wagers on their favourite. A pot of dollars went to whoever hung on the longest.

Amy's hustle was simple. Working with the guy running the show, Amy would pose as a passer-by.

They'd drum up as much interest as they could by selecting a burly man from the crowd to compete with her. Everyone laughing, cheering and filling the pot with green. Once she'd squeezed them dry, Amy would dangle next to the sweating beast until he inevitably let go of the bar before she did. Amy made it look like a close contest. Her sinewy arms looked the part and her short shorts kept everyone's attention as she wiggled around, supposedly trying to hold on. No one ever suspected the little cuff around her wrist that hooked over the bar. Amy and the man who owned the pull-up bars would split the winnings, then she'd come back a few hours later and do it all over again.

I winked at Amy as she panted beneath a palm tree after her last performance. She got up and followed me along the sidewalk a short way. The stench of the woman was overpowering. It was enough to dissuade me and I was about to walk away when she said:

'Ain't nothing you wanna do that I ain't done before, mister. You ain't gonna surprise ol' Amy.'

She wasn't old, of course – my late mother would have said that Amy had just had a rough paper round. Perhaps she was twenty-five, but her own bad choices made her look almost double that. I slipped her a hundred-dollar bill, and told her to clean up and meet me on Santa Monica Pier that evening.

She wore baggy hippy pants and a bikini top, and was much more fragrant after her shower. We rode the rollercoasters and played in the arcade. I wore shades and a baseball cap at all times.

Afterward, we took a stroll down the beach. We walked a long way. When we hit a secluded stretch, Amy stopped and tried to kiss me in the moonlight, but I could still see the brown of her teeth. I feigned shyness and she called me 'sugar', and started telling me about her older brother who fucked her in her granddaddy's barn. She said the old man had thrown her out when she told him what the boy had done. Called her a cock tease. Perhaps one day, a pathetic police profiler will speculate that I, too, am impotent or was myself fucked in a barn as a child. Profilers are oxygen thieves.

It was Amy who decided to strip naked and run into the sea. Her body was youthful, firm and strong. She whooped as the cold waves hit her. After much cajoling, I agreed to join her and we frolicked together in the salty water. Amy hung her arms around my neck and tried to kiss me again. I was becoming annoyed, so I held her underwater for a while to drown her lust. When she resurfaced, instead of being angry, she was more aroused than before.

'Do it again,' she spluttered, 'but put your hands around my neck this time.'

Only too happy to play whatever game this was turning into, I obliged. This time, I kept her below for a little longer and when I let her up she was desperate. Rubbing at my cock and thrusting her buttocks into me.

'Fuck me,' she begged. I realized then that this was one seriously unhinged woman. I dunked her again – longer this time. She took a while to catch her breath, but when she did, she said the strangest thing. 'You want to kill me, don't you?' she said. I couldn't believe my ears but I've always found dishonesty distasteful, so I nodded.

'Mmm, yes,' she moaned. 'How do you want this to go?'

'Well,' I said, a little off-guard and needing to think

fast, 'I'm going to nick your arm. Then you'll bleed out – the salt water will make sure of that . . .'

'Mmm,' she said, rubbing my chest with her tiny breasts.

'Then you'll fuck me as I'm bleeding?' she asked.

'Sure, you'll be well and truly fucked,' I said, honestly.

'What's the safe word?' she asked, and I thought about it.

'Let's keep it simple,' I said. 'The safe word is "Stop".'

She nodded and held out her arm. I took off my glasses, popped a lens and with some considerable force managed to crack it in two. I cut deep, long and vertically right up the forearm. It was far more than the 'nick' I'd promised her. She bit into my shoulder, which was not entirely a turn-off, but not something I could ever get into. She wanted to begin immediately of course, but my ardour was slight, so I let her fondle me but avoided her kisses. I've always found kissing to be the most distasteful element of human copulation

It didn't take as long as I'd expected for her to start to shiver and weaken. In the moonlight, her tanned skin had a greying pallor and I held her in my arms as she no longer wanted to tread water. I took a few steps deeper. Being significantly taller than her, the water barely lapped my shoulders.

'Gee, I'm feeling a little woozy here,' she said. 'I think you cut a little deep. We should stop.' She pushed back from me slightly and made to swim to shore. Not realizing how weak she was, she floundered and turned back to cling on to my neck.

'Take me in,' she slurred. 'Stop.'

I stepped a little deeper. I was up to my chin in the water, balancing on my toes.

'P . . . please,' she whispered. 'Stop. It's the . . . safe word. I'm saying, "Stop".'

Her body clinging to mine was as light as a tiny, trembling bird. She tried to swim ashore again but didn't get far before she began to drown. Somehow, she made it back to me. Gripping on for dear life. Her nails dug into my shoulders. I ran my hands over her nipples.

'S-s . . . stop,' she begged through chattering teeth. Her whole body shuddered against me. She tried to scream but she was close to passing out. 'Please . . . s . . . stop.'

I liked her. I admit it. I liked a lot of my victims, to be truthful about it.

I didn't want Amy to die without me fulfilling her initial desires. I'd feel bad about that later . . . maybe. Then I made sure I stayed with her in the water until I'd been unable to find a pulse for a good ten minutes. In my sentimentality, I kissed her on the forehead and bid her a gentle goodbye. The fish would take care of her now.

I flew home to the UK and didn't read or watch the news for a while. A few months later, though, I did do some searching. Amy had wound up mangled in the propeller of a fancy yacht coming into harbour at Marina del Rey, just south of Venice. The news article was short. There was no picture and that made me genuinely sad as I can't remember her face. Nor, indeed, any of their faces.

I'd very much like to see them all again.

# 14

Amy is stunning. Dark skin and multi-coloured dreadlocks, with piercings aplenty and a bright, white smile. The woman speaks in a creamy American accent and Chloe Spears blushes from her neck to her forehead. Sam takes in Chloe's mirrored body language as Amy explains that she believes she has met Denver Brady.

'Firstly, Amy, before we get into that,' Sam interjects, 'does the name Charlotte Mathers mean anything to you? Other than what you may have seen on the news.'

'No, ma'am,' Amy says, 'I'm here about Denver only. I believe I am the Amy character in his book.'

'What makes you think that?'

'I wasn't sure at first,' Amy says. 'To be honest, I skimmed the whole thing for a book club I joined. I just moved to London and wanted to meet new friends, so, I figured . . . Anyway. Sorry. Why do I think I'm Amy? Firstly, the location is right: Venice Beach. I still have a place there, as well as the one here in London. I'm a professor. I split my time between UCLA in the States and, here, at London Birkbeck.' She flicks a pink dreadlock back over her shoulder. 'That said, the "Amy" person isn't explicitly black and, as you can see, I'm a woman of colour. Plus, the Amy in *How to Get Away With Murder* is a hustler, a poor drug addict, and I'm far from that.'

'Yet you're here, claiming to be Amy?' Sam presses.

Amy doesn't respond but smiles and reaches with her forefinger to tap her pearly front tooth. Sam gets it immediately, but she can see that Chloe is confused.

'Denver says that Amy had a gold incisor,' Amy explains to Chloe.

'I paid a small fortune to have my gold tooth replaced with white enamel. Plus, other details in the chapter match a really dodgy date I had several years ago with a British guy. Finally, Denver is a rare name and my date was with a guy named Denver.'

'Tell us about the date,' Sam says, leaning forward in her chair.

'I knew from the get-go something was wrong.' Amy sighs. 'He looked nothing like his profile picture. Then again, they never do. This is why I don't date guys any more.' Next to Sam, Chloe nods eagerly, as if there's some kind of second conversation happening between the two women that Sam can't hear.

'His profile name was Denver. No surname. We chatted a little before the date and he said he had no social media presence, which I quite liked, but that also meant I couldn't check him out in advance. He said he ran a business in London and was in LA to see about opening a branch in the US.' Amy pauses, sips her water and then continues. 'We met round about sunset, at the kidney.'

'The skateboard park in Venice Beach?' Sam checks. 'Yep. My family have always called it the kidney, after the bowl that's almost the exact same shape,' Amy draws a bean in the air with her finger. 'Anyway, I knew immediately the guy was not it. The first thing he did was hand me a business card, as if to demonstrate his level of importance. He'd said he was six feet tall, but he was closer to five nine. He was sickly-pale – looked like he lived in a windowless basement. His British accent kept slipping into something strong . . .'

'Could it have been Romanian?' Sam offers, but Amy shakes her head slowly.

'No. I'm sure he was a native English speaker. It felt to me like he was actively trying to sound like a British Royal, but he couldn't stop switching to something else – like a Liverpool accent, Scottish maybe? Or perhaps whatever Ant and Dec speak.'

'Geordie,' Sam says, smiling to herself. It would fit perfectly with Betty's nephew.

Amy shrugs.

'Please describe for us, in detail, what happened next,' Chloe says.

'We walked along the promenade towards Santa Monica Pier and rode the Ferris wheel. We stopped on the way and watched a woman doing pull-ups. Trying to beat a man from the crowd. Denver was determined she was hustling – faking it. He said she must have some kind of hidden hook on her wrist. But to me, she was just a strong woman who was great at pull-ups.'

'Please try to remember everything he said to you,' Sam says.

'It's difficult, but I remember having the distinct impression that he was a bullshitter. For example, he said he had various degrees and ran a business and volunteered at a hospital and had a secretary. All kinds of lies, or what I took to be lies.'

'Why are you so convinced he was lying?' Sam presses.

'Hmm,' Amy looks up at the ceiling, concentrating. 'Because he just didn't seem that smart. I felt like he was maybe starting with a truth and then lies just built all around it.'

'How so?' Sam asks.

'For example,' Amy says, 'I teach a literature module and when I mentioned that fact about myself, he said he'd read everything Charles Dickens ever wrote. Like, he always needed to be a step beyond me. Then, when I tried to talk to him about *Oliver Twist*, it was clear to me he'd maybe seen the movie or stage show, but definitely hadn't read the book.'

'How can you know?' Chloe asks. 'Surely the story is the same?'

'Not at all,' Amy says. '*Oliver Twist* is a tragic book. It's crammed full of murder, infanticide, child abuse, domestic violence, animal cruelty. It's really, truly heartbreaking.'

'But when I saw it in the West End—' Chloe begins.

'Exactly!' Amy almost yells with enthusiasm for the topic. 'You saw little kids tap-dancing, right? And singing 'Food, Glorious Food!' Not in the book. The book is something to cry over, not sing about. It really quite annoys me that *Oliver* is so glamourized.'

'So Denver pretended to be smarter than he really is. Anything more?'

'We left the rides and walked back towards Venice,' Amy continues, 'It was dark by now and I was ready for the date to end. So I told him honestly. I thanked him for his time and wished him well.'

'Ouch,' Chloe says. 'How did he react?'

'He thought I was joking,' Amy says. 'He was so far up in his own ego, he thought I was flirting. Then – and I'll never forget this – he started unbuttoning his shirt.'

'What did you do?' Chloe says.

'I said "*Na-ah*. Don't you get that belly out!"' Amy says, and Chloe suppresses a smile. Sam gestures for Amy to go on. 'He just kept on stripping. Right there on the beach. He said he loved skinny-dipping. And I told him that I was leaving now, that no man should behave as he was doing, and asked him not to contact me again.'

'Good for you,' Sam says, genuinely impressed. She knew so many women don't voice their rejection for fear of triggering a bad reaction. Treading on eggshells, just like her mother did, doesn't keep people safe for long.

Amy shrugs. 'He blew up. Told me I had no idea who he was or what he was capable of.'

'Woah,' Chloe says.

'Mm-hmm,' confirms Amy, nodding. 'I ended it right there. I didn't even make another excuse, just walked away. I went and met some girlfriends and we laughed about it.'

'And next thing you know, you're a victim in *How to Get Away With Murder*?' Sam asks.

'Yes, ma'am,' Amy replies. 'It reads like some kind of revenge porn to me.'

'Revenge porn . . .' Sam ponders the idea. 'That's exactly what makes it the strangest chapter in the book by far, and you've just explained why. It's violent sexual fantasy.'

'Guys don't take rejection well,' Chloe states. 'Not that I'd really know.' Amy smiles.

'Amy, can you confirm if this is the man you met?' Sam asks, showing the woman a picture of Andrei Albescu on her phone. Amy takes her time, staring closely and zooming in.

'Well, I'm one hundred per cent sure that he is *not* Denver,' Amy says. 'Denver had blue eyes and a softer jawline. He had a milky complexion and mousey-blonde hair – he wasn't dark-haired and heavy-browed like this guy. Denver was completely average-looking.'

'And around five foot nine, you say? Not a tall man?' Sam continues.

'That's correct.'

Sam is keen to draw the interview to a close so she can think through the repercussions of yet another chunk of the book proving to be a lie. 'I'll need you to sit with our sketch artist and our technical expert,' she says, to wrap things up, 'so they can prepare an image and information for public circulation—'

'Wait a second, ma'am,' Amy says, 'I haven't told you the juicy bit yet.'

'There's more?' Chloe asks.

'It's in another chapter of the book. The chapter about the old lady?'

'You mean Betty?' says Sam.

'Poor, lovely Betty,' Amy sighs. 'Betty reminds me of my

Grammy. Anyway, Betty had this ring, right? A ring that he stole? Guess what our boy Denver was wearing on his pinky finger. In the moonlight, it looked like it was glowing.'

Sam knows it'll take the sketch artist a while to draw Denver's face from Amy's memory, and DC Chen said there was little hope of finding an online dating profile from years earlier, but he'd agreed to try. So, Sam spends the evening reading statements from Charlotte Mathers' family, friends, teachers and those who came into and out of her home. She knows she should be finishing Denver's book – there are only two chapters left – but she's still only got limited concentration and she's desperate to figure out who placed that tracker in Charlotte's bag. Even though she trusts that Tina is focusing on the detail, she can't resist thinking about Charlotte's case instead of Denver's book. She's more convinced than ever that Charlotte's killer and the author of *How to Get Away with Murder* are two separate men, and finding the child's murderer has always been her priority.

Toni rests his head on her leg and occasionally licks her hand or the piece of paper in it. In the background, the TV is on mute, but it's not an *Only Fools and Horses* re-run tonight. It's Harry's press conference, requesting Andrei Albescu to come forward as a person of interest in the Denver Brady case.

Sam works through the countless sheets of paper, separating those with alibis from those without. Plenty of people had access to Charlotte's school bag and could have placed a tracker in it, but only a handful of them have no alibi for the night Charlotte was murdered. Sam places Nigel Mathers, Jack Mathers, Mr Patel and Jim the gardener, along with two teachers and five school friends, in the suspect pile to be re-examined. In the absence of physical evidence, they need to build a net of circumstances that point to one individual.

She picks up Nigel Mathers' statement and reads again how

he came home and followed his usual routine: treadmill, shower, glass of whisky in his favourite chair as his dinner warmed in the oven. Then, he fell asleep. *Something isn't right*, Sam thinks, and circles a few words in the statement to revisit later.

Next, she rereads Jack Mathers' statement. He left home around 6 p.m. for a retirement party, not long after Nigel had got back from work. He didn't see Charlotte that evening and she didn't call or text him. *Odd*, Sam thinks. Why didn't she call her uncle when her father failed to show up? A little prickle runs down her neck and Toni licks her hand, sensing a change in her. She reads on. Jack left his retirement party to buy a vape refill, and his phone shows that he was there for the rest of evening until he shared a taxi home – his return was captured on the doorbell camera. He comes in and heads straight to bed, having found nothing amiss. Something niggles, feels like it's about to click into place, when suddenly Toni goes wild. The little dog leaps from the sofa with bone-breaking urgency. His fur sticks up and he barks with a rage that Sam hasn't heard before.

A moment later, there's a knock on Sam's front door. Despite knowing she's safe inside, her heart pounds as she moves into the hallway. It's past 10 p.m. – late for any caller.

'Who is it?' she calls out, feeling silly at the tremor in her voice. Maybe she should have taken her police baton from her belt.

'It's me,' says Adam Taylor.

Sam lets out a breath she didn't know she was holding, and opens the door. Toni bounces over to their visitor, who reaches down and scratches behind his ears.

'Well, you're a good guard dog,' Taylor says. 'You heard me coming a mile off, didn't you?'

'Is everything OK, Taylor? It's pretty late. I—' Sam begins, but he cuts her off as he moves through the hallway and into her lounge as if he's a frequent guest in her home.

'I need to talk to you,' he says, then adds, 'ma'am.'

Sam doesn't like his tone or the raised colour in his cheeks. Clearly, this is serious. She follows him into her lounge and quickly picks up a cup, bowl and Crunchie wrapper, dumping them in the kitchen. She returns to the lounge, flicks on her jasmine-scented plug-in diffuser and sits down on the sofa. Taylor faces her, lowering himself into her mum's old rocking chair, which squeaks at him.

'Is it about Charlotte?' Sam asks.

He shakes his head. 'I've fucked up, Sam,' he whispers. It's the second swearword Sam's ever heard him say. He looks at the floor, wipes his face. 'I've really fucked up.'

'You're scaring me, Taylor,' she says, honestly. When he looks at her, she tries to smile reassuringly, but he just holds his head in his hands. She tries Dr Thomson's technique and sits patiently, waiting for him to speak. A moment later, he stands and steps into the middle of the room, leaving the chair rocking behind him like a scene from a horror movie.

'I . . .' he tries, pacing a little, his tall body filling her tiny lounge. He sits down next to her on the sofa. It's a three-seater, but they're both tall and their knees almost touch as they face each other. 'It's just that I really care about you, Sam. I mean, ma'am. *Fuck*.'

Sam feels her throat tighten and something else. A flutter in her chest that she hasn't felt in a long time. Yes, she likes and has even come to trust Adam Taylor in the weeks they've worked together, but—

'Remember when we went to Newcastle?' he asks. Sam frowns, taken aback. She nods. 'You had that panic attack and . . .'

'And as I've said several times, I'm sorry, Taylor. That shouldn't have happened.' Sam face burns and she fiddles with the tassel on the sofa cushion. 'Like I told you before, I don't drink, honestly. I'm on medication, so I can't, and even before that I didn't —'

'Can you try to remember anything else that happened that night?' he asks. She shakes her head. 'Can you remember what happened when ... when we got back here?' His eyes flick between her and the floor. Sam feels the air leave her lungs. Her mind is wild with possibilities. Had she tried to seduce him? Been sick on him?

'Really? Nothing?' he implores, turning to face her more fully.

She feels her cheeks burning up. His eyes are much too intense. She looks away and finds herself grasping the tassel on its own, which she's unintentionally torn from the cushion.

He continues through the roar in her ears. 'I've come to really respect you, Sam. I had no idea what you were wrestling with back then. I didn't know about the—'

'PTSD?' She cuts in, not wanting to hear the letters from his mouth. 'Lots of police officers have that. One in five, would you believe?' She tries her best to ignore the wobble in her chin. 'For me, it doesn't come from work-related trauma, but things that happen at work can trigger it. Like DS Lowry running his fingers up my skirt in a pub corridor and whispering in my ear that he knows I'm gagging for it. Like my own godfather convincing me we don't have enough evidence against Lowry when it was just my word against his. *He said, she said, so ...*' She lets her words die away. It's the first time she's spoken out loud of Harry's betrayal. Even with Dr Thomson, she's maintained that Harry did the best he could for her and always has done. But now? Considering Harry's recent behaviour, it's time she faced up to the truth.

Sam feels a tear run down her cheek and lifts a hand to rub at it viciously. She hates crying. Taylor catches her hand and takes it in his, using his fingers to gently rub the tear away. His fingers linger on her cheek.

'Sam ...' he starts.

'No, Taylor,' she says and he drops his hand, leaning back to give her a little space.

'I need to tell you—'

They both jolt as Taylor's phone rings, loud and insistent. Toni jumps up, barking once again. Taylor stands, slides his phone from his back pocket, his other hand in his hair. He paces and talks for a moment, then hangs up and turns back to her.

'That was the DCI,' Taylor says. 'Andrei Albescu is at the station.'

The custody suite feels chaotic at night. Bright strip lights buzz and flicker, several guests complain loudly about the accommodation and a woman wails in the waiting room. Sam and Taylor press through and are directed to interview room number one. Sam prepares herself to take her first look at Andrei Albescu. The man who burned down the printers of *How to Get Away With Murder* and is receiving profits from the sale of the book. The man who much of the evidence points to as the most likely candidate to be Denver, whether Sam agrees or not. She tries to quell her instincts, but as soon as she turns the corner and sees Andrei, she knows. *That's not him*, she thinks. *That's not Denver Brady.*

The man is very tall – around 6ft 5. He manages to appear simultaneously skinny yet strong. His face puts him around fifty, but his dense, dark hair and heavy black eyebrows suggest he's younger. He's covered in dust and grime, and wears a labourer's outfit: navy work trousers, a tatty sweater and a beanie hat that he's removed and is kneading between his hands. Rigger boots. A couple of days' worth of stubble. Brown circles under his eyes. A nervous sweat-sheen on his brow.

None of them speak; they have instructions to wait for Harry. Albescu leans against the wall and closes his eyes, exhausted. Sam and Taylor simply stare at the man from their seats.

'He's lanky,' Taylor whispers, 'just like Richie Scott said. He'll have an accent, too.'

Sam doesn't reply. Richie Scott would love Denver Brady to confess to killing Melanie. That would be Richie's ticket out of jail, and Sam is determined not to do anything to help that along.

*Fuck Harry*, thinks Sam. 'Let's begin,' she says smoothly. 'Take a seat please, Mr Albescu.'

Taylor opens his mouth to object, but catches the look in her eye and starts the interview recording. He goes through the formalities – the caution, the introductions, recording protocols – and assures Albescu that this is an interview to aid with an investigation and that he isn't under arrest. The 'yet' is silent, but loud. All the while, Sam takes the man in.

'Mr Albescu – may I call you Andrei?' Sam begins, and he nods and tries to smile. 'I'm sure you're a busy man, what with a wife and little ones to get home to, so I'll dive right in. Do you recognize this child?' Sam slides a school photograph of Charlotte across the table, letting her eyes rest on it for a second before returning them to his face.

'I seen her on the news.' He speaks with a light accent that's an unusual hybrid of cockney and Romanian.

'What about in real life?'

'No.'

'You know nothing about her murder?'

'No.'

'Do you own any tracking devices?'

'No.'

'Have you ever been to Holland Park?'

'No.'

'Can you tell me why someone carved this girl's initials, and Denver Brady's, on to a tree in Holland Park?'

'Yes.'

'Do you—wait, what? Yes?' Sam blurts. 'What can you tell me about that?'

'I think the killer read *How to Get Away With Murder* and copy.'

Sam sits back and takes a sip of water from her plastic cup. Taylor clicks and unclicks his pen, his knee bouncing up and down beneath the table, making her drink vibrate when she puts it back down.

'So, you recognize this book, Andrei?' Sam pushes her copy of across the table. Its cover is scuffed, the spine cracked and a corner is turned down, marking her place. There's not much left for her to read.

'Yes,' Albescu says, stroking the cover. 'I wrote it.'

Taylor's head snaps around to look at Sam. *Keep cool, Taylor*, she thinks.

'You wrote this book, Mr Albescu?' Sam asks cautiously.

'Yes. I wrote this book.'

'Alone?' Sam asks, trying to keep the incredulity from her voice.

'Yes. I wrote this book. Alone.'

'Is this book crime fact or crime fiction, Mr Albescu?' Sam asks.

'I do not understand. I wrote *How to Get Away With Murder*. I am author.'

'Is the story in the book true, Andrei?' Sam tries again.

'I write how-to guide for serial killers,' he says.

Sam sits back, a little breathless and unsure of how to proceed. She can't believe what Andrei is saying.

'Tell us explicitly: are you confessing to the murders outlined in this book?' Taylor presses.

A pause, then Andrei says, 'I confess.'

'What we mean, Andrei,' Sam tries again, 'is, did you kill people and then write a book about it? Are you a serial killer?'

'My name is Denver Brady.'

'I need to tell you at this point, Mr Albescu,' Taylor says, 'that I am arresting you on suspicion of murder. You do not have to say anything, but it may harm your defence if you do not mention when questioned something that you later rely on in court. Anything you do say may be given in evidence. Do you understand me?'

'I would like to speak to my lawyer, please,' Andrei says, sliding a business card across the table. Sam stares at it. She knows she has every piece of this puzzle; she just can't, for the life of her, see the full picture.

Sam and Taylor take adjacent seats in the tiny meeting room, with the door firmly closed. They each stare into their steaming tea and say nothing. Every few seconds one of them sighs or shakes their head. Four floors below them, Andrei sits in his cell as his lawyer is contacted. Sam has also asked for a translator to be brought in urgently.

'I know what you're thinking.' Sam blows on her tea, not meeting Taylor's eye.

'Yes,' he sighs, 'and I know you don't want me to say it aloud. You don't want to hear that Andrei matches Richie Scott's description of the man who came to his home the evening his girlfriend was murdered.'

'It's true,' Sam agrees, 'I don't want to hear it, but the arson, too, is leading us to Andrei.'

'Plus, his confession,' Taylor adds cautiously. 'And the money from the book sales.'

Sam sighs, taking a tentative sip of her drink. 'We'll have to get a warrant to hold Andrei longer.'

'You don't think he's Denver, do you?' Taylor slurps a steaming mouthful.

'I really don't,' Sam admits. 'More importantly, I don't think he's the man that killed Charlotte. But, sticking with Denver for the moment, Amy confirmed that Andrei looks nothing like the creep she remembers. Sean said Denver is a northerner, born and bred. Only Richie Scott claims Denver is tall and dark-haired with a foreign accent, and Richie's as reliable as a chocolate fireguard.' Sam swallows more hot liquid, feeling it burn its way down her throat. 'Andrei said one thing that I do believe, though. He said that Charlotte's killer simply read *How to Get Away With Murder* and copied it. I think he's right.'

Taylor nods. 'Two killers. The man who killed Betty and potentially others, and the man who killed Charlotte.'

'Yes,' Sam says, 'and I think both of those men are still on the loose.'

'So, what now?' Taylor stifles a yawn. 'Sorry, ma'am. I'm completely shattered. The hours we're working are . . .'

Sam nods. 'Try and get some rest, Taylor, before we get to question him further.'

She doesn't say that she needs to finish the book off once and for all, and that it's time to put Denver Brady's sick cocktail of truths, half-truths and outright lies to bed.

## When Things Go Wrong

We're coming close to the end of our time together. I'm sure you'll agree, having arrived at my penultimate chapter, that I've almost fulfilled my promise to you. You now know how to get away with murder.

Let me briefly take you back to how this journey started – with a list of reasons you may be caught. We'll conclude my personal story with the final item on that list: that 1 per cent of us will be killed by our victims.

It can happen to the best.

It almost happened to me.

It wasn't very long ago – about two years, I'd say. I was an advanced practitioner, well beyond killing little old ladies and talking young men into jumping off bridges. I'd abandoned the gamery of lacing wine bottles with drugs and I'd let go of most of my disguises, too. I was at a point in my career where my victim count was so high that I knew I'd made it. I knew Mary Ann, Teddy, Jeff and the gang would all welcome me to warm my hands by Satan's fireside as one of the greatest serial killers of all time.

I need to tread carefully here so as not to give too much away, so I will say nothing about how I selected this next victim. He was called Basil and he lived in a castle, although he referred to it as 'The Lodge.' It had dozens of grand rooms, including a library with those rolling ladders like in *Beauty and the Beast*. (What? You think serial killers don't do Disney?) There was a sauna, steam room, stables, fountains, and staff who cared for the gundogs and hunter horses.

Basil was a little shocked when I stepped into his kitchen, masked and ready, but he offered me a stiff drink and proceeded to pull his cheque book from the drawer. No one in the real world uses cheque books any more, I told him. But he just tutted.

'Name your price, my man,' he said.

I always source my weapon from the victim's home and you should too. I pulled a knife from Basil's giant block. Embarrassingly, I'd selected the bread knife and had to quickly slide it back in and take out another. I stepped toward Basil with a large chef's knife in my hand.

'Now, now, old chap,' he said, eyeing the knife. 'Let's be reasonable here.'

I lunged, and he dodged.

'This is rather silly, old boy. Just name your price,' he insisted.

I have no idea what happened next. He managed to clobber me with something and it's possible I blacked out. The next thing I knew, he had a knife himself that he held to my throat and had activated a panic alarm – a button that rich people have whereby they can summon the police without the inconvenience of dialling 999.

'Now you've done it, old chap,' he said. 'The police are on the way.'

Anyone who's ever watched a horror film knows that the second the killer is incapacitated, you need to kill them properly – otherwise, they'll just get up again.

Basil was more of an *Only Fools and Horses* kind of guy, though. I took a few seconds to catch my breath. It was difficult to concentrate, what with the wailing alarm throbbing in my skull, but I decided to appeal to his sense of class and decorum.

'May I please sit up?' I asked.

Basil hesitated for a second, the knife pricking my throat, then he nodded and stepped back slightly. I sat up and in one swift motion whacked his wrist, sending his knife skittering across the waxed wooden floor. It took me a moment to climb to my feet, and I felt dangerously dizzy as I chased the old man up the stairs.

He locked himself In the bathroom. I threw myself against the door. A central panel broke free and I was tempted, for a split second, to stick my head in the gap and yell, '*Heeeeeere's Johnny!*' But I figured that my genius would be wasted on Basil. I did, however, peek inside to try to determine where Basil was positioned and what the layout of the room was.

He was quick as lightning. I felt no pain in the first seconds, only the warmth of my own blood pouring from my neck and running down my chest. I stumbled backwards, knocking over a laundry basket and falling most of the way back down the stairs. 'The bastard got me,' I heard myself saying to no one.

The alarm was still wailing. From the amount of blood running through my fingers, I supposed he'd nicked an artery and I had about eight minutes left to live. It didn't scare me. I wasn't in pain. Then I had a thought that terrified me to my core: no one would ever know who and what I was.

I scrambled to my feet and somehow managed to get myself out of Basil's house, to the electric bike

I'd hidden in nearby undergrowth, and back home. I crashed through my own front door and scraped my way upstairs to my office. The blood from my neck was sticky now, and I was covered in mud. I grabbed a sheet of paper and a pen. Then I paused. I was losing consciousness. I doubted I'd regain it. I had seconds – not enough time to write down my full story. So, as my vision clouded over, I managed to scrawl one sentence. The one that whoever found my body would hopefully release to the police and the press, and secure my legacy for ever.

*My name is Denver Brady, and I am a serial killer.*

# 15

When she arrives back at her desk the next morning, her brain still reeling from Andrei's 'confession', what she sees makes her wonder if she's finally lost it. Sitting in her chair, sipping tea from their least-chipped mug and nibbling on a Hobnob, is a young nun. Sam knows she's a nun because she's dressed in full nun gear, complete with white headdress and black veil over the top. To make the scene even more bizarre, officers are standing around the nun and seem to be laughing at a joke she's just made.

As Sam approaches, the group disperses and the nun looks over at her before standing and dusting the crumbs from her chest.

'Ma'am,' Chloe says, smiling, 'we have a visitor.'

'I see that.'

The nun stands. 'Detective Hansen, I presume?' She takes Sam's hand, grasping it in both of hers, and smiling warmly up at her.

'Yes. How can I help you . . .'

'Sister. Sister Mary Louise,' the nun says, her accent lightly northern. 'There's been some confusion, you see, because I've been calling for a week or more now but the lovely Grace and Hannah, on your civilian team, thought I was *your* sister. I'm not – just in case you weren't sure!' The nun tilts her head back and laughs heartily at her own joke, drawing a smile from Sam and a bewildered look from Taylor, who's hovering over her shoulder. 'Oh,' the nun says, 'and who might this handsome fella be?'

'Trainee Detective Constable Adam Taylor, ma'am,' he says, stepping forward and receiving an equally genuine hand-hug.

'Well, didn't the Lord bless you both,' the nun says, admiringly. 'You're the SIO in the Denver Brady case, I hear. I've only just learned what it means – Senior Investigating Officer. You're so young to be called that, don't you think, dear? Senior. Anyway . . . Denver Brady. Evil himself.' Sister Mary Louise makes the sign of the cross. 'Denver is why I'm here and why I've been telephoning.' Her blue eyes glint and Sam's certain there's a hint of tears behind them.

'Please, Sister, let's take a seat in—' Taylor starts.

'Oh, no fuss. No fuss.' She wipes her cheek. 'There's a lovely young man in a black cab waiting outside for me, so I'll be quick. It's about Sarah. Sarah Lawrence . . .' The nun swallows hard. 'She was my best friend. She's in that dreadful *How to Get Away with Murder* book that's in the news and my godson, he spotted it. Knowing my own personal story, he brought the book to me and I read the chapter on Sarah myself. That's by-the-by. I'm here to tell you that this Denver chap is a liar. Plain and simple.'

'I hate to ask, Sister,' Sam says, 'but how can you know—'

'The Lord detests lying lips, but He delights in people who are trustworthy. Proverbs Twelve.'

'Amen,' Taylor says, shrugging at Sam's incredulous look.

'In the chapter about Sarah,' the nun goes on, 'Denver describes a rounders scene. Sarah loved rounders. Just like he says, she had red hair, as orange as the sunset. We wore brown uniforms, ugly things they were, with yellow trim, and dreadful boater hats in the summer. The convent playing field backed on to another field, with a few trees at the end by our school, including a giant oak. Beyond that, the grounds of the local grammar school and sixth-form college. The lads would come over of a lunchtime and linger by the convent walls. '

'So he's telling the partial truth?' Sam asks, then turns to at Taylor. 'Like he did with Betty, Melanie and the other victims.'

'But Denver didn't kill Sarah. She was in trouble, you see. The kind of trouble a convent girl from a strict Catholic family can't afford to be in. She hanged herself from the big oak. It was my fault. She came to me for help and . . .' Taylor hands the nun a tissue and she takes his hand, as if sharing his strength. 'It was me who carved the love heart on the trunk of the oak tree, and just *her* initials inside it.'

'Is it possible, Sister,' Sam asks gently, still trying to piece the story together, 'that Sarah's death could have been made to look like suicide when—'

'Sarah wasn't murdered,' the nun says. 'I know Sarah killed herself because she left me a note. In her own hand, saying things that only she would say.'

'I don't suppose you kept that note, Sister?' Sam asks.

'I did.' She gestures to a small wooden box with a carved crucifix sitting on the edge of Taylor's desk. 'I brought a few photographs, other things you might need.' Tears slide down her face, which is pale and youthful. A small sob seeps from her lips and Sam steps forward, bending down and embracing the woman in a way that Past Sam would never have done. The nun slides her arms around Sam and heaves silently for a few moments.

'That explains why we found nothing in the database,' Taylor says quietly, once Sister Mary Louise has composed herself. 'Because without a crime involved, we'd have no record. I ran internet searches too, though, and still found nothing, which is odd.'

'*Och*, well you wouldn't,' the nun says. 'The family and the church kept it all quiet. There wasn't even an obituary in the local paper.'

'Oh my God—ness. Goodness. Oh my goodness,' Sam stutters, suddenly grasping what the nun has told them, without her having to spell it out.

'Yes, you've got my meaning now, haven't you?' she says.

Taylor looks from Sam to Sister Mary Louise. 'I'm not following.'

'I am.' Sam swallows. 'We need a list of all students of that grammar school from 1995 to 1998. I bet Betty's nephew is on it.

It's a strong piece of circumstantial evidence connecting him to Sarah and *How to Get Away With Murder*.'

'Oh, you are a clever girl,' the nun says.

'Ma'am, could you explain in—'

'Taylor, how could Denver know about Sarah's death and the Sister's carving on the oak tree unless he was there and saw it for himself?'

The sister shakes her head, misery etched on her face. 'I've inspired a serial killer's creativity, by all the saints!'

'That's so risky,' Taylor scoffs. 'Surely Denver wouldn't be that stupid?'

'Certainly risky for us,' the nun says. 'Denver has been to our little village.'

'Which is where, Sister?'

'Wolsington, a tiny place near Easington Colliery,' she says.

Sam gasps. 'That's where Betty Brown lived,' she exclaims. 'Everything leads us back to Betty. With or without the physical evidence, we need to bring the nephew in.'

'Betty Brown, did you say?' The nun's face tightens. 'As in, B. B.? Well, that makes no sense at all . . .'

'What is it, Sister?' Sam asks, and the nun hesitates then begins to rifle through the box on Taylor's desk.

'It's these,' Sister Mary Louise says, pulling out a plastic bag containing a wad of paper. 'When I cleared out Sarah's room in the convent, I found them and well . . . I hung on to them. But they weren't written by a Betty, that's for sure. It wasn't a Betty who got Sarah in trouble.'

Sam feels the blood leave her face and her skin tingles all over as she takes the item from the nun. Through an aged freezer bag, Sam can just about make out a few words written on the outside of an envelope in a delicate script, surrounded by love hearts: 'LETTERS FROM B. B.'

'Denver's letters to Sarah,' Sam whispers, barely breathing. 'You kept them.'

'I've never read them,' Sister Mary Louise rushes to clarify. 'They weren't mine to read. I just wanted to keep them safe.'

Sam blinks. 'You're saying you've never taken the letters out of the envelope?'

'Upon my soul, I have not,' the nun promises.

Taylor beams. 'That means . . .'

'The only fingerprints on these will be Sarah's and B. B.'s.' Sam grins. 'Taylor, pull up Betty's file and find the nephew's name – I think Duggan said it but my memory . . .' They wait as Taylor quickly navigates the multiple digital documents stored in HOLMES.

'Next of kin,' he reads. 'Barry Brown.'

'B.B.' says the nun.

'We need to find him,' Sam says. 'Right now. Today. I am certain he is the man who wrote *How to Get Away with Murder*. When this comes back from forensics, we should finally have the evidence we need to prove he's Denver Brady.'

Sam can taste Denver Fever in the London air. The city has gone mad with it. *How to Get Away with Murder* has gone viral and, according to Chloe Spears, original copies are selling on eBay for over a thousand pounds a pop. Sam does her best to block out the rhythmic chants of the protestors and the clipped voices of the reporters as she returns from a quick lunch. There's only one name on their lips, and it's not Charlotte's. She does her best to take in the faces of the crowd, knowing that he could be there. Watching the show. Revelling in the fear and chaos. Looking for his next victim.

'NO, NOT ALL MEN! YES, ALL WOMEN!' cries a voice through a megaphone.

Sam is grateful for the vacuum of the elevator and ascends to fourth floor with her eyes closed and her breathing even. Several floors below, Andrei Albescu is inside interview room two, liaising with his lawyer. DCI Blakelaw has the entire team working to prepare files for the Crown Prosecution Service, and the fourth floor is so loud that Sam inserts her earphones and double taps until Bob Dylan's voice is all she can hear. Through the glass, Sam sees Harry on the phone, no doubt speaking to the Commissioner, who is insisting on twice-daily updates. It's not Charlotte they're talking about, Sam guesses, but Denver.

Sam suspects that, given the volume of publicity *How to Get Away With Murder* has received, the ten grand that ties Andrei to the book's sales is far from the total revenue by now, and she believes that somehow, Barry Brown is getting his hands on the rest. A second examination of Andrei's bank statement has also revealed that several months ago he withdrew a large sum of cash, matching the amount Swinton's charged to print the book. For now, Andrei has been charged with arson, buying more time to investigate his connection to the murders described in *How to Get Away With Murder*. Because currently, there's nothing actually connecting him to them. Not a single piece of evidence. And several of the murders didn't even happen: Amy is still alive, as is Sean; Jono's drowning was an accident; Sarah committed suicide; and if Basil even exists, he survived. Betty and Melanie were the only victims of murder. No matter how hard Harry rages, the CPS will never support charging Andrei with their murders unless they find physical evidence or he makes a plausible confession. So, why would Andrei confess to killing Betty and Melanie when there's so little evidence against him? Any good lawyer would advise Andrei to give a 'no comment' interview. Something teeters on the outskirts of Sam's memory, but she can't grasp it.

Sam sits heavily in her chair, and for a few moments more she does nothing but think. She can smell Taylor's aftershave, but pushes away the memory of his visit to her home yesterday. The feel of his fingertips on her cheek. She fiddles with the little netball keyring. She'd agreed to work on the book investigation and leave Charlotte's murder with Tina, but she can't stop herself thinking about who might have placed that tracker in Charlotte's bag. Her phone rings through her headphones, cutting off her music and making her jump. She double taps to answer.

'It's Duggan.' The Geordie officer sounds like he's in a wind tunnel and Sam presses her earpod harder into her ear. 'I've got the school records you asked for. They haven't been digitalized so I had to drive there in person. What a fanny-on I've had. Anyhow, we have Barry Brown and Robert Brown both listed as former pupils there. Wolsington College. Bobby went on to Northumbria University, then we have a death certificate. Died by—'

'Drowning, I know. Tell me about Barry.'

'Betty's nephew, grew up in Easington Colliery, did a degree at Northumbria University but I have nothing on him after graduation, until he inherited everything from Betty's estate and no one knows where he went after that.'

Sam frowns. 'I thought Betty changed her will?'

'She told her neighbour she'd done that, but apparently the copy of Betty's will leaving everything to the Salvation Army was never lodged with her solicitor, and never found.'

'So Barry got her money, then disappeared?'

'Yes. At least, there's no criminal record. I've submitted a request to the banks and registry office, but right now it looks like he just vanished. He likely changed his name. That's far more effective than we like to admit,' Duggan says ruefully. 'But I heard on the grapevine that you've got Denver Brady behind bars and he's Romanian?'

'It's early days,' Sam says, before asking Duggan to keep searching for Barry and ringing off.

Sam is tempted to spend time tracking down Barry herself, to stop Harry telling the world that Denver Brady is a man named Andrei Albescu when she knows full well he's not. But finding Betty's killer and the author of *How to Get Away With Murder* isn't her top priority, despite her agreement with Tina and Harry's orders. With Duggan and Taylor pursuing the Barry Brown lead, she decides to treat herself to a few minutes' consideration of the case she's burning to solve. She makes a cup of tea, holes up in the small meeting room and goes over Charlotte's crime scene photographs again. Her heart races uncomfortably, and she has to sip her tea every minute or so to flush away the salty taste, but she makes her way through each image carefully. She takes notes, then closes her eyes and lets the facts of Charlotte's case, and only that case, flow through her.

Something needles her about Charlotte's behaviour the night she was killed. Sam turns the sequence of events over in her mind. She feels so close to grasping something, when Harry calls everyone into the briefing room. He's smiles and nods as people file in, patting one or two amicably on the shoulder. Despite the team's exhaustion, it's clear Harry is in a good mood. Chirpy, even. He no doubt expects that he'll soon be able to tell the press that he's bagged a serial killer. In the meantime, he's gathered them to say he wants them all focused on Charlotte Mathers.

'I'm sorry to do this, folks, but we need one last push to get this over the line. I've no choice but to ask for overtime this weekend, please.' Harry keeps his tone light and talks through the stony silence, describing how they are all playing a vital role in securing justice for a child. He ends by literally applauding the officers as they begin to leave the room and she notices that he's humming under his breath.

'Detective Inspector Hansen,' Tina Edris says to Sam as they walk out, 'you need to stand up for yourself. You're supposed to be on a phased return. The DCI has already made you joint SIO. You can't work weekends too. I say this as an ally, not a rival; as a friend.'

'Tina—' Sam begins, but the other woman just holds up her hand and walks away, giant bucket bag banging against her hip.

Sam rests her forehead on her arms and rests on her desk. She hates to admit it, but Tina has a point. Just like Dr Thomson has told her, it's too much. Sam yawns deeply and sits up, her eyes landing on Charlotte's photograph on the whiteboard. *Fourteen years old*, Sam thinks. *Dead. Strangled. Posed like a doll, on a tree trunk. For a man's pleasure. And I'm sitting here, yawning.* Sam chides herself. She rises to her feet. This isn't about Denver Brady, she thinks. This isn't about *How to Get Away With Murder*. It isn't about the Romanian in a cell downstairs. It's not even about the brutal murder of a nice old lady from the North East. This is about a girl. A child. That beautiful child with the green eyes. She's all that really matters. *Screw the rest*, Sam thinks.

'Ma'am,' Taylor says, coming over from his desk as he sees her get up. He speaks in a low voice. 'I was thinking, it's going to be another late one. I'm going to grab some food and I thought—'

'No, thanks, Taylor,' Sam says, and gathers up her things. She's already decided where she's going and it's not out for dinner with her trainee.

Sam orders an Uber and steps out at Jessica and Jamil Patel's home. Using the map that DC Chen had built from CCTV alongside her phone app, she traces Charlotte's precise route to Holland Park and arrives at the entrance. Dog walkers are everywhere and she wishes she'd brought little Toni – he'd love the park. She's been teaching him how to play fetch, using treats and a squeaky ball. *Next time*, she thinks.

Sam follows in Charlotte's footsteps, going in through the gate and taking an immediate left, passing the miniature hedges and flower beds. The path sweeps around in a large arch and Sam follows it until she comes to a small path shooting off to the left. It leads away from the main route and has lower-level solar lighting, rather than the tall, overhead streetlights of the larger path. *Why would you go this way, Charlotte?* Sam thinks to herself. It might have saved the girl a few minutes, but surely . . . ? She must have been really worried about Nigel. But why?

Sam takes the footpath until she comes to the oak trees. A pair of green parakeets sit preening each other on a branch. The park is less cultivated here, and feels more wild and natural. The grass is longer and the bushes provide a lot of ground cover. The path rises slightly and drops back down, creating a hidden area of undergrowth to Sam's left. She has no trouble finding the tree. There's a mountain of teddy bears and flowers beneath the oak that mark it out.

Sam walks over the grass, stands in front of the tree and looks around. At night, this place would be invisible from the main path. Why would any girl come this way? Even if Charlotte was highly concerned for her father. Unless she was with someone? A raw section of trunk catches Sam's eye. She steps closer, recognizing the spot where the love heart with CB + DB used to be. The forensic team have carved away the branded bark, but the tree will bear the scar for ever.

The pieces are all in front of her – she can feel it.

'Why can't I get it?' she mutters. 'Why can't I solve it?'

Sam looks from the scratched-away love heart to the cards and teddies, flowers and letters, their ink running inside of plastic packets. She picks a few up. Notes from friends, teachers, strangers. Sam replaces each one and begins arranging those that have fallen over into a neat pile. Sam's breath catches when she picks up a card titled 'Niece'. She prises it open, but the ink has run and is no longer legible.

'Why didn't Charlotte call you that night, Jack?' Sam asks aloud. 'Was it just because she knew you were out? Or . . .'

Mind whirring, Sam pulls her phone from her pocket and opens a map application, typing in the name of the pub in Brenham where Jack Mathers was the night his niece died. Over five miles away. Feeling like a rookie private investigator, Sam googles how long it would take to run that distance. Between thirty and seventy-two minutes for the average person, Google says.

'Well, that's helpful,' Sam mumbles frustratedly to herself. Jack Mathers couldn't have left the party for more than an hour without his absence being noticed. His phone didn't disconnect from the pub's Wi-Fi at all, even though he claims to have left to go to a shop. No witnesses reported him being sweaty or out of breath, so he can't have run. The pathologist confirmed that it would have taken at least fifteen minutes to murder and pose Charlotte, and then there's the carving of the love heart on the tree, which would also have taken time.

The love heart on the tree . . .

Sam feels the pieces slotting slowly into place, and lets her eyes continue to roam to the wound on the trunk where the carving was. She remembers that the expert confirmed the carving itself was fresh, and that it would have taken at least half an hour to make, and required tools. That's a long time to risk lingering at a crime scene, with a bag of chisels and a dead child beside you. It must have been carved before the murder. Some time earlier that day. But that would only have been possible if the killer had known Charlotte's route in advance.

Sam's skin prickles and she knows she's close to something. She lets her mind run over the sequence of events once more. Someone concealed a tracker in Charlotte's school bag. Carved the love heart. Then waited for Charlotte to walk through the park on her way home. Charlotte only came this way because it was an emergency and she was concerned for her father, who wasn't answering the phone. No one could have known that Nigel would fall asleep and fail to pick Charlotte up that particular night . . .

It clicks.

Just like that, Sam knows who murdered Charlotte Mathers. She knows how. She even thinks she might know why.

'My God,' she says under her breath. She gives herself a moment, staring skyward and letting the tears come. She takes deep lungfuls of air, feeling a new, heady lightness in her chest, then pulls out her phone, a trembling finger hovering over the call button. *Call Taylor,* she thinks. *Get a warrant, make an arrest.* She'll be the hero who solved Charlotte's murder. She'll prove everyone wrong who thought she wasn't up to the task: Tina Edris, Dr Pete Thomson . . . Even herself.

Tina's words roll through her mind once again: *Blakelaw has only made you joint SIO because he needs plenty of heads in line to roll before his own.* Then Sam pictures the moment she told her godfather about DS Lowry grabbing her and sliding his fingers up her inner thigh. She remembers the look in Harry's eyes as he sighed and asked her if it was a case of *he said, she said.*

'You know I believe you, Sam, but we both know how these things go,' he'd said. 'I only want what's best for you.' She'd thrown up in his wastepaper bin. He'd taken her home, told her to leave it with him and he'd see that it all *just went away.* Sam remembers finding out a few days later that Harry had pulled strings, called in favours and seen Lowry transferred to another police force. Transferred with promotion, that is. Sam remembers the weeks that followed. The nightmares, the depression, the fear. Then the giant panic attack at work that saw an ambulance called and Sam carried out of the fourth-floor office, not strong enough to return for six months.

Sam takes a deep breath.

'Fuck Prozac,' she says, 'and fuck Harry.'

Sam hits dial.

It's time to start doing things differently. It's time for her to take back control of her own story.

# 16

The room erupts in applause and whoops when DI Tina Edris steps out of the lift. She smiles and raises her hands in a gesture of thanks. Her eyes meet Sam's and the women exchange an imperceptible nod. Four floors below them, Jack Mathers sits in a cell, waiting for DI Edris and Harry to interview him on suspicion of murdering his niece.

'I still don't get how Jack did it,' Chloe says from somewhere behind her. 'Jack was miles away. He has an alibi. He didn't have time to kill Charlotte and carve that heart. He couldn't have known she'd be walking home that night.'

'He followed Denver's advice,' Sam says, sitting down at her desk.

'He didn't have time, ma'am,' Taylor argues. 'The heart would have taken—'

'To be honest, we should have realized sooner.' She sighs. 'Jack simply put a tracker in Charlotte's school bag, then he drugged Nigel a couple of times and watched Charlotte's route home. He carved the heart into the tree in advance and then he—'

'Why, though?' Taylor asks. 'This is his family.'

'Money,' Chloe says flatly. 'Nigel inherited all the family wealth because Jack was on drugs and all sorts back when their father – Charlotte's grandfather – died. Jack wanted the money.'

'But Nigel's still alive,' Taylor says.

'Maybe Nigel was next,' Chloe says.

'I think you're right,' says Sam, nodding. 'Jack was probably relying on Nigel committing suicide but he may well have planned to stage that later – then as next of kin, Jack would have inherited everything. Charlotte knew that something wasn't right about Jack, which is why she didn't call her uncle that night when her father failed to collect her from Jessica's house. I refuse to attribute Charlotte's wariness of Jack to simple instinct – there is no special intuition that alerts women and girls to the predator in their midst. Jack must have done something to put Charlotte on her guard. We'll never know.' Sam gives a sad shrug.

'Perhaps,' Taylor ventures, 'Charlotte caught her uncle reading a book called *How to Get Away With Murder*.'

That idea hadn't occurred to Sam, but she thought it was a good one. 'Charlotte was a smart girl. She figured Jack out a lot faster than we did.'

'Edris still got him, though,' Chloe chimes. 'Even with Denver's book to help him, Jack still didn't get away with murder, thanks to her.'

'Don't underestimate how much you've helped, Chloe,' Sam adds. 'And you, Taylor. We all played our part. We can't bring Charlotte back, but we gave her everything we had to give. Well done, everyone,' Sam smiles. They all watch through the glass as Tina and Harry chat animatedly in the DCI's office. Tina is beaming, nodding, as Harry shakes her hand and pats her shoulder.

'Looks like the DCI is pleased with her,' Taylor says. 'A quick arrest will be great for his precious stats. All he needs now is for us to find the real Denver, then Blakelaw will go down in history as one of the most successful DCIs the Met has ever seen. I hope he gives Tina the credit she deserves when he speaks to the press later.'

Sam turns away and heads for the kettle. She'd love to tell Taylor that she was the one who had finally pieced together the bits of Denver's book that Jack had used to try to get away with murder. How she had realized Jack lied in his interview when he claimed that he didn't read or exercise much – Jim the gardener had confirmed the opposite to Sam. How Jack had followed Denver's instructions about tracking devices, planting the pregnancy test, using bicycles and disguises, as well as creating a physical and digital alibi. How Jack had very likely persuaded his grieving brother to throw *How to Get Away With Murder* to the press and deflect attention away from Charlotte's actual killer.

Sam had pieced it all together, slowly but surely – yet she'd decided to give the win to Tina. Her reasons were not pure. In fact, they were selfish. Sam didn't want to vindicate Harry's decision to make her SIO when he knew she was not ready. Moreover, she felt that, in some small way, helping her colleague secure her first arrest as a Met detective might go some way to guard Tina's future with a police force that desperately needed more strong women. Sam knew that the institutional misogyny plaguing the Met wouldn't be cured by Sam going without credit so another woman could have it, but she was already confident that she had found Denver Brady, and just as soon as Sam had cleared up the confusion around Andrei Albescu, she would have her own big arrest to celebrate.

Sam was perceptive enough to know that if she had simply called Tina and told her what she'd realized about Jack Mathers murdering his niece, Tina would have insisted that Sam receive full credit for solving the case. So, she'd been a little cunning in her approach. When Sam had called, she'd led Tina just far enough down the path to be sure that her colleague would reach her own conclusions and make the arrest. When she'd hung up, Sam had felt weightless and free, knowing that she'd helped to bring Charlotte the justice she deserved. Knowing that Charlotte's killer would soon be behind bars left Sam feeling like she could breathe properly for the first time in many months.

'DI Hansen . . .' A colleague interrupts her thoughts. 'Call from the custody suite. Your suspect, Andrei Albescu, is ready to talk. The lawyer and translator are ready, too.'

'Damn,' Sam says, then turns to Taylor. 'I forgot to ask Duggan about Barry Brown.'

'Ask him what?' Taylor says.

'What degree Barry did at Northumbria University,' Sam says.

'Why?' Chloe asks.

'It's just a piece of the puzzle I think might be important.'

'Ma'am,' the woman presses. 'They're waiting for you.'

'You go,' Taylor says. 'I'll call Duggan, then join you.'

# 17

Inside the interview room, Andrei Albescu waits with man in a crisp suit and a woman who sits in the corner, a notepad and Romanian dictionary on her lap. Sam and the translator exchange a polite nod and Andrei's lawyer stands to introduce himself.

'Julius Windsor,' he says, shaking Sam's hand, 'of Windsor, Rogers and Knight. King's Counsel.' The pale, jowly man hands Sam a business card and smiles at her with watery blue eyes. She doesn't return his smile. She thinks for a second that Toni would growl at this man, as he occasionally does when they're out walking.

'DI Hansen,' Sam says to the room.

'We've met before, Detective,' the lawyer says. 'A couple of years ago. Back when you were investigating cold cases—'

'I don't remember,' Sam cuts him off. 'Shall we get down to it?'

The man straightens and wipes his sweaty top lip with his tie, which makes Sam's insides roll. Taylor arrives just in time to conduct the formalities, and as he does so Sam takes in Andrei Albescu's demeanour. He looks remarkably calm, his hands clasped loosely on the table, his eyes neutral. He's wearing fresh grey clothes and he's showered. Her eyes drift to the lawyer's garish tie, which is baby pink with birds on it. Are they flamingos?

'It's clear to me, Detective,' the lawyer smiles, 'that you have no evidence against my client. Nothing. A misguided sentence or two, without representation and without a translator. You and I both know—'

'Andrei,' Sam leans forward, ignoring the lawyer entirely. 'I no longer need to question you regarding Charlotte Mathers. Do you understand?' He nods. 'All that I need you to do is explain to me why you burned down Swinton's Printers and why money from a website called Howtogetawaywithmurder.com is ending up in your account. I know there'll be a reasonable explanation. I know you aren't a killer. But I need you tell me the truth, so that I can get you home to your family.' Sam sits back, her mouth a little dry.

Andrei looks to his lawyer, who shakes his head.

'No comment.'

Sam's stomach drops. 'Did you agree to allow someone to use your bank account, Andrei?'

'No comment.'

'Did someone offer you money to burn down—'

'No comment.'

'Andrei, think of Nadja.' Sam leans forward. 'Please. Tell us the truth about the arson and the money from the sale of that book and I will personally speak to the CPS about—'

'No comment.'

Sam takes a deep, calming breath. 'Do you know a man named Barry Brown?'

'No.'

'How about Betty Brown?'

'Betty from book. I wrote *How to Get Away With Murder.*'

'But did you kill Betty?'

'No.'

'Did anyone ask you to confess to writing *How to Get Away With—*'

Everyone in the room jumps at a sharp knock on the door. Harry's head pops around it and says, 'The search team have found something.' Sam doesn't like the urgent excitement in his voice, but stops the recording, excuses herself and steps out into the corridor to find DC Chen waiting for her. The grin on Harry's face makes her skin prickle.

'Jack Mathers and Denver Brady,' he says, beaming. 'That's how we'll be remembered. Two in one week.' At Sam's uncomprehending expression, he gestures to Chen, who hands Sam several evidence bags, and she turns her attention to the larger one first. At first glance it appears to be a ream of paper, but a closer look shows the sheets are covered in lines of typed text, with handwriting and crossings-out along the margins.

'From the Albescu property. We found these in a storage box, wrapped in bin bags. It appears to be a manuscript, ma'am – an early draft of a book,' Chen says. 'We also have this laptop, which is running the dark web and contains only a handful of files, each named the same thing, with a simple numbering suffix.'

Sam swallows.

'Multiple drafts, ma'am,' Chen goes on. '*How to Get Away With Murder* Version One, Two, Three and so on. And that's just on the desktop. When I get done with this laptop, we'll have—'

She turns her attention to the smaller bag. Something small and blue, a hint of red and silver. She shudders.

'Earrings and a ring with a sapphire gemstone, Sam,' says Harry, rubbing his hands together. 'The proverbial nails in the Romanian's coffin. This is it, Sam. This will make you.'

Sam struggles to breathe.

'Excuse me . . .' The lawyer is sticking his head around of the door behind them, which he has opened just enough to do so. 'We haven't got all day and my client—'

'A moment, please,' Harry replies, dismissing the man, but the lawyer doesn't close the door. Instead, his eyes linger on the laptop and the bin bags. His mouth forms a tight line, then he re-enters the room where Andrei waits. 'Get the jewellery to the lab and do your magic with the laptop, Chen. This isn't a done deal, by any stretch, but I think you've got him, Sam. I'll call the CPS myself.'

'Sir,' Chen nods, then he turns to Sam, adding 'Congratulations, ma'am,' before striding away.

'Andrei Albescu is not Denver Brady,' Sam cries, an itchy heat rising up her neck. 'I don't know what's going on here, but I know in my gut that the man did not write *How to Get Away With Murder* and he certainly did not murder Betty Brown and Melanie Davison or—'

'Sam . . .' Harry holds his hands up, palms open. 'We have the money trail, the CCTV from the petrol station, and now, it seems, a lot more besides. We follow the evidence, not baseless theories.'

'He's not Denver,' Sam stares him hard in the face. 'I am certain. I have witnesses who—'

'Look, why don't you take some time—'

'Harry!' Sam hisses, feeling a little spittle fly from her mouth. 'It's not him.'

'Is this really a hill you're willing to die on, Sam?' Harry whispers.

'I *promise* you, Harry, on my mother's soul,' she pleads. 'That man is not Denver.'

'Sam, your parents would be so proud. You have caught a *serial killer*. Paparazzi from around the world are camped out on our doorstep and I can walk out there and say *your name*. Their name – Hansen. Can you grasp what that would mean? What would your father—'

'He is not Denver Brady!' Sam yells.

'God, Sam,' Harry hisses, glancing up and down the corridor. 'Haven't I always done what's best for you? I'm telling you to take this win. For both our sakes. I want this for you. And you will not take this opportunity from me.'

Harry turns and walks away, leaving Sam alone in the corridor. She shivers, runs her hands down her face and flattens herself against the wall, letting it hold her up. It would be so easy for her to go upstairs and call the CPS, outline the evidence and charge

Andrei with murder. She'd stand next to Harry, smile and nod as he told the world's press that she's found Denver Brady, then work to build a case against Andrei for the murder of Betty Brown and Melanie Davison, potentially freeing Richie Scott in the process. Sam would be the jewel in the Met's crown. All she has to do is go along with Harry's suggestion. It's not like she hasn't done it before.

A deep heat begins to stir in her stomach, then it rises to her chest and burns out through her face and neck. She stands up straight, smooths her jacket, rolls back her shoulders and marches after Harry. When the lift opens on to the fourth floor, she strides across the space and directly into Harry's office, not giving a shit that he's already on the phone,

'Yes. Quickly, please. Thanks.' Harry places the phone in the receiver and sits down, letting the momentum carry him backwards in his chair. He laces his fingers, closes his eyes and takes a few deep breaths as if he is an exhausted parent about to handle a difficult child.

'DI Hansen,' he says, 'kindly refrain from entering my office without—'

'Cut the bullshit, Harry. Do not pin Denver's crimes on some poor immigrant who—'

'Andrei Albescu is already under review with immigration as a result of his petty crimes. Not to mention the arson charges we can bring against him today. Now this. Once we put the evidence to him, he'll probably—'

Sam turns and slams the office door. It's a visceral need to move. She wants to hit something. Anything. All the anger from the last year is boiling up and finally spilling over.

'Harry. Don't do this. Albescu is an innocent man. He's being framed or ... or something. I just need some time to find the real—'

'Think about it, Sam,' Harry pleads. 'This will be the making of your career.'

'It's wrong.' Sam announces, folding her arms. 'Just like transferring Lowry instead of reporting him was wrong. I will not go along with you this time, Harry. I will not watch an innocent man charged with murder. I will not see him branded a serial killer while a real predator is released from jail and another remains free.'

Harry sighs. 'Can't you see that it's in your best—'

'Do not talk to me about my best interests,' Sam barks. 'I refuse to allow this to happen. I'll speak to the police and crime commissioner. I'll speak to some old journalist friends. I'll sing it from the rooftops like Maria Fucking von Trapp if I have to.'

By the end of her rant, Sam is panting, and Harry sits patiently, waiting for her to contain herself. They both know she knows how to cause trouble. These days, people listen to whistleblowers, and Sam's a credible one. She can see the headlines now: *WE HAVEN'T CAUGHT DENVER! DETECTIVE CLAIMS*. Harry would have to discredit her somehow and she's been nothing but well-behaved since she returned to work. He even made her SIO. *I have a strong hand here*, she thinks. Why, then, is he looking at her as though he knows something she doesn't?

'My dear girl . . .' He shakes his head. 'I've done everything I can for you.'

There's a knock at the door. A woman Sam vaguely recognizes enters the office. When she turns back, Harry has the saddest look on his face. It reminds her of the day Harry carried her father's coffin up the aisle of the church.

'Last chance, Sam?' Harry pleads.

'Fuck you, Harry.'

Harry takes a deep breath. 'Sam, this is Erica Mason from upstairs – HR. I've asked Erica to join us as I have some difficult news for you, Sam. I'm afraid we need to suspend you from duty, with immediate effect.'

Sam steps back, her throat suddenly dry. 'You can't suspend me without cause,' she tries to say, but the words come out in a rasp.

Erica gives her a calm smile. 'I'm sorry, Detective,' she says, 'but it's come to our attention that you recently suffered a panic attack while on duty. Subsequently, you went to a public house and rendered yourself incapacitated by way of alcohol. All while on duty and supervising a trainee, who managed, under difficult circumstances, to bring you home.'

Salt floods Sam's mouth and her chest seizes. How could they know? Taylor wouldn't have said anything. He brought her home and left her on the sofa under a blanket.

'Taylor called me,' Harry says.

'Why would Taylor—'

'Because he couldn't get you out of the taxi!' Harry spits, anger flaring. 'So, I came and got you on to your sofa while the boy cleaned up the dog shit from your kitchen floor. I told him I'd have his job if he didn't keep shtum—'

'You made me joint SIO the next day!' she cries. 'How could you? Knowing I'd had a—'

'What the DCI means,' Erica interjects, 'is that he directed Trainee Detective Constable Taylor to leave the matter in the DCI's hands. The decision to make you joint SIO was never formalized and nor will it be, as we have also discovered that you've failed to attend your private counselling appointments. If you remember, when you first took sick leave, it was agreed that private counselling would be an acceptable alternative to in-house therapy, but that it remained obligatory. Our well-being officer has sent you numerous emails requesting updates and meetings, and you have ignored them. All things considered, DCI Blakelaw has decided to involve HR—'

'Because he needs me out of the way for a while so he can convict the wrong man. Otherwise you'd have said nothing to H-fucking-R, would you, Harry?' Sam's words are venomous, but they lack real strength. She's already struggling to breathe properly and the room's beginning to spin. Through the glass, she sees

Adam Taylor looking in at them. His cheeks are red and she's sure his eyes are glistening, but his regret can't help her now. Sam places a hand on Harry's desk, trying to steady herself.

'Screw you, Harry,' Sam whispers, the tears spilling over and plopping on to her blouse.

Harry smiles at her calmly, then the phone rings. They both know it'll be the prosecutor calling to discuss charging Andrei Albescu with the crimes of Denver Brady.

'I'm sorry, Sam,' Harry says coolly, 'I've come to believe that you need some additional sick leave. Please excuse me now.' With that he nods at Erica, who tries to place her arm around Sam's shoulder, but can't reach and settles for holding her elbow instead.

'Let me see you to a taxi, Detective Hansen,' she says, 'and I'm afraid I'll need your work phone and badge.'

# 18

Time melts into a blur of miserable sleep. Sam has come to know these as her dark days. There have been a lot of them in her life. Ever since she found her mother at the bottom of the stairs when she was nine years old, the dark days have hovered in the background. They hit her again when her father died, ten years after her mother. And more recently when DS Phil Lowry assaulted her and her godfather destroyed her fragile trust all over again.

She should get out of bed. She should take a pill and call someone, but she has no one to call. Apart from Dr Thomson, and she can't face him. Sam knows she'll do none of the things she should do to feel better. Things like showering, taking a walk, eating a healthy meal. That's possibly the worst thing about this, Sam thinks. Knowing how to help yourself and being utterly incapable of fighting the overwhelming urge to do the exact opposite.

Sam pulls her duvet closer around her and curls into a ball.

She ignores the need to eat. She ignores Adam Taylor calling her name through the letterbox. She ignores the hurt that Harry doesn't even try to visit. She lets the dark days roll into one another, until they become a week, then two. The most she manages to do is empty a whole bag of kibble into a casserole dish and put new puppy pads down for the dog. Toni barely leaves her side. The little scruff rests his head on her waist and it feels like someone who loves her is holding her. When she cries, he whines and tries to lick her tears away. When she drags herself to the toilet, he waits for her outside the door. When she turns over in bed, he pushes his warm weight into her.

It's black outside when the dark days ease into grey ones and Sam makes it to the kitchen for a slice of toast from a freezer loaf and a single tablet. *Fuck you, Prozac.* The kitchen is in an unspeakable state and Toni watches as Sam puts on some kitchen gloves then cleans up the dirty pads and sprays bleach over the lino before mopping it down. Once she's sorted the kitchen, she crawls back upstairs, washes her hands and face, and climbs back into bed. The next morning, when the birds start to sing outside, Toni barks and jumps around on the duvet.

'Sshhh,' Sam says, but he won't stop. Eventually, she sits up and the barking ceases. She lies down again and it starts once more. She sits back up. 'OK, OK, I'll get up. But the sofa is the best I can do.'

They curl up on the sofa together and Sam uses her old laptop to order a pizza. It'll be the first full meal she's eaten in a fortnight and her stomach cramps in expectation.

As she waits for the takeaway, Sam flicks on the TV, ready for the familiar comfort of *Only Fools and Horses*. Instead, she's immediately hit with the headlines. SHOULD SERIAL KILLER'S FAMILY BE GRANTED ANONYMITY? scrolls across the screen. Sam switches channel. DCI BLAKELAW ANNOUNCES RETIREMENT FOLLOWING RECENT TRIUMPHS. There are photographs of Jack Mathers in handcuffs alongside grainy images of Andrei 'Denver Brady' Albescu. The only relief Sam can feel is that there are no pictures of Nadja or the children; they seem safe, at least for now.

A news presenter standing in front of New Scotland Yard's famous rotating sign lets her know that Andrei Albescu has been charged with the murders of Melanie Davison and Betty Brown, plus arson and other offences. Words like 'overwhelming evidence' and 'expected to plead guilty' make Sam throw the TV remote at the wall. She instantly regrets the decision, because she now can't quickly turn off when the camera cuts to Harry's face.

'Thank you, yes, this is indeed a great day, a great time, for the Metropolitan Police. Two killers behind bars. I cannot say much more, as we will be working hard to secure convictions of these men, which I'm convinced, in the face of significant circumstantial and forensic evidence, we will achieve. The dedication of my team, my SIO Tina Edris and her colleagues, has been exemplary. That's all, thank you.'

Sam curses, retrieves the remote and switches channel once again. She watches as reporters livestream from around the country. A camera pans to a large group gathered outside 10 Downing Street, then cuts to another at Albert Dock in Liverpool, before settling outside York Minster. 'Jesus Christ,' Sam says to Toni. 'It's everywhere.'

A reporter asks a young woman with red lip-stick why she's protesting.

'The British public is sick and tired of dead women and girls. There are dead women everywhere. Dead in their homes. Dead in our parks. Husbands killing wives. Dads killing daughters. Strangers killing anyone. We've even got policemen killing and raping women. We want it to stop.' The small crowd stands behind the camera and the woman turns to them, her fist pumping the sky as she shouts, 'Make Britain safe for women! Make Britain safe for girls!' The chant gets picked up instantly and the camera zooms back out, the reporter handing back over to the studio.

Sam sighs and flicks over to *Only Fools and Horses*.

# 19

The next morning, Sam wakes on the sofa under an empty pizza box, feeling more human. Her stomach is still full and she brews herself a cup of black tea and swallows a tablet, noticing that there's only one left.

For the first time since her suspension three weeks ago, Sam showers. Toni sits outside the bathroom as she washes her hair multiple times to penetrate the layers of grease that have accumulated. Her pyjamas are ripe and could probably stand up on their own; she pushes them into the washing basket and dons her Nordic jumper and sweatpants. Then she feeds Toni and as he eats, she mops the kitchen lino once again with hot water and bleach. His meal finished, Toni scratches at the door. Sam shakes her head. He barks.

'OK, boy,' she says, pulling out a denim jacket. 'Only a little walk, though, and while we're at it we can call at the pharmacy for my Prozac.' Sam grabs Toni's new collar and his extendable lead. He jumps up at the front door while she searches for her keys and phone before remembering that she'd had to hand in her work phone when she was told to leave. She digs about in her kitchen drawer, the one with everything from sticky tape to tampons in it, and finds her personal mobile, which she hasn't used since being back at work. Mercifully, the screen comes to life when she plugs it in. The battery symbol flashes and she leaves it to charge, fitting Toni's collar and clipping on his lead.

It's bright outside, and Sam supposes it's about midday. There's a blue sky and not much traffic. Perhaps it's the weekend, Sam thinks. Making her way down Matrimony Place, past St Paul's Church, she passes a queue of brunchers lined up outside Bubbles and Beans. The pharmacy that Dr Thomson sends her prescription to is only a five-minute walk along the high street, but Sam is sweating by the time she arrives.

Now that she's managed to leave the house for the first time in weeks, Sam decides that she wants to make the moment last. So does Toni. He struts and sniffs, looking back at Sam and waiting for her if he gets too far ahead. She notices that his hip bones are no longer visible and there's a spring in his swaying step. A little smile creeps over her face, feeling strange but pleasant.

They head north towards Battersea Park. She's always loved to stroll around the Rosery Gardens, the Ladies' Pond and the rest of the lake there, and she wonders if that might boost her mood. There are some street food vendors by the water and Sam buys Toni a doggy ice cream, which he licks once and growls at, so she gives him half her hot dog instead.

Taking a different route home, down an unfamiliar high street, most of the shops Sam passes are the usual franchises: Costa, Subway, Currys. Toni gives a little yelp as Sam jerks to a halt outside an electrical shop. The window is filled with huge televisions. The latest curved flat-screen dominates the display. On the screen, a smart presenter sits behind a news desk, talking to MP Cecil Taylor. But it's not the man's face, an older version of Adam's, that's caught Sam's attention. It's the words scrolling across the bottom: *CONVICTION OVERTURNED: MET POLICE APOLOGIZE.*

Taylor Senior and the presenter disappear and a new presenter begins to talk from outside an old building that Sam knows is the city courthouse. There are no subtitles, so Sam enters the store and heads directly to the nearest TV, grabbing the remote that's attached to it by an anti-theft chain and upping the volume. As if sensing Sam's prickling armpits, Toni lets out a low whine and licks her shoe. Sam's pulse is racing. A throbbing strikes up in her temples. Behind the presenter, Sam sees a familiar figure, his arms raised in the air as if he's just scored for Bristol City. She can just make out the Union Jack tattoo. Bile rises in Sam's throat as he steps on to the podium and the camera closes in on his grinning face as he reads from a piece of paper.

'Excuse me, miss,' says a voice behind her, 'no dogs in the store.'

'Today,' Richie Scott says, 'justice has been done. Justice for me and justice for my beautiful Mel. I always said I was innocent and now everyone knows what Denver Brady, now identified as Andrei Albescu, has done to her. Not what I done. I loved my Mel.'

'Excuse me,' the voice says again. 'I'm sorry but there are no dogs allowed in here.'

'I want to thank you lot, the public, for your support. I want to thank my mates what stuck by me and I want to thank my lawyer here, for getting me out.' Richie gestures to the man by his side who is standing back from the crowd, only his torso momentarily visible as the camera quickly skips out and then back to Richie's grinning face. Sam gasps.

'What will your first act as a free man be, Mr Scott?' calls out one journalist.

'I'm off to the pub.' Scott grins. 'First round's on me, boys!' Another cheer rises from the crowd.

'How do you respond to women's rights groups who feel that you still belong in prison, Mr Scott?' asks a different voice.

'I done my time for that, and I'm sorry for it. Mel could really push my buttons, but I'm sorry I rose to it. I don't accept violence against women.'

'What do you say to the Met police, who wrongfully arrested an innocent man?' asks another journalist.

'Everyone makes mistakes,' Scott shrugs. 'Police are just humans. But not catching Denver Brady sooner. Not even knowing a serial killer was—'

'Security. We've a woman with a dog in the TV section. She's refusing to leave.'

Sam's feet find motion and she walks from the store and back the way she's come. Her mind begins to whirr and clunk like an old car that's stood still for too long but is made of strong stuff. For weeks she's struggled with so many pieces of the Denver Brady case. Like a jigsaw that she couldn't quite finish. But in that moment, looking at Richie Scott without his prison jumpsuit and out in the open, it all comes together.

Sam knows who killed Betty.

Sam knows who killed Melanie.

Sam knows it all. Because she recognizes that dreadful tie.

Sam rushes home. Ignoring the bunch of flowers on her doorstep, she fumbles her way inside and grabs her mobile, navigating immediately to her work email and finding herself logged out. Her password doesn't work. She logs on to her personal email and drafts a message to Neil Duggan. She's not 100 per cent sure of his email address, so she sends several, with varying combinations of forename and surname and initials. Within ten minutes, she's had half a dozen bounce-backs and one reply.

Hansen,

Pleased to hear from you. I've been calling but been stonewalled Met end. What's going on down there?

I found Betty's nephew. Barry Brown is a lawyer in London – see attached.

We need to talk. My (personal) mobile is 07700 900458.

Neil

DI Neil Duggan

Northumbria Police

Sam slumps on to the sofa, panting, and clicks on the attached PDFs, reading them quickly. Then she smiles a great, wide smile. There's a certificate of name-change.

'I knew it,' she says to the dog. 'I've found the real Denver Brady and his name is not Andrei Albescu.'

## *Legacy*

We have arrived at the end of our time together. I truly hope you've concentrated on my words, taken notes and underlined. It's important that you re-read this guide to murder before you begin your own career. Repetition is an important component of learning and understanding for average people, such as yourself. I say this not to insult you, but rather to protect you. I call you average as you are now. I doubt that I will call you average for long. Not if you've paid proper attention to my advice. Once you've become what I've taught you to be, you'll leave average behind for ever. This is why I need my final lesson to be on legacy.

My legacy, your legacy. For nothing but the art lives on and everyone knows the name of the artist.

After my own near-death experience at Basil's hands, everything changed. I started to give due care and attention to what I would leave behind for the next generation.

When I woke up on my office floor, the day after Basil had slit my throat, I couldn't believe I was alive. I was not, however, filled with *joie de vivre* after not having not succumbed to my wounds and perished. Instead, a great anxiety consumed me. As my wounds healed, my mood didn't lift. It was my dark night of the soul. I kept the piece of paper with my scrawled sentence on it and, one evening not long after, it gave me the answer.

I needed to be known. I needed to tell my story. That very day, I began writing this book. As part of my journey, I've given a lot of thought to how I want to be remembered, and I'll pass this learning on to you here, in my final meditations.

Whoever you are right now, today will soon be gone. Once you fulfil your potential as a serial killer, you will leave behind this world of jobs and public transport, poor healthcare and women who say no. You will be more than everyone around you.

However, it's important that when you embark on your career as a serial killer, you shape your legacy from day one. How do you want to be remembered? What do you want the headlines to say? What will they call your Netflix documentary? Providing that you have devoted yourself fully to the advice in this guide, you will become an infamous serial killer and, despite our efforts, the nature of your fame will be decided by others, and this can be difficult to stomach. Once a legacy is formed, the real version of you becomes irrelevant. To repeat: once a legacy is formed, the real version of you becomes irrelevant.

However unimpressive, average or outright disappointing you are right now, it won't matter. A legacy transcends this reality. You can be a spotty virgin from a Welsh sheep farm and, providing you follow my advice, you will become the most fascinating creature in any room.

My own legacy, I have sought to shape with this book. As I intend to continue to get away with murder for the rest of my days, I have found a way to shape my living legacy. Should I be caught – which I won't be – the man behind the mask will not matter. All that will matter is the art and the legacy I have built for myself within these pages. I have no doubt that once this book receives the attention it deserves, men will line up pretending to be me. Men will revere me; they'll think of me when they fuck. They'll wear T-shirts with my name on. They'll talk about me down the pub.

Providing that you shape your legacy as well as I have shaped mine, it doesn't matter who the man behind the mask is. If you're so disappointing that they can't wrap their little minds around it, they'll simply refuse to believe that the police have caught the right guy. Either way, the fan mail will come, women will fall at your shackled feet, and Trevor MacDonald and Piers Morgan will fight for your attention. God, I hope Sir Trev is still alive and kicking when you're reading this.

I'll say it again: once you have created your legacy, the real you ceases to matter. You could be anybody – a toothless bricklayer from Peckham, a skirt-wearing Glaswegian with moobs, an illegal immigrant with a dozen kids and zero prospects. No matter how disappointing you may be in real life, you'll be like God in the eyes of the world. Better than God. No one believes in that loser any more. Everyone will know that you exist.

With that notion, I leave you.

You, my beautiful reader, have been wonderful.

Denver Brady, SK.

# 20

Sam looks up at the office building of Windsor, Forbes & Knight. It has a narcissistic presence, giving the impression of power and self-importance, even though it's no better than the other towering structures on either side of it. Its tinted windows capture Sam in their reflection and twist her out of shape, distorting her until she barely recognizes herself. A revolving doors swirls silently, and Sam lets herself be pulled into its current.

A few seconds later, Sam is ejected into a whoosh of air conditioning that smells like a chemical replica of garden jasmine. The scent is perfectly complemented by the tinkling of piano music that seems to echo off the white walls, floors and furniture. A single, curved white desk sits in the centre of the tiled expanse and it takes Sam an uncomfortable amount of time to reach it, causing her to look down at her feet accusingly, as if they're deliberately dawdling. A lone receptionist grins at her for the duration of her approach, only to direct her to an iPad for the purpose of checking in.

Sam touches the screen and scrolls to the bottom to click on 'W'. The solicitors' stylish black crest appears alongside several other businesses also beginning with that letter. She wonders how she didn't make the connection before.

An electronic whirring announces the arrival of a printed badge, which Sam slides into a lanyard taken from a waiting wicker basket. Also white. Sam looks around, uncertain where to go next.

'If madam would like to pass through security, she'll find a lobby and complimentary refreshments inside,' says the receptionist.

Sam nods and walks towards a scaled-down version of an airport hand-luggage check, placing her phone, keys, tissues and gum into a small tray. Just as she does at Heathrow, Sam takes a deep breath before walking through the body scanner as innocently as she can. The light turns red, and Sam glances at the guard. The woman is handling Sam's phone, turning it off and dropping it into a thick cloth bag, which she secures with a plastic device that looks similar to the anti-theft tags shops use on clothing.

'What are you doing?' Sam asks, bristling. The woman simply points to a sign: *Guests' devices will be stored securely for the duration of their visit.* Interesting, Sam thinks, wondering what else goes on inside this building besides the writing and editing of murder manuals. Sam's eyes move instinctively to the corners of the ceiling. No cameras.

She turns away from security and heads to the whitewashed sea of sofas and armchairs. She's surprised to see a glossy white piano in the centre of the seating area. No one is sitting at it, yet the keys are moving, as if the ghost of Bach has signed a zero-hours contract in SW1.

'Amazing tech, isn't it?' says a young man from an egg-shaped chair. He looks a lot like Adam Taylor, so Sam smiles. He holds up the pouch containing his phone and looks at it longingly. 'I'm lost without it. This is like torture.'

'Fans have to put their phones in pouches just like these at Bob Dylan concerts,' Sam says. 'He feels it makes the experience more authentic.'

'Either that, or he sounds rubbish live and doesn't want any recorded evidence,' the man suggests.

Sam rolls her eyes and turns to make a frothy coffee using a machine with an unnecessary number of buttons. She takes a croissant. It's warm and fresh and dusted with icing sugar.

'Who are you here to see?' smiles the man. His nosiness is striking and he looks her up and down casually, dissecting the detail of her. She does the same back. He looks well dressed but his shoes aren't the real deal like Taylor's, suggesting he's not as well paid as he wants people to think.

'You're a journalist,' Sam concludes through her croissant.

'Guilty,' he nods, impressed. 'Well, an investigative YouTuber, actually. You must be a detective, with those powers of observation.' He's smiling but his face drops when Sam doesn't deny it. 'Shit,' he says, leaning forward. 'Are you here to see Denver Brady's lawyer? I'm interviewing—'

'I'm meeting an author,' Sam cuts in.

'Oh, right. Must be a big name to afford a desk in SW1?'

Sam shrugs in a way that conveys that she won't be falling for any questioning techniques.

'Fair enough.' The man slumps back in his chair and sends a waft of musk Sam's way. They sit in silence for a moment, watching the piano play itself. 'You know,' he says, spinning his egg-chair like a child, 'I heard on the grapevine that there are over two thousand companies registered in this building. That's over three hundred million quid a year, this real estate costs. What are all of those companies really up—'

'Why interview the lawyer?' Sam interrupts again, already bored.

'Are you kidding?' he says, 'Denver Brady himself – Andrei Albescu is his real name, you know, but I stick with Denver because, let's face it, it's cooler . . . Anyway, Denver won't give interviews. His family – he has a wife and three kids – they've vanished, so I can't entice them to speak to me.'

Andrei has four children now, Sam thinks. She doesn't correct the YouTuber as he describes how interviewing the lawyer is as close as anyone will ever get to speaking to the biggest serial killer of our age – possibly the biggest ever, because who knows how many other murders Denver has committed and hasn't put in his book, he says, the egg bouncing with enthusiasm.

'... this interview would be groundbreaking. Could give us insight into the mind of a serial killer. What makes the monsters do it, kind-of-thing. I'm hoping to make him an offer he can't refuse and, in exchange, I want insight into Denver's childhood, his mother and how she raised him. Plus—'

'I'll give you some insight,' Sam says. 'These men are losers who kill women because they can, and because they want to. It's power, control and sex. Nothing more sophisticated than that. It's not his mam's fault and his dog didn't pass on a message from God or Satan. There is no great philosophy to it, and murder victims are not entertainment. You're wasting your time, anyway. He won't grant you an interview. Not because he doesn't want to, but because he can't be seen on TV.'

'I can pixelate his face,' the YouTuber argues, 'and change his voice. I'm offering him six figures for—'

'Miss Hansen?' the receptionist interrupts. 'You may go in now. Please take the lift to the third floor. Mr Windsor's office is room 1408.'

Sam stands, stuffing the last of her croissant into her mouth.

'Wait,' the man says, his brow puckering. 'I thought you said . . . Why are you here?'

Sam shrugs, but it's a good question, and one she's been wrestling with since she made the appointment. Why does she feel the need to confront this man? To come to his lair and look at him; to question him; present him with everything she knows, even though she has no legal power to act on anything he may say? For the most part, it's self-indulgence. Sam wants her showdown. Her *Scooby-Doo* moment, where she alone unmasks the killer. Denver's readers want it too, she supposes. A trope of the genre that she derives too much satisfaction from herself to subvert.

'You want a real story?' Sam asks. He nods. 'Why not do an

exposé on the number of criminals and suspected criminals changing their names and becoming untraceable? Now *that's* something that's *really* scary. Anyone can assume a new identity and our software is so archaic that no one ever knows. Nothing is monitored because the systems don't talk to each other. Everyone assumes that a name-change is a big deal, and that the police know about it. We don't. No one does. Paedophiles, rapists – anyone can change their name and then vanish. HOLMES knows nothing about it. Politicians talk about closing the legal loophole, but it's never happened. Even if that comes into force, it'll only stop known offenders – those already convicted.'

The journalist thinks for a second and then says, 'Nah. I think the *Guardian* already covered that story,' he says, then adds, 'Who's Holmes, anyway?'

'HOLMES2. Didn't you read *How to Get Away With Murder*? Denver talks about HOLMES in detail.'

'I tend to skim-read,' he says.

'You can't skim-read books like *How to Get Away With Murder*,' Sam admonishes. 'Endings make no sense that way, and we're almost there.'

He sighs. 'If I read too deeply, I start feeling like I'm just another character on someone else's page and the other people around me are just characters, too. Some days, I feel like I'm not even an important character. That I've been cheaply thrown into a scene, probably at the last moment, because the author forgot to convey significant information earlier on. Or needs me to challenge some convention or hint at something a hundred pages in the distance . . .'

He's still talking as Sam walks away, deciding to herself that the young man has really missed the point – he's tantilized by the villain and hasn't been paying attention to the bigger picture.

Sam is surprised to feel the lift descend as she pushes the button for the third floor. When it pings open, she feels that the strange

YouTuber might have a point, because nothing in front of her seems real or right. Gone are the gleaming white tiles, the fake jasmine scent and Bach. Here is motion-activated strip-lighting and grotty carpets that don't quite meet the skirting board. Sam doesn't step out. Instead, she pushes the button again for the third floor. *Beam me up*, she thinks, but the doors just bounce in place, sealing her fate.

Sam squeezes Charlotte's little netball keyring as she steps out into the dark corridor. Something that had once been a pressure-laden reminder of a murdered child now soothes her and gives her confidence in her abilities and conviction. The air is stale and her shoes cling slightly to the floor as she lifts them, implying a stickiness to the carpet that she doesn't want to consider. As she walks, the lights behind her turn off and those ahead flicker to life. Arriving at room 1408, she knocks and a male voice invites her to come in.

*This is it*, she thinks.

The dragon's den.

Julius Windsor, as he is known now, sits behind his desk and doesn't bother to stand when Sam steps into the room and closes the door behind her. She's immediately struck by how tiny the space is. She had pictured the lawyer's office as resembling Charles Dickens's study: giant bookshelves, a mahogany desk, a typewriter. Instead, Windsor sits behind a faux-oak desk that's uncomfortably small for an adult and accommodates only his laptop, his legs clearly visible beneath it. He looks like a man at a primary school parents' evening, crammed into a child's chair. The seat for guests is a foldable yellow plastic thing and Sam notes the creak it gives as she tentatively sits down. There's a small table to the side of Windsor's desk with a browning pot plant, two used blue china cups and a teapot covered with a floral cosy. Sam heats up as she recognizes Betty's precious collection.

In contrast to his grim surroundings, Julius Windsor gleams in his tailored new suit and brogues that are polished to a high shine. The man is average height, with sandy hair and pale skin. He's slightly built and hides a paunch beneath a patterned shirt and garish tie. The tie.

He waits patiently as Sam plonks down her bag and removes her beige trench coat. She's gone over and over what she'll say to him, but as he sits smiling pleasantly, she finds that she's lost for words.

'Good morning, DI Hansen, how lovely to see you again,' he says.

'Good morning, Denver Brady,' Sam counters.

He simply raises an eyebrow slightly. 'Hansen,' he says, as if musing. 'Like that dreadful long-haired boy band from the nineties? 'MMMBop', wasn't it? You must get that a lot.' He gives her a jovial grin.

'Not really,' Sam says. 'I quite liked that song, actually and the band's name is spelled with an O not and E. Speaking of names: Julius Windsor is pretentious as fuck. Especially given that you chose it yourself. It's a bit of a leap from Barry Brown. I guess you needed something posh-sounding for your big-city law firm. A firm you set up with your ill-gotten inheritance.' There's more emotion in her voice than she intended and she focuses on slowing her breathing.

'I don't deny changing my name,' he says carefully, 'and moving to London to set up a law firm with the inheritance from my Aunt Elizabeth. Bettering oneself is hardly illegal.' His accent is pure RP, with perfectly formed vowels and no dropped t's. He even pronounces the word 'aunt' like the word 'aren't', rather than 'ant', as a northerner would. He must have taken elocution lessons to finally rid himself of his Geordie twang.

'Let's talk about *How to Get Away With Murder*,' commands Sam, redirecting the conversation.

'Ahh. Catchy title, wouldn't you say? A solid four and a half out of five on Goodreads, you know.' He winks.

Sam takes a deep breath. This conversation isn't going how she expected. She'd imagined it feeling like a police interview, her pressing and him defending, but he's cracking jokes.

'You murdered your Auntie Betty,' she accuses.

'Dreadful Yorkshire puddings.' Denver/Brown/Windsor chuckles, sitting back in his tatty chair.

Sam feels her cheeks flushing so she takes her eyes from him and lets them roam the small room as she tries to collect her thoughts. There's a dusty mouse trap in the corner. She notices a pile of jiffy bags and imagines the man kneeling down and packing up copies of *How to Get Away With Murder* for posting. She casts her gaze about for surgical gloves, a hair net, or any of the protective clothing that he no doubt wore as he stuffed the books into the waiting envelopes. She wishes she had a warrant to search this place properly.

Taking a deep breath, Sam begins again. 'Your motive was financial, but you also tortured Betty. I'm guessing that she'd tried to disinherit you. She saw you for what you really are. Perhaps you tortured her so she'd tell you where she'd hidden her will, or maybe you're just sick. Probably both. You killed her and used her money to set up this firm – Windsor, Forbes and Knight. But there is no Forbes or Knight. It's just you, isn't it?'

'This practice is highly rated. Feel free to read our client reviews.' He yawns, stretching his arms high above his head. Then, one by one, he bends back each of his fingers until it gives a little pop. He makes a satisfied moan, cracks his neck to one side and then begins to twiddle his thumbs. Sam swallows, sits up straight and clears her throat, deciding to begin at the beginning.

'Jono drowned accidentally in a quarry – you read about that tragedy in the newspaper and even kept a clipping hidden in your aunt's scrapbook. Sarah killed herself – you heard about it and noticed the carving on the oak tree that her best friend made in her memory. Sean Lister isn't dead—'

'Shame.' He shrugs. 'Homophobic loser.'

'You put him in your book as payback,' she says. 'Daisy, you simply lifted from the newspapers and twisted. Amy is a university professor, a wealthy, beautiful woman who rejected you so you wrote some disturbing revenge porn about her. I dare say Basil doesn't even exist – you simply needed to create a narrative for why you wrote the book.'

Windsor's lips twist and he silently, slowly claps his hands together in sarcastic applause. 'That dreadful fellow wouldn't let it drop,' he says. 'No wonder police officers are all in therapy and popping sertraline like smarties. You lot can't let anything go.'

She smiles. 'You're talking about DI Duggan, I presume?' He nods. 'He had you rattled,' she says. 'Reopening Betty's case would have been a disaster for you. That's the real reason you wrote *How to Get Away With Murder* in the first place.'

'I'm thinking about book two,' – he licks his lips – 'although one has to take great care with any sequel. I suppose *Die Hard* and *Star Wars* managed it. Even *Home Alone 2* was all right. Are you a connoisseur of—'

'But Richie Scott killed his girlfriend, Melanie, not you and not Andrei,' Sam snaps. 'I don't understand why you wanted to free Richie. Did you need him just so you could create a convincing serial-killer character to cover up your *one* murder – Betty Brown?'

'I wonder who will play Denver in the film version of *How to Get Away With Murder*,' he ponders out loud, his eyes glistening. 'I'm thinking Henry Cavill or Hugh Grant? Be nice to have a Brit. I suppose Efron is out because he did Bundy, and even Zac can't do more than one serial killer in a career. God, I hope they don't go with Toby Jones; he's an odd-looking—'

'But you're not a serial killer!' she spits. 'You're just another average loser who killed one woman he knew for the most banal of reasons. You're ten a penny. Common. Literally, a daily occurrence.'

'Ouch!' he slaps a hand to his chest and chuckles. 'Maybe Christian Bale could play me—'

'Play *you*? Denver Brady is a character you created; you're nothing like him! You're not Christian Bale in the shower. You're not even Chris Martin. You're a regular man. Squidgy around the edges. Dull. Boring. Like all the serial killers before you. Bigged-up into an idea of something more. Flawed and weak. You are simply the most disappointing Denver I could ever have imagined.' Sam pants slightly in the airless room.

'And yet, the world can't get enough of me. Of us. Serial killers.'

'You planted the evidence at Andrei's home,' Sam pushes on.

He sighs, rolls his eyes and begins to fiddle with a paperclip on his desk, bending it one way then the other, as if he's bored.

'You had Betty's sapphire ring yourself and I'm guessing Richie told you where he'd hidden Mel's earrings, didn't he? You put them with your laptop and hid them at Andrei's house.'

'Serial killers get more fan mail than Harry Styles, and nearly as much pussy,' he says, without bothering to look up at her. 'Andrei has no idea how lucky he—'

'Andrei Albescu is your victim, too,' she says, her voice ripe with hatred. 'It's easy to exploit illegal immigrants, isn't it? The narrative is always reversed in the press. They exploit us, right? I guess he came here, to this very office, for legal advice. You probably offered to pay him to use his bank account, then paid him to burn down Swinton's. Then induced him to confess to writing *How to Get Away With Murder*. Did he know you'd be framing him for murder? Nadja knew you were up to no good. She tried to tell me. She had your business card right there in her hand—'

'Immigration,' he says in a schoolmaster's tone, 'is destroying this great nation. Do you know that in fifty years, half of the UK will be Muslim? Doesn't that scare you? It should. It scares me. Even Brexit can't save us now, because they're already here and they're at it like rabbits. You should be thanking me for—' As he nears the end of his sentence, Denver slips into a Geordie accent that seems to surprise him more than Sam, bringing him to an abrupt stop. He takes a deep breath, and twists the paperclip hard.

'What about Bobby?' Sam whispers. 'Did you kill him, too? Push him into the Tyne the night of his graduation because he started to suspect something wasn't right with you?'

Something flickers, then. Genuine emotion, perhaps, a hint of remorse. It lasts barely a second and then he gives his head a shake, as if to rebury his humanity.

'It feels to me like your boss,' he hisses, snapping the paperclip in half, 'DCI Blakelaw, has decided to close the book on Denver Brady. See what I did there? Close the book?' She ignores his question. 'My genius is wasted on you,' he says. The echo of words from the book in this man's mouth makes Sam's fists clench in her lap.

'The police will—'

'Samantha, you're on your own with this theory of yours. I'm guessing you tried to tell your superiors but you've been told to let it go, haven't you? Your boss landed himself a serial killer and that man who killed his niece on the same day. Do you think he'll let you drag this up again? Of course he won't. Some two-bit copper, probably crippled by daddy issues and up to her eyeballs on antidepressants? You're just—'

'Shut the fuck up,' Sam snarls, her skin burning with anger.

He smiles, snake-like. 'Our time's up, Samantha. I'm a very busy man.'

'I still have questions to—'

'This isn't a children's fairy tale or a cosy crime novel. Not every thread will be tied up, and there is no dramatic third-act happy-ending coming your way. *How to Get Away with Murder* is finished. *Over.*' He grins at her, his lips parting to reveal sharp white teeth.

'We'll see about that,' Sam spits.

'No, we won't,' he sighs. 'By now, you should have somehow realized that you're a minor character in *my* story.'

Sam stands, and turns toward the door; this time she's the one with a smug smile on her face

'What could you possibly have to smile about?' Denver asks. 'You think you're going to be the one that brings me down?'

Sam gives him one final, contemptuous look. 'You're not the only one who loves a good plot twist.'

# 21

Sam wakes early the day after her meeting with Windsor and is soon rattling along the M4 in her little Ford Fiesta, with Toni in the back seat looking smart in his new harness. They're following the same route that Sam and Taylor took a couple of months ago when they visited Richie Scott in HMP Bath, where he belongs. Sam taps along to classic rock on the radio, but flicks channels when any of the many rape songs of the eighties, nineties and noughties come on. 'My Sharona' by The Knack. 'Don't Stand So Close to Me' by The Police. 'Young Girl' by Gary Puckett. Sam's dad had loved all of these songs but they make Sam feel sick, despite the catchy refrains and superb musicianship.

Sam wonders, for the hundredth time that week, what is wrong with men? Then she pictures Adam Taylor and knows deep down that it's not all men, just too many of them. Not Dr Pete Thomson, either. She paid for a final two sessions with him, then thanked him and signed herself off. He's recommended a few female PTSD specialists who she'll reach out to in the future if and when she needs them, and she's engaging with the police psychologist as far as is necessary to get her suspension lifted.

Sam crosses Bath city to the borough of Twerton and parks up a couple of streets away from the house of recently released murderer Richie Scott. From the passenger seat, she spends a few minutes stuffing her own long hair into a wig cap, before sliding a man's wig over the top. She looks like her younger brother in his emo stage. If she had a younger brother, that is. Then she slides a beanie on top of the wig, leaving just small bits of hair visible. She's already wearing men's jeans that conceal her curves and now pulls on a leather biker's jacket. Finally, she attaches clip-on lip and nose-rings, then slides on her sunglasses. Outside the Fiesta, Sam checks her reflection in the windows of the car. *Bloody hell*, she thinks, *I look cool*. If Green Day and Metallica had a son.

Sam and Toni wander the streets casually in search of a certain address. After five minutes, she spots the duck-egg-blue door of 39 Acacia Gardens. The front garden is a jungle, but the street is quite pleasant. Most residents take care of their homes around here. Except for Scott. The lights are on in the house, but Sam can't see any movement. She takes a seat in the bus shelter opposite and lights a cigarette, trying not to cough as she moves it to and from her lips without inhaling.

Sam has a feeling that Richie Scott is the kind of man who heads to the pub around 2 p.m. on a Saturday to get a good seat for the three o'clock kick-off. She glances at her phone screen: 1:02 p.m. A bus pulls up and Sam shakes her head to the driver, who pulls away again. Toni sits patiently, and she pats his back. Without appearing obvious, she tries to check for cameras. She can't see any inside the bus stop or on the street, but the buses themselves will all be fitted with some kind of recording gear. Her head itches underneath the wig, but she can't get at it through the layers.

After thirty minutes she's seen nothing, and Toni begins to whine. She picks him up and he sits awkwardly on her lap. His little body has filled right out and his coat feels much thicker than it originally was when she strokes his back.

'We need some more dental chews for you, boy,' she says as he licks her face, almost making her gag.

Sam's so busy wiping away the saliva that she doesn't notice Richie Scott leave his house. By the time she looks up, he's already through his garden gate. Sam stays seated, her stomach tightening at the sight of Richie without his handcuffs. He's wearing a black football shirt that's at least one size too small. Snug jeans and no coat. He stops, lights a cigarette and hovers. *What's he waiting for?* Sam wonders. For a heart-stopping moment she thinks he might have clocked her as his eyes roam up and down the street, but after a second they pass over her and he looks up at the sky in the way that recently released men tend to do.

'Hurry up, Lindsay!' he yells.

Moments later, the duck-egg door opens and a blonde woman steps out. She looks a lot like Melanie, Sam thinks. Bright-blonde hair. Deep tan. Eyelashes and nails. Gorgeous, if a little overdone for Sam. Far too beautiful to be with this monster. She locks the door and totters down the garden path on skinny stilettos, pulling her denim jacket around her. Richie begins gesturing to her before she's reached the gate. Sam frowns, unable to make out what's going on. He seems to be pointing to Lindsay's shoes and then he pinches her coat. Lindsay says something in return but he shakes his head and she goes back inside the house.

They wait again. Toni is fidgety on Sam's lap, but she doesn't want to move and attract attention. Richie scrolls through his phone, oblivious. Lindsay re-emerges, this time wearing flat shoes, and the jacket is gone, revealing a tight, red tank top and noticeable cleavage. She really is stunning. Richie takes her in from head to toe, nods and they set off down the street. They walk strangely, switching sides of the path now and then. Richie always initiates the movements. It's like a badly choreographed dance and Sam frowns again, baffled. Lindsay rubs her arms as if she's cold. Why did she take her jacket off?

It takes Sam a few more moments to finally realize what's going on.

Richie Scott is a man who likes to control how his women look. The cleavage needs to be out. The make-up and nails done. She's just an accessory to him, like a polished car. Lindsay looks like Mel, but she's taller and surpasses Richie Scott's 5ft 5 by at least two inches. That's why he made her change out of her heels. That's why he's making her walk on the lowest part of the footpath. He needs to be as tall as possible next to her. *What an egomaniac*, Sam thinks, as Richie manoeuvres his girlfriend again.

'He's making her walk in the actual gutter,' Sam mutters to Toni, who ignores her.

After ten minutes of Sam following at a distance, the couple enter a pub. It looks like a nice local, with baskets of flowers along the red-brick front and a few football flags adorning the window-sills. Sam walks past the pub and heads back to the car to sit for a while, so her presence isn't noticed.

When she enters the pub two hours later, she hears Richie before she sees him. As expected, he's clearly several pints in and sits opposite a large screen showing a football game. Sam orders a shandy and sits a few tables behind the couple. They've been joined by some other men in football shirts, whose eyes move from the screen to Lindsay's cleavage and back again. The place smells of hops, BO and cheap aftershave. Occasional cheers and regular profanities fill the air. It seems that the home team is winning.

Sam sips her drink and Toni settles on the floor at her feet. He seems very comfortable in this environment and she wonders if the little scruff frequented similar old-man pubs in his previous life. Despite not being remotely interested in the game, she forces herself to watch it. She allows her eyes to roam across the Lindsay's body from time to time but sees no evidence of bruises or other abuse. If anything, the atmosphere between her and Richie feels positive.

He leans in and whispers to his girlfriend, who discretely takes a twenty-pound note from her purse and passes it to him surreptitiously, as if it were cocaine. He then gets up and buys four pints, which he places in front of each of the men at the table, pocketing the change. He's using her money but wants it to appear that he's using his own. No drink for Lindsay, either. What a knob.

Suddenly, the men erupt in shouting. Toni jumps on to Sam's lap, sending shandy down her sleeve. The men swear and point at the scream. An opposition player is carrying the ball towards the penalty spot. The atmosphere for the remaining seven minutes of the game is hostile. The barman eyes the group as they become more agitated. When the whistle blows, Richie Scott slams his glass down on the table. Lindsay places a hand on his shoulder and he shrugs her off, jumping up and storming out of the pub.

The remaining men chunter among themselves, ignoring Lindsay, who starts looking around for Richie. She's clearly uncertain whether to follow him or await his return. One of the other men speaks to her and she smiles politely, then spins as she hears the door crash open behind her.

'You coming, or what?!' Richie yells at her.

'Sorry, love, I wasn't sure if you'd just gone for a ciggy.'

'You'll say anything, you will. You'll sit all day and talk to any man that'll look at ya. Fuckin' whore,' Richie hisses, and Lindsay blushes.

'There's no need for that. I was just coming,' she says.

Richie Scott grabs Lindsay by the arm and pulls. She appears well made and strong, but she is no match for Scott and flies off her stool, which clatters on to the floor.

'Hey!' calls the barman, but Richie has already dragged his new girlfriend through the pub's front door, letting it swing shut behind him. Sam watches as the barman shakes his head and picks up a glass to polish. 'Some men,' he says to no one in particular.

*Don't worry mate*, she thinks, clipping on Toni's lead. *I'll make sure he gets exactly what he deserves.*

# 22

Sam watches through the window as the woman from the estate agent wrestles to erect a 'For Sale' sign in her jungle of a front garden. The online ad for the home on Acklam Terrace, which Sam has lived in since she was a teenager, describes it as 'dated but homely' and on a 'sought-after street' in a 'desirable borough' of London.

The house sale will leave Sam a wealthy woman. Free to start again somewhere new. She's tempted by an advert for a Detective Sergeant position at Northumbria Police. It's a step down from DI, but she's happy to go easy on herself for a year or two, given everything she's been through. From her initial searches, she's discovered that she can afford to rent a three-bedroom apartment on Newcastle's Quayside for less than the interest fetched by the money from the sale of her tatty house in London. *Toni would love a little garden*, Sam thinks to herself as she sends an enquiry form to North East Properties.

'Can you say, "*Wey aye, mate?*" Sam asks Toni, who raises an eyebrow and scratches behind an ear.

The sign finally erected, the woman waves to Sam and she returns to watching the news. MATHERS CLAIMS INNOCENCE, the headline scrolls across the screen, as the presenter describes how Jack Mathers has pled 'Not guilty'. His brother Nigel has refused to visit him or pay for legal representation. Jack is on remand pending trial, which won't begin for several months.

Although she's accepted calls from Harry, Tina, Chloe Spears and DI Neil Duggan, Sam is still cancelling any calls from Adam Taylor. She's been busy, she tells herself, trying to bring two killers to justice. More honestly, though, she's ashamed. She knows she put Taylor in a terrible position after her panic attack in Newcastle and she doesn't blame him for calling Harry – as far as Taylor was aware, he called the man who was like a father to her. It's not Taylor's fault that Harry has suspended her. She's embarrassed, too. Embarrassed that she keeps thinking about the way his fingers lingered on her cheek. She shakes her head, pushing away the idea that any man would be interested a forty-something year old with PTSD and a wonky-legged mongrel.

She kills time until Saturday packing boxes and emailing back and forth with Erica from HR to discuss a transfer to a different police force. When the weekend comes, she drives out to Bath again.

She parks her car in the same spot as before but wears a different disguise: a brown bob with an oversized knitted sweater, leggings, and brown contact lenses behind chunky reading glasses. Toni wanted to come, but she's left him at home this time. Sam orders fish and chips at the bar and is seated long before Richie and Lindsay arrive. Sam keeps her head in her magazine as Scott searches for a seat. When her meal arrives, Sam casually looks around and sees the couple a few tables to her left. She knows instantly that things have escalated since her last visit. Lindsay has a black eye. A burst lip. The poor woman has tried to cover them with make-up, but it's obvious even from across the room.

Sam struggles to enjoy her fish and chips. The potato clings to her throat and the mushy peas cool on her plate. The waiter carries food over to Scott's table and Sam notices that Lindsay eats one-handed, leaving her left hand lying on her lap. The couple eat in silence.

When she sees Lindsay standing up, she quickly rises herself and walks briskly to the Women's room. From inside a cubicle,

Sam hears Lindsay enter and lock the adjacent door. Then there's the sound of a struggle. Then a little sob. Sam steps out and knocks on Lindsay's door.

'Won't be a sec,' she calls.

'I was just wondering if you're OK,' Sam replies.

Slowly, the cubicle door opens. 'I'm all right,' Lindsay sniffs, 'but, can you, er, can you undo my jeans for me?'

Sam stares. 'Pardon?'

'Undo my jeans. Just the top button? I'm right-handed and my wrist is, er, injured.'

'Oh. OK,' Sam says, stepping closer and using all of her fingers to force the button through the stiff denim buttonhole. 'What happened to your hand?'

'Accident,' Lindsay mumbles.

'I'm not surprised you couldn't undo that. Those jeans are practically painted on to you,' Sam says, smiling up at Lindsay, but the other woman's eyes are brimming with tears.

'Sit down, love,' Sam says. 'We need to talk.'

## 23

Harry looks older than ever when they meet for dinner the following week, but he's full of the joys of spring. As he examines the menu, Sam takes him in – this man, who had been her only family, her only rock for so many years. He's smart, in a suit, his almost entirely grey hair slicked back. Sam runs her hands through her own hair, which is soft, styled and freshly highlighted.

After their brief encounter in the Women's room, she'd arranged to meet Lindsay at a hairdresser's today, so they could chat without Richie becoming suspicious. They'd sat together in a quiet corner of the salon, tinfoil in their hair, and Lindsay had sobbed as Sam told her the truth about Richie Scott. Lindsay had confessed that he'd become more 'hands on' not long into their relationship. Just the night before, Lindsay confided, he poured his drink over her head and then pretended it was a joke. As they were talking, Lindsay was constantly texting, fearful of not replying quickly enough to Richie. Even though he was tracking her location, he still asked for a photograph of his girlfriend in the hairdresser's holding up his chosen number of fingers, and then a photograph of the hairdresser so he could be sure it wasn't another man.

'. . . Earth to Sam,' Harry says. 'Pete's arrived.'

Dr Pete Thomson takes a seat at the table and greets her warmly, and she's relieved he doesn't seem uncomfortable about socializing with a former patient. Sam sips her water as Pete and Harry catch up. As the men chat, she takes in Harry's familiar face, the bushy eyebrows that have more grey than black in them now. For all his flaws, Harry is probably the person she knows best in this world, since her dad died. In many ways, she owes Harry more than anyone, her father included. Without him, she'd never have joined the police. She'd never wanted to follow in her father's footsteps – she'd seen what the job can do to someone – but Harry had been determined that the police force was the right path for Sam. The night she'd wept on Harry's shoulder, as her father's body lay cooling in the basement at Acklam Terrace, he'd told her that she was made of the right stuff. So, Sam had joined the police, determined to catch the bad guys. She'd just never expected Harry to be one of them.

'We'll take the Château Montrose,' Harry says to the waiter.

'Very good, sir,' the man says and walks away.

Sam hates red wine. It's something she's always wanted to like, but she just can't. She smiles anyway. Maybe this time it'll taste better. She looks to Dr Thomson, who says nothing about the choice of wine. If anything, the doctor looks as surprised to be here as he sounded on the phone when she called last week to invite him.

'Well, this is nice,' he says. 'You both look so well. Especially you, Samantha. The change in you is impressive. Love the new hair by—'

'Don't call her Samantha, she hates it,' Harry says, tearing open his bread roll.

Pete turns to her, astounded. 'Oh, really? In all our time working together, you never said!'

She shrugs. 'It's just Sam.'

'Like her old man,' Harry adds. 'DI Sam Hansen, mark two.'

Pete smiles. 'Sam it is, then.'

The waiter returns and performs the tasting ceremony to perfection. Harry sniffs and swirls, then nods. The waiter fills Sam's glass first, then Dr Thomson's, and finally Harry's, before placing the bottle in the centre of the table. They raise their glasses in unison, holding eye contact as they chink. A waitress arrives to take their food order and Sam opts for pasta, as does Pete. Harry orders a blue fillet steak and a side of chips. Sam momentarily worries about his cholesterol, but Pete interrupts the thought with a question about her move out of London.

'My packing is well underway,' she answers. 'I'm hoping for a transfer to Newcastle, or perhaps Cumbria. If not, I might just travel for a while. I've a few odds and ends still to tie up.'

'I can't fathom it, myself,' Harry says, 'quitting London for the grim North. There's nothing in Newcastle but Greggs and pubs.'

'Sounds fine to me,' says Pete, and he winks at Sam.

'It's the arse-end of nowhere,' Harry continues, dipping his bread in the shared ramekin of fluffy yellow butter. Sam sips her wine and tries not to wince at its taste. She knows she'll never finish a whole glass, so she pours herself some water from the carafe. 'She should just come back to the Met. You'd sign her off again, wouldn't you, Pete? She can try another phased return.'

Sam can't speak, too afraid of what she'll say. Mercifully, Pete doesn't mention that she's no longer his patient and tactfully switches the subject.

'When's your last day, Harry?'

'End of the month, officially, but the new DCI has already taken over. He's moved into my office and put dreadful art on the walls. I went in today to say my final cheerios and eat cheap cake.'

'How's Tina doing?' Sam asks.

'Who?' Harry wonders. 'Oh, her. Fine, fine. I never doubted her. Better than your trainee. What's-his-name hasn't stopped moping about the place since you decided to take some time off.'

'Taylor,' Sam mutters. 'His name is Adam Taylor.'

'I'm sick of him,' Harry says, 'wandering about like a lost puppy. First, asking when you'd be back. Then how were you doing. Just yesterday he had the nerve to ask me to pass a message to you.'

'What message?' Sam asks, her skin tingling.

'How should I know?' Harry scoffs. 'Told him I'm retired and I'm not taking up a new role as a postman.'

'I can't believe you're actually retired,' says Pete quickly, possibly noticing Sam's white knuckles clenched around her butter knife. 'I was so surprised to hear—'

'Used to have compulsory retirement, you know,' Harry says through a mouthful of bread, 'the Met did. Fifty-five. Ridiculous, isn't it? Retiring us at fifty-five. But I'm a fair bit older than that now and I just thought, I'll go out on a high. It's a good time and, well, let's just say I have a friend who thinks I might do well in politics. He's made a few introductions. There's always the local council and even . . . well, we need some damn good MPs if we're going to sort it all out. Hmm. Say no more for now.' Harry taps his nose and Sam takes a deep breath.

'You'd make a great MP,' she forces a smile. 'You'll move out of London, I suppose?'

'Yes, I let my little flat go, so I'm back home in Broadstairs with the wife. Thank God for the golf club.'

'How is Beryl?' Sam asks.

'Good days and bad. She's more forgetful than ever. Mind you, she can still remember what I did wrong yesterday, last week, even last year. I've even started walking to keep out of the way. Me, walking. Like those fuddy-duddy old men in beige coats. It'll be a flat cap next, you watch.'

'Where do you walk?' Pete asks, clearly keen to change the subject.

'Along the tops at Botany Bay,' Harry says.

'Toni loves that beach,' Sam says. 'We might join you one time. Before we head to the arse-end of nowhere.'

'Yes. Well. I'm not much for dogs, but . . . I thought you were getting rid of it, anyway?'

'Steak, sir?'

The waiter brings the food and Sam's pasta is exquisite, but she could eat it twice. The gourmet portion-sizes aren't enough now that she's jogging again. The three of them make small talk through dinner and all order dessert – with a round of brandy for the men, at Harry's insistence. Sam's surprised to discover that Pete is married and is in the process of adopting a six-year-old boy.

Pete asks about the Charlotte Mathers murder trial – apparently, his husband is a true-crime buff and is following it all keenly. She admits to Pete that she's no longer centrally involved in the case preparation for trial, but she believes that the evidence is limited. A conviction is possible, she tells him, but without a confession the prosecutor might struggle. It depends on the jury on the day.

'I always liked the uncle for it,' Harry says through a mouthful of steak.

Sam takes a deep breath, but says nothing.

Pete asks about Andrei Albescu. Of course, Pete calls him Denver, his real name as lost to him as his freedom. In truth, she's done her best to push thoughts of Andrei in a twelve-by-five-foot cell out of her mind. The media have made that difficult, though. There have been linguists and profilers on every TV show since it happened, analysing *How to Get Away With Murder*. Claire, the linguist who helped Sam, has been offered fifty thousand pounds to feature in the latest docuseries. If only they all knew, she thinks. She gives Pete a measured response about Andrei, hoping to turn the conversation away from that topic – one that's highly likely to keep her awake tonight, just as it has every night for weeks.

Sam's eyes grow heavy as the meal draws to a close. The packing and the planning are really sapping her mental energy. She's relieved when the waiter finally puts the padded black book containing the bill next to Harry and produces a card machine from his belt. Harry takes out a gold credit card.

'Let's just split it evenly, eh? Far simpler,' Harry says, and taps the machine after the waiter has keyed in the amount.

Pete catches Sam's eye, but neither of them says anything. They each produce their own debit cards and pay their portion of the bill. The waiter brings their coats and tells Harry that his driver is waiting.

'Casino, old boy?' Harry turns to Pete.

'I'm guessing you'll also say no, Sam?' Harry says after Pete declines, forcing his arms into his coat. 'Your old man and me, we had some nights, I can tell you.'

Sam smiles as best she can as she shakes her head. Harry kisses Sam on both cheeks before turning for the door, and she and Pete watch him leave. She thinks he looks aged, a little unsteady on his feet. No longer the tall, lean man with pitch-black hair that used to spend hours in their living room, talking about antique shotguns with her father and pretending not to notice her mother's bruised arms.

'It's great to see you both getting on so well again,' Pete says, once Harry's left the restaurant. 'It's a shame you lost that relationship when you needed it most. I don't think Harry ever understood how much damage he did when he promoted that officer who—'

'Harry's always been like a father to me,' Sam says, cutting Pete off and tapping on her phone screen. 'He's not perfect, but I love him dearly. Where are you headed, Doc?'

'Same direction as you, I think. Share an Uber?'

'Great idea.'

'I'll get it,' Pete says. 'At least I enjoyed the overpriced wine. Fancy splitting the bill – what a bugger he is sometimes, eh?'

Sam just smiles.

'One last drink before I order the taxi?' Pete asks.

'No thanks, Doc. Hangovers last a lot longer now I've turned forty.' Sam slides her arms into her jacket sleeves. 'Plus, Toni's waiting at home and we have a lot to get done before we move.'

'Of course,' Dr Thomson says. 'No rest for the wicked.'

'Exactly,' Sam says.

# 24

Toni watches as Sam tapes down the final box and writes 'LOUNGE' on it in marker pen. Renting a place without seeing it in real life is risky, but Neil Duggan has assured her that the flat she's chosen is in a good area, 'in the posh part of toon'; and it's near Northumbria Police HQ, the Quayside, and the green and pleasant Exhibition Park, perfect for dog-walking. Sam still finds the cost of rent Up North too good to be true and struggles to believe that she can rent a three-bedroom apartment with a small garden, located 'in the posh part', for less money per month than a room in a London HMO.

As she finishes up, she skims through the messages from Lindsay on her phone. The messages are essays, but she goes back to the beginning and takes the time to read each word carefully before replying. Sam knows the dangers of skim-reading and missing important words or phrases that hint at a meaning entirely different from the surface level. Sam's reminded of the journalist she met in Windor's office reception and what he'd told her about skim-reading Denver's how-to guide, and of how he'd failed to grasp the facts. She had taken her time, never skimming a single word of the book, not that she'd ever felt the urge to. Rather than subjecting the reader to chunks of description and filler text, the book had simply credited them with the intelligence to assume that time had passed and things had happened, and that they'd be saved from mundanity and offered only the bits they needed. The best bits.

Sam slides her phone into her back pocket and decides to take one last look around the terraced house that's been her home since her late teens, and check that everything's ready. She runs upstairs and trips at the top step, sending herself flying across the landing. As she lands, she laughs, amazed at how hopeful she's feeling now, compared to this time last year. She jumps up and works her way through the upstairs rooms. Everything is in place. The empty rooms look so much bigger now, with all their contents in labelled boxes against the wall. There are marks on the carpets where furniture has stood for two decades, leaving a completely different shade in the now-exposed pile that once hid beneath. She does the same downstairs, Toni trotting wonkily behind her. He'd cocked his leg against one of the boxes when Sam had begun packing, so she's trying to keep an eye on him.

Finished in the main house, she pulls back the lino in the corner of the kitchen to reveal the cellar door. Lots of old London houses have a basement, her dad had explained the first time he brought her down there: a cavernous space designed to protect the main house from ground water and often used for shelter during the Blitz. Cellars then became man caves – places where husbands worked for hours on model train sets or, in her father's case, polished his antique pistol collection. Now, according to the estate agent, they function as wine cellars or games rooms.

The old stairs are solid English oak, and she walks down them without making a creak. Using the light on her phone, she examines the now empty room. Her dad's desk is still in the corner, a huge lamp next to it, strewn with cobwebs. She doesn't need to close her eyes – she can see him there still. Slumped over his desk, antique pistol in one hand, a pot of polish open in front of him. Brains splattered up the wall. No note. That's odd, the police had said.

Sam jumps as her phone pings, and Toni whines from above. She takes one last look at the old desk and turns, walking back up the basement stairs. The message, as she expects, is from Lindsay, and Sam fills the kettle and sets it to boil as she begins reading. Lindsay tells her that she'd like to meet up again at the cafe in Bath. It'll be their fourth meet-up since the day Sam spoke candidly to her in the hairdresser's.

It's a long drive for each hurried cuppa and conversation, but Sam agrees to it immediately and sets a day and time. Lindsay's been doing really well; her arm is healing and the women have become like friends. Sam suspects that she's getting ready to leave Richie, and wants to be there to see her to safety. She knows it takes victims of domestic abuse an average of five years and around half a dozen attempts before they finally leave for good. Lindsay would be a bit of a miracle if she got out this soon, but she's living with a murderer so perhaps she's more motivated.

'And I can't wait longer than one more month,' she says to Toni, who scratches at the door, asking to go to the beach, 'because we'll be moving away.'

The kettle boils and she warms the teapot, adds two tea bags, then lets the water hit them with a hiss – the strike, it's called. Sam fires off a few more messages and checks the news for anything new on Andrei Albescu or Jack Mathers. DENVER BRADY SENTENCED TO LIFE, she reads, and takes a deep breath. She knew the day was coming: Andrei pled guilty and thus skipped a jury trial and went straight to sentencing, so it was only a matter of time. She suspects a deal was offered: a life sentence, rather than a *whole life* sentence, meaning he'll serve twenty-five years. For burning down a building and making a few bad choices. Sam swallows. She desperately wishes she could help the man, but it's impossible. All she can do now is ensure those responsible are brought to account. Sam pours her tea from the pot when the timer sounds and adds milk.

She carries the cup to the lounge, where she and Toni sit

together on the sofa. Sam polishes her police baton and sips her tea. On the TV, Del Boy tries to sell an oversized trench coat to his mate. Sam chuckles. She knows the words to this episode; it's one of her favourites. Once the baton is polished, she places it on the shelf in the entry hall. It's supposed to live on the leather belt that police officers wear around their waist, and Sam promises herself she'll put it away soon.

After she's finished her tea, she clips on Toni's lead, grabs a coat and unlocks the front door. Outside, Toni runs towards the car, tugging her along.

'No, boy, we're not going to the beach today,' Sam says, and the little scruff falls into step beside her. Toni loved their strolls along the clifftops, but Sam's already closed that chapter.

Instead, she turns towards the high street. After purchasing a small bunch of daffodils, she hops on the next bus and they disembark near Holland Park. She walks the full length and breadth of it today, in no hurry to reach her destination. When Toni starts to shiver, she turns towards the cluster of oak trees.

The teddies and flowers are fewer, but still fresh, lying against the tree where Charlotte Mathers was murdered by her uncle. There's a warm breeze, but Sam is cold under the oak's shade and can't take her eyes off the scratched trunk where Jack Mathers carved his niece's and Denver's initials to throw the police off his scent. Now there's a plaque instead:

C, SLEEP WELL, MY ANGEL. DAD XXX.

Sam lays her daffodils against the tree and closes her eyes.

'Hello, Detective Hansen,' says a small voice from behind, and Sam turns, wiping her eyes. Jessica and Mrs Patel stand together, each holding a bunch of fresh flowers. The woman nods a greeting then walks away from her daughter to place the flowers against the trunk.

Jessica smiles up at Sam. 'Thank you for catching him,' she says. 'This increases your solve rate to ninety-nine per cent.'

Sam smiles, saying nothing. Toni approaches tentatively and the girl bends to stroke his head, giving Sam a second to think. She reaches into her jeans pocket and holds out her clasped hand. 'I think this belongs with you,'

Jessica steps closer and takes Charlotte's netball keyring, running her thumb over its now well-worn surface. The C in the middle of the ball is barely visible, and the chain is twisted from so much handling.

Jessica holds the keyring to her chest. 'I'm one hundred per cent certain that I'll remember you always, Detective Samantha Hansen.'

'Just Sam is fine,' she says, blinking away tears.

Without warning, the girl throws her arms around Sam's waist, then just as quickly detaches herself and walks away. Sam watches as Jessica goes over to the great oak tree, lays down her flowers and, beside them, places Charlotte's little netball.

# 25

Sam's sick of the sight of the M4, but she taps the steering wheel as she drives, singing along to her favourite dad-rock-band, Journey. The song finishes and the presenter announces that the news is coming up, followed by 'Delilah'. Sam flicks stations and lands on a Taylor Swift song, 'Love Story'. She remembers singing along to it with Adam Taylor and she shifts stations again, picking up a country-music station. This time a woman is singing about a pretty little souped-up four-wheel-drive. It's a happy song that feels like summer, even though the skies are a perfect shade of British Grey.

Lindsay is already there when Sam pulls up outside Bath Swimming Pool, hovering in the doorway, teeth chattering. Not for the first time, Sam wishes she'd wear a proper coat. Sam folds her arms around her friend gently, as if she were embracing a bruised bird, then they go to the desk, pay and walk through the turnstile to the swimming pool's cafe. The smell of chlorine is overwhelming, but Sam quite likes it, the same way she enjoys the fumes at a petrol station. They order their usual drinks and sit at their table in the corner; Lindsay likes to have her back to the wall and see the entrances and exits of any room she's in. Her teeth continue to chatter and she looks around nervously, even though she knows Richie is at Ashton Gate football stadium, fifteen miles away. Sam is still waiting for her to speak when the drinks arrive. The tea is good, and Sam warms her hands on the cup.

'I'm ready,' Lindsay finally says, picking a marshmallow from the top of her hot chocolate. As she strokes her hair back from her face, Sam sees that her ear is black and swollen. Bruised and out of shape like a rugby player's. Like Melanie's.

'Are you sure, Linds?' Sam asks. 'I don't want to discourage you, but if we do this, we have to do it right. Leaving an abusive partner is dangerous.'

'I know I chickened out before, Sam, but this is different,' Lindsay promises, her words sounding thick, as if she's talking with her mouth full of food. 'Last night . . .' She trails off, staring into space.

'Linds?' she says, pulling the other woman's focus back.

'Sorry. My head is battered. Literally. I think I might have concussion. My ears are ringing, too.' Lindsay pushes her fingers hard against her temples. 'It's like this high-pitched sound, but all the time.'

'It might be tinnitus. My mum had it. I know it's awful.' Sam smiles sadly.

'It's because he hits me round the ears, isn't it?'

Sam doesn't respond. She doesn't have the heart to tell Lindsay that the bruises will fade and the bones will knit back together, but there are some things Richie has done to her that she will have to live with long-term.

'Richie's angrier than ever,' Lindsay says. 'He thought he was going to be famous, what with all the press attention he got when he was released from prison, but that's died off. He thought he was gonna be rich, too – his lawyer promised him they'd sue the police for wrongful imprisonment. That's not happening because the lawyer says he doesn't have time for it any more and Richie needs to find someone else to represent him. He's not sleeping. Not eating. Just drinking and being angry. It's scary.'

'Is that what's made you think now is the time to leave?' Sam asks.

'Not just that,' Lindsay says. 'The beatings are getting worse.

Last night, he put a pillow on my head and sat on it.' Sam's hand flies to her mouth, even though she's heard stories like this, worse even, hundreds of times.

'That's awful, Linds,' she mutters.

'I thought he was gonna kill me. I couldn't breathe. My eyes felt like they were popping out and I . . . I . . .' Lindsay looks down at her untouched hot chocolate, her cheeks flushing pink.

'It's OK, Linds,' she reassures her. 'Go on.'

'I pissed myself.'

Sam doesn't speak. What can she say?

'Not only that,' Lindsay continues, 'I bit through my tongue. I didn't feel it at the time, but it's killing me now. He only got off me when I passed out. I honestly think he thought I was dead. When I came to, I found him crying.'

Sam slides her hand across the table and holds Lindsay's cold, bony fingers in hers.

'I'm ready, Sam. I'm really ready this time.'

'Once we set the ball rolling, there's no going back,' Sam warns.

Lindsay nods.

'OK,' Sam says. 'We leave now. Right now.'

Lindsay gapes at her. 'But I haven't—'

'We've got some time before the football finishes. It's not much of a head start, but it's enough. We'll go back to Acacia Gardens together. You can pack your stuff and then I'll drive you straight to King's Cross. You're taking the first train to Newcastle. My friend Neil will meet you at the station and you'll stay in my new apartment for two weeks.'

'I don't have any winter clothes,' Lindsay says, panicking. 'It's cold up North. I seen it on *Geordie Shore*.'

'Are we doing this, Lindsay?' Sam asks, her voice firm.

'Richie would hate the thought of me going out on the Quayside. And this Neil – who's he?'

'A friend. He's a police officer. You can trust him, I promise.'

'Wow. Newcastle,' Lindsay says. 'Yes. I'm doing this. Today. Else Richie will kill me. I know he will.'

'I've already got you a travel pack sorted,' Sam says. 'It's in the boot of my car. I've put a bit of cash in there for you, plus a new phone, but it's not a smartphone. You can't go online after today. Not until this is over with. I've put some clothes in there, too. And snacks. Even my favourite book for you to read on the train. I'll need you to give me your phone, Linds, and tell me the passcode and any passwords.'

Lindsay looks at Sam doubtfully. 'Why?'

'It's common in domestic violence cases for abusive partners to plant hidden tracking on phones,' Sam says in her official voice. 'Over and above the tracking you might consent to. You can use the new phone I got you, and I'll get this one checked and back to you as soon as I can.'

'He tracks me everywhere,' Lindsay sighs, taking her iPhone tentatively from her pocket and stroking it. The case is bubble-gum pink. Slowly, she pushes it across the table to Sam. 'That's why we have to meet at the swimming pool cafe and I have to jump in the bloody deep end every time so I smell of chlorine.'

'What's the passcode?' Sam asks, picking up the phone.

'Richie doesn't like passcodes,' Lindsay says, 'and he changed all my passwords to "LindslovesRichie".'

'I'll take care of it,' Sam slides the phone into her pocket.

'What'll happen to Richie?' Lindsay asks.

Sam shrugs and stands to leave. She can't lie to Lindsay about the outcome she anticipates for Richie Scott. Instead, she says, 'Look on the bright side, Linds. At least you don't have to jump in the swimming pool today.'

They drive to Acacia Gardens and Sam sits in the car as Lindsay heads into the house to pack. Sam takes the pink phone from her pocket and accesses Lindsay's Facebook, unfriending and blocking Richie Scott. She switches the phone to silent and checks that no alarms are set to go off. Then she attaches a charging cable and plugs that into a power bank. She pops them all in a plastic ziplock bag and leaves the little package sitting in her door pocket for later.

On her own phone, she texts Neil to let him know that the plan is in motion. She books Lindsay on to a train out of King's Cross, up to Newcastle. Rail strikes mean that there's only one train they can take, otherwise Lindsay will have to stay in London tonight and that's too risky. Sam pulls up Google Maps. Richie will be tracking Lindsay's phone as soon as the Bristol City match ends, if not before. Plus, she needs to make one stop-off along the way. The timings are certainly tight, but not impossible if they leave now.

Lindsay emerges through the duck-egg door carrying a pink duffle bag and a large teddy bear. When she sees Sam eyeing the toy, Lindsay explains that it's a childhood favourite that she couldn't leave behind. Sam smiles, seeing the teddy as a sign that Lindsay is leaving for good this time and intends to never step foot inside Richie Scott's house again.

Lindsay falls asleep as soon as they hit the M4. Sam hopes that she isn't severely concussed or damaged after Richie's latest beating. She tunes the radio to a sports station and listens to the scores come in. Bristol City is two-nil down. Richie will be furious. *Good*, Sam thinks. She checks the time. It's getting late. Soon the crowds will flow out of Ashton Gate and he'll see that something is amiss. The women have a few hours' head start at most. She prays that Richie doesn't track Lindsay's phone before the full-time whistle blows. She pushes her foot down on the accelerator. The little Fiesta rattles as it tops eighty miles per hour.

They hit a huge traffic jam waiting to enter London, and by the time they pull up outside 132 Stafford Terrace, Sam is sweating. She'll have to be quick or they'll miss the train, and she knows that, by now, Richie Scott will be after them.

'Where are we?' Lindsay asks, waking up for the first time since Bath and taking in the fine London city street that they've stopped in. 'This isn't the train station.' The area is impressive and reminds Sam of Charlotte Mathers' home. There are flowering hanging baskets and gloss-black railings adorning towering white houses that are worth millions.

'Just dropping something off, Linds. Then I'll get you to King's Cross.'

Lindsay glances at her watch and pales.

'The football's finished, Sam.' Panic suffuses her voice. 'Richie will be coming for me. Can't you do this later? Please, just get me out of here!'

Sam offers a quick word of reassurance but is preoccupied with looking in her car mirrors, waiting for the street to be clear. She pulls a hat and sunglasses on as a rudimentary disguise, but would much rather avoid being seen anywhere near this house. When the street is as empty as it's going to be, she jumps out of the car, slipping the plastic package from her door pocket. She climbs the steep steps to a black front door with an ornate brass knocker, then pauses, looking around her, before standing on tiptoe and reaching into one of the hanging baskets. If she were a woman of average height, she wouldn't have a chance, but she manages to push the bag deep into the soil in the basket. She stands back, examining the basket from all angles. Nothing of the package can be seen. She descends the steps three at a time and jumps back in the car.

'What were you doing that's so important?' Lindsay asks, her voice shrill.

'Just a quick errand,' Sam replies, then slams the accelerator and skids out of the street.

'You have posh friends,' Lindsay says, relaxing a little now that they're on the move again.

'Not a friend. Just a lawyer,' Sam states, taking the road towards King's Cross station. 'He's a rotten guy, to be honest with you.'

Lindsay pulls her teddy bear to her chest. 'Aren't all men rotten?'

'Not all of them, Linds,' Sam says. She has the sudden urge to text Adam Taylor, to ask him to meet her for dinner, or even just a walk around Battersea Park with Toni. She doesn't have long left in London, but if it's his weekend off they could do something together. She knows he'd answer on the first ring if she called.

Still, she can't help picturing how it would be. Perhaps he'd arrive with an expensive bouquet of flowers that she'd have no vase for and that would look completely out of place in her empty lounge. He'd stroke Toni behind the ears and the little scruff would walk treacherously at Adam's heel instead of hers. She'd take him around the lake and he might say, 'This is beautiful, Sam. It's a shame you're thinking about moving away from here. We could do this kind of thing more often.'

After the Rosery Gardens, where they'd pretend to be a Victorian couple taking the air, they'd sit on a bench in the Old English Garden and she'd feel the press of his body against hers.

'Newcastle is only three hours away, Sam,' he might say, and she could smile and let her brown eyes rest on his blue ones for long enough to mean something. His hand would reach over and take hold of hers, pretending to rub her cold fingers for warmth, but really asking a question. And she might nod and exhale as he leans in, his eyes closing and his lips moving towards—

'There it is!' Lindsay almost yells. 'King's Cross. Shit, Sam! You missed the turning.'

'Sorry!' She indicates and pulls into a side street. 'My head was somewhere else.'

'I'm running for my life here, Sam,' Lindsay squeaks. 'Please can you concentrate?'

'Sorry, Linds.' She works her way through the traffic until she finds a vacant space along the station's western wall. She hugs Lindsay and talks her through what to do next, then watches as her friend and her teddy bear vanish into the crowds of King's Cross.

Sam breathes a sigh of relief, then takes out her phone, her finger hovering over Taylor's name.

*Maybe*, she thinks. *Maybe.*

# 26

Sam hears about it second hand, of course. It doesn't make the front page, because that's still being wasted on Andrei Albescu; apparently serial killers are evergreen news items. But she does receive a text from Adam Taylor. She pauses *Only Fools and Horses* and reads the message several times over:

> Julius Windsor (the lawyer with the pheasant tie) has been attacked. We're looking for Richie Scott – he's on the run. Thought you'd want to know. See you soon? Axx.

Sam doesn't reply, but she smiles to herself.

'Not very satisfying, really,' she remarks to Toni, who's sprawled over her lap. 'If this was a book, readers would want details. They'd want to see everything play out scene by scene. But sometimes, imagining is better.'

She closes her eyes and tries to picture the prick of a lawyer who wrote *How to Get Away With Murder*, to cover up his murder of his aunt. He's walking towards the front door in his fancy house to answer a knock. He looks through the peephole, because even killers take precautions. A man waits on his doorstep. He recognizes the man. A client. A fellow criminal. The lawyer opens the door and Richie Scott steps inside. Richie's ranting about his girlfriend, Lindsay, saying that he's tracked her phone to this address. Richie suspects she's trying to leave him and has hired herself a lawyer. The lawyer, of course, denies all knowledge of

Lindsay's whereabouts. Unfortunately, Richie doesn't believe him and, more unfortunately still, Richie has a temper. What follows is a bone-crunching, lip-bursting, rib-cracking montage in Sam's imagination.

She forces the smile from her face, takes out her phone and calls local hospitals until she lands on the right one. She tries to lace her voice with concern and to sound much older than she is when she speaks to the nurse.

'Windsor, Julius Windsor,' Sam says, 'I'd like to know how he's doing, please, dear.'

'Are you family?' the nurse asks.

'Oh, yes,' Sam says. 'I'm his Aunt Elizabeth. But you can call me Betty.'

The nurse tells her that she's very sorry, but Mr Windsor is in a critical condition. If Betty can possibly make it to the hospital, she should come soon. Sam explains that she can't come but would the lovely nurse please hold Julius's hand and tell him that Aunty Betty is thinking of him? She will? How kind.

Sam hangs up and laughs hard as Del Boy pours Maxwell House coffee over Uncle Albert's Christmas dinner. It takes a few minutes for her to regain her breath, then suddenly something makes her spine tingle: a noise. The gentle click of her garden gate. Movement outside. A footstep. The crunch of glass underfoot. An outside security light flashes on. She holds her breath, straining to hear more. Then, the unmistakable sound of someone trying the handle of her front door. Sam grabs the TV remote, hitting the off-button and plunging the room into darkness.

It's time.

# 27

Sam's armpits prickle and her ears flood with a roaring sound. She hears the door click as it opens. A footstep on the hallway tiles. She can hear someone breathing. Then, the door closes softly. Another footstep in the hall. Someone is inside her home. Sheer panic runs through her and she's frozen, unable to move. Some distant part of her knows she should find her phone and dial 999, but she just sits there, paralysed. Fear makes her pelvic floor muscles drop. She can hear herself panting. She can taste her fear – a familiar, salty flavour at the back of her throat.

A bright light shines in the hallway. Perhaps a mobile-phone torch.

A man steps into the lounge.

He's dressed all in black leather that squeaks as he advances into the room. A balaclava covers his features but Sam knows exactly who he is. She rises slowly to her feet, her dressing gown heavy around her. Her movement draws his attention and he turns, shining the light in her face.

'Hello Samantha,' he says, his voice muffled by the fabric over his face. He flicks his left wrist and a long, thin shape extends in front of him. 'Find your weapon in the victim's house,' he says, paraphrasing Denver Brady and waving her own baton at her. 'This is better than a bread knife.' She never returned the baton to her utility belt after polishing it. It was there, in the hallway, for him to pick up. He laughs cruelly through the open mouth of the mask.

'I thought I might see you again,' she says, trying but failing to level her voice. Legs jelly. Heart pumping. Her hand extended to shield her face from the torchlight.

'You thought you'd see me again, but you still didn't have the sense to lock your front door?' he asks.

'What do you want?'

He doesn't answer. Instead he growls as he steps towards her. Sam jumps but can't go anywhere. She's in the corner of the room and he's still standing in the only doorway. She notices his muddy footprints on the old carpet and wonders fleetingly if he's wearing boots that are his own or have been bought especially for tonight, as Denver would have advised. 'Where's my girlfriend?' he growls.

'You murdered her, remember?'

'I'll fuck you up,' he hisses.

She can't help but bark a laugh at how predictable he is.

'Don't you dare fucking la—'

'OK, Richie,' Sam says, holding her hands up. 'I know where Lindsay is, and I'll tell you. But first, tell me what happened with Julius Windsor. I want details. Did he beg?'

'You're one twisted—'

'Bitch?' Sam suggests. 'Julius told me I had daddy issues.' She shrugs. 'He was right, I suppose. But I dealt with my daddy issues when I was nineteen.'

'Lindsay's here, isn't she?' He demands, spinning to look towards the hall and stairs.

Sam reaches calmly into her pocket and pulls out her taser. 'Freeze!' she shouts, in as firm a voice as she can muster. 'You're under arrest for entering—'

'Lindsay!' Richie bellows, lunging for the hallway. Sam deploys her taser, firing it directly across the room and hitting him in the hip. It's a good body shot. Clean; well timed. He falls to his knees, and her baton skitters across the hall tiles. But the leather protects him from a strong jolt, and he begins to stand again.

'Taser! Taser!' Sam shouts, more out of habit than to warn Richie that she's about to deliver another shock. Richie wobbles as she presses the trigger and gets him again, but remains in a kneeling position. He twists around, pulls the taser from his bike leathers, drops it on the carpet.

'Fu . . . ck . . . ing . . . bitch,' he wheezes. The only light in the room now comes from the streetlamp outside. Richie is just a silhouette. He tries to stand. Sam has a split second to decide what to do. Richie's in the doorway between the lounge and hallway, blocking her only exit. But the front door is unlocked and she has plenty of neighbours to run to. So, the stairs or the door?

Sam charges at Richie, careening into his side like a rugby player. They both fall heavily, her on top. She pushes herself off him, to her feet, and makes a run for it. He grabs at her dressing gown, yanking her back. She slides out of it and runs into the hallway. Turns right. Up the stairs.

She's lived in this house almost her whole life; she needs no light. Two stairs at a time. She hears him right behind her. He flicks the hall light switch; it doesn't work. He pounds after Sam, up the unlit staircase, reaching the top step. Then trips and crashes down heavily. Air splutters from him; he's winded. Prone on the small upstairs landing. Sam looms over him, a large, steel baseball bat in her hands. She doesn't hesitate, just swings. A strange whooshing sound comes out of him but he doesn't scream. Sam strikes once more, hears a crack. She quickly pushes open her bedroom door and flicks the switch, sending light spilling across the scene on the landing.

On the floor, Richie rolls on to his side, clutching between his legs. He's struggling to pull air into his lungs. Sam swings the bat at his back. He cries out and then whimpers, still clutching his genitals. She must have ruptured a testicle. Sam swings again, another blow to the back. He's barely moving now. Just lying there, trying to breathe.

'How does it feel, Richie?' she whispers. 'To be the helpless one?' There is liquid pooling on the carpet. It's coming from Richie's waistline. He must have pissed himself, she thinks. She swings the bat casually in front of his face. He tries to push himself away from her, but can't.

'Please,' he wheezes, 'wait.'

'Did Melanie say please? Did Lindsay say please?'

'You . . . you . . .'

'Bitch?' Sam says. 'That is so boring. Find a new word for us.' She swings the bat again, but he curls into a ball and she just catches his ankle. A small crack and a squeal.

'You won't get . . . away . . . with . . .'

'That's where you're wrong, Richie,' she says slowly. 'This is exactly how to get away with murder. You would have learned a lot more about it if you'd paid attention to what *I've* been up to, rather than Denver.'

She lands a final blow on the side of Richie Scott's head. There's a crunchy squelch that Sam thinks may have killed him. At this point, she's not too bothered either way. It's one hell or another for this arsehole.

She takes a few deep breaths to gather her thoughts, then gets to work. On tiptoe, she tightens the landing light bulb that she'd loosened and turns it on. She can now see the scene in all its glory, just as the police and, later, the forensics team will.

She moves to the top of the stairs and unties the cable she'd fastened across the top step three weeks earlier, the day after her meeting with Julius Windsor. She coils it neatly before stepping into her bedroom and placing it into her waiting laptop bag. She's pleased it's back where it belongs, having tripped over it herself once or twice while packing up her things. It's the price you pay for booby-trapping your own house, she supposes. Just like in *Home Alone*.

Behind her, Richie begins to make a strange bubbling sound.

Probably dying, but she can't be sure. She removes the glove on his left hand, takes her baseball bat and wraps his fingers around it several times. Replacing the glove proves tricky, but she manages, then she leaves the bat next to Scott. Given that his fingerprints will be all over it despite the gloves he's wearing, all evidence will suggest that he brought it with him Arriving at her home armed will make Richie's crime more serious, and her less likely to be charged with excessive self-defence. If Richie dies, a post-mortem will show that she only inflicted a few blows with the bat – hardly excessive. If he lives, it's back behind bars for him.

She stands and considers the scene for a second. Richie lies bloody, on her landing, next to the bat. He's still breathing. She walks back downstairs. It's over. It occurs to her that Julius Windsor and Richie Scott could even end up in the same intensive care unit, and she begins to hum. Something she hasn't done in a long time.

Calmly, she collects her baton and taser, wipes them down with an alcohol wipe from the kitchen then places them in her utility belt, which is hanging in the under-stairs cupboard. She reconsiders, and hides the taser in the drawer of her dad's desk, in the basement. She shouldn't really have a taser at home.

Finally, Sam stands at the front door and breathes for a second with her eyes closed. Then she walks the entire house again, making sure that everything looks how it should – like a lone female has had no choice but to defend herself from a criminal on the run.

After her walk-through, Sam perches on the sofa and takes some panting breaths, each one faster and shallower than the last. Once she's sure she's ready, she pulls her phone from her pocket, where it's been the whole time, and dials 999.

'This is DI Samantha Hansen ... I need police and an ambulance,' she says, infusing her voice with panic. 'A wanted man ... Richie Scott ... Please, send help ... He's just tried to kill me in my home . . . My God . . . he had a weapon – a bat . . . I've defended myself . . . Oh Jesus . . . I think I'm going to . . .'

Sam lets the phone slide to the floor, then rests her head on the arm of the sofa, slows her breathing and waits for the cavalry to arrive. Was her phone call overly dramatic, bordering on suspicious? She doesn't think so. She might be a detective, but she's also just a woman. She suspects her female hysteria will be deemed perfectly natural.

# 28

Sam spends the night in hospital. It's precautionary, they tell her, as she was unresponsive when the paramedics arrived. She must have passed out. Adam Taylor is there when she opens her eyes. He's brought Maltesers and daffodils. Sam closes her eyes again. Adam sits for hours as nurses come and go. To pass the time, he talks non-stop, in that awkward way people talk in hospitals. He goes on about the case he's working on, the London weather, and his mother's UTI. Adam only leaves her bedside to go to the bathroom and Sam takes one such opportunity to text Neil and check how Lindsay is doing.

Sam must have nodded off, because when she next opens her eyes, Taylor's fingers are resting gently on her hand and he's nodding off himself in his chair. One of the good ones. She smiles to herself, laces her fingers through his and closes her eyes again.

By lunchtime, Sam is ready to shower and get out of the hospital, but there's zero privacy and she's wearing a crinkly, open-back gown, as the police took her clothing into evidence. When she asks Taylor to leave, he initially refuses, so she begins to pull back the covers.

'I'd like to preserve the innocence of your eyes.' She grins and he blushes, taking the hint.

'Call me when they release you,' he says gently. 'I want to drive you home and make sure you're OK. I can stay over if—'

'Actually, Taylor,' she says. 'Could you do me a favour?'

'Of course.'

She gives him instructions and her house key.

When Sam is discharged later that day, Taylor has been sent to a crime scene, so she calls Chloe Spears, who picks her up and drives her home. Sam stays quiet, like any traumatized victim of an attempted murder.

When they arrive back at Sam's terrace, she asks Chloe to come in with her, just to check that everything is safe. From outside, they can hear Toni yapping. The little scruff continues to bark as Chloe checks the house. Sam even has her colleague check under the bed, as if Richie Scott might have awoken from the coma she put him in and secreted himself under her mattress.

'Gosh, he's noisy!' says Chloe as Toni launches himself directly on to the sofa, whining for Sam to sit with him. Chloe goes into the kitchen to put the kettle on and too quickly re-enters the lounge with a pair of steaming mugs. They can't be properly brewed, Sam thinks, but she sips gratefully. She'll make herself a decent cuppa once Chloe's gone – though, given that Chloe has moved several boxes and taken a seat in the armchair, that might not be for a while.

'How are you really doing, Sam?' Chloe asks, concern etched on her face. 'Don't just say "fine" to me again.'

'It's tough.' She shrugs. 'It just seems like there's been so much . . .'

'Trauma, lately?' Chloe offers.

'Yes,' Sam says, helping Toni to get comfortable on her lap. 'Exactly.'

'You've been through so much,' Chloe says, 'what with Harry's accident last week and now someone trying to murder you in your own home.' Chloe slurps her tea, which no one should ever do. 'You and Harry were close, weren't you?' She says it casually, but Sam detects a hint of something else in her voice. Something that, to Sam, sounds a little like suspicion.

'Yes. Harry was my dad's partner. They went through the

academy together. Inseparable. I was nineteen when my dad died. He shot himself in the head with a collectible firearm. He was in the basement and I was upstairs in the bath. I didn't even hear the gunshot. Harry stepped in and became like a father to me. Luckily, I inherited this house, but I had no job. It was Harry who helped me get into the Met. We drifted apart last year, with my breakdown and what-have-you. But we'd put that all behind us and then . . . then . . . I lost Harry too.' Sam rubs the plaster on her wrist where a cannula had been.

'I'm so sorry, Sam,' Chloe says, and slurps again.

'I'd just had dinner with him the weekend before he fell. Things were good. Our mutual friend, Pete Thomson, was there too. He's a good guy, Pete . . .' Sam lets herself think back to that meal and the one time she'd seen Harry after it. Their walk along the cliffs by Botany Bay. That had been a lovely day. Sam finds herself humming again.

'I'm so sorry, Sam,' Chloe says, and swallows some more tea. 'Harry's accident was tragic. He can't have realized how close he was to the edge.'

'I feel so scared, back here. In this house. In this room,' Sam says, changing the subject.

'Richie Scott can't hurt you any more. Besides, you're about to move to Newcastle, aren't you? You've already got a place there? Taylor was saying he might come up for a visit once you get settled,' Chloe says, but Sam isn't interested in small talk.

'How's that lawyer doing? The one Richie attacked before he got me?' she asks.

'Julius Windsor. He's still alive but unconscious, last I heard.'

'Richie Scott's a monster,' Sam mutters.

'Not for much longer,' Chloe says. 'I think they'll switch him off later this week. They're trying to find next of kin but he's estranged from his brother and there's no one else. It's looking like his girlfriend Lindsay will make the final decision.'

'Mmm,' Sam says, wishing to God that Chloe had left the teabag in longer. 'You still seeing . . . Gosh. What's her name? The woman who met Denver?'

'Amy,' Chloe smiles, blushing, 'Yes, we're still seeing each other. Although she's back in the States at the moment.'

'Nice,' Sam says.

'Can I ask you something?' Chloe says.

'Of course, but I'm tired,' Sam says, ready for Chloe to leave so she can enjoy a good cup of tea and some *Only Fools and Horses*.

'I suppose I was just wondering where Toni was when you were attacked? If he'd been here, he might have barked. Given you a few seconds to dial 999.' Chloe delivers the question casually, but Sam hears the challenge behind it: nowadays, people are never more than metre from their phone, so why hadn't Sam called sooner? Sam smiles to herself. Her instincts were right about Chloe Spears. She's a good officer, with good intuition.

'Yes, Toni would have barked, little hero that he is.' Sam ruffles his head. 'He was at the vet's. He needed his teeth cleaning and a minor operation on his back leg. I'd put it off; to be honest, I was thinking of handing him over to a shelter. Now I can't imagine how I ever contemplated giving him up. He's my best friend. Taylor brought him home for me earlier today.'

'So Toni happened to be at the vets the same day that Richie Scott's girlfriend chose to run away from him and, for some reason, Richie thought—'

'Look, Chloe, can we talk about something other than last night?'

'Of course. Sorry, Sam. Tell me about your move to Newcastle.'

'I can't wait to start afresh in a new place.' She smiles. 'I just hope that the North is ready for my brand of justice.'

Chloe smiles back. 'Newcastle's not going to know what hit it.'

# *Bonus Chapter*

Let's talk about killing people you know.

I know I said I wouldn't, but I will.

I guess you just can't trust a serial killer, eh?

My advice comes with a warning and disclaimer: proceed with caution – you can never truly unknow a thing once it is learned. When a world has been opened to you, that door can never again be fully closed. Once you taste the sweetness of killing without consequence, you may not be able to stop. You may not want to.

Now the housekeeping is out of the way, let's get down to it.

There are many reasons that you might have picked up this book, but I'm going to assume that not every one of you is an aspiring serial killer. I'm guessing that many of you had a specific person in mind when you reached for this opus of mine. Disappointment is a terrible feeling, so I'll try to go a little way towards delivering what I promised you.

People want to kill for all kinds of reasons. Those reasons can't always be pure, like mine. Killing simply for the joy of it is liberating, but I suppose that you might want to kill your dickhead boss, an abusive parent, or people who leave bags of dog shit hanging from bushes.

So, if you want to murder someone you know and get away with it, you need to be *especially* careful and *especially* patient.

By far the best way to go about such a murder is to avoid it being labelled a murder at all. To do this, find your prospective victim's weakness and exploit it. You can do this in a variety of ways. It could be very literal, in that you know that they have weak lungs and are prone to asthma attacks while hiking in the heat. Simple – off to a remote desert location you go, faulty inhaler at the ready. Allergies are perfect, too – bees, wasps, nuts. You have it very easy if your chosen victim has such a weakness. Addictions work well – drug addicts OD all the time. Alcoholics frequently fall; you can push one down the stairs and it's likely the police won't look at you twice. Even things like diabetes can work beautifully. Maybe your victim can't swim – rent a boat and, oops, they fell in the water. Do your research, then execute your plan. It's best if you can make it happen while you're not even there. Be creative. Have fun.

If your intended victim has no such weakness of the body, perhaps you can exploit a weakness of the mind. This could be someone's depression (easy pickings), someone's ego, their temper, greed, lust, pride, obsession. If you're smart about it, you can use any one of these things to create the perfect conditions for murder.

A really great example is Hetty Blister, an American woman who married a famous film producer. Naturally, he was a philanderer and by some accounts a rapist. Hetty had been made to sign a prenup that would leave her with nothing, so divorce was out of the question. If he died, however, she got everything, plus a hefty insurance cheque. Hetty began extra-marital relationships with several men. She selected them well. They were ugly, stupid and quite poor. Most importantly, they all had a violent temper. Hetty had them fall in love with her, then began to 'confide' in these men about her husband's behaviours – his affairs, his beatings, his money that could be hers. *Money that could be theirs.* It wasn't long before one of Hetty's beaus ran over the film producer with a stolen car. Twice. Hetty was never implicated in the crime as there was no evidence she ever actively encouraged her boyfriends to hurt her husband. She lived happily ever after. Persuading one person to kill another, as she did, is a brilliant way to get away with murder.

Obviously, you must take care not to communicate anything in writing. And don't ask your dupe outright to kill your nemesis. Otherwise, you risk being charged as an accomplice. If your intended victim already has an enemy, or if you can create an enemy for them, that could work. If you can convince someone with a proclivity to violence that another person has wronged them, one or both could go on to end up dead. You won't even be there. You'll get a phone call one day and find out like that. Brilliant. Not wholly satisfying, as you'll have to hear about it second hand, but it gets the job done.

Paying someone to kill for you is an option, but not one I'd really recommend. If you want to pursue this route to murder, re-read my chapter on the dark web.

Next up we have the self-defence ploy. Basically, you entice the person you want dead to try to kill you. Unbeknownst to your victim, you've secretly learned Krav Maga or you have a pet tiger. I jest. You could very simply have stashed weapons in your home so that when they attack you, they are dispatched swiftly. To get away with such a murder, you not only need to survive, you also need to demonstrate that your reaction, i.e. killing them, was proportional, otherwise it's not self-defence. To do this, you'll need to take a few blows yourself and look badly beaten. Or, the person needs to come to your home armed, and you 'end up' killing them in a fight. Double points if you can set a booby trap or two in advance. Think *Home Alone*. The self-defence ploy works really well for women if they can prove a history of abuse or if the victim is already a known criminal, because the police will care less that you killed them.

Then there's the accident method. Be careful with this one because this is riskier than you might first think. The best accident to use to kill someone is a fall. Preferably from a substantial height, such as a cliff or a balcony. Staircases aren't fatal enough. Car accidents are very hard to cause nowadays, as modern vehicles are difficult to sabotage. However, accidentally setting someone's home on fire or leaving the stove on, causing monoxide poisoning, can work. But, as I say, in my opinion a fall is best.

In the run-up to the accident, keep a low profile in the person's life, but keep things on good terms with them. If you need to spend time with them (your spouse, for example), ensure that it's a happy experience. Buy them gifts with your debit card. Book cinema tickets together. Never, ever arrange an accident for someone who you've been seen arguing with recently. Ensure that there are plenty of recent witnesses of good standing in the community (think doctors/dinner ladies) who can testify that you and the deceased were on good terms last time they saw you together. Whatever you do, don't rush things. Wait for the moment when they're naturally on the edge of something very high and then, poof – gone. You want their death to be utterly mundane. Like one of those chapters in a book that people skip or the author doesn't even bother to include. Boring and pointless. Hardly worth the effort to write or read about.

Finally, I'm sure you've all considered the staged suicide option. This is a lot harder than it looks and needs careful planning. It's much easier if you live with the person (a parent, spouse or child). If you can persuade them to kill themselves by subjecting them to prolonged abuse, that'd be best. Hanging someone is nearly impossible without a lot of help. Lacing their liquor with fatal tablets may work but most toxins will show up in a forensics test, so do your research carefully. The easiest way to stage a suicide is to wait for the victim to fall asleep on the sofa or at their desk, sneak up quietly and shoot them in the head. I know, who has access to guns these days? If you are one of the lucky ones, be sure to place the gun in their dead hand afterwards and fire it again, as if they had themselves misfired the first time. This will ensure that the gunshot residue is on their hands. Take care to wear gloves yourself or take a long, hot bath afterwards.

And just like that, we've arrived at the end. I'm sure that, providing you're not a real dummy, you now understand *How to Get Away With Murder*. I really hope you've enjoyed reading me. If so, I'd appreciate top marks – all the stars, please, on Amazon, Goodreads or wherever you can. This is my debut, remember. I'll only get better, you know.

I hope you'll hear my voice in your head for many months to come. I hope you'll miss me. I hope you'll lie awake at night, wondering who I am, where I am. Maybe I'm your golf buddy. Your uncle. Your friendly neighbourhood bobby. I hope you'll keep me in your heart, and on your shelf.

As you close my book, I wonder what you'll do next? Turn on the kettle and watch another episode of the latest addictive true-crime series? Personally, I think I'll take the dog for a nice long walk. To the park, or to the beach.

Maybe.

## *Acknowledgements*

Thank you to the people who believed in this book and helped to make it everything it could be. My incredible agent, Stephanie Glencross, who took a chance on a new author and saw the diamond in the rough early versions of the MS. The hugely talented author and agent Danya Kukafka, thank you for bringing the book to North America. Thank you, Team Transworld: Alison, Finn, Alex, Anna and especially Thorne Ryan; I'm eternally grateful for your vision for this book, your stunning editorial skills and your candour. Kelley Ragland, you've been beyond brilliant – I'm forever grateful to you and the Minotaur team. Thanks to the fantastic translation team at DHA, especially Giulia and Sam. My publishers in each territory – thank you for taking this book to so many readers in so many languages, it means everything to me. Thank you to my UEA cohort, amazing authors all, and my UEA lecturers, especially Tom and Nathan. My draft readers: Rachel, Jessica and Holly.

As well as the people who believed in the book, I need to thank the people who believed in me and my dream of becoming an author. My Mum, Carol – for raising me to be resilient, unafraid to dream big and always teaching me to know my worth. My sister and best friend, Claire Elizabeth – for loving me as I am and being the best person on the planet. My brilliant, beautiful girls, Rose and Grace – I hope you find something that fills you with as much purpose as writing books does me. My fiancé and rock-solid foundation, Dean. The young ones: Ellana, Ash and Hanny. My aunties Judith and Lesley. My Dad, for being a fantastic business mentor. Those I've lost, especially Si and Christine. My wider family. My friends Hannah, Gemma, Laura, Elliot and Anna. My Newcastle crew. My netball family. My writing group friends, especially the North East Novelists and Teesside Writers Group.

Thank you all *so* much.